Seekers

A World Within A World

Liz Morris

Carpenter's Son Publishing

Seekers: A World Within a World

©2014 by Liz Morris

Published by Carpenter's Son Publishing, Franklin, Tennessee, in association with Roaring Lambs Publishing, Dallas, Texas.

Published in association with Larry Carpenter of Christian Book Services, LLC
www.christianbookservices.com

Scripture quotations are from the New Revised Standard Version Bible, copyright © 1989 the Division of Christian Education of the National Council of the Churches of Christ in the United States of America. Used by permission. All rights reserved.

Cover Image by Sky Morris

Cover Design by Debbie Manning Shepherd

Interior Design by Suzanne Lawing

Edited by Robert Irvin

Printed in the United States of America

978-1-940262-03-1

Dedication

Cassie Bernall
Long live your fearlessness . . .

To JWM:
For believing in the power with me

To JAM:
May the gifts pass on to you

To SWM:
Your creativity never ceases to amaze me. Thanks for all you did.

To JTS Jr., KRS, JMD, ROD:
Thanks for all your prayers and support.

To AOS and JTS:
If it weren't for you, I would not be who I am today.

To the readers:
May your life never be the same again!

For more information about *Seekers* and the series, or to enter
a contest for the chance to contribute to the upcoming trilogy,
please visit our website at www.readseekers.com.

CHAPTER 1

No Man's Land

The air was thin as Nettle drifted up out of her body toward the ceiling. You could see her boyfriend, Tommy, crying as Nettle hopelessly stretched out her arms trying to tell him that everything was going to be OK, but he couldn't hear her. She wanted desperately to talk to him. Her mother and father were crying and hugging over in the corner of the room as though she was dead. Was she? Suddenly, the atmosphere changed; she was now outside and the sun was bright. Nettle could see everything, as if the whole world were opening up to her. Traveling through the distance at warp speed, her mind began unlocking clues to the future.

"Nettle?" she heard someone say. She turned to look.

"Yes," she replied, not seeing a soul.

"The answers are there."

"Where?" she asked.

No response.

"Who are you?" she tried again.

Interrupted by a terrible screeching sound, she turned to see a massive eagle heading straight for her. The sound was almost deafening. He looked seriously angry, and she knew immediately that if she didn't fly away, he was going to have her for lunch. Her heart began to race. *Where can I go?* She spotted an enormous mountain close by and directed herself toward it. She descended down and ran for cover. *Whew . . . that was close.* All appeared tranquil now—picturesque, if you must. This majestic, magnificent mountain had sex appeal. Nettle instantly knew this was where she was supposed to be. It was almost as if she could hear the whistling sounds of the wind calling her name again. *Is this place going to give me answers to the unknown element I've been searching for all of my life? I desperately want to know. But . . . if I'm dead now, where is everyone?*

She made it over to the other side and began assessing her options—something she was always good at doing. Noticing her clothes appeared luminescent, she concluded this was all a part of the afterlife. *But wait a minute. My body looks the same. What is happening to me?*

As she walked around, the place began to feel creepy, so she climbed down to what looked like a long hallway wrapped alongside the mountain. It looked as though someone had built the corridor eons ago. She stepped inside and noticed old Indian symbols etched on the interior walls. Glancing around, she spotted seats built out of carved stone. They were filthy. There was broken glass everywhere from all the broken-out windows. As she walked over to sit down, she immediately felt something there with her: a presence, possibly not from this earth. She looked over to her left and saw a large black and white king snake slithering along the corridor wall. *What is this place? Is there anyone else here besides me? Is this all there is to life's exit . . . broken glass and filth?*

"Help!" she heard someone yell. Looking over to her right, she spotted two men holding a young boy at gunpoint. He appeared to have bruises up and down his arms, and his clothes looked tattered. Nettle knew right then, if she didn't do something quick, they were going to shoot him. She screamed, and immediately they turned and saw her, at once letting the young boy go.

Run! she said to herself, but her legs were frozen. She was shaking all over. She couldn't move.

"That's her," one of them said. They marched toward her, and she screamed again, this time waking herself up.

* * *

Nettle lay in her bed, drenched in sweat. Completely awake now from this horrifying dream, she peered over at her college roommate, Chrissy, to see if she was awake. But Chrissy was sound asleep. Nettle's heart was pounding so hard it felt like it was about to beat open her chest. The thought of being dead literally haunted her. She glanced at her clock and noticed it was only five-thirty, so she lay there until daylight trying to figure out why she had been having so many puzzling dreams lately. She wanted so badly to put two and two together. She really wanted to know the meaning of this one. It seemed the most bizarre. Nettle had studied dreams and was highly aware that some were signs of future events. Pulling out her flashlight and a piece of paper, she began writing down the details. Her hands were shaking.

She remembered dying signified that an issue or era of a person's life was coming to an end. Maybe this dream was a sign, foreshadowing something in her search for the unseen world. She had dreamed about this mountain several times before. It was severely mysterious.

Even as a young girl, she knew there was more to this world than everyday existence. She started her journey after reading about a supernatural encounter a young boy had at the age of ten. His experience perplexed her and she wanted to know if it had validity to it. Now, after studying nearly all the ancient religions, she knew that man comprehended there was something out there. She just wanted that "something" to find her. She was not going to settle for someone else's experience . . . she wanted her own. *I have to be alone to find my answers*, she determined. Quietly dressing, she grabbed her tablet and slipped out the door.

She headed first to a Denny's to grab some pancakes. Waiting on her food, she began researching the Internet to find something—anything she could find—of her dream's meaning. She went to the only site she trusted: *Streams International*. Her findings were intriguing. *Wow, a tunnel means you are about to experience a transition in your life. Imagine that . . . and being chased means an enemy is trying to generate fear.* She could not stop reading. It was as though she knew this dream was a prediction of her future. Feelings of curiosity were beginning to get the best of her, so she quickly paid her bill and headed out toward Corridor Mountain, just on the outskirts of Tucson. *Hopefully this place will have some significance or, at least enough similarities, so I can interpret more.*

Some of the mountains in Arizona were quite different from the ones she grew up around in Colorado, but she loved them all the same. Mountains were Nettle's hiding place. They represented strength and power, allowing her to draw from their majesty a still, quiet inner peace. Pulling in the parking lot, she noticed a corridor of sorts wrapping around the side of the mountain. It all looked very familiar, almost déjà vu-like. Her stomach felt the anticipation, and her heart began racing a little, remembering that no one knew where she was. *Tommy would probably kill me if he knew I was out here all alone. I love him so much,* she thought as her mind raced from thought to thought. Opening her car door, she quickly dismissed any fearful thoughts and placed her entire focus on the mountain before her.

* * *

Tommy and his best friend, Josh, woke up early to head to the desert for some target practice. "I can't wait to unload this puppy. This is the most incredible gun I have ever bought," Tommy said.

"I hear ya," Josh said. "I can't wait to shoot it either. I think we should go someplace different today than usual. Let's go farther out and see if we can find someplace really unique."

Tommy thought about calling Nettle to let her know what he was doing this morning, but chose not to. He had a desire to teach her how to shoot a gun so she would be able to protect herself if need be.

Josh began showing Tommy the direction they needed to go. They grew up in the area together, so they were pretty familiar with all the mountainous terrain.

"Look, over to your left," Josh said. Tommy quickly spotted what looked like a deserted road winding up a beautiful mountain. It had a couple of safety cones in the middle of it, but they would be easy to move in order to get by. The area did appear different than anything they had ever seen before in the desert.

"Is that a pond over there at the base?" Tommy asked.

"I think so," Josh said.

"Now that is something you don't see often out here."

"I wonder what's at the top," Josh mused.

"I have no idea, but it sure is beautiful," Tommy answered, looking all around.

With both turning to look at each other as if they were reading each other's minds, Josh hopped out of the truck to move the cones. Driving slowly up the road, they began to notice a dense, lush, almost tropical-like forest.

"Man, this is amazing," Tommy said. "It looks almost make-believe. I have never seen anything tropical like this in the desert before."

"Me, either," Josh replied, eyes peeled and stuck on the setting before him.

"Look, there's a house. Someone must live up here," Tommy said in amazement, staring at the rather odd topography. There was a large white cottage-like dwelling with a white picket fence situated several feet from the road. You could have easily missed it.

"It looks like the lights are on inside," Josh said as he was scoping out the place. "I wonder if they own this mountain."

"Who knows? Let's just keep going and see what's at the top," Tommy said.

As they continued up the mountain, the road suddenly dead-ended. "Well, it doesn't look like it has a place for us to set up a good target. I think we could find someplace better than this." Tommy began making a U-turn when Josh spotted a huge tent back from the road.

"Stop!" Josh shouted. "What are all those people doing under that tent?"

Tommy slammed on his brakes; they could see a couple hundred people sitting and listening to some guy standing at a podium.

"Are those wheelchairs they are passing around over their heads?" Josh asked.

"I don't know, man; it kind of looks like it. Let's park and go find out." Quietly getting out of the truck, they began to nestle down behind a set of bushes. The man at the podium was telling the audience about an unknown kingdom. He began asking people to come up on the platform, where he spoke something—and they were instantly cured.

"What the heck was that?" Josh asked in utter disbelief.

There was no response from Tommy; he was almost hypnotized watching the unbelievable encounters. Totally fascinated by what was happening, Tommy and Josh began inching closer when, suddenly, dozens of men in red ski masks came out of the woods firing bullets into the crowd of people. The gunfire jolted Tommy and Josh to their feet. In a nightmarish frenzy, they stood frozen, watching people go down left and right. Screams of horror were all they could hear.

"Run!" Josh yelled.

People were yelling and scattering frantically for their lives as the bullets were whizzing into the crowd. Tommy and Josh knew it was only a matter of time before they would be hit.

"Hurry, unlock the door," Josh was yelling as Tommy was grabbing for his keys. Panic-stricken and shaking, Tommy turned the engine on and took off.

"Do you think they will come after us?" Tommy yelled as terror engulfed them both in the escape.

"I don't know," Josh responded, looking back to check.

"Call 911!" Tommy's voice was loud and demanding as fear gripped his mind. Josh fumbled for his phone and, just as he was about to dial the number, Tommy realized the white farmhouse, the only thing on that road, had disappeared.

"Hang up quick!" Tommy roared loudly at Josh. Josh anxiously hit the off button.

"What?" he asked, confused.

"The farmhouse disappeared."

Josh turned around, and sure enough, it was gone.

"Where did it go?" he yelled, as Tommy was flying all over the road, trying to get away.

"I don't know, man, but this is messed up."

Josh kept turning around. "Just hurry, Tommy, get back to the apartment and we can decide what to do then." You could hear the terror-stricken panic in his voice.

"What in the world was all that? Who were those men in the ski masks?" Tommy shouted out again.

"I don't know, but there were at least a dozen of them," Josh said, continuing to turn around to check things out. "Oh my God, Tommy, here they come—they are behind us now. Faster, you have got to drive faster."

Tommy floored the gas pedal, desperately trying to get away. His new truck was flying, gulping up ground at more than a hundred miles an hour, trying to escape.

"OK . . . I think they stopped," Josh blared. "But don't slow down; keep going."

"You think they got my license plate?" Tommy asked.

"I don't think so. I don't think they ever got close enough."

"We can't say a word about this until we see it on the news. Not a word," Tommy said.

"OK."

They drove the rest of the way back in sheer disbelief and silence; Josh's legs were trembling. Once safely inside their apartment, Tommy tried to call Nettle to see if she was up. He was desperately trying to get his mind off everything. Her phone went straight into voicemail, so he hung up and began texting her. There was no response back. *I'll wait a little while then try again. She and Chrissy are probably still asleep.*

CHAPTER 2

The Stranger

Nettle saw that the stairs leading up to Corridor Mountain were extremely steep. She left her cell phone in the car so nothing would disrupt her. Approaching the entrance to the corridor, she began to feel a little edgy. She knew this was a place where the homeless and destitute slept at night, but she thought it would be safe to visit now. But something felt odd . . . not quite right. Her anxiousness grew as she heard strange sounds echoing through the passageway. Anticipation tingled down her spine. Her palms were getting clammy and her heartbeat unsteady. *This place is creepy.* Walking carefully to the middle of the corridor, she noticed a bat lurking at the top of an outcrop, protruding from the ceiling. The tunnel definitely reminded her of her dream. *Why am I feeling a sense of uneasiness? This is not what I was expecting.*

Walking farther inside the corridor, the atmosphere began to feel threatening, and she could hear the echo of a muffled voice. Instinctively, she squatted down, when all of a sudden a sharp, thunderous clap jolted her back to her feet. *Get out; get out now,* her mind said, but something deep within her gut was drawing her to stay. Looking up and down the long hall, she heard another sound.

"Who's there?" she asked.

No response. Silence filled the empty corridor. Nettle stood still as a statue, unmoving.

"I said, who's *there*?" This time Nettle saw the shadow of what appeared to be a young boy running from one side of the corridor to the other. Determined not to leave, she mustered all her courage and proceeded to walk toward the shadow. Peering out from behind a bench was a frightened, dirty young boy.

"What are you doing?" she whispered.

"I'm looking for my dad," he whispered back.

"Is he up here?"

"No, ma'am."

"Well, then where is he?" The whispering continued.

"I don't know for sure."

Nettle was a bit puzzled and yet curious at the same time. Realizing they were alone, she continued her questioning in her normal tone of voice.

"Is your mom out here with you?"

"Nope, she's in heaven."

"Excuse me. What did you just say?"

"I said she's in heaven. She died a few months ago, and no one could find my dad, so I was put in a foster home. I hated it there, so I ran away to find my dad."

"Seriously?" Nettle asked, deep concern in her question. "Does the foster home know you've run away?"

"Well, I'm guessing they probably know something by now."

"How old are you?"

"Eleven."

"So, your dad lives here in Tucson?"

The boy looked down at his feet, trying to decide whether to trust this young woman or not.

"I'm not sure. He left my mom and me a few years back, and we have not heard from him since. I know he is out west, though, so I took the bus from Birmingham, Alabama, out here to find him."

Nettle was intrigued by his resolve but not sure what to do. "So, what is your name, young man?"

"Jackson."

"So Jackson, how do you know he is out West and that Arizona is the right place?"

"I know it in my heart," the boy said intently. "My mom always told me he was probably in Arizona or Nevada. So what's your name?"

"My name is Nettle. Come on . . . let's get you out of here so we can look for your dad."

Nettle turned around to lead Jackson out when they heard some men arguing vociferously. As they rounded the corner, she could see several men starting to fight. Without saying a word, Nettle grabbed Jackson's hand and took off running at high speed in the opposite direction. All she could think about was her dream. Running to the other end of the passageway, a man suddenly stepped out on front of them.

"Stop!" he yelled, holding his hand in the halt position. "You must not go any farther or you will go off the side of the cliff," he said with urgency.

Nettle had no clue whether this man had anything to do with the other guys but was not going to take any chances.

"Run," she yelled to Jackson as they frantically took off in the opposite direction again.

"Wait, don't go that way, or you might run into them. I am not going to hurt you. Please let me help you," the man pleaded. "I live up here and I know the place very well."

With that, Nettle stopped and turned around to check him out. Scared of heading in either direction, she had to make a choice. He did seem to look pretty docile. He also looked to be older, like in his sixties. She knew if she headed back the other direction, it might be far more dangerous.

"I know the back way out. Let me help you both to safety, please . . ."

Moving quickly back toward the man, Nettle decided to trust him. "So you live up here?"

"Yes'm," he replied while looking down toward his shoes.

"What is your name?"

"My name is Ollie. Now come on. Let's get you guys out of here. Follow me."

Nettle could sense the urgency in Ollie's voice and could tell he was worried about their safety. Cautiously, she followed him to the other side of the mountain. *Is this encounter more than coincidence?* She would have to think about that later.

"You must be careful up here. There are men who are up to no good; sometimes, it is not safe," he said as they arrived in the parking lot.

"Thank you," Nettle said.

Reaching for her purse once they were at her car, Nettle insisted Ollie let her pay him for his help. He refused.

"You two get out of here now, and be careful. It was nice to meet you."

"It was nice to meet you, too, and thank you so much for your help."

He just smiled and nodded his head good-bye.

"He seemed like a nice man," Jackson said once they were in the car.

"Yes, he was. I feel sorry for people like him that are down on their luck.

"So Jackson, I meant to ask you. What's your dad's name?"

"Arlice Beasley."

"Did he remarry?"

"No, but he did have a girlfriend. Actually, she was my mom's best friend. Her name was Miss Amanda."

"What? He left with your mom's best friend? That's terrible!"

"Yeah, that's what I thought too."

"So, you don't think he married Amanda?"

"Well, I'm not sure, but I don't think so because he never divorced my mom. He just left us with no explanation or anything. We woke up one morning and poof—he was gone. No note or anything. We were so upset. I think that's what made my mom die."

Nettle could feel his pain. She, too, had felt this kind of hurt before.

"Is that what the doctor said?"

"Well, the doctor said it was a heart attack. But my Aunt Maribeth said it was from a broken heart, and I think she is right. My mom was only forty-two, and for her to die so suddenly . . . it had to be because my dad hurt her so much."

"What was her name?"

"Kathryn."

"Why do you feel the need to find your dad if he did that to you and your mom?"

"Because he's the only family I have, and I am never going back to that foster home. I will die before I go back there. Can you take me to your house so we can look him up today? Please?"

Nettle felt conflicted about the whole situation but knew she had to help in some way. She would have had a younger brother around Jackson's age, but he died at three months. His name was Aaron Kyle. It was something she didn't share much.

Driving back to the dorm, she knew her roommate, Chrissy, would have difficulty understanding why she brought Jackson back there . . . but that was OK. Something had risen inside of Nettle, compelling her to take on his cause. Was he the boy in her dream?

CHAPTER 3

Corridor Mountain

Chrissy had been studying all morning for a test. She was always worried about passing since schoolwork was a challenge for her. Examining herself in the mirror, she decided to pull her long blond hair up in a comb and call her friend Jackie to go get some lunch. She turned and opened the door, and there stood Nettle and Jackson.

"Hey girl, I have been texting and calling you all morning. Where in the world have you been? And who is that?" Chrissy asked.

"Oh, I'm sorry . . . my phone must be on vibrate. I've had a lot going on this morning, so I haven't paid any attention."

"No problem."

"Oh, this is Jackson. Jackson, this is Chrissy."

"Hi," Jackson said.

"Hi . . . and you are Jackson who?"

"He is Jackson Beasley, he's lost, and I am going to help him get back home."

"OK. That's cool. So where were you all morning?" she asked as they all walked back inside the dorm room.

"I got up early to go to Corridor Mountain."

"Let me guess. To search for answers to all those puzzling questions you have."

"Yes, and when I find them, you are going to want to know them."

"I'm sure I will, Miss Brain," she said, laughing loudly. "By the way, Tommy called a few minutes ago and sounded like he needed you right away. I told him I had been trying to call you, too, and couldn't get you either. He said he left you a couple of voicemails and several text messages. You might want to call him now. He sounded kind of upset," Chrissy said.

Nettle reached for her purse when a loud knock pounded on the door. Chrissy opened the door, and there stood Tommy. He looked white as a ghost.

"Nettle, where in the world have you been?" he asked, his voice almost trembling. "I have been looking all over for you. Why didn't you tell someone where you were going? I was really starting to get worried about you. I left you several voicemails and texts, and when you didn't respond at all, my mind started going crazy with ideas about someone kidnapping you."

"Kidnapping me? Why would you think that? That's absurd, sweetie. I have been preoccupied with things today, and I left my phone in the car, so I didn't even know you had called. Are you OK?" she asked, noticing he was acting strange.

"It's just not like you to go off for so long without letting anyone know you're OK."

Nettle could tell by his overexcited tone that he was not going to let this one go.

"Tommy Jones, you know how contemplative she is! You can only guess she was out on some mountain probing for her answers again," asserted Chrissy, trying to help her best friend out.

"I appreciate her depth, Chrissy, but I was really worried for her this morning."

Nettle was sensing something different about Tommy, but reasoned that he was just bothered by this. She had never seen him act this distressed before.

"You're right, I should have told someone. The truth is, I had this dream last night, and it correlated perfectly with Corridor Mountain. I actually saw two men trying to hurt a young boy in my dream. So maybe that's why I was supposed to go there, to find Jackson. Tommy, this is Jackson . . . Jackson, this is Tommy."

"Oh . . . Hi, Jackson."

"Hi. You sure are tall. Do you play sports?"

"Yeah, I play football."

"What position?"

"Quarterback."

"Oh man! That's cool. I have never met a real college quarterback before."

Tommy chuckled.

"Can I come watch you play sometime?"

"Sure," Tommy responded, looking at Nettle like, *Who is this kid?*

"Awesome, thanks! I can't wait!" Jackson replied excitedly.

"You know, Nettle, Corridor Mountain is where a lot of homeless people sleep at night, and I have heard some really weird stories about that place. I've lived here all my life and I've never even been there," Tommy said as he continued on his trail of questioning.

"Well, it has always looked like a cool place from far off and the shape of it is so interesting. Then when I dreamed about a similar mountain, I had to go there. You know, growing up in Colorado, I went by myself all the time up in the mountains. It was my hiding place. The mountains were my refuge away from the rest of the world," Nettle said, trying to comfort him a little.

"So, that's where you found Jackson?"

"Yes, he was hiding there. He is kind of lost."

"What do you mean 'kind of lost?'"

"He's been looking for his dad and just needed a place to spend the night . . . so I brought him here, thinking I would call you, so you and I could help him find his dad." Chrissy slowly moved to the other side of the room, trying to stay out of this one.

"Well, where is his dad?"

"He doesn't know for sure," Nettle said, giving Tommy a poor, pitiful look.

"What? How old is he?"

"I am eleven!" Jackson blurted.

"So, let me get this straight. You went to meditate in a place you knew nothing about, and brought back a homeless kid?"

"I'm not a kid."

"Yes, Tommy. I couldn't just leave him there all alone."

"Well how do you plan on finding his dad?" Tommy insisted. They were both speaking as though Jackson was not standing there. Suddenly Jackson jumped up on Nettle's bed, trying to look this six-foot-five athlete in the face.

"Please, I need your help. My mom died and I was put in a foster home and the people were horrible to me. I had to get out of there. When I got off the bus this morning it started raining, so I had to find a place to stay dry. Some place where I could hang out for a while and no one could find me. That's when Nettle found me and helped me get out of the place. Please don't be mad. She is only trying to help me. And I really need her help. Please, will you help me too?"

Tommy could see the sadness in the boy's eyes. He also noticed the tears in both Nettle and Chrissy's eyes. Tommy's family had housed many hurting people through the years. Some of them were like brothers to him now.

"I'm not mad at anyone, Jackson. I am just worried that we won't be able to find him and that the police will be looking for you. We could get in big trouble for harboring a runaway child. I will let you stay with me tonight, and we will try to find your dad, but if we can't locate him, then I'm afraid tomorrow we have no choice but to call the police and let them help you out."

Jackson's eyes lit up.

"We will find him. I just know it. He is here somewhere close, I can just feel it."

"OK . . . but tomorrow we have to come up with a plan if we don't."

"Thanks, sweetie. I love you," Nettle said, smiling in a really big way at Tommy.

"I love you, too. Now that I know you are OK, I have some errands to run and an essay to write, so Jackson can come on with me." Tommy felt relieved knowing Nettle was safe. He wasn't sure if anyone saw him and

Josh today, or not. But he felt he needed to be aware of his surroundings for awhile. In the meantime, he had to focus on helping Jackson.

"Great, sweetie, I will call you later on this evening. I have to write an article for the school paper and study for a test, so after that I will touch base with you," she reassured him.

"That's fine. I'm sure Jackson and I can find plenty to do."

* * * * *

Nettle finished writing her article and was starting to feel sleepy from being up so early. She decided to take a nap before studying for her test. Nestling into her small twin bed, she closed her eyes and fell into a deep sleep for a few hours. Upon waking, her mind immediately started racing with thoughts about her dream the other night. *Was it related to Corridor Mountain? What made me feel the need to go there?* She couldn't help but think about her encounter with Ollie today . . . *Was he angelic?* Her mind was filled with vivid imaginations as she sprang up and exclaimed to Chrissy, "I've got to go back!"

"Back where?" Chrissy asked, startled from her studies.

"Back to Corridor Mountain!"

"Are you crazy? Tommy will kill you! Besides, it will be dark in a couple of hours and you should not go out there alone."

"I'm not. You are going with me."

"Oh, no I'm not! I don't have any desire to go to a creepy place in the dark. I sure don't want to bump into anyone out there either."

"Oh, come on, Chrissy. What happened to your spontaneity?"

"Look Nettle, I just don't think we should go looking for trouble. It doesn't make sense to me. Tommy said it was a weird place anyway. Let's wait until tomorrow and I will go with you then."

Chrissy knew there was nothing she could really say to keep Nettle from going. From a young age, Nettle had many premonitions and an instinct to follow them. Once she made up her mind, that was it.

"Stay here if you must. But I know I need to go tonight. I think something is going to happen there that I have never encountered . . . something intense." Nettle sat straight up in her bed and wrapped her arms around her bended knees. "You know, Chrissy, all my life I have been searching for answers to life's most complicated questions. I know my melancholy mind tends to wander. But I think there is more to this life than we know. I have thought that since I was a kid. I think there is another world out there . . . involving supernatural power. I need to find out for myself how to get to it, and I think that I will discover a few answers at that corridor. I don't know why, but I just feel that our place in history seems to be more uncertain than all the previous centuries before us, and I have to know why. We have more medicine and technology than ever before in history, but more sick people, more depressed people, and more suicidal people. What are we in search of that we are not finding? That's what I am seeking.

Oh boy, here goes Miss Magna Cum Laude's explanation of history, Chrissy thought to herself. *She is talking way over my head.* However, Nettle always seemed to end up being right about these things.

"I just feel like our world is spinning without direction . . . kind of like a ship without a compass. Somehow I believe we are intended not just to simply exist . . . I think there's something more. You can see it and feel it in the landscape."

"Wow!" Chrissy said. "You are so different from me. I never think about those kinds of things. I just take life as it comes and leave the figuring out about it to someone else. I suppose I need to think about it deeper, because if there is more to it, then I would never know it. So you really feel like the corridor is the best place for you to find these answers?"

"I don't know. But I do think I'm being drawn there for some purpose. Why else would I dream about it so clearly? You would think I'd be peaceful about it. But I'm a little apprehensive to find out what it is."

"I just hope once you find it I can understand it," Chrissy said, laughing. "I still think you've lost your mind for wanting to go up there when it's almost dark. But you go do what you think you need to do. But if you don't call me by eight o'clock, I'm calling the police—got it?"

"I got it! I will call you at eight o'clock sharp. Oh, and by the way . . . if Tommy happens to call you again, don't answer the phone. I don't want him to know I'm going back, so please don't answer."

"OK, I promise. But hurry back. I could never forgive myself if something happened to you."

"I will." Nettle grabbed her purse and took off for Corridor Mountain.

CHAPTER 4

The Engagement

Thinking back about her childhood, Nettle reflected on all her escapades in the mountains. The quaint Colorado city she grew up in gave her a sense of safety. Here in Arizona the mountains were different; although still beautiful, they just had a different charisma from those in Colorado. Everything back home was green and lush and peaceful. Many times she had gone to those mountains to mull things over, simply to think. Here, the mountains almost presented an atmosphere of danger, future expectancy, and adventure. She welcomed the difference and was excited to see what she was about to discover there.

Her father John's small grocery store always provided a good living for her family and allowed her mom, Katrina, to homeschool Nettle in her elementary years. Nettle was able to focus on her interests at a very young age; she had always been very inquisitive. Her parents had done a good job teaching Nettle right from wrong. She thought about what they would think of her driving back to Corridor Mountain at dusk. She was sure they would oppose it. However, she knew this was something she had to do.

Transitioning her mind to Tommy, she realized that he truly was the love of her life. He was a man of strength, he had great character, and

Tommy was full of fun. Hoping he would not find out about her journey back to the mountain, she quickly dismissed her remorseful thoughts for going anyway.

Nettle found a place to park close to the corridor entrance. The gusts of wind made an unusual whistling sound, seemingly warning her not to enter. The wind caught her car door and swung it wide open. She could see the dust swirling across the desert while it was moving throughout the valley. The pictorial golden-ginger sun was starting to set deep behind the mountain as Nettle locked her car door. At this point, everything was peaceful. Over to her right she could see a couple of nomadic men searching a big trash bin, looking for food. They never noticed her. Walking briskly down the sidewalk, she made her way to the corridor entrance. The upward route was elongated, steep, and filled with cracks, so she climbed with caution. What once was the city's favorite tourist attraction had now become the home for unsettled nomads.

Out of the blue, a large flock of migratory birds flew closely overhead, causing Nettle to flinch. *What is it about this place that can look so peaceful, yet feel so disturbing?* The sun shrinking behind the mountain made her more cautious as she held her mace close at hand. The nightlights inside did remove some trepidation from Nettle's mind. She sauntered down the hall; she was in no hurry to find the right place to sit. Observing the ornate rock carvings and becoming totally enamored with the absurd structure of the place, she walked right past the place where, earlier, she had heard noises. Settling in on a nearby bench, Nettle began her engagement.

She shut her eyes to block out any distractions. She put her head in her hands and bent it down to her lap . . . and began to articulate her thoughts. "To believe or not to believe . . . This is man's uncertainty. The supernatural—a speculation that puzzles man. An obscure question, so vitally important, yet so futilely misunderstood. How can we ever understand that which we do not recognize?" Eyes still shut, Nettle stood to her feet. Something inside her heart felt illuminated. "An undertaking impossible to achieve without surrender," she said loudly. "We are disillusioned souls searching for truth and value, but we're finding the counterfeit instead and missing our whole identity. Is there really a world within a world, whose kingdom is unfolding right before our own eyes?" These rather visionary words began flowing into her mind effortlessly, as if someone or something was putting them there. She continued the discussion out loud. "You are present in the atmosphere—floating carelessly about for me to grab." Eyes still shut, Nettle raised her arms as if she were reaching to the sky. "Speak; I am listening. Please, speak to me. I sense your presence."

Then . . . not audibly but deep within, the voice began to declare, "Eyes that look are common; eyes *that see* are rare, revealing secrets to its servants. You carry the future, you breathe the air of inspiration, and you are nourished by the spirit of the future. You are unquestionably controversial: a villain of today, a hearer of tomorrow. At night the future comes to your door and knocks; you refuse to let it walk away silent. You, Nettle, are a unique copy of an ancient gift, a unique reverberation of an ancient manuscript."

Nettle opened her eyes in hopes of fully grasping her encounter with the unseen realm only to see two men standing directly in front of her. They grabbed her by the arms, totally destroying the moment. "Stop," she screamed. "You're hurting my arm."

"Tell us. Tell us right now."

"Tell you *what?*"

"What that was."

"I don't know what you are talking about."

"What you just received."

Nettle refused to discuss her encounter or let these men know anything. She remained silent.

"Look, lady. Just show us your powers. We don't want to hurt you."

They began to push Nettle over to the outside of the corridor. She could tell they were antsy and not sure what to do with her.

"Hawk, grab the tape and duct-tape her hands and mouth."

Nettle tried to spray him with her mace when, immediately, Hawk grabbed it out of her hand. She wasn't strong enough to pull it away from him. Abruptly, he placed the duct tape around Nettle's hands and over her mouth. "I am only going to say this once. You tell us what your powers are and we will spare your life," demanded this obscure, evil-looking man.

"Ransom, do you think we need to torture her a little?"

"Shut up, stupid. You just said my name."

"Oh . . . sorry, boss."

Nettle could not figure out what they wanted. *What powers? Who were these creeps? Were they deranged homeless men? Or did they see something from the outside world that she didn't a few minutes ago?* The experience was so incredible, she felt something happen. Something was different. *Did they see this 'something' in the physical—or the supernatural?*

All of a sudden, Nettle's thoughts were interrupted by the sound of people running. She could hear them but couldn't see them. The voices began to echo and were moving closer to where they were. *If only I could scream.*

"Nettle, are you here?" she heard Tommy yell. Tommy and Jackson had showed up to convince Nettle to go home.

Suddenly, Ransom pulled out a gun. Nettle tried to wrench herself free as Hawk held her tight.

"Not this one," a voice said from behind them.

Turning around toward the voice, Ransom and Hawk glared at the man, then at each other. It appeared as though they knew him. Nettle instantly discerned the unspoken glares.

"You can't stop us," Ransom said.

The man walked closer. Nettle's eyes widened as she feared for his life.

"I said, not this one."

Suddenly a rock plummeted through the air and hit the back of Hawk's head. He started to fall down, so Nettle was able to tear away. As she looked up she saw Tommy and Jackson motioning her to run toward them. The stranger challenged Ransom so Nettle could get away. The two men wrestled; a shot was fired.

"You pelted him right in his head," shouted Jackson as they darted back towards the corridor entrance. "I guess it pays to be a quarterback."

Ransom ran over to Hawk to help him up. Hawk was stunned, but OK.

"Get up!" Ransom ordered. "We have got to get the girl!"

Approaching the entrance, Tommy stopped for a moment to carefully pull the tape off Nettle's mouth.

"Oh my God, Tommy, I think they shot him."

"Shot whom?" Tommy asked as he carefully pulled the tape off Nettle's hands.

"The homeless man, Ollie. We have to do something; we have to call the police!" she said frantically.

Suddenly, out of nowhere, the two men lunged out from behind the corridor wall, hitting Tommy over the head and knocking him out cold. Nettle screamed while Jackson started running back into the corridor as fast as he could. Violently grabbing Nettle by her arms, they began forcing her back into the corridor. She was fighting them with everything she had, trying to get away.

"Help!" Jackson screamed, hoping someone would hear him. As he neared the end of the passageway, an arm reached out and grabbed him. A hand covered Jackson's mouth.

"It's OK, Jackson. It's me, Ollie." Ollie pulled Jackson over behind a huge pool of rocks on the side of the mountain.

"You're bleeding."

"I will be OK. Did they get Nettle?"

"Yes, and they knocked Tommy out. We have got to do something."

"You must be quiet, Jackson, so they don't hear us."

"What are we going to do?"

"Shhh . . . " Ollie whispered again; he could hear the men approaching.

Ollie was losing a lot of blood and knew he didn't have much time to help Nettle.

"Look, lady, we don't want to hurt you, but if you don't shut up, we will make you."

"You had better let me go. You are going to be sorry if you don't," Nettle shouted, jerking left then right.

"Tape her mouth again, now!" Ransom ordered.

Nettle wrestled Hawk again, trying to get away. "Hawk, do I need to shut her up myself?"

"No, boss. I got this."

Tommy sat up, still a bit stunned from the blow. He began running back down the long corridor to find Nettle.

"Nettle, can you hear me? I've called the police and they're on their way. Nettle, can you hear me?" he kept yelling, hoping the men would let her go.

The two men quickly pulled Nettle farther outside to hide from Tommy. At this point, they were just about ten feet from where Jackson and Ollie were hiding.

Jackson couldn't stand it anymore, so he leapt out from behind the rocks and took a swing at Ransom, hitting him in the face. Ransom swiftly grabbed him by his shirt and held him tight. Removing his gun and holding Jackson by one arm, he prepared to shoot Tommy when he arrived.

"Tommy, run! He's going to shoot you. Turn around and go back!" Jackson screamed. Ollie, bleeding and in extreme pain, knew he had to do something.

Ransom sternly pulled Jackson close to his chest and held him tight, covering his mouth. Squirming feverishly trying to get away, Jackson bit Ransom hard and immediately the thug let go. Jackson's heart was pounding out of his chest as he took off running back into the Corridor in search of Tommy. Ransom fired two shots in the air, hoping to scare them both so he could get away with Nettle.

Sirens were in the distance, approaching quickly. Jackson found Tommy and they went to meet the police.

Ransom and Hawk dragged Nettle over off the side of the mountain into a place filled with a lot of debris and brush.

"As long as you do what we say, you will be fine. Try and get away, and we will shoot you. Got that?" Ransom snarled at her.

Police swarmed into the parking lot as Tommy and Jackson made their way back down the entrance. The sirens echoed throughout the Corridor Mountain valley. The flashing lights were a symbol of protection to Tommy, as he motioned the police over to where the two of them were standing. The first officer arrived and introduced himself as Officer Whitmore. He began asking Tommy questions.

"We have to move fast. They've called the police on us," Hawk whispered.

"I know the back way out," Ransom said. "Grab her and bring her with us." They fled down the back side of the mountain.

Extremely weak from bleeding, Ollie stood up. He was in excruciating pain, but knew he had to do something. He was Nettle's only hope at this point.

Hawk and Ransom took Nettle to the exact spot that Ollie expected, and he arrived shortly after the three of them. "Stop!" he demanded as he slowly felt his body falling. Nettle tried desperately to pull away and help Ollie, but there was nothing she could do. She was trying hard not to panic.

Ollie was down. Hawk roughly rolled him over and taped his mouth, then kicked him in the head.

"Leave the old man alone," Ransom said. "He is no use to us or anyone anymore. Besides, by the time the police get here, he will have bled to death."

"If we keep her with us, we might not make it out of here," Hawk whispered.

"Yeah, we better leave her here. We can come back tomorrow and take her to the rest of the people then," Ransom said.

"Hand me the tape. I am going to bury her underneath that brush over there. We can trash all the evidence in the pond later," Ransom said. "Just hurry so we can get out of here."

Two other officers arrived and met Tommy. They were Officer Holmes and Cothern. Quickly they made their way up the steps and into the corridor in search of Nettle.

CHAPTER 5

The Sketching

"Send for an ambulance now. Someone has been shot. We need a ten-fifty-six," Officer Holmes shouted.

Officer Whitmore did not look up as he proceeded to call for an ambulance. A car came driving up extremely fast and pulled into the parking lot next to where Tommy was standing.

"Chrissy, what are you doing here?" Tommy asked.

"I told Nettle if she didn't call me by eight o'clock, I was calling the police. When neither of you answered my million phone calls and texts, I did just that. I came as fast as I could."

"Nettle has been kidnapped and we think someone has been shot. That is what the officer is calling in now."

"What?" she said as she started to cry.

Tommy put his arm around Chrissy as they waited in anticipation of hearing whom the ambulance was for. Chrissy and Nettle had been friends almost their entire lives. Chrissy's loyalty and admiration for her best friend ran deep.

How will I ever forgive myself if something has happened to Nettle? No sooner had this thought come to Chrissy's mind when a description of the man that was shot came through. Everyone stood frozen.

"Thank God it's not Nettle, but I pray whomever it is, is OK," Chrissy moaned. Her throat was feeling sore as she held back the tears. Tommy hugged her tight; only moments before, each had feared their best friend, Nettle, had been killed.

* * *

Nettle lay still, thinking about what Ransom and Hawk had just said. What did they mean "the rest of the people"? Maybe they had kidnapped others, or maybe it was something she didn't want to know. Whatever the case, she was glad they had decided to leave her there. Now it was just a matter of the police finding her.

The ambulance arrived to retrieve Ollie. As Jackson stood watching, sorrow filled his heart. He was familiar with pain and loss and was beginning to close his emotions off to stop the hurt. He walked off to be by himself for a moment. Over to the side, he could see Officer Whitmore questioning Tommy. He knew it was just a matter of time before someone recognized him.

Officer Holmes returned to help Officer Cothern in the hunt. It was very dark and the moon was not giving out much light. They continued to scan the area with their flashlights.

"Hey, I think I see something over here." Nettle was moving her legs around fiercely to get their attention.

"I found her!" Officer Cothern shouted. He gently removed the duct tape from her hands and feet.

"Are you Nettle Gray?" Cothern asked.

"Yes, sir, I am. Did you catch them yet?"

"Not yet, but we will," the officer said.

"Are you OK?" the other officer, Holmes, came over to ask.

"I am fine, but what about my boyfriend and the little boy? Are they OK?"

"They're doing fine," Holmes said.

"How about the homeless man, Ollie? Is he all right?"

"We're not sure, ma'am," Cothern said.

"I was afraid you were going to say that."

"Can I go see my boyfriend now?"

"Yes, but after that, you need to go on to the hospital and get checked out. The detectives will be there to ask you some questions."

As they walked back toward the others, Jackson saw Nettle first. He ran hard to hug her. Right now, she was his only true friend.

"Jackson, I am so glad you are OK. I was worried about you. I can't believe you punched Ransom in the face like that. Way to go!" she said as she high-fived him. Jackson smiled big—he felt needed for the first time in a while.

Tommy moved to embrace her. For several minutes his strong arms held her tight. No words were exchanged, just the feelings of joy and safety and the unspoken "I love you."

Chrissy hugged Nettle and told her how much she loved her and pleaded with her to never scare her like that again!

"Who were they, Tommy? Did the police say anything?"

"Not yet, but they will find them, I'm sure. I'm just grateful you are all right."

Officer Whitmore instructed Nettle and Tommy to head to the hospital and told them there would be detectives present to question them once they finished their medical checks.

"I will take Jackson back with me to the dorm room. You guys just call me in the morning and I will bring him over," Chrissy said. "I'm assuming you'd rather stay over at Tommy's tonight for your own safety."

"That sounds great," Nettle said. "Why don't we just all meet for breakfast tomorrow morning at Mimi's Cafe at ten o'clock?"

"Perfect," Chrissy said. "We will see you there in the morning."

As Tommy and Nettle drove in silence to the hospital, neither of them could get their minds off all that had happened to them today. *Was it just a coincidence, or had they been following me around before today?* Nettle reflected to herself. She didn't want to scare Tommy or make him worry anymore, so she just kept her thoughts to herself.

* * * * *

"You must be Nettle Gray," the first detective said, standing inside the emergency room.

"Yes, sir," she replied.

"I'm Detective Moll."

"Nice to meet you, sir," Nettle said.

"And you are?" the other detective asked, extending his hand out to Tommy.

"Tommy Jones."

"Oh, the quarterback for the Wildcats?"

"Yes, sir."

"Nice to meet you, Tommy. I'm Detective Gibbs," he said as he shook Tommy's hand.

"Likewise, sir," Tommy said.

"After you both get checked out by the doctor, we would like to ask you a few questions," Detective Moll said. "It won't take too long."

"Sure, that's fine," Nettle responded, somewhat cautious.

"No problem," Tommy replied.

The emergency room was pretty empty. Wendy, the nurse on duty, called them both back fairly quickly. Nettle had a few bruises on her arms, but nothing major. Wendy took all of Nettle's vitals and told her the doctor would be in shortly. A rather tall, stately looking African-American man walked in and introduced himself as Dr. Wallace. He asked Nettle a few questions as he looked at her bruises.

"Does this hurt?" he asked, touching her arm.

"No, sir, not too bad. It's just a little tender."

"Well, I think you are fine. If anything starts hurting or you start feeling any different, be sure and contact your regular doctor first thing in the morning. I see nothing wrong with you physically. How are you emotionally after seeing someone get shot?"

How does he know that? "Well, I was a little shaken at first, but I think I am fine now."

"Is he alive?" Nettle inquired.

"I'm afraid he didn't make it," Dr. Wallace answered. "But I do know a great psychologist who deals with people who have had similar traumatic situations. Her name is Dr. Ann O'Daniel. Here is her phone number; you might want to give her a call. Sometimes in these instances, people start having bad dreams or experience a little anxiousness. Ann's a little ball of dynamite and is excellent at her job. Just tell her I referred you."

"Thank you. I will keep that in mind."

Tommy was waiting in the room down the hall when his nurse, Angela, said that the doctor wanted to get some X-rays of Tommy's head. She took his blood pressure, temperature, and pulse.

"The aide should be in shortly to take you to get some X-rays of your head, and then the doctor will be in to see you."

Tommy could hear whistling approaching as a young, enthusiastic man entered his room.

"Hey, I recognize you. You're the quarterback for the University of Arizona."

"Yeah, man," Tommy said as he stuck out his arm to shake the guy's hand.

"Well, it's nice to meet you, Tommy. My name is Kort, and I will be taking you down to X-ray. Man, I love watching you play football."

"Thanks. We've had a great season this year."

"So, what happened to you?"

"I got hit over the head by some random dudes tonight up at Corridor Mountain."

"Really . . . that's strange. We've had a few other people that were up at that place come in here recently with something wrong."

"Like what?" Tommy inquired.

"Well, for one, there was a man that got shot up there tonight."

"Yeah, I was up there when that happened. Those were the same guys that hit me over the head. They tried to kidnap my girlfriend."

"Yeah, we heard about the kidnapping attempt up here in X-ray, but," he lowered his voice to a whisper, "between you and me, I think there's more to it than they're telling us."

"I beg your pardon?" Tommy whispered.

"Well, I am not for sure, but I think the police know more than what they're telling us."

"Really, like what?" Tommy was hoping Kort would tell him what he knew.

"I don't know, man. I better not say." Kort grew a little antsy; he didn't want to say anything that might get him fired.

Tommy, sensing his restraint, let it go. But he made a mental note to remember what Kort told him when talking to the detectives. Kort wheeled him down to X-ray.

Nettle was released and proceeded back to the front desk to check out. Wendy had informed her that the detectives were waiting for her in Conference Room A, down the hall to the left.

"Just be careful," Wendy whispered. Nettle was about to ask why when the front desk clerk came back from the restroom. Wendy quickly turned away from Nettle, as if she had not said a thing. It puzzled Nettle. *Why did she say that?*

"The detectives are waiting on you," the front desk clerk, Niki, reminded her.

"Oh, yes. Thanks." Nettle proceeded down the hall and decided to decipher all that later.

Walking into the conference room, she was introduced to Sheila Niño, a sketch artist. Although exhausted and really wanting to go home, she politely responded. As they all sat down around the table, Nettle began to notice uneasiness in Detective Moll's mannerisms. He looked rather uncomfortable for some reason.

"I know you are tired and this has been a really long night for you, but while everything is still fresh on your mind, we need to get as many details as possible," he said. "First, though, we want to start with a sketch of what they looked like. Sheila will try to draw a description of the two men as you give her the particulars. Try and be as detailed as you can."

"I am very sorry for what has happened to you this evening," Sheila said. But, if you can be really descriptive of the two men, I will do my best to sketch them perfectly. Let's start with Hawk."

"OK," Nettle said as she began describing Hawk, wishing the whole time that Tommy would hurry up so he could be with her. For some reason, she had a bad vibe.

"He looked to be around fifty years old and about six feet tall. He had dark brown hair shaved very close to his head, kind of like a military haircut. He had a small tattoo of a skull on his right arm. Oh, and his face was kind of heart-shaped. He had dark brown beady eyes and really thick dark eyebrows. His teeth were a little crooked, and his nose was small and pointy and his mouth was kind of wrinkled. Like a smoker. He actually looked older than he probably was . . . like he had lived a hard life. His cheeks were very rosy, almost like he had on blush. And he was not the leader, Ransom was."

"What was he wearing?" Sheila asked.

"He had on a black, no-sleeve T-shirt with the words 'Seek to Destroy' on it. He also had a red camouflage bandanna tied around his right bicep, right above the tattoo of the skull. He was wearing camouflage pants and black boots." Sheila continued drawing. . . .

* * * * *

Tommy was waiting on the doctor and anticipating meeting with the detectives. He was starting to get a little antsy and wanted the doctor to hurry up. Finally, after what seemed an eternity, Dr. Wallace stepped into Tommy's room.

"Well, Doc, everything OK?"

"Yes, for the most part. It doesn't look like you have a concussion."

"Then I can practice football this week?"

Doctor Wallace thought for a moment. "Why don't you refrain from practice for a couple of days? That will give the knot time to go down a little."

"Sounds great, I can do that. Can I go now?"

"Yes, and take care of yourself. If your head does start to hurt, just take some ibuprofen." As Tommy was getting up to leave, Dr. Wallace lightly grabbed his arm. "And, oh, Tommy—be careful. Sometimes it's hard to tell the good guys from the bad guys out there."

"Yes, sir." Tommy wondered what in the world Dr. Wallace meant by that, but chose not to ask; he was ready to get out of there. Arriving back at the front desk, Niki came around and escorted him to the conference room. She thought Tommy was really hot and had always wanted to meet him. *Too bad he has a girlfriend* was rolling through Niki's mind. She handed him her phone number anyway.

"Come in," Detective Gibbs said.

"What did the doctor say about your head?" Nettle quickly asked.

"He said I'm just fine. How are you?"

"I'm fine, too."

Tommy happened to look down and saw Sheila sketching Hawk. "Wow, is that one of them?"

"Tommy, this is Sheila Niño. She is a sketch artist for the police," Nettle said.

"Nice to meet you, Tommy," Sheila said, holding out her hand to shake his.

"Likewise," Tommy said as he sat down next to Nettle.

Sheila completed the sketch of Hawk and turned it around for everyone to see.

"Wow, that's awesome . . . it really does look like him. You did a fantastic job." Turning toward the detectives, Nettle offered, "I sure hope you guys can find them."

"OK, now let's describe Ransom," Sheila said.

"Evil, he looked extremely evil. He's probably around five feet, ten inches tall and weighs somewhere in the neighborhood of 170 pounds. His hair was very long, dark brown, and stringy. He was somewhere close to, I'd say, thirty-five years old and had a rather thin frame. His eyes were almost black and very round, and he had somewhat of a wide nose. His face was scruffy because he hadn't shaved in a while. He had on all black: a black T-shirt, black pants, and black boots. His left arm had tattoos up and down the whole way with all kinds of birds on it. It was creepy. His right arm had the words 'One World' tattooed all the way down the forearm. He was definitely the one in charge and barked all the orders. He told me that if I would just cooperate, then he would not hurt me. I also remember him, or maybe it was Hawk, saying something about the rest of the people in the desert, but I don't know if he meant more of his cronies or maybe other people they had kidnapped."

"Did you notice any accent when he spoke?" Moll asked.

"No, sir. Neither of them had a strong or definitive accent."

"Did they seem to have a plan?" Gibbs asked.

"A plan, I'm not sure. I don't think this was intentional. I think they wanted to take me someplace in particular. But I'm not sure where or why. They said they wanted what I 'received,' which made no sense at all. That's why I thought they were just some delusional homeless men." Nettle was as intentional as she could be in her statement to the detectives.

"What did you *receive?*" Moll asked.

"I'm not sure I received anything," Nettle said. She wasn't quite sure where their line of questioning was going. She wasn't about to tell them about her encounter. It was as if they weren't asking the right questions—or enough questions having to do with the kidnapping situation.

"Nettle, is there anything else I need to know about the way Ransom looked before I show you the sketch?" Sheila questioned.

"Not on his looks, but his shirt did say, 'I Hate Seekers' on the back of it. I wasn't really sure what that meant, so maybe you guys can tell me," she said, hoping to shock the detectives to try and get a feel for their response. Both Moll and Gibbs glanced at each other as if they knew something they were not telling. Then they both shrugged, acting as if they did not know, either.

"We have no idea. Seekers? Huh. We will look into that," Gibbs offered.

Sheila turned the sketch around to show everyone the drawing of Ransom.

"OK, now that is actually eerie how much it resembles him. You did an excellent job!" Nettle blurted.

"Thank you."

"You never know about these kinds of people," Moll said. "This is probably two deranged derelicts that hang out up at Corridor Mountain trying to rob people."

"I don't think they were there to rob me. I think they were more intrigued with getting information from me. They wanted me to tell them something I couldn't. That's why this is so bizarre. I'm curious to know why they were asking me those weird questions."

"What weird questions?" Moll was finally probing a little.

"Like I told you, they wanted to know what I 'received,' as if I had something they wanted."

"Well, we will keep that in mind and let you know the minute we catch them," Gibbs said.

And just like that, their meeting was over.

* * * * *

"Something's not right, Tommy," Nettle said as they were leaving. "I don't have a good feeling about either of those detectives. I get a weird vibe from them, and I don't like it. Why would two homeless weirdos carry a gun and not ask me for anything if they were just trying to steal from me?"

"I hear ya. But we are tired; maybe we just need a good night's rest. I think we need to tell our parents about all this tomorrow. Maybe they will know how to handle this situation better than us."

"That's fine. I just hope this whole thing is over and we don't have to worry about it anymore."

Once they got back to Tommy's apartment, Nettle nestled up on Tommy's couch and immediately fell asleep. Tommy covered her up with a blanket. Then he went on to bed and laid there for a few minutes thinking about what he and Josh had witnessed earlier that morning.

Surely it wasn't related to Nettle's kidnapping. . . . How could anyone know? No one saw their faces, and we did not tell anyone. But why wasn't it on the news today?

Too tired to worry about it anymore, he fell asleep.

CHAPTER 6

The Sign

Nettle's phone alarm went off and she hopped up to get ready. Tommy made his way to Josh's room and quietly knocked on the door.

"Josh, I need you to come eat breakfast with me and Nettle. I need to talk to you about something that happened last night that's very important. You know I wouldn't wake you up this early if it wasn't important."

Josh sat straight up. "What time is it? Is everything OK?"

"It's nine o'clock and we are meeting at Mimi's at ten. I need to bring you up to speed on what happened to me last night after all we saw yesterday morning."

* * *

Back at the dorm, Chrissy and Jackson were up getting ready when Chrissy's cell phone began to ring. Chrissy's mom, Julie, always called Chrissy on Sunday mornings to chat about her week.

"Sweetie, your dad and I were up early this morning drinking our coffee and watching the news when they showed a sketch of two evil-looking men on television. They said they are on the loose in Tucson and tried to kidnap a university student last night, but she was able to get away. The reporter also said they killed a man. Have you heard about this?"

"Ahh, well . . . yeah, Mom, I do know about it."

"Well, you and Nettle need to be very careful. Don't go out at night by yourself until these madmen are caught. Do you know the girl they tried to kidnap?"

"As a matter of fact, I do."

"Is she OK?"

"Yes, Mom, she is fine."

"OK, good."

"Well, I have to go, now. I am meeting some friends for breakfast, and I don't want to be late."

"OK, sweetie, but you girls be careful, and tell Nettle hello from us."

"OK, will do. Bye."

Chrissy's parents, Gary and Julie, were good friends with Nettle's parents, John and Katrina. Chrissy wondered if her mom had said anything yet to Katrina about the incident.

* * * * *

Tommy got out of the shower and decided to invite Sam to breakfast. Sam played middle linebacker on the team; they had become close friends.

"Hey, Sam. You up?"

"No, I'm not, and this better be good, dude. You better be dying or something 'cause I was planning on sleeping in today," Sam snarled.

"You know I would not wake you up unless it was important. I need to ask you a favor."

"What time is it?"

"Nine-fifteen. I need you to meet me at Mimi's Café at ten. Can you be there? It's really important."

"Well, it better be, homey. Again, I was planning on sleeping late today."

"I know, man, but I need your advice on something. Can you make it?"

"Yeah, I'll be there at ten."

"Thanks, man."

"No worries. See you soon."

Sam was extremely tough and had a rather sarcastic side to him. He was recruited from a small high school in Arkansas, where he played middle linebacker. Six feet, four inches tall, weighing around 220 pounds, the pros were already looking at him, too; he was one of the toughest college middle linebackers in the nation.

Mimi's Cafe was always crowded on Sunday mornings. Nettle got a table for six in the back corner, where it was quiet, and sat down. Everyone arrived on time except Sam. He was always a few minutes late.

"Hey guys, hope this is worth the wake," Sam said, approaching the table laughing. "Who is this little dude?" He pointed at Jackson.

"My name is Jackson, and I'm a friend of Nettle, Tommy, and Chrissy's."

"OK, nice to meet you, Jackson. My name is Sam."

"Nice to meet you too. Do you play football too?"

"Yes, I am the middle linebacker."

"Oh, cool!"

As they all settled in, the waitress arrived at their table.

"Hello, my name is Cindy, and I will be waiting on you today. Do you guys go to the university?"

"As a matter of fact, we do," Chrissy answered.

"Did you hear about that kidnapping last night?"

"What kidnapping?" Nettle responded abruptly.

"The kidnapping that is on the front page of the *Arizona Daily Star* and all over every major television network right now. It's on every channel—some girl from the university. They haven't said her name yet, but she was kidnapped last night by two demented-looking guys. She got away. The reporters said they think it's the same guys that kidnapped those teens from Pusch Ridge Christian High School that they haven't found yet."

"Really," Tommy said. "What else did they say?"

"Well, they said these guys are very dangerous, and they were up at Corridor Mountain last night, and for everyone not to go there until this passes over. They even shot and killed a homeless man up there. "The news reporter said he was trying to help get the girl free. It's a scary place up there at that mountain. I hear there are ghosts up there and all kinds of spooky characters. No telling what really goes on up there," Cindy continued. "I just don't know what a nice girl would be doing up there at that corridor alone at night by herself anyway. She must've been crazy or something."

She scratched the side of her face with her pencil eraser, then sighed, "Well, I'll be right back with your drink orders."

"Well, guys, that is why we asked you to come here today. The girl they tried to kidnap last night was Nettle," Tommy said. You could see Josh and Sam's eyes widen.

"What?" Josh said, a little confused.

"Nettle, before you tell them anything, you need to know my mom called me this morning. Apparently the waitress is right; this thing is all over the news. You probably need to call your parents as soon as we leave here," Chrissy said.

"Look! It's them. They're on the TV now!" Jackson interrupted, excitedly. "They are showing Hawk and Ransom right now."

"Oh my gosh," Chrissy said. "It's a sketch of them."

As they all turned to look at the TV, the room got quiet. Cindy went and turned up the volume. The reporter went on to say that the two men were still at large and were very dangerous. They believed the kidnapping was targeted, and that university officials were being notified today to put extra police on campus.

"They targeted you?" Chrissy asked, looking anxiously at Nettle.

For the next twenty minutes, Nettle shared the details. She also told them all about finding Jackson and the search for his dad.

"The thing that bothers me most is that last night when I described the two men to the detectives and told them that Ransom had 'We Hate Seekers' written on his shirt, they just looked at each other like they knew something they weren't telling us," Nettle said.

"I noticed it too. Something's up," Tommy said.

"What are seekers?" Sam asked.

Josh gave Tommy the eye; he was wondering if it had anything to do with what had happened to them yesterday morning as well. *Were those people up on that mountain, seekers? Is that why they were being shot at?* He pondered, trying to figure out the definition of a seeker.

"We are not sure yet what seekers are. I guess they are people who are just searching for truth," Tommy said.

"Like Nettle?" Chrissy asked.

"Yeah, probably like me," Nettle responded, giggling.

"So, Nettle, the homeless man . . . Did you see him get killed?" Josh questioned.

"Well, I had just turned to run, so I didn't look back. I wasn't sure who got shot until later, when we walked back up on him bleeding to death on the ground. It was horrible; they put duct tape over his mouth and then kicked him in the head. They're sick. It was weird, though, because when Ollie originally walked up to help save me, and they saw him, they hesitated for a minute, as if they knew him. Then Ollie said, 'Not this one.' Maybe it was just my imagination, but it felt as though they all knew each other. I thought to myself, had they kidnapped others Ollie knew about? I guess we'll never know now."

"Why didn't you tell the police that, sweetie?" Tommy asked. "Don't you think that was important information?"

"I don't know, Tommy. Something inside me said not to share that part," she told him. Cindy brought out their food, and Jackson's eyes got as big as the pancakes.

"I have not had any pancakes since my mom died. These look awesome," Jackson said, digging in. Everyone ate and tried to get their minds off of what had happened the night before. Cindy brought out their checks and told them all to be careful.

"Do you plan on telling Coach about this?" Sam asked.

"I don't know. I have to think about it. Please don't say anything yet. Let me be the one to tell him."

"No problem, man, but if you have a slight head injury, he's going to ask you how you got it, and you know Coach, he has a way of getting things out of you."

"Yeah, I know. I'll cross that bridge when I get there."

"OK, dude, call me later . . . I'm going home and back to sleep."

"I will take Jackson back with me until you guys have time to tell Tommy's parents about everything," Josh said. "Just give me a call later and we'll hook back up. We can go online and start looking for his dad."

"That sounds great," Nettle said.

"Yeah, that sounds awesome!" Jackson blurted.

Tommy drove Nettle to get her car, and she followed him to his parents' house. It was almost one-thirty on Sunday, so Tommy figured his parents would be home soon.

Exiting his truck Tommy stopped dead in his tracks. He stood there, shocked. He could not believe his eyes.

There it was in broad daylight, a sign that said, "We hate seekers," sticking straight up in Tommy's parents' front yard.

The hair on Nettle's arms stood up. Instantly she knew this was intentional. She tried hard to remain calm.

"I really thought this thing was random, but not now."

"Hold on; don't get too upset. We don't know for sure. We don't even know what a seeker is yet."

"Well I must be one . . . Why else would they want me?"

CHAPTER 7

The Big Question

Tommy and Nettle waited anxiously for his parents to get home. You could feel the tension in the air. Tommy had pulled up the sign and stuck it in his truck.

"Let's first tell them about last night, and then we can discuss the sign."

"OK, that's fine," Nettle said. "Tommy, can I ask you a pretty deep question?"

"Sure."

"Have you ever struggled with your beliefs about there really being an unseen world? I mean, coming from a home where your dad is a pastor, I was just curious about it."

"Honestly, yes. Still do. Through the years I have seen and heard so much religion. I sometimes felt like I had to be perfect because of it. That everyone was judging me and watching to see if I would perform correctly. When I was sixteen I started getting high just to take the pressure off. But it didn't take me long to realize that was a sure way to mess my life up. I have old friends that still smoke, not realizing they are destroying their lives. Most of them just don't know how to cope with stress, and it's the only thing they think that will relieve it. But all it does is numb the pain until they need more. I still have a lot of questions. I really would like answers just like you; it's just that I guess I am too lazy to seek them.

"That's what intrigues me so much about you, Nettle. You are one of the most nonjudgmental, discerning, intellectual people I have ever met. You don't allow any system of belief, science, or tradition to stand in your way. You love both science and nature. I guess because you were raised totally different than me, it makes it easier to discover. I have heard it all my life, and that really sucks sometimes, because I should know how to decipher out what is real and what's not. It is so hard for me to get my eyes off the individual. There are just so many other voices today trying to come in and disprove and discredit divine intervention. Yet somehow, deep inside, I know there's more. How could anyone not know there's more? Just look at the cosmos. But more than that, I witnessed a person in a third-world country that had something evil living on the inside of them . . . it manifested itself and literally spoke through the person. I heard it with my own ears. It was the vilest thing I have ever witnessed. So, I know there is another world, no matter what any professor or theologian tries to dispel. That is the one thing that lets me know for certain we are not alone."

"You know, Tommy, I believe the problem for most people is that they are seeking answers instead of the entity. We can't allow anyone to try and convince us of anything intellectually, emotionally, or even physically that has not been experienced ourselves. The mind will try and discard the unknown world if we listen to other people. However, there is another element involved. You must go after the supernatural . . . If there is an outer world out there, whether scientific or not, we will find its source if we believe. I don't give a flip what anyone supposes or doesn't accept as true; truth is truth, and when I find real truth, I am going to master it. But, one thing I do know, it will speak," Nettle said. She was firm and carried deep conviction in her voice.

"You know Nettle, Josh and I have had several conversations because he was raised in a home much like mine, but without the pressure of being a preacher's kid," Tommy said. "I really think he gets it even though he might not talk it all the time. He has told me on numerous occasions he thinks there is more than we actually understand from a kingdom well within our reach. He believes that mortals of the twenty-first-century have not understood truth as a whole because of the vast division of doctrines and the pride most take in their theology. Everyone seems divided. Just look at our government. He also thinks there is an evil luminary who heads up an army of detrimental adversaries. He thinks they have the power to deceive many people and keep them from discovering truth for themselves. His mom has witnessed several supernatural things in her life that he told me about—things that a mere human could never do. You need to ask him about it. It will make the hairs on your arms stand up and chills run down your spine."

"That's incredible; I will definitely ask him about it. Your mom and dad are so well respected in the community. They are always willing to lend a helping hand to people in need and are always supporting the poor. Hasn't their life been a barometer for your beliefs?"

"To some degree . . . I guess. They have taught me to be my own person and not let any outside influences curb my inner knowing of truth. And I am so very grateful for that."

"So then your question must be: What's it going to cost me?"

"Pretty much."

"What if it costs you your life? Or it costs you your career in football? Would you still go for it, if you knew for certain it was absolute truth?"

"Yes."

"What if you could perform supernatural powers in its kingdom?"

"What do you mean?"

Nettle smiled at Tommy, knowing that something big was about to transpire. She hugged him tight just as the front door opened.

"Hey there, kiddos, what a pleasant surprise to see you both," Tommy's dad, Richard, said as he and his wife walked into the den.

"It's good to see you guys too," Nettle said, hugging Richard and Tommy's mom, Joan.

Tommy knew that what he was about to share was going to cause great concern to his mother. She was a bit of a worrier when it came to him. He didn't want either of them to overreact until they had this thing figured out.

"We came here today because we have something we want to tell you."

"Sure, Son. Have a seat. What's on your mind?"

"Have either of you seen the news at all today?"

"No, I'm afraid not."

"Well, they are reporting that two evil-looking men tried to kidnap a university student last night," Tommy began. "We just wanted you to know that it was Nettle."

"What?" Joan exclaimed.

"What in the world happened, dear?" Richard asked. Nettle told the Joneses about the ordeal.

"Well, I have been keeping up with that high school student kidnapping incident very closely. Do they think they are the same kidnappers?"

"I don't think they know yet, Dad."

"Well, I think you both need to stay here a few days until everything blows over," Joan said.

"I know the police are hot on their tracks by now," Tommy said, trying to reassure his mother. "Dad, nothing strange has happened around the church, has it?"

"No, Son, why do you ask?"

"Well, when we drove up, there was a sign in your yard saying, 'We Hate Seekers!'"

"Well, what's that supposed to mean? Let me see it," Richard said.

They walked outside and Tommy pulled the sign out of his truck and showed it to his parents.

"What do you think they are talking about, Dad?" Tommy asked.

"I'm not sure, Son, but I will try and get to the bottom of this. Your mother is right; you both need to stay here with us for a while, at least until they are caught."

"Nettle, honey, have you told your parents about this yet?" Joan asked.

"No ma'am. I was going to call them after we told you guys."

"Well, let's go back inside and do that right now," Joan suggested.

Suddenly they heard a loud car horn blowing frantically. Chrissy screeched into the driveway and jumped out of her car. She had a terribly worried look on her face.

"You all are not going to believe this," she said, talking ninety miles an hour. "When I got back to the dorm, there was a sign stuck to our door that said . . . 'We hate seekers!' At first I thought it was a joke. Then, when no one admitted putting it there, I began to think it was them. How in the world did someone put that on our door without anyone seeing them? What does this mean? What do they want with us? I don't like this and it makes me scared, knowing they know exactly where we live."

"My parents had a sign in their yard that said the same thing."

"Do you think someone in your dorm is connected to these guys?" Joan asked.

"I don't think anyone knows the answers right now," Richard said. "But I do think you girls just need to stay here at our home the next few days until we get this all figured out. Right now, you both need to call your parents."

Nettle and Chrissy informed their parents, then went back and gathered their things at the dorm. Tommy called Josh to let him know what the plans were. He agreed to keep Jackson with him for the night.

CHAPTER 8

Another Dream

The next morning, Nettle awakened from another really fascinating and somewhat perplexing dream. She rolled over to see if Chrissy was awake. After all, it was seven o'clock already.

"Chrissy . . . Chrissy," she whispered loudly. "Wake up." She nudged Chrissy's arm. "I have something to share with you and Tommy."

"I'm already awake. What is it, Nettle?"

"I think I had a dream about our future. I really want you and Tommy to hear it and tell me what you think before I forget any of it."

Chrissy followed Nettle into Tommy's room.

"Tommy, wake up," she said as she rubbed his arm. Tommy opened his eyes only to see Nettle and Chrissy standing directly over him, looking intently down at him.

Tommy sat upright, startled. "What is it? Is everything OK?"

"Yes, everything is OK," Nettle said. "I just had a really bizarre dream. I think it was a premonition of things to come. I wanted you and Chrissy to listen to it and tell me what you think."

"OK. Let me get dressed, and I will meet you in the kitchen."

They all gathered around the kitchen table anxious to hear the dream.

"First, let me start out by saying that I really think this dream was some kind of revelation or disclosure of some sort," Nettle began. "I know that sounds weird, but it was very real, and I have such peace about it. I remember every detail. It started out with a group of sick people that needed curing. They were people of all ages, from babies to the elderly. They were all in this big room, inside a barn, about a hundred to two hundred of them waiting to be made well. It was just about time for the meeting to begin, when all of a sudden a big eagle swooped down and picked up one of the little children and started carrying him away. All the people got quiet and watched as the eagle flew away with the child.

"Next, I was standing on top of a mountain and could see the child. I could tell he was sick and needed help. Something inside me knew that my purpose lay in saving this young boy. A definitive voice spoke and said, 'Just believe.' At that moment, that very instant, I knew I could fly. I knew that if I believed the voice completely, I could help this child. So I decided to accept that I could fly, and away I went. Soaring through the sky with my arms outstretched like a bird, flying over the mountains, rising through the clouds, over all creation. For a brief moment, I was so excited I forgot about the child. Higher and higher I went, faster and faster, until finally I spotted the eagle carrying the child. I knew I must be clever and not let the eagle see me so he wouldn't drop the child and kill him. The eagle seemed to be on a mission, too. Suddenly, I looked down and saw far below. There were people walking all around this farmhouse, but it had an electric fence around it so the people could not get out. I realized this wasn't a good place even though it looked nice. As I continued to look, I noticed there was no one else around and that the farmhouse was way out in the desert. The strange thing is that this is the second or third time I dreamed I could fly. I had another dream the night before last about a mountain, an eagle, and flying. I think this dream might just be a continuation . . . I'm not sure. I find this all very intriguing."

"What does flying mean?" Chrissy asked.

"Well, I looked it up, and it means that you have the ability to move in another realm and rise above your problems and circumstances."

Tommy had a real look of concern on his face. Nettle thought it was just because of the dream. However, Tommy's secret seemed to be unfolding in Nettle's dream.

"So anyway, I began to see military-like equipment all around—tanks and all kinds of barricades around the place. The eagle started flying around and around the top of the farmhouse, when all of a sudden, it swooped down and dropped the child into a large pond right in the middle of the desert. Immediately, a woman wearing an African-looking outfit dove in and pulled him out. Then a man appeared in front of everyone, and they all started bowing down to him, even the small child. It was as if he was a god or something. I knew I must hide and not let him see me, so I flew over and landed on top of a large tree and watched to see what they would do next. Suddenly, over to my left, vans full of people pulled up and got out. I could tell they didn't want to be there. They must have been kidnapped because their faces were forlorn and their heads were held low. It was as if they knew their lives were over. Then, men who appeared to be guarding the farmhouse drew their guns and told everyone to bow down to the leader. Everyone obeyed. I watched a little longer when I realized that I had been given the answer. It was kind of like a golden scepter of authority, if you will, to help these people escape. I don't know if they were all sick or if they just needed to escape, but I knew it was my place to help them get out. I needed additional help, because I knew I could not do it in my own strength. Then that voice spoke again, telling me I had the answers, just like in the first dream when it said that I would find the answers. And then I woke up!"

Chrissy's eyes were as wide as golf balls as she sat staring at Nettle. Tommy, sitting quietly, had a look of near-dread on his face as he wondered deeply about Nettle's dream and his escapade yesterday morning. *Who gave her this dream?* It was not coincidental. Tommy would continue to keep his secret to himself for now.

"Nettle, you are the most unordinary person I know, and that's why I love you so much," Chrissy said. "You experience so many uncommon occurrences. That was the most amazing dream I have ever heard. Maybe that's why you were drawn to the corridor—to find out about these people and lead the police to them. Maybe there are others out in the desert."

Tommy sat there, still thinking deeply on what Nettle had just shared with them. Cautiously, he agreed with Chrissy. "Nettle, you have to study this out and make sure you understand what it means. This is serious and you could be killed getting involved with something like that," he said, a look of distress on his face.

Before Nettle could ask him what exactly he meant by that, Tommy's cell phone rang.

"Hey man, when are you coming home?" Josh asked. "Jackson is really getting antsy to see Nettle. He's been up since six o'clock talking about some dream he had last night."

"Alright, tell him we will be there by ten."

"Sure thing, see you then," Josh said.

"Do you think your parents would let Jackson stay here too?" Nettle inquired. She had heard what Josh said through the phone.

"I'm sure they will," Tommy answered. "It's time to tell them about him anyway. I can't believe his face isn't plastered all over the news. What's up with that? You think he is telling us the truth?"

"Well, I hope so. He better be, or he might just get turned in sooner than later," Nettle said. "But I believe him; he hasn't given any of us reason not to yet. And I take full responsibility for bringing him here."

"Maybe you should tell Tommy's parents about your dream, Nettle," Chrissy said. "Maybe Tommy's dad can give you some insight on the meaning."

"Sure, I can do that."

* * * * *

Ten o'clock rolled around and they walked into the entrance hall to leave when Tommy's dad called them into the den.

"Take a look at this," he said, turning up the volume on the TV. It was Officer Cothern describing Ransom and Hawk. "They just said they now have information that ties the two men to several kidnappings, including the kidnapping of a four-year-old little boy last night," Richard said. Nettle glanced over at Tommy, thinking about the dream she just had.

The officer went on to tell the reporter that the four-year-old's name was Stephen Beasley, that he was diabetic, and that he needed his insulin badly. *Beasley*, thought Nettle, *that's Jackson's last name. Surely he doesn't have a relative named Stephen. I need to remember to ask him.* The news media then skipped over to the corridor shooting, showing a picture of Ollie. They said his name was Oliver Cook and that he went by Ollie. They portrayed him a hero, dying while trying to rescue the young girl. The news went on to say that they were not going to release photos of the girl, or her name and whereabouts, so the men could not locate her.

"I recognize Ollie," Richard said. "He came to our church a couple of times. He was a kind man. He shared with me that a gentleman passing through town spoke in the park one morning and it changed his life. He said the man's life story was similar to his."

"Yes, that's right," Joan said. "Ollie told us this gentleman actually had a gift to cure people. He said he saw it with his own eyes as he watched several people get cured. It really made us stop and think if this was possible today."

This was all becoming very bizarre to Tommy. He was starting to think that everything was somehow connected—even Jackson. He was concerned for everyone's safety.

"That's cool about Ollie. Too bad we will never know now. Well, we have to get going. We have to go pick up someone at my apartment and bring them back here. When we get back, we want to tell you about a dream Nettle had last night," Tommy said.

"OK," Richard said. "Please be careful, and be aware of your surroundings."

"Oh, we will," Chrissy said. "You don't have to worry about that; I am very observant. I'll be watching everything; you can count on that!"

"Nettle, can you believe it? A four-year-old boy was kidnapped last night. Just like in your dream," Chrissy said as they stepped outside.

"I know, and I don't think it is just a coincidence . . . I have a feeling we are about to encounter my dream in the near future."

"I have something I want to tell you guys once we are with Josh. It might shed some light on everything," Tommy said.

"OK," Nettle answered. "Don't forget."

When they pulled up to Tommy and Josh's apartment, two other cars were outside.

"That looks like Coach McClain's car; I wonder what he's doing here," Tommy said. They walked inside and there sat Josh, Jackson, Sam, Coach McClain, and one of the assistant coaches, Coach Hartsfield.

"Hey guys, come on in," Josh said. "Coach found out about the other night and wanted to talk to us about it."

"Hello, everyone. Coach Hartsfield and I just stopped by to let all of you know that Officer Holmes contacted me last night. He wanted us to be aware of our surroundings just in case these guys were to try something else. Tommy, I want you to be very aware of your environment at all times. Officer Holmes seemed to think the kidnapping was targeted."

You could hear Chrissy sigh as she turned and shrugged her shoulders at Nettle. "I have called a team meeting since the biggest game of the year is in five days. I want the team to know and be on the lookout for anything out of the ordinary or anything suspicious. I also called Dean Pogue at the university and made him aware. He said he hasn't heard anything from anyone on the school staff but that security would be put on high alert. I want practice today to go as usual, OK?"

"OK, Coach," all the guys said, seemingly at once.

"There is something else you should know, Coach," Tommy said.

"What's that, Son?"

"I have a slight head injury. The doctor said I should miss a couple days of practice, but I think I am good to go. I just wanted you to be aware of it."

"Well, when you get there today, we will have you checked out again, just to make sure."

"Yes, sir . . . sounds good."

Coach McClain stood up, and you could tell that at this moment more than ever, he felt like a father to these boys. He had been a coach for thirty-two years and had never experienced anything like this before. He wished he could protect his boys around the clock. He was a man of few words, but when he spoke, they listened.

"You guys are the leaders on my team. I need you, now more than ever, to lead. Take care of yourselves. Be careful. I will see you at practice this afternoon."

"Yes, sir," the boys said as they walked the coaches out to their cars.

"Wow, this thing is really bad, isn't it?" Jackson said. "I can't believe all this has happened since I left my foster home. I can't wait till those guys get busted. Oh, by the way, I had a dream last night that they got caught. And all of you were in my dream."

"Yeah, he has been talking about this dream ever since he woke up," Josh said. "I think this whole thing has kind of freaked him out a little. He has probably seen too many scary movies."

"No!" Jackson exclaimed. "This dream was too real; I just know it . . . just like I know we are going to find my dad."

"Oh, really?" Tommy said, now starting to consider some of these dreams. "What happened in your dream?"

"I just remember that Nettle found the bad guys. She also helped the kidnapped people escape. They were all locked up in some weird place. It almost looked like a cave, but that's really all I remember. But she was their hero," he said, smiling as though his dream was real.

"Jackson, speaking of finding your dad, do you have a four-year-old relative named Stephen Beasley?" Nettle asked.

"Not that I know of . . .Why?"

"Well, we saw on the news this morning that these guys just kid-napped a four-year-old boy last night, who is very sick with diabetes. His name was Stephen Beasley. I was just wondering if he was related to you."

"I don't think so."

"Let's talk about all this in the truck. We need to head back so we can tell my parents about both your dreams," Tommy said. You could tell by his quietness—he seemed almost despondent—that something was weighing heavy on his mind. Nettle decided to ask him later; she had never seen him like this before.

"Look, there is a sign on the side of your truck," Jackson said.

"Someone must have just stuck it there, because it was not there a few minutes ago when we walked Coach Hartsfield and Coach McClain to their cars," Tommy said.

All six of them stood there, as though frozen, looking around the complex. Tommy glared at the rooftops. Josh looked around the side of the place. The girls looked down both sides of the street. Sam looked behind both vehicles.

"Look, there's also a note on your windshield," Sam said.

As the six-foot-five-inch rough and rugged quarterback opened the letter, chills ran down his spine. A look of fury came over his face; Nettle noticed it quickly.

"What does it say, Tommy?" Nettle asked.

Feeling nervous over the look on Tommy's face, Chrissy suggested they go back inside before they read it.

"First of all, there is a picture sketched of all four of us at the top of the note. There is one of me, Nettle, Chrissy, and you, Josh. Then at the bottom there is one of Jackson, some other man, and a small boy."

"Well, what does it say?" Nettle inquired, urgency in her voice.

"It says, 'We will let the man and the boy live, if you give Nettle to us. We know she has special powers. She will not be hurt.'"

"Let me see that," Nettle said, reaching for the note. "Whoa, that is the little boy we saw on the news this morning . . . that is Stephen Beasley."

"Can I see him?" Jackson asked.

Nettle carefully handed the note to Jackson, waiting to see his response once he saw the young boy.

"That is my dad. That is a picture of my dad, Arlice! They have my dad; we have got to do something to save him." Tears began to well in the boy's eyes.

"Who is the little boy, Jackson?" Nettle asked. "Do you recognize him?"

Through his teary eyes, Jackson looked again. "I don't know. I don't recognize him, but that's my dad. That is Arlice Beasley."

Chrissy walked over to hug Jackson; she told him not to worry. She assured him they would find his dad and everyone would be OK.

"Does the note say anything else?" Josh asked.

"No, that's it," Tommy said.

"I wonder why they drew all four of us if all they want is Nettle?"

Josh asked.

"Probably to try and scare us. To let us know they are watching all of us, since we're friends," Tommy said.

"Well they don't scare me," said tough-man Sam. "Bring it on. I will have something big waiting on them."

"I believe what they are saying in the note is true," Nettle said. "As most of you know, my quest has been to try and search for significance. I have some serious questions that I can't seem to shake. I knew the only way I could get answers was to get alone and see if I could prove out this supernatural entity by him speaking to me. That night while I was standing on Corridor Mountain, these words came very clearly to me: 'Eyes that look are common; eyes that see are rare, revealing secrets to its servants. You carry the future, you breathe the air of inspiration, and you are nourished by the spirit of the future. You are unquestionably controversial, a villain of today, a hearer of tomorrow. At night the future comes to your door and knocks; you refuse to let it walk away silent. You are a unique copy of an ancient gift, a unique reverberation of an ancient manuscript.' I think I was about to receive those powers, but when I opened my eyes, there stood Hawk and Ransom. I don't know how long they had been standing there watching me."

"What in the world does that mean, Nettle?" Chrissy asked.

"That means she carries a foretelling voice," Josh said.

"A what?" Sam asked.

"My mom has tried to convince me that she hears him speak, too, but I was just too young and uninterested to really pay attention before," Josh said.

"Nettle . . . I have known you nearly all my life, and you have never said anything to me about having extraordinary powers," Chrissy said, an air of near-suspicion in her voice.

"Or to me, either," Tommy said.

"That's because I don't understand the entirety of it yet. I know bits and pieces. A few parts have been revealed but not the whole thing yet. I have been asking for more. I was receiving a lot of it just before I was taken.

"I have got to get back to the corridor. Especially now that those bozos seem to know I have powers."

"This sounds like something in the movies. Like *The Avengers* or *The Expendables*," Sam said.

"Well, if you have special powers, I need you to use them to go and save my dad," Jackson said. "Just like in my dream, you are going to save all those people."

"Now hold on a minute, Jackson," Tommy said. "We don't know for sure that Nettle is anyone's liberator right now."

Almost energized, Nettle looked at Jackson and said, "I had the same dream, Jackson, just like yours, only more detailed. I don't think we have much time.

"We have to come up with a plan, and come up with one quick. You have gifts, too, Jackson."

"I do?"

"Just you wait and see."

"But we have no idea where they are located," Chrissy said.

"Did your dream tell you the exact location?" Josh asked.

Out of the blue, and with a look of apprehension on his face, Tommy butted in before Nettle could answer.

"I have something to tell you all, and it is very confidential."

Finally, thought Nettle. She could tell that whatever it was had been weighing heavily on his mind for some time now.

CHAPTER 9

The Announcement

"Josh and I have a secret we have not told anyone yet," he announced. Josh sat there, mentally preparing himself for what their reactions might be.

"You all know we used to drive out deep in the desert on Saturday mornings to just hang for the fun of it. Sometimes we would go target shooting and sometimes just check things out. So last Saturday morning Josh and I decided to go for target practice and drove out in a different direction. A few miles out we discovered this area that I would describe as a lush, tropical forest. It was crazy; we had never seen anything like it in the desert before. It was a beautiful, enchanted-like area. It even had a pond. So we decided to drive the road that led up a mountain."

"Yeah, he's absolutely right; the place was very unusual-looking," Josh added. "About a quarter of a mile up, we saw this cottage-looking, white farmhouse. It was relatively large with a white picket fence around the property. Something about it looked eerie, though." Josh held his hands up and wiggled his fingers for effect.

"Yeah, it literally reminded us of a place the government would use secretly, to do classified work." Tommy was now continuing the story. "We didn't see anyone around, but we did notice there were lights on inside the place. It was a beautiful, sunny, cool morning. We kept driving until the road dead-ended. As we made a U-turn to leave, we noticed a huge open tent with at least a hundred and fifty people inside. But most interestingly, there were no cars. Not one car parked anywhere."

"So what were all those people doing? Was it a party?" Jackson asked.

"We couldn't tell at first. All we could see were a bunch of wheel-chairs being passed around over everyone's heads. We decided to park the truck and get out so we could see better. We noticed a man standing on what looked like a stage, talking to the crowd. We snuck up closer and hid behind some bushes to listen."

"Tommy Jones, why didn't you tell me about this?" Nettle interject-ed.

"Just wait. When you hear the end of the story, you will know why."

Sitting on the edge of her seat, anticipating the rest, Nettle recalled her dream. Foreseeing where this was going, she knew this incident was going to connect—somehow.

"What did you guys do next?" Jackson, extremely anxious, prodded.

"Totally captivated by what we were witnessing, we moved closer," Tommy went on. "The gentleman speaking at the podium told everyone they could be restored to health. When he said that, I looked around, and sure enough, there were a lot of people there that looked handi-capped or sick in some way. Then we watched as the people went for-ward and were instantly made well. There were wheelchairs, crutches, and canes all over the place. We saw a blind man receive his sight. I had never seen anything like it in my entire life. And my dad's a pastor."

"Yeah, it was really surreal," Josh said. "But the most remarkable part was what the guy told the people. In fact, Jackson, now that I think about it, that man looked a little like that sketch of your dad."

"Yeah . . . he did," Tommy said. "He definitely resembled him."

"Well, what did he say that was so profound?" Nettle asked. She, too, was anxious to hear the rest.

"He started telling the people about this 'supernatural kingdom' that is not of this world."

"That's right," Tommy said. "I've heard a lot of spiritual stuff in my life, but never have I heard anything like what this guy taught before."

"Me either," Josh said. "He called himself a seeker, a spiritual scientist or kingdom investigator of sorts. The information was so compelling that we couldn't wait to hear more. He spoke about an integrated message system that bears evidence to everything supernatural. He said the messages vastly exceed the insights of the individual people that developed it and provides the answers to everything. He began asking everyone that was sick to come forward again. This time we had moved up so close, you could have heard a bug fart."

Everyone laughed, but desperately wanted to hear more. Tommy went on. "The first person that went up was about a sixty-five-year-old man. People were helping him get up on the platform. He had an amputated leg from the knee down. When they finally stood him up, the seeker man—that's what I will call him—asked him his name and what happened to his leg. The guy said his name was Dan and that his leg had been blown off in war. The seeker man went on to say, 'Well, I have good news for you tonight. There is a supernatural power around us right now.' He said it was not energy like many talk about. It is an individual.

"He went on to say that we can all have possession of this comprehensive message system. That it was given to us from outside our hyperspace—from outside of the time dimension itself. It is a power available to us from our 'master' and his 'kingdom,' and he can heal anyone. You no longer have to live under the earth curse anymore. Then he looked at him and said, 'Are you ready to have a new leg?' Then Dan, beaming with anticipation, shook his head yes. What happened next just about blew our minds. That seeker man reached down and touched the amputee's nubby knee with his hand. Then, he closed his eyes and said, 'Grow, I command you to grow now, according to the kingdom authority I have been given.' And there, as Josh is my witness, right before our eyes, that guy's amputated leg grew out. Immediately, he started crying and running around on the platform with his new leg. The people roared and clapped, and some even danced around, they were so astonished."

"Yeah," Josh said, "it was incredible and it was real! Tommy and I were close, so we could see it clearly."

Nettle, feeling tightness in her stomach, wanted to know more. She knew there was more to this life than what she had been taught. "What else happened? I want to hear it all, Tommy."

"All kinds of things happened. We saw blind eyes opened; we saw a crippled woman get out of her wheelchair and walk. It wasn't that stuff you see on TV where people are just moved by their emotions. These people were cured, Nettle." You could hear the excitement in Tommy's voice.

"Now, why is it you have never told me or anyone else about this yet?" Nettle asked again. "Especially when we had our talk yesterday."

"Dude . . . this is awesome," Sam bellowed.

"I wanted to tell you, Nettle, especially yesterday while we were talking, but I just couldn't yet."

"Then, completely out of nowhere," Tommy continued, "a shot was fired, and then another and another. Suddenly the seeker man went down—he was hit. Josh looked at me with terror in his voice and said, 'We've got to get out of here, now!' Run!"

"We began running as fast as we could back to the truck. We couldn't stay long enough to see if the seeker man was dead or not. People were going down left and right. I don't know how many masked gunmen there were, but it sounded like shots were being fired from everywhere. I don't know how we escaped without being hit. Thank God we were parked close."

"Unbelievable," Chrissy said. "That's the scariest thing I have ever heard." She had a look of dismay. Her look let the guys know they were right in keeping their story a secret before now.

"What happened next, Tommy?" Nettle asked. She looked in his eyes with alarm.

"We ran as fast as we could to my truck and headed back down the road. But here's where it gets really weird: when we got to where the farmhouse had been, it was gone! Nothing was there—nada, nothing!"

"What?" Nettle exclaimed. "What do you mean 'not there'? Houses just don't disappear."

"Well, this one did," Tommy said. "It wasn't there anywhere, I promise."

"Are you sure you guys were looking in the right spot? I mean, you must have been freaked out by the gunfire and not really paying attention," Chrissy said.

"No, Chrissy," Josh said. "The farmhouse was the only thing on that road besides the trees, and it was gone."

"I believe you," Jackson said.

"So where did you go next? And why didn't you tell the police?" Sam asked.

"As we were driving back, our hearts were beating ninety miles an hour," Tommy said. "Our adrenaline was rushing and our endorphins were off the chart. Then Josh realized they were following us."

"Oh my God, are you serious?" Chrissy said.

"They finally stopped once we turned off that road into the desert. It was then we discussed not saying anything until we knew it was safe. We wanted to see it on television first, and then go to the police."

"But that was the problem," Josh said. "It was never on television, not one mention of it. To this moment there has been nothing said."

"Did you see any of the gunmen's faces?" Nettle asked.

"Nope, not even one of them. All we could see were their red ski masks," Tommy said.

"Did you ever hear the seeker-man's name?" Chrissy asked.

"No, we never heard it mentioned," Josh answered.

"And you think I'm crazy for wanting to go to that corridor, when you went way out to some deserted desert place and saw people killed and never said anything?"

"I know, Nettle. That is why I was scared for you . . . These might be the same deranged people. I have a feeling they are connected somehow. I don't have any proof of that, but it feels like it."

"If it is related, all the more reason to get to them first," she said. Remembering her dream about the desert, she suddenly had thoughts about something that might link both incidents. She recalled Ransom mentioning a pond. She had almost forgotten that until now. Tommy mentioned a pond where he was, too. *We have to go to that pond. Maybe it will give us answers,* she thought to herself.

"She's right," Sam said. "I think we need to go kick some kidnapping butt."

They loaded up and headed back for the Jones' house; Sam went back to his dorm. Sam was so intrigued by all the things Nettle had said that he could not stop thinking about it. He had a gut-wrenching feeling he was supposed to be involved, too, and really wanted to know more about this so-called "other kingdom" thing.

Sam was deep in his own thoughts. *Could I have powers, too? I really need to know more about this stuff.*

CHAPTER 10

The Visitation

After sitting comfortably in the Jones' den, Tommy began to go over everything in his head.

"You know guys, I was thinking. I really don't have a concise plan yet, but I really do think we all should take a ride out to that place tomorrow in the daylight and check it out again," he suggested.

"Let's do it," Jackson said. His little mind was going in circles with this new information. "Maybe we can find my dad. Maybe this will help us know what to do next. So what time tomorrow do you want to go?"

"Hold on a minute: I don't know about this," Chrissy said. "Don't you guys think we have had enough excitement the last couple of days?" Chrissy was frightened.

"I think we should go too, Chrissy," Nettle said in a serious tone.

"You can't be serious!" Chrissy retorted. "I think we need to think this thing through and not make any rash or emotional decisions."

"I'm very serious," Nettle said. "Besides, who knows, there may be tons of people that need our help. We might be their only hope. I think that both dreams prove that we are on the right track."

Nettle leaned back in her chair. "I want to share something with you guys that I think you might find intriguing." Nettle was beginning to realize she would eventually have to share what she was encountering with many others once she understood it all. No matter what anyone thought or alleged.

"Before you start, do you think you are discovering answers for all people?" Josh asked.

"Well, first, let me start by saying this, Josh. I have been researching a ton of information about our generation. Some of the facts I have found are really disturbing. The suicide rate is higher than ever before in history. The number of kids without dads in the homes right now is the highest it's ever been, so that leaves them feeling they have no direction in life. It also leaves them with a fear about getting married themselves. Did you all know that 60 percent of all first marriages fail and 80 percent for second marriages? I have two friends whose dads have both been married five times, and they are only in their forties."

"Good grief," Chrissy responded.

"Teens are using more drugs than ever, and it is reported that the number of teens on antidepressants is at an all-time high. Let alone all the ADD and ADHD medication teens are on. The porn industry is making a killing and a larger number than ever, now, are addicted to pornography, both boys and girls. The highest number is men, but they usually become addicted as teens. Statistics claim that porn is a major accomplice in destroying marriages. How many times have we heard *Nightline*, or whatever, reporting stories about men going after under-age girls for sex online? Then we have thousands of little girls being stolen in our nation, and all over the world for that matter, and sold into sex trafficking. What is wrong with us? What are we looking for that we can't seem to find? We make more money in America than anywhere in the world, yet we are the most depressed, addicted, and miserable."

"Yeah, I know three girlfriends that are taking Prozac right now and can't seem to shake their depressing thoughts," Chrissy said.

"I know that you guys love me and won't judge me, so I feel I can share some of my recent encounters and information with you," Nettle said. "My motto is always investigation before condemnation, so I hope you adopt that philosophy as well and investigate what I am about to tell you before you choose to condemn it."

"I don't think you have to worry about that here with us, Nettle," Josh said. "We enjoy hearing and learning from you. At least, I do."

"I just don't see most religions giving people what they need today. I am discovering something different," Nettle went on. "You can't find it unless you go seek it out intentionally, and then it will come to you. You see, the seeker-man was right. The earth had a curse hanging over it for a long time, but not anymore. Many people don't believe, accept, or even know this. Most are wedged in the boundaries of their family tradition. Some are trapped in the confines of institutionalism; they are literally stuck in their humanness. Others are too smart for their own good and deny it because they can't see it, feel it, or touch it. Or, some famous scientist claimed to disprove it, and that settled it for them. They will never be able to transcend past the human mind into the spirit part of their being. Most people are totally unaware of this available power. We are supposed to learn from our parents, and they have been wrong. They have been so preoccupied with making money and a living that they have missed the most important part of why we exist. Some people are scared to depend on anything but themselves.

"Have you noticed how everyone wants to know their purpose but are too lazy to dig and search for it? I find it rather intriguing that the most intelligent, those with the highest IQs, are the least reputable in understanding man's unique design in seeking for more, beyond our own minds. It's baffling to me," Nettle said, quizzically. "They end up becoming the most detrimental to society because of their vocal hatred of people who find the unknown realm. They usually are people who have been hurt by someone, so that nullifies any inquisition further into the truth.

You could have heard a pin drop as Nettle went on. "This impenetrable force, you must take very seriously. It is not something to play with. He has been sent to help only those who believe in him. The answer is always up to man to believe in *this unseen world*. And that is all I can tell you now."

"So, what you are saying, if I am hearing you correctly, is that you think this all has something to do with a supernatural world?" Josh asked.

"I don't think; I know so," Nettle said. "I have experienced it myself. There is an additional world out there, Josh, a kingdom, and it has everything to do with us here on earth. It is a vast expanse of a timeless place—a kingdom or empire that rules the times and space. A way into which man can have hope and security about the afterlife. I think that seeker-man must have seen it and tapped into its power."

"So you are what they're after," Tommy said.

"Do you actually hear this force or power talk to you?" Jackson asked.

"Oh, yes, Jackson. Very clearly on most occasions."

"Am I old enough to get a hold of it?" he prodded.

"Absolutely," Nettle replied.

"How do I find it?" Jackson questioned. He was so intrigued by what Nettle was telling him that he was sitting on the edge of his seat—about to fall off—with curiosity. Whatever this power was or whatever this realm was about, as young as Jackson was, he still wanted to know more. Something . . . maybe this force, was moving on the inside of him and he could feel it right then. What an awesome peace he had.

"I've learned that in order to find it, your opinions must vanish. The reason is because the one who imparts it is from another dimension, Jackson. The one who imparts it to you is called *Parakletos*. He is part of a kingdom that exists both here and in the outer world. He gives you wisdom way beyond your years if you just ask for it."

"Well, that's an unusual kind of name," Jackson said. "It's pretty tight, though. Can you see him?"

"I have never seen him," Nettle said. "I have only heard him. He can literally tell you the answers to things. He even informs or warns you of future events."

"Are you sure about all that?" Tommy asked.

"Trust me, Tommy. I am telling you this from experience. Try not to allow any religious doctrine to get in your way," Nettle said softly as she smiled sweetly at him. "He can impart a lot of things to mortals—things they aren't even aware of."

The others were beginning to believe. They could tell Nettle had experienced something that was from the supernatural. You could almost see it, visually, on her.

"Come on; let's get back to your house," Nettle said to Tommy. "We probably need to tell your parents about the sign." She knew in her heart they were about to experience some things that would prove she was right. She would never push Tommy toward her viewpoint; she would talk to Parakletos about showing him directly.

Tommy headed straight to the bathroom when they got home; suddenly, his cell phone rang.

"Hello?"

"All we want is the girl, just like we said in the note. Give her to us and all this will stop. We know she has extraordinary powers, and we want her to use them for us. We are not going to hurt her," the deep, muffled voice said.

"What girl?"

"Don't play stupid with me, Tommy! Nettle; we want Nettle."

"Well, you can't have her!"

"Look, buddy, you think a disappearing farmhouse is something? I can make your whole family disappear. You don't want that to happen, do you?" Tommy heard the phone click suddenly. He had to think. This infuriated him. He was now beyond scared; he was livid.

Nettle had gone to her room to lie down for a little while. Tommy went into his room to be alone and think. As he lay there, just about to fall asleep, Nettle ran into his room in a state of excitement.

"Tommy, I just had a vision. It was almost like I was in a trance. You are never going to believe what I have just seen," she announced while pulling him out of bed to follow her into the den.

"Hey everybody, I need to share something important with you right now before I forget it. Chrissy, could you write it down as I go, please?" Tears were welling up in Nettle's eyes. Her heart was beating intensely as if she was about to give a speech. Tommy hoped it was something that would help in breaking the news to her about his alarming phone call.

"I just had a premonition; I think it was a forewarning of some kind. It was different than a dream because I was awake. It almost felt like I was in a trance, or it was a vision."

Instantly, their curiosity was extremely peaked.

"In this vision, I saw several kings coming up from the earth. They were from all over the world. They were standing together in a circle, chanting, 'We will prevail, we will conform the world. The nations will bow down in devotion to us.' They kept repeating these same phrases over and over."

"Where were the kings from?" Jackson said.

"They were from four different countries . . . Italy, Greece, Iran, and Iraq. As they stood there together, I could literally see four strong whirlwinds blowing in every direction, covering the whole place while they chanted. Then I saw two men walk up to the kings, and I just knew it was Ransom and Hawk, except they were dressed in long white robes and the kings called them 'Mighty Men of Valor.' It was weird."

"Oh man; that's what's up. It sounds like a sci-fi book I read not long ago," Jackson said. "Keep going. What else happened?"

"All of a sudden, this massive eagle flew over their heads and dropped a scroll down in the middle of their circle."

"Was it the same eagle you saw in your other dreams?" Jackson asked.

"No," Nettle said. "This one was much larger and seemed to have radiant power. His wings where huge, and his eyes were fiery red and they glowed. When he flew over, everyone fell to their knees in fear. Then the eagle flew off and the king of Iran picked up the scroll and examined it. He read, 'Blessed be the name of the king, forever and ever, for wisdom and might are His. And He changes times and seasons, He removes kings, and He raises up kings. He gives wisdom to the wise and knowledge to those who have understanding. He reveals deep and secret things; He knows what is in the darkness, and the light dwells with Him.' As soon as he finished reading it, the king of Italy said, 'What does this mean?' Then Ransom said to him, 'Oh magnificent king, I will bring the astrologers and magicians in to interpret this scroll.' Then the vision was over."

"Well, what in the world do you think that means?" Chrissy asked. "And how in the world did you remember all that?"

"I think it means that we are about to encounter something way beyond our human abilities. I think we are about to encounter an apocalyptic journey into a realm we don't know much about. But I do know this: it is very real and it involves us. I think our generation will be used to fight in this melee."

"That is pretty far-fetched, Nettle. But I will say your vivid details are amazing," Josh said.

"I must ask: what is a melee?" Chrissy asked.

"A melee is a violent free-for-all. Like a fight or brawl," she answered.

"Thank you so much, Miss Dictionary," Chrissy replied, smiling really big at Nettle.

"You are most welcome," she replied, blowing Chrissy a kiss back.

"What does 'apocalypton' mean?" Jackson asked, while everyone chuckled at his pronunciation.

"'Apocalyptic' just means when the world comes to an end as we know it."

"I'm just glad I know you well enough to know you are sane," declared Tommy. "After the phone call I just got, it makes me think there might be something to all your dreams and visions. What I am about to tell you might validate it even more." Now everyone was on the edge of their seats again. "While you were in your room having that vision, they called me."

Without hesitation, Nettle inquired, "What did they say?"

"They said that all they want is you, and if we would just cooperate, then the rest of us would be safe. But if we don't do as they wish, then my house and my family would disappear just like the farmhouse."

"What?" Josh asked. "They knew about the farmhouse?"

"Yeah, man."

"So it is them. They must have kidnapped all those people we saw out there."

"Oh my God, this is awful," Chrissy said, a look of dismay on her face.

"And my dad is out there," Jackson said. "We have to go soon or they might kill him, and then I won't have any parents left to raise me."

"So here's my plan," Tommy said. "After my parents go to bed tonight, we all go out there. They won't expect us and we can at least see if the place is still there. My dad has several guns; we can take them with us."

"Oh, that's great; this is going to involve guns?" Chrissy spouted.

"Would you rather go without them?" Tommy asked.

"Well, no, but I'm not sure I like this plan. It all sounds so scary."

"But if we go now, they won't be expecting us," Nettle said.

"OK, let's do it," Josh said. All in all, he was pretty pumped at the idea.

"So when we get there, Tommy, what is your plan then?" Chrissy asked.

"Just to go and search it out. See if we can find anything that would give us clues about the kidnapped seekers. I want to see if there is more than just the farmhouse out there. Then, when we know for sure, we can get help. So tonight we will leave at midnight. Wear black clothing and running shoes in case we need to run. We will take my Tundra since it's black and big enough for all of us, plus it has four-wheel drive."

"I sure hope you all know what you are doing," Chrissy said. "This could be very dangerous."

* * *

After football practice, Tommy, Josh, and Jackson went to the apartment and gathered more of their clothes.

"Tommy, do you think they're going to hurt my dad?" Jackson inquired.

"I don't think so . . . we just have to play the game smarter than them. It is kind of like outsmarting the opposing team in football. We just need to develop our strategy and outplay them."

"OK, good." Jackson was beginning to really look up to Tommy, and he enjoyed being with him.

They grabbed a bite to eat on the way home and were all anticipating what might happen that evening.

CHAPTER 11

Midnight Hour

The moon was bright and the night was still as the clock struck midnight. Quietly, everyone snuck into the truck. The stars had brilliancy about them, as if they would light the way. The cool breeze gave everyone a sense of mystery in the air.

"I sure hope we're doing the right thing tonight. I have a feeling that we are about to embark on something way out of our league," Chrissy said.

"And I think you are right, Chrissy," Josh responded. "But aren't the greatest moments in life when human impotence and divine omnipotence intersect? This will be a journey way out of the ordinary; however, I think once we see the place, we will all know we are doing the right thing. I can't imagine being trapped in the desert against my will by some lunatics like Ransom and Hawk. Maybe this should be your first story, Chrissy. Your journalism professors will love this. I can see it now, 'Miss Chrissy Matthews, the world's leading reporter, saves the planet from total disaster,'" Josh said, half-serious and half-joking.

"I don't know, Josh. We might all end up dead if we dared something like that."

As they approached the edge of the desert forest, Tommy turned off his headlights. He made sure he pulled the truck up to the edge of the trees so it would not be easy to spot.

"I've never seen a tropical forest out in the middle of the desert before," Chrissy said. "This is pretty awesome."

"Let's get out and walk the rest of the way," Tommy suggested. Carefully opening their doors, they dared not make a sound. One by one they cautiously filed out of the truck. By now it was around twelve-forty. Tommy passed out the handguns to everyone except Jackson. Nervously, Chrissy held her gun down by her side. Walking very close to the edge of the forest, they approached the road leading up to the farmhouse. Over to the right, they observed the beautiful large pond standing still as the stars themselves, glistening under the moonlight. Without warning, Tommy stopped dead in his tracks, holding his hands out for the others to follow suit. Without delay, they all squatted down to their feet.

"Shhh . . . don't make a noise," Tommy whispered very softly. Immediately they spotted a large creature coming up out of the pond. Tommy quickly motioned for the group to crawl into the forest and hide behind the trees. Watching this unbelievable scene, they froze when they suddenly realized there were three more. This was so far out they could not even blink.

Each creature looked different. The first one looked like a lion but had eagle's wings. The minute it got out of the water onto the land, its wings disappeared, and it stood up on the ground on two feet like a man. Then, the second creature, which looked like a bear, came out of the water with three ribs in its mouth between its teeth. The third creature came out and looked like a leopard, with four birdlike wings on its back. It had four heads coming out from its neck, each one looking different. The fourth creature that crawled out looked the most dreadful and terrible of all. It looked exceedingly strong and had huge iron teeth. It had ten large horns and then a little horn right in the middle of the large horns. It was covered all over with human-like eyes. It came out speaking strange things, but they could not tell what it was saying.

The four creatures stood there for a minute making all kinds of strange noises. Some sounded like words and some like sounds. It was the most bizarre moment any of them had ever encountered. Then a loud clap of thunder roared in the sky, which made them all jump, and all the creatures roared back, as if responding to the thunder. The sound sent shrills down their spines.

"We've got to get out of here before they see us. They will kill us," Chrissy said.

"No," Nettle said. "Don't be afraid; we are supposed to be here." The moment Nettle whispered that to Chrissy, lightning filled the sky. It was magnificent. A profound sense of knowing this was right entered each of their minds.

"Whoa . . ." Josh whispered. "Now that was amazing!" Josh grabbed Chrissy's hand, signaling to her that it was going to be OK. "Stay close to me," he whispered.

Unexpectedly, the four creatures started walking toward the forest, where the road to the farmhouse was located.

"Lay down, quick!" Tommy said. All their eyes remained glued to the situation. They watched as each creature started evolving into a man. Each man was dressed in a royal robe.

"You've got to be kidding me!" Nettle whispered. "Those are the four kings in my vision. Those are the men I saw in the vision, Tommy. I know they are. There, on the left in the purple robe, is the king of Iran; next to him, in the maroon robe, is the king of Iraq; next to him in the middle, in the dark blue robe, is the King of Greece; and on the far right, in the white robe, is the king of Italy."

"Are you sure?" Tommy whispered.

"I'm positive. I recognize their faces."

"Look, over there!" Jackson whispered, almost frantically. As they all turned to see what Jackson was talking about, there appeared to be two men running at full speed to greet the kings. Right before their eyes, only a few feet away, they realized it was Ransom and Hawk. Upon their arrival to the kings, they fell to their knees and began to worship them.

Then, boldly, the last and dreadful king, the one with the iron teeth, and now the purple robe, lifted up his hands and proclaimed, "The kingdoms of this world are at our fingertips, and soon we will have dominion over them all. For the hour has come, our supremacy is near, and shortly, all power will be ours to conquer the world." As they all began chanting, a truck drove up with a huge cage on the back of it. Once it arrived beside them, the driver got out and opened the cage. Unexpectedly, the most mesmerizing and fascinating creature of them all stepped out. It was a fiery red dragon with seven heads and ten horns. Crowns started appearing incrementally on each one of its horns. His tail whipped back and forth as he surrounded the kings, as if he was threatening to devour anyone who would get near them.

"I think Jackson was right. We are in the middle of a science-fiction movie. I do not believe this," Tommy whispered.

"I think I'm going to faint," Chrissy whispered.

"No way," Jackson whispered. "You can't faint now; it's just getting started . . . This is awesome!"

Frozen, almost mummy-like, everyone sat there witnessing the most mystifying incident of their lives. *What will we tell others? Who would ever believe us? Is this really real, or is it some kind of deception?* As these types of thoughts bounced around in all their heads, a trumpet began to blow. It sounded almost militaristic, and a multitude of people came walking down the mountain road. The dragon stood steadfast, roaring vehemently at the sky, daring anyone to come near him or the kings. *Did we just witness alchemy? Are we being catapulted into a futuristic realm of reality?* Nettle thought. *What the heck is this?*

"Look, over to your left," Tommy whispered. Six almost Hulk-looking men were carrying a huge bronze statue on an altar down toward the four kings. Tommy pulled out his tiny binoculars so he could get a better view of the statue. He began to tell the others that it looked like the body of a man, but its head was like a snake with seven eyes.

"There is something written on each of its eyes," he said.

"Can you tell what it is?" Nettle whispered.

"It looks like names," he said, squinting hard to see the inscriptions. "Each eye has the name of a country written on it. One eye has the word Iran; the next one has Iraq; the next one Libya; the next one Ethiopia; the next one Turkey; the next one Syria; and the last one has Russia on it." By this time the people were starting to make a lot of noise. It was as if they were eulogizing the kings. Then, all of a sudden, another creature came crawling out of the pond. This one looked like a leopard, only his feet were like the feet of a bear and his mouth like a lion. Then the king of Iran walked over to the creature, raised a golden scepter, and touched its head, as if giving him power. The creature began roaring loudly. Then, the king of Iraq walked over to the creature and placed a royal robe of many colors around his back and led him back over toward the other three kings, who were standing before the statue. Immediately, all of the people, a crowd of around three hundred, along with Ransom and Hawk, fell on their faces and worshiped the kings, the creature, and the bronze statue.

"Come on, we need to go and search the place while they are all out there worshiping," Nettle said. She got up and the others followed her as she started through the forest and up the mountain. They climbed higher and higher, and in looking back, they could see a huge fire starting below. No one said a word; they just climbed. Suddenly, Nettle stopped and put her finger over her mouth as if to say, *Shhh . . . be quiet.* She had spotted a cave, or at least it looked like the entrance to a cave, with two men sitting by it. She turned to huddle everyone together and said, "Maybe the people are in there."

"What should we do now?" Chrissy asked.

"It doesn't look like the two men are moving at all," Tommy said. "I think they are asleep."

"I don't know, Tommy," Chrissy said. "Let's just watch for a few minutes to make sure." Tommy picked up a small stone and threw it to make a little noise to see if they moved. Neither of the two men stirred.

"I'm going to walk up there," Nettle whispered.

"Wait!" Josh said. "I think Chrissy and Jackson should go back to the truck. That way, if we are caught, they can get away and go for help."

"Good idea. You and Jackson go back to the truck," Tommy instructed as he handed Chrissy his keys. "If we are not back in one hour, then you guys head back to town and tell Tommy's parents to call the government, or someone, for help."

"But I want to stay here. My dad might be in there," Jackson said.

"No," Tommy said. "You have to go back so you can describe all of this if something happens. They will believe you more than us," Tommy said, trying to come up with something to convince Jackson to go back so he would be safe.

"Come on, Jackson, I need you," Chrissy said. Somewhat discouraged, Jackson agreed to go with Chrissy back down the mountain.

Nettle reluctantly agreed to Tommy's plan for him to enter the cave instead. She hugged his neck and told him to be careful.

"If I'm not back in thirty minutes, you take Nettle and get out of here, and I mean it, Josh," Tommy said.

"I will, man," Josh said. "I promise."

Tommy made sure his handgun was off of safety and started walking slowly toward the cave. The two men did not move and appeared to be asleep. Inside, tunnels were everywhere. As he walked further in, he couldn't believe his eyes. Every tunnel was color-coded, so he decided to go to the right and follow the one that had the bright green paint on the cave walls. As he got further down the hall, he could hear snoring. He peeked around the corner and there was another guard, sound asleep, with a machine gun in his lap. Tommy knew it wasn't just mere luck that all the guards were asleep. He came up on a huge door, and over it, the words "First Battalion" were inscribed. As he began to turn the knob, he noticed a tripwire attached to it, so he stopped.

Something very important must be in that room. Walking further down the hall, he came upon a door that had the words "Babylonian Kingdom" emblazoned over it. He carefully began to turn the knob, when suddenly, black widow spiders began to crawl all over his hand. He quickly pulled his hand away and began shaking it profusely. While he was ridding himself of the spiders, the door and ground began to move, and at once he was inside the Babylonian room. Slowly turning around, he was mesmerized by the eloquence of the room. It was as if he had entered a Persian castle. The walls were extremely ornate and looked as though they were made of gold. There was a smell of incense burning, and the lighting was dim like candlelight. Buckets dripping with costly jewelry and gold bars lay before him.

I feel like Nicolas Cage, in National Treasure, *or, Harrison Ford in one of his* Indiana Jones *series,* Tommy thought. He noticed a large statue in the back corner of the room. It was similar to the one outside. *It must be over twenty feet tall.* Tommy didn't recognize who the figurehead was.

Walking slowly toward it to get a better look, he began to hear strange noises. *That sounds like a cross between a screech owl and a large cat,* he thought. Moving around all the expensive furniture, he crept closer, and then he spotted them . . . two live dragons with jewels all over their heads. Not taking any chances, he turned to leave when he stumbled across a dead body . . . all that was left were the bones. Tommy jumped over the bones and tore out for the entrance. His heart racing, he twisted the handle and quickly advanced through the door. Twenty minutes had now passed; he knew his time was running out. Wanting desperately to discover if there were seekers there, he looked around one more time. There it was, as if in broad daylight. The door was emblazoned in red; the words read: "Seekers—Numbers One through Twenty." Time running out, he ran over and turned the knob. It was locked. *Should I knock? What if there is a guard inside?* He knew time was short, and the others would go without him if he was late. Hesitantly, he decided to leave, knowing he could come back later. He at least had his answer.

Realizing now the cave probably held the kidnapped people he and Josh saw, and possibly more people, he knew Nettle's dreams were indicative of something far greater than anyone could comprehend at this point. *I better ask her more about this quest she's on and what else she has discovered and ignore my previous opinions. Was Jackson's dad in that room? How many people had they captured?* Slipping past the guards, Tommy ran quickly back to the spot where he had left Nettle and Josh.

* * *

Chrissy and Jackson had made their way to the truck, when all of a sudden, she couldn't hear herself think. A deafening noise was hovering directly over their heads. As they watched in silence, two helicopters landed in the middle of the desert. Two men dressed in a most dignified way stepped out of the helicopters, walking toward the kings.

"Do you have any idea who that is?" Chrissy asked.

"Maybe Jason Bourne and Batman," Jackson said laughing.

"Oh no!" Chrissy exclaimed.

"What?"

"That is Paul Clemmons, the president of the United States, along with the Prime Minister of England, Tobin Dunn. What in the world are they doing here?"

Chrissy watched as she saw them hand several gifts to the kings. Then, in utter horror and sheer disbelief, she and Jackson witnessed firsthand as the president and prime minister bowed down to the kings.

"Well, I guess we won't be telling the government now," Chrissy said. "It looks like they are in on whatever this is."

"Get out of here . . . this can't be good," Jackson half-whispered, half-shouted.

"I wonder if the others can see this from where they are," Chrissy said.

Running down the mountain in search of the truck, Nettle, Tommy, and Josh had stopped dead in their tracks upon hearing the helicopters. Tommy explained, while watching through his binoculars, what was still taking place.

"The king of Greece is now walking over to lay the gifts they received on top of the large bronze altar. Right now they are all exchanging bows, and the president and prime minister are walking back over to the helicopter."

"That was quick. I wonder what it was all about," Nettle questioned.

"I don't know, but let's get out of here fast before anyone else appears," Tommy said.

Almost out of breath from running so fast, they finally reached Tommy's truck. By now, the people were growing more and more intense as they listened to the king of Iran's speech. Applauding and yelling as though he was their savior, they began to chant, "Hail to the final king." Lasting about twenty minutes more, the king of Iran finally finished his speech. The crowd, led by Ransom and Hawk, turned around and marched back up the road toward the cave. Now alone again, the four kings shook hands and began walking around in a circle, arms on each other's shoulders.

"What are they doing, playing ring-around-the-rosy?" Nettle scoffed. "They look ridiculous. This has to be some kind of power play or some kind of creepy sacred dance."

"Whatever it is, I wish they would just end it so we can get out of here," Chrissy said.

Round and round they marched, embracing and chanting profusely. Then, as they turned back toward the pond, the conversion took place again. Altering themselves from human kings back into those ugly creatures, they glided back into the pond.

"This is some of the weirdest stuff I have ever encountered. You could not make this stuff up if you tried to," Chrissy said. "I never expected to see mythological-looking creatures out here. No one is ever going to believe us."

"Oh, I think we are in for a lot more," Nettle said. "I think this was just the tip of the iceberg. I find it rather intriguing, if you ask me. I have always known there was evil in the spirit world; I just didn't think I would ever witness it."

"Well, the ancient scripts talk about these types of things quite a bit," Josh said. "I do know that."

"Yes, but I thought they were just allegorical," Chrissy said.

"Alla ... what?" Jackson asked.

"Never mind," Chrissy said. "You will learn that later on in English. And apparently, I have a lot more to learn about this spirit stuff as well."

"I wonder where that pond leads to," Tommy questioned. "Obviously they can breathe underwater. I think there is more to this than meets the eye. God only knows what those half-human and half-creatures were. The government probably created them, and, who knows, there may be plenty more like them."

"They were trans-human," Josh said.

"Maybe ... but when they were in human form, they were kings, just like in your vision," Chrissy said.

"Did you guys see the president land in the helicopter?" Jackson asked.

"Yes," Josh said. "What was that all about?"

"Yeah," Tommy said. "I watched through my binoculars. One of those gifts looked like a scroll. It had jewels on the outside of it. The other gift was some sort of black box, and it had feathers all over it. I saw one of the kings walk over and set them both on the bronze altar. Then

I watched as they both bowed toward the kings."

"Yeah, that was the outlandish part," Chrissy said. "I don't know why anyone would bow to four kings, a golden altar with a scroll, and a black box on it . . . ridiculous."

"Who knows? But I will say, this is even more bizarre than a farmhouse disappearing," Josh said.

"Yeah!" Jackson said. "It's like a wild, futuristic movie; you never know what could happen next!"

"For real," Tommy said, trying to digest all they had just witnessed.

"Speaking of bizarre, tell us what you found in the cave, Tommy," Nettle asked. "Was it as weird as what we all just saw out there?"

"Yes, it was. Inside the cave were all kinds of passageways, all marked with colored paint on the walls. I took the hall with the green paint; it headed to the right. There were guards inside, as well, and the one I saw had a machine gun, but he was asleep, too, thank goodness. I tried to open one door, but it had a tripwire on it. I think it might have something very important inside it. The guard was sitting really close to that door, too. Then I came to another door, and the writing over it said, 'Babylonian Kingdom.' When I touched it, freaking black widow spiders crawled out all over my hand. As I started to shake them off, suddenly I was thrust inside that room."

"OK, now that would have freaked me out," Jackson said.

"Yeah … right?" Tommy said. "The first thing I saw inside the room was a huge statue about thirty feet tall. Obviously, they're into statues out here. It was the figure of a man, and it might have been one of those kings we saw, but I couldn't tell. The room was filled with gold, jewelry, gold bars, and really expensive stuff. As I looked across the room, tied down on the floor were two live dragons with jeweled heads. Apparently, they didn't hear me or see me, but that's when I decided to get out of there in case they started making too much noise."

"What kind of noise do dragons make?" Jackson asked.

"I'm not sure exactly, but these sounded really strange," Tommy said.

"I didn't think dragons were real until tonight," Jackson said.

"Well, I didn't think anything that we have seen so far was real," Chrissy said. "But apparently it is! The government can make anything appear real."

"What do you make of all this, man?" Josh questioned.

"I don't know, bro. This is some weird, funky stuff."

Nearing the house, Tommy had many questions rolling around in his mind. *Was this life his or someone else's . . .* He really wanted to know.

CHAPTER 12

Game On

The campus of the University of Arizona was buzzing with students everywhere. Nettle, Tommy, Josh, and Chrissy made their way to class. It was the first time in years the Wildcat football team had promise. In just a few days the team would know if they were on their way to a bowl game. The commentators were forecasting the Rose Bowl for next year and possibly even a Bowl Championship Series. They had predicted Tommy to be a top NFL prospect by the end of his second season. He had become the talk of the town. The local newspaper called him a "six-foot-five, 240-pound Adonis, built like a steel tank." Coach Hartsfield had informed him that he had already completed more passes with more yards than any quarterback in NCAA history. He really was a dual threat—run and pass—tested by the fires of high school wrestling (where he won his weight division). As a sophomore, he was being heralded as the toughest quarterback in the Pac-12 Conference and maybe even all of college football.

"The newspaper is really promoting you boys this morning," Richard said as he began to read to the group. "The three sophomores, Tommy Jones, Josh Hayes, and Sam Sully have skyrocketed this Arizona team to new altitudes. Tommy Jones is getting the chance to experience what it's like to be the most talked-about player in college football, according to sports commentator Jonathon Myers. The pro scouts are all over this determined quarterback. This savvy and cerebral sophomore has everyone's attention with his strong arm, passing ability, and leadership qualities. These boys not only play with passion but with stamina like we have not seen in years at Arizona. It's amazing and exciting to watch. Pretty soon, I predict, Tommy Jones will be a household name. In fact, the University of Arizona is going to become known as a real powerhouse very soon, Jonathon went on to speculate," Richard read.

"Wow, that's amazing … a household name … that's awesome," Josh commented, patting his best friend on the back.

Josh knew that Tommy had never really considered the fame that would come with this level of success. Call it crazy or naïve; whatever it was, he had never reflected upon it. It was somewhat hard for Tommy because of his internal shyness. But Josh never doubted his abilities and always encouraged and complimented his best friend's unique strengths.

"Both you boys are incredible," Richard said. "I am proud of you both. It is going to be exciting to see what lies in store for all three of you. Sam included."

Finishing up their coffee, Richard and Joan left for work.

"You know we have football practice today at four," Josh mentioned.

"Yeah, but with all this other stuff going on right now, that is the least of my worries," Tommy said.

"Maybe we should tell a couple of the guys and get them to go back out there with us," Josh suggested.

"Like who?" Tommy asked.

"Like our group: Sam, Carver, Tay, Tenya, and Cory."

"I don't know, man; I'm just not sure we need to bring anyone else into this."

"I just thought the more of us out there who are armed, the better. You know Sam is a great shot."

"Yeah, I know … let's think about it."

"You know Tommy, I think Josh had a good suggestion. Maybe it's not a bad idea to get the guys to help us out. We could use a few more people to scout out the place. But only our core group: Sam, Carver, Tay, Tenya, and Cory. That's it. Can you ask them to meet with us after practice tonight at eight, your apartment?" Nettle asked.

"Sure, I can ask, but you really need to think about this, Nettle, because all of our lives at some point might be in danger," Tommy responded.

"I realize that, but we might be saving hundreds of lives in the meantime."

"Wow, Nettle, I never knew you were a G.I. Jane kind of girl," Chrissy laughed, entering in on the tail end of the conversation.

* * * * *

As the day went on, Tommy wrestled with involving the others. However, he knew they would probably need them to help out.

Practice was intense and it was hot. The team was ready and the coaches were anticipating a win. Tommy hesitantly invited his friends over to his apartment after practice. The first to arrive was Sam.

"I just want you to know that I have your back on whatever it is you want to discuss with all of us," Sam said before everyone arrived.

"Thanks man, I appreciate that very much."

Nettle and Chrissy made brownies for everyone and Jackson was putting the icing on as the rest of the group arrived. They were all eager to hear what Tommy had to say.

"What we are about to tell you tonight, you cannot tell a soul. Not your girlfriends, not your friends, not even your parents at this point. If any of you do not feel comfortable with me saying this, please feel free to leave right now." By the tone of his voice and the intense look on his face, Tommy's friends were dying to hear what he had to say. No one moved while they all glanced around at each other. Their faith in Tommy ran deep, so leaving now was not an option. Sam, without hearing anything else, piped up and said, "I'm in!" He was the first one, but respectively, everyone else followed suit before they even heard what was to be said.

"Wait! Look who's on TV!" Jackson exclaimed.

Nettle quickly walked over to turn up the volume. It was Officer Whitmore, Detective Moll, and Detective Gibbs. They were announcing they had two men in custody. They strongly believed these were the two men who kidnapped the high school students and who attempted to kidnap the University of Arizona student. Strong evidence linked them to the shooting of the homeless man, Ollie Cook, as well. As the cameras panned over the two men's faces, Officer Whitmore identified their names as Ransom Lee Pearce and Hawk Marcus Williams.

As the cameras panned across their faces for the second time, Jackson yelled out, "That's not them!"

"How do you know?" Tenya asked.

"Because I have seen them," Jackson responded.

"Yeah," Nettle said. "You're right, Jackson, that is not them."

"Oh, this is not good," Chrissy said.

"We really have to be careful about who we decide to trust," Josh said.

"Trust about what?" Cory questioned.

"Yeah, what are you guys talking about?" Carver asked.

Tommy went on to enlighten them about everything that had happened so far. He told them about seeing the kings, the creatures, and the president of the United States. He informed them they wanted Nettle because they thought she had extraordinary powers; that was the reason for trying to kidnap her. The whole time Tommy was talking, Nettle was observing their facial expressions. She could tell Carver and Tenya were a little skeptical.

"So when do you plan on going back?" Tenya asked.

"A week from this Sunday," Tommy answered.

"Ahhh man, I'm not so sure about this," Tenya said. "I mean, I want to help you guys, but this sounds really dangerous, and I want to go on to the NFL and play football or become a doctor ... not die or get caught by some sinister, evil characters."

"I understand," Tommy said.

"Yeah, but sometimes we have to look beyond ourselves and our own ambitions for the sake of others, which is hard to do sometimes," Josh said.

"I will admit that I like doing what I want to do. I also think long-term and about consequences. So this is really hard for me. But, I guess I will trust you on this one, so count me in," Tenya said.

"Yeah, count me in, too," Carver said.

"OK…so we are all in?" Tommy asked one more time.

"Yes," they said in unison.

"Do you plan on telling the police?" Carver questioned.

"Not at this point. We just aren't sure who to trust yet," Tommy said.

"I have a question," Tenya said. "Let's say we get in there and we find three hundred people. How in the world are we going to get them out safely if we are twenty miles deep into the desert?"

"All we plan on doing this trip is to find out more of what is going on out there. If we discover a bunch of people being held against their will, then we will cross that bridge when we get to it," Nettle replied.

"Remember, you are going to see strange creatures out there, like dragons and four-headed animals with multiple eyeballs, and you might have to shoot them," Josh reminded.

"Bring it on!" Sam said. "I have hunted many a duck and deer in my life. I think I can slay a dragon."

"You go, homeboy! I can see it now: Sam, the dragon dynasty dude," Tay laughed.

"I don't think that will be a problem for any of us," Cory said, smiling. "Me, Josh, and Tenya dominate on C-O-D!"

"What's C-O-D?" Chrissy asked.

"*Call of Duty,*" Jackson said. "It's a video game of war."

"Oh …well I guess you think that makes you all expert marksmen," Chrissy said.

"It sure does," Cory said, laughing his head off.

"OK, so the plan is to meet at my parents' house a week from this Sunday night around eleven-thirty. They are usually asleep by then, and we can head out. We need a good five to six hours to accomplish everything. I will take my truck, and Sam, you can take your truck and follow us. Remember: you cannot tell anyone yet: not your girlfriends or your parents," Tommy reminded his friends.

"Also, I want you all to know that tomorrow I've decided to go to the police station and pretend I think the two men they captured are Ransom and Hawk," Nettle announced. "I want to see if I can get a feel for their reaction when I ask to see them. Those two men vaguely resemble the men Sheila sketched the night I described them. I find it very interesting they didn't contact me to come and verify that it's them," Nettle said.

"Good idea, Nettle; I want to come with you. I am really good at discerning those kinds of things too," Chrissy remarked.

"OK, we will go early in the morning."

"Good night, guys, and thanks for coming and supporting us," Tommy said.

* * *

The next morning the sun was bright and the breeze was cool. Entering the police station, Nettle and Chrissy noticed only one lady was on duty at the front desk. The girls approached the counter and asked to see either Detective Gibbs or Detective Moll. The policewoman, Olivia, asked for their names and then made a call to Officer Whitmore's office instead.

"How can I help you ladies?" Officer Whitmore asked after arriving in the lobby.

The two girls looked at each other with surprise; there had been no hello or anything. Nettle was not even sure he recognized her.

"Well, we are here to see Ransom and Hawk, so we can put this thing to rest. We saw on the news that you guys caught them, and we were so relieved," Nettle said.

"Why don't you both come with me?" he said. He took them down to the jail and slowly unlocked the door. He showed them two men that were definitely not Ransom and Hawk. Nettle knew that both men would easily recognize her if they were Ransom and Hawk, yet they acted like they had no clue it was her.

"That's them all right," Nettle said, trying to sound convincing.

"Yep, we caught them last night. You girls are safe now." He ushered them back up front and left the room rather quickly.

"What was *that?*" Chrissy asked.

"Who knows … I can't worry about that now; we just have to figure out if there are people kidnapped out there. Then we will work on finding out whom to tell."

CHAPTER 13

Forcing a Safeguard

After class, Nettle and Chrissy picked up Jackson to attend Tommy and Josh's football practice. As they were driving toward the campus, Nettle noticed a black car following pretty closely behind her.

"Don't turn around, but I think someone is following us."

"What?" Chrissy exclaimed.

"They are in a black car that almost looks like the government cars you see in the movies. I'm going to pull in and get some gas at the next gas station. Chrissy, you go in and get a drink and see if you can write down the license plate number and description of the car. Jackson, you pay attention to what they are doing and try and remember what they look like. I am going to focus on getting my gas so it doesn't look like I know anything is going on."

Chrissy got out and went inside the station. The black car pulled up as if to get gas close to Nettle. She acted like she didn't see them. However, no one got out of the car. The windows were tinted, but Jackson was looking hard to see in. Chrissy bought a drink and an apple, and when she walked back outside she acted like she accidentally dropped the apple and rolled it in the direction of the black car. As she advanced toward the car, it slowly moved forward. She could see the two men clearly in the front seat but did not recognize them at all. She did notice there was also a man in the back seat. As the car began pulling forward, Nettle noticed a government sticker on the back. The car pulled up next to the convenient store and the driver hopped out to go inside. Jackson, seeing the driver get out, immediately opened his door and headed toward the inside as well.

"Jackson," Nettle whispered loudly. "Get back in the car now!" Jackson kept walking. He was so determined to find out who it was, he did not even hear Nettle. He walked into the store but immediately came right back out and advanced toward the car. Nettle quickly finished pumping her gas, got her receipt, and hopped back in the car with Chrissy. Just as she was about to close her door, she heard Jackson yell.

"Dad! They've got my dad!" He tried to open the back door of the car, but it was locked.

"What's he doing?" Nettle yelled to Chrissy.

"I don't know," Chrissy said. "It looks like he is trying to get in their car. Quick, pull up there."

As Nettle was pulling up, the driver ran outside, grabbed Jackson, and shoved him inside the car.

"Oh my gosh," Chrissy said. "They just kidnapped Jackson. Go, go, go, Nettle, we have to stop them. We can't let them get away or we might not ever see Jackson again. They could kill him."

Nettle started shouting for Chrissy to get the license plate number. "Hurry. Now call 911 and tell them we just saw a young boy being kidnapped."

"Are you sure, Nettle? What if the police are all in on it?"

"OK, OK ... don't do it, then."

"Just don't let them get away!" Chrissy screamed. All of a sudden, they saw the back door of the car open and shut, open and shut.

"Look, I think Jackson is trying to jump out. Oh, no, he's going to get killed," Chrissy shrieked. Suddenly the man in the passenger's seat leaned over into the backseat, raised his arm, and hit Jackson. Jackson stopped opening the door.

"Are you kidding me?" Nettle said. "They just hit Jackson. I don't think so. I am going to ram into the back of them!" Her heart was pounding as she pressed the gas pedal to the floor.

"Be careful," Chrissy said. "I don't want to die." Winding through neighborhood streets, driving all over the road, Nettle tried to get close enough to ram the back of their car. Determined to catch them, she sped up to try and stop them.

Both cars were veering all over the road. Nettle was not going to back off. She got close enough to lightly touch the back of the car. They were up to sixty miles an hour on a neighborhood street. Nettle finally got close enough to the car to ram the back of it, and just as she was about to do it again, the passenger leaned out the front window and fired a shot at Nettle and Chrissy, missing the car only by a few inches.

"Oh, dear God," Chrissy yelled. "He's shooting at us. Pull back, Nettle, pull back."

"I can't," Nettle said. "I will lose them. You just duck down. I'm going after them."

Chrissy ducked down and started praying. Nettle sped up, and just as she was about to bump the back of their car, the man fired again, this time hitting one of the front tires on Nettle's car. It started spinning out of control until it finally hit a curb and stopped.

"They're getting away! Dang it, they're getting away!" she screamed as she brought the car to a halt.

The government car sped off quickly, but Chrissy had written down the license plate number, make, and color of the car.

"Are you OK?" Nettle asked.

"Yes, are you?"

"I'm fine, just aggravated that they shot my tire. Let's call Officer Cothern. I think we can trust him." Chrissy, pretty rattled, was able to call the police station; she got through to Cothern. She told him she and Nettle had been shot at, and they had also witnessed the kidnapping of a young boy. He asked her if anyone else knew about this and she told him no. She told him their location, and he told her he was on his way and not to call anyone else.

"That's odd," Chrissy said as she hung up.

"What did he say?"

"He said he is on his way and not to call anyone else until he gets here. I guess that could be good or bad . . . we will just have to find out once he arrives. Who are these people, Nettle?"

"I don't know who they are, but they are tied to the government somehow, because that was a government sticker on the back of that car. If Jackson was right about the man in the backseat, we know for sure now; they have his dad too."

"Do you think they are planning on kidnapping all of us?" Chrissy asked.

"I don't know," Nettle replied. "This is getting crazier by the minute."

"Where do you think they will take him?"

"Who knows, but I bet we get a phone call from them soon. I expect now they will try and use Jackson to get to me."

"Are you going to tell Officer Cothern all this?"

"I'm not sure yet; let's play it by ear. We have to be certain we can trust him. This is majorly critical now."

Fifteen minutes later, both Officer Holmes and Officer Cothern drove up. They could see the girls were both shaken up a bit.

"What happened?" Cothern questioned.

"Well, we stopped to get gas at the 7-Eleven on East Speedway Boulevard. Just as I was about to finish filling up, we saw a man come out of the restroom, grab a young boy, throw him into his car, and take off," Nettle told them.

"How do you know it wasn't the boy's dad, or uncle, or something?"

"Because he was kicking and screaming, and you could tell he did not know them," she replied.

"Them?" Holmes asked.

"Yes," Nettle said. "There were three of them in the car. Chrissy and I kind of freaked out watching this happen and decided to follow them. Then, when we got up close to the rear end of their car, the guy on the passenger side leaned out his window and shot at us. The second time he shot at us it hit my tire, and that's when I lost control, because my car started spinning. As Nettle was talking, Chrissy was closely watching the officer's facial expressions and reactions.

"Did you happen to get the license plate number and description of the car so we can call it in?" Officer Cothern asked.

"It was a black Ford Crown Victoria, and it looked almost brand new. I think it was a government car," Chrissy said. "Both men had on black suits, too. They didn't look like your normal kidnappers." She waited to see the expressions on their faces.

"Really?" Officer Holmes said. "Did you get a good look at the men's faces?"

"Just the one coming out of the bathroom," Chrissy said. He had light brown hair, cut very short, and was about six-foot-two. He was almost bald, and like I said, was wearing a black suit. The man who shot at us was a light-skinned black man, and he was wearing a black suit with a red tie."

"You said there were three men. Did you happen to see the one in the backseat?" Officer Cothern asked.

"No, but we did notice that every time they turned a corner, he kept rolling back and forth in the backseat, like he couldn't use his hands to support himself. So maybe they kidnapped him, too, and his hands were tied up," Chrissy said.

"Don't you want to know what the kid looked like?" Nettle asked.

"I think we know already," Officer Holmes said. "It was Jackson, wasn't it?"

Nettle took a deep breath, glanced at Chrissy, and said, "Why would you think that?"

"We have been waiting for this opportunity to talk to you privately, Nettle, but we had to wait until the right time. Why don't the two of you get in our squad car and take a ride with us."

"Oh, I don't know about that," Chrissy said.

"You have to trust us, Chrissy; we are the good guys. Officer Cothern and I are on your side, and there's a lot we have to tell you."

"But what about finding Jackson? Aren't you worried about that right now?" Nettle asked anxiously, again sounding very alarmed.

"We know where they are taking Jackson, and he will be OK. They have been trying to find him for a while. They have been following him and were about to get him when you discovered him at Corridor Mountain. They were going to try and use him to get to his dad."

Officer Holmes ran the license plate number. It was a government car, originating from Washington, DC, and driven by Hans Manchanson, a White House aide to the Defense Department.

"Why does the government want to kidnap Jackson's dad?" Nettle asked.

"They think he is a threat to them. They probably were just surveilling you guys today. But when things went wrong, they had no choice but to capture him so their cover would not be blown. Now that you know we are on your side, can you tell us the whole story again, this time with complete accuracy?" Officer Holmes asked. Nettle revealed how Jackson thought he saw his dad, Arlice, in the back seat, and that was why he started screaming so loud.

"This is all getting really odd," Chrissy said. "Please tell us what is really going on here!"

"Why don't you both come with us, and we will show you other seekers. We promise we are here to help you. There is more you both need to know. We will share inside information that will help you stay safe," Cothern told them. Nettle and Chrissy got in the squad car.

Shortly thereafter, they reached a country road and drove for another fifteen minutes or so. The road was pretty desolate and felt a little isolated. It put both girls on edge, thinking they had made a mistake trusting them. Finally, they pulled up to a large gate, and Officer Holmes got out and punched in a code. The gate opened. They followed a long, winding driveway lined with lush palm trees to a very large house. The property was beautiful. The home was built of stucco with a beautifully ornate tile roof. It was set on about twenty acres and had a large pond off to the side. The landscaping was gorgeous. It looked like something out of *Architectural Digest* magazine.

Holmes pulled inside the garage and told everyone to wait until the door came down before they got out. As they entered the home, they couldn't help but notice its magnificence. The floors were marble and the chandeliers were grand. The ceilings were about thirty feet tall, and the room had two huge columns going up to the top of the ceiling. It seemed like a normal but very elegant home. The girls were both wondering who lived there.

"We'll explain everything here in a minute," Cothern said.

"I hope so," Nettle replied. "This is all beginning to get a little difficult to understand."

"Yeah, and she's the smart one, so you can just imagine how I'm feeling," Chrissy said, managing to crack a small smile.

Both officers, and Nettle, laughed, putting Chrissy more at ease.

As they followed the two officers up the stairs, they came to a room with double doors that were closed and locked. There were two armed guards standing on both sides of the doors. Cothern leaned into the wall and allowed a retinal scan inside one eye so the door would open. The room was huge but was set up like a hospital. Immediately Nettle saw Dr. Wallace and two of his nurses from the hospital. They also noticed a hospital bed facing away from them toward the window.

"Hello, Nettle."

"Hello, Dr. Wallace."

Nettle introduced him to Chrissy. *Why in the world is Dr. Wallace here? What is going on?*

"Now, we would like you two ladies to meet someone else," Officer Holmes said. "Would you follow me over here to the bed, please?" As they approached the hospital bed, Nettle gasped and held her hands up to her mouth as she realized who was in it.

"Ollie, you're alive!"

"Yes, Nettle, thanks to Dr. Wallace."

"So, this is Ollie?" Chrissy asked.

"Yes, and you must be Chrissy. Very nice to meet you," he said, sticking out his hand to shake hers.

"Well, it is nice to meet you too, sir. I have heard a lot about you."

"I don't understand," Nettle said. "I thought they killed you."

"Well, Dr. Wallace and his nurses rushed me into surgery and saved my life. But no one knows except a few people. Right after surgery they brought me here to recover. I am doing much better now. But it is imperative we let the world believe I am dead."

"Why?" Nettle questioned.

"Well, I think that's what they are about to tell you," he said as he smiled sweetly at the girls.

"Why don't you both have a seat over here?" Holmes said. "What we are about to share with you can never be told to anyone other than those we allow you to tell. Can I have your word on that?"

"Yes, sir," the girls both agreed.

"There is someone else we would like to introduce you to."

The door began to open as Nettle and Chrissy waited anxiously to see who was there.

CHAPTER 14

Global Alliance

Immediately, Nettle recognized the handsome, debonair, stately looking gentleman. As he walked over, everyone else in the room stood up. Nettle and Chrissy followed suit. He introduced himself as General Todd Kerwin, chief of staff to the president of the United States. Nettle and Chrissy shook his hand and told him it was a pleasure to meet him.

"Nettle," he said, looking deep into her eyes. "Officer Holmes and Officer Cothern informed me that you saw a young man by the name of Jackson Beasley get kidnapped today by two men in an undercover government vehicle. Is that true?"

"Yes, sir, but there were actually three men, sir."

"Yes, you are correct. There were three men, but the third gentleman was not with our government. We believe it was a man by the name of Arlice Beasley, Jackson's natural father."

"OK . . . " Nettle said.

The general went on to say that Arlice Beasley was kidnapped not long ago while holding a crusade out in the desert. The girls were listening intently, thinking about Tommy and Josh's story. He told them there were close to two hundred people at the gathering. He said that out of nowhere, shooters came from the woods and took them all hostage.

"Fortunately, the shooters had rubber bullets, so no one was actually killed. Hurt, but not killed. They have also kidnapped many more people who have been held prisoner there for over a year now," he informed them.

"How do you know all this?" Nettle asked.

"I was there every time."

Nettle's eyes widened as he went on to tell the girls that the place that Arlice had found to hold his crusades was a secret hiding place for the government.

"They have been watching Arlice for several months up there because he has the power to cure people. At first, the government thought that Arlice was a spy. They were convinced he was trying to thwart their plan to unite the world. When they realized that was not the case, that he was simply up there curing sick people, they became interested in his powers. They called in their masters of the universe . . . their wizards, magicians, diviners, and astrologers. They wanted to see if they could match or outdo what they thought were Arlice's powers. When they realized he had supernatural powers they could not match, they decided to kidnap him and the others to investigate. That's when the brainwashing began. They have been brainwashing many others of this type for over a year now. It was never in the news because they informed all their families they were dead. The government has paid for a whole lot of fake funerals."

"How awful!" Chrissy exclaimed.

"Why were you involved if you are against all this?" Nettle asked.

"The last thing they need to know right now is that I am not really on their side. The United States government is deeply entrenched in a secret operation, and I'm the only one privy to most of that top-secret information. Since I am the president's chief of staff, it is my duty to oversee all actions of the White House. I also manage the president's entire schedule and decide who is allowed to meet with him and who is not. So I am privy to all confidential information. I guess you could say I am his gatekeeper; therefore, I know pretty much everything he knows. I have also been appointed to be one of five generals in the new governmental hierarchy of the New World Neighborhood. So I am positioned very well to stop this madness."

"Then why are you telling us?" Nettle asked.

"Two reasons. One, because the kidnapped people have become part of a brainwashing experiment that you need to know about, and two, because I am part of the kingdom you are searching for. There is a small group of us in this modern world that has tapped into its ultimate power. We also listen to Parakletos and understand the reason we are all here. We live out from under the earth-curse."

Earth-curse, Chrissy thought, remembering that Josh talked about that.

"It is a realm that most people never discover, but you are different, Nettle. You know the kingdom exists, and you believe in it; therefore, you will find what it has to offer," General Kerwin said.

Nettle had to pinch herself. Who was this guy, and how in the world did he know what she was searching for? How did he know about her quest for more revelation? Was it really going to be revealed through something so odd, so intimidating, and yet so intriguing? She could only hope he would tell her more.

"Are there any other people like you within the government?" Nettle asked.

"A few, and you will meet them eventually."

"What about Ollie? Is he one?" Chrissy asked.

"Ollie was once part of Ransom's group, but became a severe alcoholic, and they kicked him out. They made him live on the streets like a bum and threatened to kill him and everyone in his family if he ever mentioned it to anyone. He was very lucky they let him live. One night, a man was teaching in the park by the old Westward Hotel, and Ollie happened to be sleeping on the park bench. He stayed and listened to the message. It was the night that changed his life forever. The gentleman teaching was Arlice Beasley."

Nettle's eyes widened with excitement. "Seriously?" Nettle said. "I can't believe it was Jackson's dad."

"Arlice entered into the realm of Parakletos and received one of his many powers—the power to heal. That night Ollie became a follower too. Anyway, there is a huge plan that has been going on now for years, involving an elite governmental group from all over the globe. The goal is to take over the planet and establish a New World Community run by four kings. Under these four kings, who will all work as one, will be five generals, and I am one of them. Then, under the five generals, there will be five colonels. There are also two ambassadors.

"They want increased global connectivity within new global structure. They will call it 'The Great Transition.' This new revision will be formed and implemented when nations begin to change themselves by an extreme shift in the structure of their own societies and their relation to each other. It will transform values and knowledge culturally. Out of this turbulence of transition, very different forms of global societies will emerge. The only hindrance they foresee is getting Israel—or anyone who allies with them—on board. Their defining feature is the ascendancy of a New World Religion. This will validate global unity, cultural cross-fertilization, and economic interdependence, so they say. However, we all know it will be a kingdom of control, power, and dominance, which always leads to hate, human massacres, and the formation of evil.

"So to put it simply, under their rule, every society must change, merge together, and form a common government and religion," Chrissy said.

"Pretty much," the General answered.

"If nearly every leader in the world is in on it, then how are we going to stop them?" Chrissy asked.

"From the inside out, and, of course, with your help," General Kerwin said.

"Yes," Ollie said. "I know that place like the back of my hand. I know where they hide the weapons and where they keep the dragons. I know where the control center is. I used to be their Ransom."

Nettle's mind was spinning as she was running the information through her internal filter. She could not believe what this had turned into. It was a true government conspiracy. Never in her wildest dreams did she think her kidnapping was government related.

"Who are the other four generals and the four kings?" Nettle asked.

"The other four generals besides me are Dan O'Donnell, England's chief of staff; Abdul Sahaad, the king of Saudi Arabia; Igor Mutko, Russia's prime minister; and China's president, Mai Fan Zhoo. The five colonels are from France, Germany, India, South Africa, and Japan."

"The four kings have a little bit of a different story," Ollie said.

"Yes, you will have to use your imagination when I tell you about them," the general said. "In order for them to be protected and not be recognized by anyone, they underwent a major physiological experiment that made them half-human and half-creature. Their creature-like appearance is similar to something you would see in a science-fiction book, but when they are kings, they look normal."

"So, do they have a ranking order?" Nettle asked.

"Yes," General Kerwin replied. "King Mohammed Darius from Iran—everyone calls him 'The Divine Snake'—is the top king. He's the number one guy—at least for now."

Instantly, Nettle remembered the black and white snake in her dream. She knew that a snake symbolizes lies, accusations, and distortions. Never did she know that it would be on this wide of a scale.

"Right under him is King Faisai Salam from Iraq. The king of Italy, Charles Otto, is next, and then the king of Greece, Constantine Alexander, is last. However, I have suspicions that there is another who will assist King Darius other than them, but I am not at liberty to say who it is yet. I believe he will be the monster of power in the New Community."

Nettle and Chrissy weren't quite sure what that meant, and did not ask, but they knew it couldn't be good.

"What about our president? How is he involved?" Nettle asked.

"President Paul Clemmons and Tobin Dunn, the prime minister of England, are the two ambassadors in the New Global Neighborhood. They will have ultimate veto power if anyone should get too power-hungry."

"Are their headquarters heavily guarded?" Nettle asked.

"Only when necessary," Ollie said. "They keep it heavily guarded after they kidnap people or have a meeting, but lately we've noticed they have let their guard down a little. Why do you ask?"

Nettle hesitated for a moment and looked at Chrissy. "I'm asking because we have seen the place."

"You went out there?" Ollie asked.

"Yes," Nettle said. "A few nights ago we took a trip out there. It was the night when our president and the prime minister of England flew in on a helicopter. We saw them give the four kings some gifts. We also saw the four kings turn into the creatures you were describing."

"Have you told anyone?" General Kerwin asked.

"We only told a few of my boyfriend's friends, whom we wanted to go back out there with us a week from Sunday. However, that was before Jackson got kidnapped . . . and before we knew all this."

"Well, just make sure they are sworn to silence, and don't tell anyone else. Our plan is to destroy the kings and stop the kingdom they are trying to build. We wanted to talk to you about all this because you are now a main target. They really want what you have to offer. They are only being nice to you right now to try to persuade you to come willfully. After a while of trying to persuade you and you not giving in, they will then start to force you. Do you know the extent of your powers yet?" Nettle's eyes widened as she thought: *How does everyone know I have unusual powers, when I don't even know what they are?*

"No, sir," she answered.

"Well, I advise you to start seeking hard to find out. Just follow the dream."

"How did you know I had a dream?"

"Parakletos."

"Wow! I thought maybe you were clairvoyant," Chrissy giggled.

"Parakletos reveals much," the general reminded her. "Otherwise, I would not be doing what I am about to do." There was intensity to his voice; he was all business. Nettle knew this was not a joke and that she needed to go discover her powers. Chrissy quickly got the picture.

"Once Ollie is up and ready, which should be next Tuesday, we will get you all together to show you our plan. In the meantime, I want you both to know an ancient truth: All seekers can find their unique powers; unfortunately, only some choose to believe in them, and they are the ones who accept. They are like gifts given freely to all who ask. Tell your friends this so they can tap into his powers too."

They are talking code . . . Chrissy thought. She was realizing for the very first time in her life that she was a seeker only in her mind, if that.

What was going on between the two of them? Whatever it was, she was determined more than ever to find this Parakletos herself. She resolved right then and there to start listening to Nettle and her visions from this higher place.

"There is one more thing I want to show you two. Follow me." Dr. Wallace and his two nurses, Angela and Judy, waved good-bye as Nettle and Chrissy followed General Kerwin, Officer Holmes, and Officer Cothern to a different part of the house. They headed back downstairs and into the laundry room. There, General Kerwin pulled out the washing machine using a remote control and opened a small door leading down into a secret underground tunnel.

"Do you have a wife and kids?" Nettle asked.

"Yes, my wife's name is Mabry, and I have one son, named Lee. He serves in the United States Air Force as a pilot. My family does not know any of this yet, but I will be sharing it very soon. Follow me," General Kerwin said as he motioned his hand for them to follow.

As they approached the end of the tunnel, General Kerwin punched in a code and did his own retinal scan to open the door. When it opened, Nettle and Chrissy could not believe their eyes. The underground room was as big as the inside of a Super Walmart, and from the looks of it, they perceived it to be the control center. Everyone was busy doing their jobs. On one of the huge screens was a surveillance camera showing the compound in the desert—a camera that revealed what was going on 24/7. Apparently they had a satellite that kept them informed of everything.

"So I guess you already knew we went out there."

"Yes, I was informed. You guys took a big risk going there alone, but I understand why you did. I want to give you both a special radio. If you get into trouble, just dial 911 on it. It will show us your position, and we will send you help."

"OK, thank you," both girls responded.

"Outside of our operation, the only other politicians you can trust locally are Jeff Morrey, the governor of Arizona, and Senator Rostene Waller of Arizona. If anything ever happens and you cannot get a hold of me, contact one of them and use the code word, *Blizzard.*

"Next Tuesday we want to meet with all of you. Have everyone meet at Brenda's Pizza Parlor at 8 p.m. Once you are at Brenda's, we will radio you what to do next. Whatever you do, keep up with those radios."

"Yes, sir," the girls said.

"Officer Holmes and Officer Cothern will get you back to your car. Your tire has already been replaced, and you are good to go. I look forward to our next meeting, so please stay safe and attuned to your surroundings. Oh, one more thing: don't worry about Jackson. Our intent is to try and rescue him."

The officers dropped Nettle and Chrissy off in front of the bus station; her car had been moved to this location. The girls thanked the officers and then drove back to Tommy's house. It was now almost seven o'clock, and Tommy and Josh would be home soon.

CHAPTER 15

Inside the Cave

Government agents Hans and Logan had dropped Jackson and his dad off inside the desert cave. Arlice was so grateful to see his son. Jackson could not stop hugging his dad.

"What's going on here, Dad?"

"Before I tell you, I want you to know how much I love you, Son. I have missed you more than you will ever know. I think about you all the time and how awful it must have been for you. I was wrong for doing the things I did, and I want to ask for your forgiveness. Can you forgive me, Son?"

Jackson was trying hard to hold back the tears. He desperately wanted his dad's love and approval. He wanted his dad to want him. His dad's words brought so much emotion to Jackson that he finally broke down and cried.

"I love you, Daddy, and I forgive you. I just want us to be together."

Arlice could tell this was hard for Jackson, and he wanted to make sure his son felt his undying love for him now.

"Look at me, Son. I want to tell you something important. Less than a year ago, I had a supernatural encounter. Not long after that encounter, I discovered Parakletos. He began revealing mysteries to me. I began to understand a new authority I possess. I took hold of the powers I learned about through him. I learned I had a gift of curing people. The more I trusted him, the more the people were cured. I had never seen anyone miraculously cured before, much less be used to do it myself. But I believed, Jackson, and I began interceding for sick people. Everyone I requested for was cured immediately; it was incredible. The word got out. One night I got a call from a woman whose son had just died at home in bed, and she begged me to come to her house before she called 911: she begged me to plead for his life. I went, Jackson, and right before my eyes the young man was raised from the dead. I guess this has become my mission of sorts. What I learned is that Parakletos will help anyone who believes in him. I was not a good person before, Jackson. But once I found out the truth about life and that I am only a harbinger of sorts to show others the truth, my life completely changed.

But I could not get you and your mother off my mind, and I knew I had to call her and apologize for my horrible behavior. When I tried to call, the number had been disconnected. I tried information, and there was no Kathryn Beasley. I could not find her online, either. I tried looking her up by her maiden name, but that was not there, either. I called her parents, Emily and Randy, but their number was no longer valid. I tried to find your Aunt Maribeth and couldn't. I even called the State of Alabama, and they were unable to help me. I am so sorry for what I did to her and to you, Jackson."

"Mom died several months ago, and I have been in a foster home, because no one could find you, either. I ran away a few days ago, and that's how I ended up here. I was trying to find you."

"I'm sorry, Son. I had no idea." Arlice grabbed Jackson again and held him tight, tears streaming down his face.

"Why did they kidnap you if you are helping people?"

"Well, I have been coming out here a lot to hold these meetings. I was condemned by several local church groups who don't believe in healing, so I decided to take the people far away so that no one would see us. That way, we would not be ostracized."

"Why did they not want you to make people well? I don't understand."

"Some people just don't believe it's possible today. They don't want or believe in supernatural powers."

"But they're awesome powers. Why wouldn't they want them?"

"They are just deceived, Son. People have been deceived for eons now. There is an evil spirit that tries to block people from knowing about the supernatural and all its powers."

"Well, I bet if one of those people got cancer, they would start believing. I know I would."

"I think you're right, Son, and I am glad you believe. Anyway, I was out here the other morning when several men in ski masks came out of the woods and started shooting at everyone. Fortunately, they were rubber bullets, so no one was killed. They brought me here to this underground cave. I have since found out they have kidnapped hundreds of people here for an experiment."

"What kind of experiment?"

"They are brainwashing people, Jackson. They told me that the world as we now know it is about to change drastically, and the only ones standing in their way are the infidels. They are hoping I will side with them and work directly for them so they won't have to brainwash me, or better yet, kill me."

"Well, how do they brainwash people?"

"I'm not sure what they are doing to them, but it can't be good."

"Well, what do infidels do that they don't like?"

"We think differently."

"Am I an infidel?"

"Anyone who believes in Parakletos is an infidel. This truth we believe in, they will never accept. They know we won't go along with their plans of establishing a global community of sorts. They told me it would be a world of peace and prosperity, where no one would be without healthcare, food, or anything vital to existence anymore. In other words, it will be a convergence of current systems and world governments together, supposedly forming unity among the nations. They call it the New Global Neighborhood."

"So, is that a bad thing?"

"Well, Son, it is when the people at the top are corrupt. This type of thing usually means only a few will rule, and when you give few people ultimate power, it usually corrupts them. They really believe that partnerships and cooperation among nations should not be a choice but the only way. They call it advancing our common humanity. In other words, globalization is for the good of the people. But it will not be good, Jackson. Maybe at first, because there will be peace, but I promise you, not in the long run."

"So, I guess they want Nettle because she has powers to stop that, right?"

"Well, she must have some kind of authority in the kingdom, because they want her really bad. How in the world did you end up with her?"

Jackson filled his dad in on everything. Arlice knew that none of what had happened was coincidental.

"Jackson, I have one last thing to tell you."

"OK."

"You have a brother."

Jackson's eyes grew really big. "I do?"

"His name is Stephen. He is four years old, and he is here too."

"I had a feeling about him, because it was on the news that a four-year-old boy named Stephen Beasley, with diabetes, had been kidnapped. Is he OK?" Jackson asked.

"He is fine. They are keeping him in the underground hospital right down the hall to monitor him."

"Is Miss Amanda his mom?"

"Yes, and I'm sure she is still in Las Vegas and has probably been threatened not to say anything. I can't imagine the pain she's going through, losing Stephen."

"That's terrible. Why would they do a thing like that?"

"It is because they are evil, corrupt leaders. They want it their way at all costs."

"Did you end up marrying her?"

"No, Son, I did not. I started drinking way too much, and she took Stephen and left me. I just hope that we all make it out of here alive so I can find her, and maybe we can all live together as a family one day."

"I do know a secret," Jackson whispered.

"What is it?"

"Nettle, Tommy, Chrissy, and Josh are planning on coming back here. I know they will find us and get us out of here."

"Be very careful, Jackson, and do not tell anyone that. You cannot trust anyone here. Do you understand?"

"OK, Dad. I promise not to tell anyone. Have you seen any of the brainwashed people yet?"

"I have seen a few. There is one woman by the name of Ruth. I met her several months ago at a meeting. I got to know her pretty well, but when I saw her yesterday, she didn't even recognize me. She was an architect, so they probably needed her for some special project. I am really curious as to what they did to her."

"What about those high school students that were kidnapped? Are they here too?"

"If they are, I haven't seen them."

Jackson lay down on the bed and began thinking about everything his dad told him. He was glad to see his dad but felt a strong sense that danger was ahead. As he closed his eyes, he fell asleep.

* * * * *

Nettle and Chrissy made it home, trying to decide what to tell the Joneses about Jackson. Joan arrived, and Nettle quickly got up to help her carry in the groceries.

"I thought we would just order pizza tonight since it is getting so late," Joan announced.

"That sounds great. I'm starving," Chrissy said.

Joan called Brenda's Pizza Parlor and ordered several of their delicious pizzas. Joan set the table and called everyone in to eat.

"Where's Jackson?" Richard asked.

"Yeah, where is the little fart?" Tommy asked.

"Jackson was kidnapped today!" Nettle blurted. She figured there was no reason to be subtle about this announcement. Joan dropped her pizza onto her plate.

"What? Did you see it happen?" Tommy asked.

"Yes, Chrissy and I both saw it happen, and we tried to chase the car down. Unfortunately, when I got too close, the man on the passenger side hung out the window and shot at us." Everyone's eyes were wide as they listened intently.

"Oh, Nettle, honey, you and Chrissy could have been killed."

"Well, there's more." As Nettle proceeded to tell them everything, Richard became aware of just how extremely dangerous this entire thing was turning out to be.

"So, let me get this straight," Richard said. "Officer Holmes, Officer Cothern, General Kerwin, Dr. Wallace, and Ollie, as well as a few others, are the only people who know about this takeover besides us?"

"Well, there are a few more," Nettle said. She rolled her eyes just a bit, as if a little apprehensive to tell him.

"Like whom?" Joan asked.

Tommy spoke up and said, "Like Sam, Carver, Tenya, Tay, and Cory."

"Oh no, Tommy. You didn't tell them did you?" his mom asked.

"Yeah, Mom, we did, because we need them to help us when we go back out there. They were all willing to go with us too."

"Don't worry, Mrs. Jones. I told General Kerwin that we told them, and he said it was OK," Nettle said.

* * * * *

After dinner, Nettle and Chrissy started helping Joan clean the kitchen. The guys sat down and began to watch the nine o'clock news. They began showing clips from a summit meeting being held at Camp David earlier that morning. Joan, Chrissy, and Nettle had settled on the couch when what they saw on TV suddenly got everyone's attention.

At the head of the table sat the president of the United States; to his right sat the prime minister of England, and the president's National Security Advisor, Lieutenant General Dale Howard. While the news report showed the president conversing with the others, four additional men entered the room and sat at the table with them.

The president introduced the group to President Charles Otto of Italy, and he began talking about the world's economy. As Nettle and everyone sat watching in amazement, Otto spoke of the beauty of nations meeting together in the United States and how their agenda was one of peace, harmony, and tranquility. Otto was a scholarly looking man with impeccable taste in clothing.

Upon finishing, Otto turned the floor over to Faisai Salam, the new president of Iraq. Salam began talking about all the new changes in that country's government and how it would always be indebted to the United States for protecting Iraq. He spoke about a future Iraq, and how one day soon, she would be a "place of provision" to the rest of the world. President Clemmons shook his head in agreement. Next, Constantine Alexander, the president of Greece, spoke about Greece's economy and how many countries, not just in the European Union, were suffering financially. He said that the world needed to look at the global economic picture as a widespread epidemic. He went on to say that people and nations needed to do something to help each other. He was a very debonair-looking gentleman with an extremely persuasive personality.

As the camera panned the room, every man was nodding his head in agreement. They all seemed very concerned about the condition of the world, and the overall tone left anyone watching feel as though these men had everyone's best interests in mind.

Finally, the last gentleman stood to speak. There was something different about his countenance. Nettle could sense a mysterious vibe in him simply by watching him on TV. He stood to speak as if showing the world he was the one in control. His name was Mohammed Darius, the supreme leader of Iran. As he began to speak, his voice was very tranquil. His appearance was mesmerizing. It was impossible not to look at him. There was something about him: his good looks, his ability to communicate, and his eyes. There was something about his eyes that drew you into believing him. Nettle realized, in that instant, that this man had the power to convince a people—a world—of just about anything because of his incredible presence, persuasive communication, intellect, and good looks. She wondered if anyone else in the room could see it.

"So let me see if I have this straight in my mind," Richard said. "In the supposed New World regime, we will have four kings that will be in power?"

"Yes, sir," Nettle confirmed.

Mohammed Darius then turned and looked directly into the camera as if to speak directly to all people. The camera panned in—extremely close. You could almost see the look of great fulfillment on his face . . . he had an incredible smile, a humbling but authoritative posture, and his English was perfect.

"Hello, my fellow constituents. We are so glad to have this time to come together and discuss the small crisis we have recently encountered."

"What crisis?" Josh said, out loud, as everyone in the room continued watching.

"As you can see, the World Council Organization has recommended that we start discussing ways for our nations represented here—and every other nation—to come together and support one another. There are many reasons why we all need each other, and there are many resources we can share. Your kind president has initiated these talks, and we are grateful to all to be here. We promise to begin an alliance that will benefit all nations and peoples of the world and bring you security, prosperity, and peace. You have my word."

The news reporter, Beth La'mon, ended the story by calling the small crisis "the lull in the world economy." News media members expressed extreme enthusiasm over the talks.

* * * * *

Nettle lay in bed that night wondering if she was ever going to understand the whole thing. She knew she must get back to the corridor. She still had unanswered questions. After daydreaming for several minutes, she finally fell asleep. Eight hours later, she was awakened by her alarm clock buzzing in her ear.

CHAPTER 16

Blindsided

Richard called Joan and asked her to meet him in his office around eight-thirty. He wanted to discuss last night's news with her. He felt a sudden responsibility to his family and congregation. While they were talking, there was a knock on Richard's office door.

"Excuse me, but can I talk to you guys before I head to class, please?" Josh asked.

"Sure, come on in," Richard said.

"Do you need me to leave?" Joan asked.

"No, ma'am."

Richard could tell Josh was bothered about something, and they were both interested in hearing what he had to say.

"You both know I am a political science and government major. The reason I chose both these majors is because I want to get involved in government and eventually run for a seat in the Senate. My Uncle Bill was a congressman, and my grandfather, Joe, worked in government his whole life. I have watched Arizona's senator, Rostene Waller, as well as our governor, Jeff Morrey, for a long time, and I have great respect for both of them. But recently I've found myself questioning my major. I want to make a difference in the world, but lately I've started realizing that if things don't change in our country, we are headed for . . . what I think is extreme adversity. After hearing the supreme leader of Iran talk last night, I began to realize that one day I might be working for a world government instead of the United States of America's government, and that frightens me a little. There have been great men who have started out good but ended up corrupt once they got on the inside. I think I'm strong enough to withstand the ridicule and scrutiny that I will probably receive, but I might not be. I guess I'm just looking for your perspective on it. I just don't ever want lies to become truth."

"Josh, have a seat, son. You and Tommy have been friends a long time, and I have watched you grow up to become a fine young man. You are intelligent, charismatic, athletic, and a great problem-solver. You seem to always count the cost in order to refrain from making a foolish decision, and I have always admired you for that. That is why we all nicknamed you 'The Philosophizer,'" Richard said as he smiled. "Joan and I have always been grateful that you are Tommy's best friend, because you take a stance for your values and passions. So in saying that, as your pastor, mentor, and friend, I will say this: When everything within you cries out with passion for a dream you know *you have been called to*, it is usually your assignment here on this earth. But every assignment isn't easy or peaceful. Some assignments are tough, some bring great reward, but, whatever the case, they are our assignments. And we must follow them with all our hearts. It is very easy for a parent or even a pastor to misdirect you.. Just remember, peace will always follow a right decision. Fear and confusion never do! Always remember that. Don't let your head get in the way of your spirit. Your *spirit* is eternal, and it was designed to tell you right from wrong—if you will listen. I know that you are a person who will make a difference in this world because you, my friend, are a strategist, a standard-bearer, and a great influence on all you meet. I think you're going to be used to affect many people, maybe even nations, and you will be given the perfect platform at the perfect time to do just that. So, my advice to you is to follow your heart . . . as long as it is in line with your spirit and there is peace."

"Thank you so much, Pastor Richard. I really appreciate your words of wisdom. I didn't want all that has been going on to affect my decision.

Deep inside, I know this is what I want. I guess I just needed some reassurance that I'm headed in the right direction. My parents have always been supportive in everything I do, and their love for politics is what has inspired me to get involved in the first place. I knew if I went to them, they would give me great advice, but it might be a bit prejudiced considering my family has always been very politically involved."

"May I say something before you go?" Joan asked. "This is totally off the subject, but you know being a woman means that sometimes we detect things and see things that men don't. Since the four of you have been staying in our home, I have noticed a precious young lady that is captivated by every word you say. I see a sparkle in her eyes when you walk in the door and a smile on her face every time she sees you. I'm not saying that you have to respond, but if you are interested in Chrissy at all, I can tell you that she is interested in you. I know that is not what you came here to discuss, but this is the only time I have had a chance to tell you when she is not around. Do with the information as you please, but I just thought you needed to know."

"Seriously?" Josh remarked, a little blindsided. "I guess I haven't even paid attention." He seemed to be thinking deeply about this. "Thanks for telling me, though. I guess because we are such good friends, I haven't even picked up on the fact that she might be interested in me."

"Well, as a woman, I know when a woman is attracted to a man, and she is so beautiful, Josh, both inside and out."

"Yes, she is," Josh said. "I promise to pay attention."

"You do what you think. I just wanted you to know."

"Thanks again, and I really appreciate you both listening to me today. You know I love you both, and I think of you as my second parents."

"We love you, too, Josh, and can't wait to see how your life turns out."

As Josh left, he couldn't help but think about what Joan just told him. Chrissy was one of the hottest girls on campus. He thought about how well they got along and tried to think of times in which she acted like she was interested in him. A big smile fell across his face as he thought about it all on the way to class.

* * * * *

Practice was long and hard that afternoon, and Josh had Chrissy on his mind the whole time. He honked his horn to let Tommy know where he was parked so they could go home.

"Well, day after tomorrow's the big day," Tommy said. "There's nothing like playing the number two team in the most important game of the year."

"Yeah, I'm psyched," Josh said. "I have this feeling that we are going to crush them. Hey, changing the subject . . . Your mom thinks Chrissy is interested in me. Do you see that? Has Nettle said anything to you about it?"

"No, Nettle hasn't said anything, but since we've been staying at my parents' house I have noticed her smiling at you a lot. She seems to always find a way to sit by you at the dinner table and when we all watch TV. You want me to ask Nettle?"

"No, not now, your mom just really thought she was. I will be more observant of the situation and see if I pick up on anything."

"Let me just say this, dude. Just like Nettle, Chrissy is probably the sweetest girl on campus. She has high standards and loves life—besides being extremely good-looking."

"I know. I guess I'm just so preoccupied with everything going on right now that I haven't even paid any attention to her. Please don't say anything to Nettle; let me figure it out."

"OK, I promise not to say a word."

* * * * *

Walking through the door of Tommy's house, Nettle and Chrissy greeted them with a big surprise.

"We've made dinner from scratch, cooked your favorite meal, Josh, and invited the guys and their girlfriends over to eat tonight," Chrissy said.

Everyone was seated in the dining room as Nettle and Chrissy began serving the food. Looking around the table, Josh realized that he and Chrissy were the only two officially not dating.

Sam and his girlfriend, Nancy, had been high school sweethearts;

Tay and his girlfriend, Jackie, met last year; Tenya and his girlfriend, Sarah, had been together a couple of months; Carver and his girlfriend, Brooke, had just gotten engaged; and Cory and his girlfriend, Jamie, started dating a few weeks ago.

"This is one of the best meals I've ever eaten," Josh said.

"Thanks," Chrissy said.

"Yeah. As you said, it's one of my favorites. It's the 'other white meat,' right?" They all laughed.

"I'm glad you like it, Josh," Chrissy said, a big smile on her face.

Tommy quietly kicked Josh's foot under the table, and they caught each other's eye and grinned. Everyone enjoyed the night and headed off to bed around ten-thirty to get enough rest for the upcoming game on Saturday. Josh and Tommy went to bed, and after Chrissy and Nettle finished cleaning, they sat down for a few minutes.

"Well, I had fun tonight. At least I got my mind off all this other stuff," Nettle said.

"Yeah," Chrissy said. "I had a great time too. I think Josh enjoyed the pork loin. I really think he is a neat guy, Nettle."

"Yeah, I know you do. You can see it all over your face."

"Oh, no, can you really? Do you think he sees it?"

"I doubt it. You know guys are oblivious sometimes."

"Do you think he would be interested in me?"

"Of course he would. You are beautiful both inside and out, and you're very outgoing. You love football and pork—what more could a guy ask for?" That set them both off, laughing hard.

"Thanks Nettle . . . I love you."

"I love you, too, Chrissy."

CHAPTER 17

Set Apart

Excitement filled the air and everyone was focused on the big game tomorrow. Students were all dressed in red and navy blue, and football banners were hanging all over campus. There was a huge poster of Tommy right outside the student union, and the cheerleaders were giving a pep rally right in front of his picture. Wilber and Wilma, the Arizona Wildcat mascots, were greeting everyone as they arrived. After class, Nettle went and bought a couple of cowbells to ring and headed over to the pep rally. Jackie, Jaime, Sarah, Brooke, and Nancy were waiting on her to arrive. Chrissy was leading the cheers and smiled at Nettle once she got there.

Chrissy had formed a tight bond with the other cheerleaders and had made each of them a special gift basket. The football players were pumped, and Coach McClain gave a really motivating talk to the players and fans. He reminded the players that if they stayed focused, determined and calm, followed their assignments, blocked and tackled well, and made good passes, they would—as he saw it—nearly be assured of a victory. Immediately after the pep rally, the guys left for their walkthrough.

The girls loved the gift baskets, and the bows Chrissy made them all were so unique that they decided to wear them at the game. The day was filled with fun—there was not a mention of the other tensions that had been happening.

* * * * *

Saturday morning arrived. Everyone woke up excited. You could feel the enthusiasm in the air. After a hearty breakfast, each started getting ready to go to the stadium. Chrissy, Tommy, and Josh had to be there early. Richard walked outside to get his newspaper when he noticed a note blowing in the wind under Tommy's windshield wiper.

"I don't want to ruin the day, but I just found a note on your windshield," he announced on returning inside the house.

"What does it say, Dad?"

Richard opened the note. "Hello, Nettle and gang . . . today is a big day for you all. Be sure and pay attention to your surroundings. Oh, and Jackson says hello."

"Is that all?" Tommy asked.

"I'm afraid so, Son."

"They are just trying to scare us," Nettle said. "I am not going to allow them to ruin my day, and neither should any of you. These bozos are crazy, and they just want us to be thinking about them and not what today is all about. Do not give them another thought."

"I understand how you feel, Nettle, and I agree to an extent," Richard said. "However, we can't avoid the fact that they keep coming around and the fact that they might be around today."

"You know what, Dad? Forget them!" Tommy said. "They are only going to make me play harder."

"Yeah, I agree, this is getting ridiculous," Josh said.

"Just be very conscious of your surroundings today. That is all I am saying," Richard said again.

"Yes, sir, we will," Chrissy replied.

Nettle had planned on sitting with Sarah, Jackie, Brooke, Nancy, and Jamie, since their boyfriends were all playing. She kissed Tommy goodbye as he left and assured him she would be carefully watching all that was going on around her and him. They agreed to meet at their normal place after the game.

As soon as Nettle walked into her room, she heard the radio go off. She turned it up and immediately heard General Kerwin's voice.

"Nettle, are you there?" he asked.

"Yes, sir, I'm here."

"Be observant of your surroundings today. They are watching you. Get word to your friends that we will pick you up at a different place this Tuesday. Go to the bus station instead, and we will pick you guys up there. Be there at 4 a.m. promptly! Get the word out to all of them today, but do it in person. Do not, and I repeat, do not text or use your cell phones for any conversations. You can write them a note or speak to them in person only. Remember, Tuesday, 4 a.m., at the bus station parking lot. See you there."

Nettle quickly got in her car and locked her doors. She knew she had to get back to the corridor, and this was the perfect time. Upon arriving, she parked and waited to see if anyone followed her into the parking lot. She didn't notice anyone. Once inside, she found a place to settle down.

All of a sudden, the corridor began to feel like it was moving. At first Nettle thought it was an earthquake. Then she began to feel Parakletos arriving through the atmosphere. She immediately fell to her knees. She knew the supernatural power was being imparted to her at that very moment. She heard him speak deep within as she had become familiar with his sound.

"I am in command of my set-apart ones. I am summoning my warriors. There is an alignment of kingdoms coming and nations gathering together. I am mustering an army for battle. They come from a distant land . . . for the day is near. For the power I hold and the kingdom I rule is not made of flesh and blood. It is a spirit world. Secret and hidden treasures are yours; get ready to receive them."

"I am ready," Nettle quickly responded. Suddenly, she heard foreign words forming in her mind like never before . . . and she began to say them out loud. Nettle instantly knew something astonishing had just happened to her. She sat still as a rock, the most tremendous peace she had ever felt coming over her. She wanted to cry, or shout, or something, but she couldn't move. Her mind had been illuminated, expanded, and transformed. This spirit's supernatural empire had just imparted into her his extraordinary gifts, here in the twenty-first century. Her intellectually stimulated being had just been changed by this powerful kingdom being . . . a wisdom not of this age or from the rulers of this age. It was something more expansive . . . only a human heart could receive it, not a human mind. Now she knew she was subject to no one else's scrutiny. No more human inclinations . . . finally, the intersection emerged into a straight pathway leading beyond mortal abilities or understanding ... this was truly the SUPERNATURAL!

Nettle immediately knew why she had been drawn to the corridor. She realized now why they wanted her. They wanted her because she was marked. The showdown of the soul: two kingdoms fighting for ultimate control of mortals. She sat there in awe, realizing for the first time in her life that humans are spirit-beings. They are in a body made of flesh and blood but have the ability, through Parakletos, to literally do things that are supernatural here on earth. Now no one could ever convince her of anything different! She knew it was real! She couldn't wait to see what would come next. The whole time . . . all he wanted was relationship . . . intimacy. Arlice must know, she thought. That's why he taught about the earth-curse. She wanted desperately to meet him and discuss this with him.

Nettle walked back to her car and headed toward the stadium. It was now two forty-five, and she knew she was going to miss the kickoff. Nettle's mind was hopping from thought to thought about everything going on in her life. She arrived at the stadium and immediately saw the scoreboard. Arizona had already scored. It was 7-0. She found her way to her seat, and the girls all stood up and hugged her.

"Where have you *been*?" Jamie asked.

"I just had to run an errand, and it made me late. Sorry!"

Sarah leaned over and said, "Josh caught a pass from Tommy and we scored, then Cory kicked the extra point."

"Awesome," Nettle said, trying to get interested in football after all that had just happened to her.

All seemed so trivial now. She looked down at Chrissy and waved, and Chrissy waved back.

* * * * *

Halftime arrived, and the cheerleaders were ready to perform their new dance. The loudspeakers came on and drew everyone's attention. "Would everyone please welcome to the field the University of Arizona's finest, performing a dance to Selena Gomez's hit, 'Shake It Up.' Let's hear it for our cheerleading squad . . . captain, Chrissy Matthews; co-captain, Ali Raymick; and team members, Allyse Perkins, Elena Tracy, Donna Bailey, Lauren Fuhrman, Lindsey Simpson, Lesley Weeks, Katie Jo Knight, Annie Laurie Lynch, and last but not least, Miss Katelyn Dandeneau." The dance began, and the girls were a fabulous hit. They had been voted one of the top college squads in America. Hardly anyone left the stands as they were all glued to the incredible entertainment. The cheerleaders rocked it out of the park. Nettle and the girls screamed loudly as they wielded their cowbells in total support. Chrissy waved again at the girls, smiling in a big way as she ran off the field.

The game went on, and Arizona played incredibly. The final score was 42-14! This guaranteed the Wildcats a bid to a bowl game, and Nettle was happy for Tommy and the team. She knew this meant a lot to him. It had been a long time since Arizona had started so many sophomores, and, on top of that, had a winning season.

Tommy, Josh, Sam, Tenya, Tay, and Cory were on top of the world as they hurried to the locker room. Coach McClain and Coach Hartsfield congratulated them on such a great game and season. "You guys played your hearts out, and it showed. I am so proud of every one of you. Now get dressed and go celebrate!" Coach McClain yelled.

Coach Hartsfield handed each player a token of his appreciation, a gift. He made sure all the players felt important. He was a young coach and had a special way of making the players feel like he was one of the guys. He was a brilliant offensive coordinator, and the players knew they were very fortunate to have him. They all knew that one day he would be a head coach.

"Great game, man," Sam said, high-fiving Tommy.

"You, too," Tommy said on his way out to go meet Nettle.

Nettle told the girls good-bye and headed down to the locker room. She quickly handed a note to Officer Ryan, the security guard. She asked him to give it to Tommy. Officer Ryan, whose friends called him Handy, was a fourth-degree black belt in karate. No one dared mess with him. One night after a game, a bunch of guys in a gang tried to attack him, and he singlehandedly took them all out. He was always cordial to Nettle and assured her he would get the note to Tommy.

Just as Tommy was getting ready to be interviewed by the press, Coach Hartsfield walked up and handed the note to him.

"What's this, coach?"

"I'm not sure. Officer Ryan handed it to me and told me to give it to you."

Tommy opened the note and read the information. He composed himself and conducted his post-game interview as he was expected to.

After the press left, Tommy called the guys together and told them the new information he had.

"We will know more when we meet on Tuesday. Remember, 4 a.m. sharp at the bus station underground parking lot, and don't tell anyone. Make sure you do not correspond by phone at all. If you need to talk, use the code words *football practice.* Then, we can meet and talk.

"Great, now let's go party and celebrate our victory!"

Everyone met at Brenda's Pizza Parlor to celebrate the big win. Sam had saved everyone a seat and was leading the victory song inside the parlor. The whole place was filled with excitement and talk of a bowl game, when all of a sudden, a gentleman walked over and introduced himself to Josh and Tommy. The others watched as they followed him outside. He introduced himself as Coach Caldwell, offensive coordinator for the San Diego Chargers. He started by congratulating them both on an outstanding game.

"I won't take much of your time, but since I was here in town I wanted to speak to you both. We are very interested in having you out to visit soon. As you probably know we have been recruiting some extraordinary players and are building one powerhouse of a team. Coach Bornstein and I know that you both would be a tremendous asset to

San Diego. I want to extend an invitation to you right now, and we will be in contact with you soon. You both played an outstanding game this evening, and your future looks very bright."

"We would love to come and visit," Josh said.

"Yes, that would be great," Tommy said.

"I will contact you soon, and we will stay in touch."

"Who was that?" Carver asked after they headed back inside.

"Coach Caldwell, the offensive coordinator for the San Diego Chargers."

"Nice," Carver said.

"Dude, that's awesome," Sam said.

"Yeah, that was really cool," Josh said.

Everyone had a really great evening and went home—for now, at least, forgetting about Tuesday.

Pulling up in the driveway at home, they didn't even begin to take notice of the car parked across the street.

CHAPTER 18

Moments of Truth

Nettle had just arrived home from school when the doorbell rang. There stood Chrissy with her hands full of books. She had a big grin on her face. As she walked in, she sat her books down and turned, facing Josh, who was standing in the den.

"Josh, can I talk to you outside, please?"

"Sure," he said, raising his eyebrows. "What's up?" They headed outside.

"I wonder what that is all about," Nettle said.

"They probably just need a few minutes together to realize that they are a perfect match for each other," Joan said.

"Mom!" Tommy said.

Josh followed Chrissy over to the outdoor bench that sat directly under a large Arizona ash tree in the Jones' backyard. Her eyes radiated an almost turquoise blue tint because of the dress she was wearing. She had a look of anticipation on her face, a sense of excitement about her.

Josh had never seen her look so beautiful. The sun was starting to set and was beaming down on her long golden-blond hair. As they sat under the tree, the wind whirled her hair gently across her face. Her excitement was contagious, and he was eager to hear what she was about to tell him.

"Josh, can I talk to you about something pretty serious?"

"Sure."

"I have been spending a lot of time trying to figure out my life and the direction I'm going. I know that I can appear a little nonchalant sometimes, but I really do have a serious side." Josh was listening intently. He couldn't help but remember what Mrs. Jones had said to him about her.

"Today at lunch, I went to be alone and just think about things. One thing that became clear to me were the feelings I have been developing for you. I know we are good friends and you are probably unaware that I even have feelings for you . . ." She grabbed his hand in hers and began squeezing tightly. Josh was smiling back at her and listening intently. His heart was beginning to race a little. "You may not even be interested in me, but I just had to tell you what I've been feeling."

"No, you're fine. Go ahead," he said.

"I know we are about to embark on a really bizarre escapade these next few days. But I couldn't go forward without telling you how I feel. I have dated a few guys that were really great, but there is something different about you." Josh's eyes widened as he listened.

"I have always considered you a special friend and enjoyed being around you. But recently, since we have been living here, my feelings have grown into something more. I'm not saying this to coerce you into anything, and I hope this is not making you uncomfortable. I just wanted to ask you if you would consider the two of us going out sometime by ourselves. I would just like to be alone and talk. I want to get to know you better. I want to spend time finding out about your dreams and goals and just hang out. It doesn't have to be anything formal."

"Sure, we can do that." And still, Josh was captivated by those eyes; it was as if Chrissy could see deep into his soul. He felt something he had never felt from any woman before looking at her in that moment.

"I think that you are the most . . ." Just as she was about to finish her next sentence, something came over Josh; he reached behind her head, pulled her over to him, and kissed her passionately. Chrissy embraced him and held him tight. Everything inside of Josh tingled, and he knew right then that he wanted to give a relationship between the two of them a shot. His heart was beating fast as he felt huge chemistry between them. *Maybe Mrs. Jones did know the right girl for me.*

Chrissy's heart was beating just as fast. *What a great kisser,* she thought. This was the moment she had dreamed about, and it was coming true.

Josh took her hand, and, looking deep in her eyes, said, "I have no idea what is about to go on in our lives or in this world the next few weeks, but I would be honored to take you out. Thanks for being brave enough to share your feelings with me. I really appreciate that. Why don't we plan on going out Thursday night for dinner?"

"That sounds perfect. What are you going to tell Tommy when he asks you what we talked about?"

"What would you like for me to say?"

"Why don't we just go in and tell them all that we have our first date this Thursday night."

"Sounds fine to me."

"Oh, one more thing . . . You're a great kisser."

"Well, thanks. You are not so bad yourself," he said, chuckling.

Everyone was getting ready to eat dinner as they entered the house.

"Well, what are you two so happy about?" Joan asked as they entered the house.

"We are going on our first date this Thursday night," Chrissy said, unable to contain her excitement.

"All right, that's cool," Tommy said as he gave Josh a big high-five.

Nettle smiled at Chrissy, knowing that later that night she would tell her all about it.

"Dinner is ready. Come and serve yourselves," Joan announced.

"It sure smells good, honey," Richard said as he walked over to see fried chicken, mashed potatoes, green beans, and homemade yeast rolls with honey butter.

"Well, I figured since the kids were about to embark on an adventure with the government, they needed a full stomach."

"Thanks, Mama Joan," Josh said.

"You're welcome, sweetie. I also made your favorite dessert."

"Yes!! That means the infamous peppermint ice cream pie," Josh boomed. "That rocks!"

The atmosphere was happy, but their emotions were all over the place. From feelings of love and devotion, to expectancy and trepidation, they continued their fun, and then parted for bed.

Later, as Chrissy and Nettle turned out the lights, Chrissy confided in Nettle how much she liked Josh.

"So did you tell him how you felt about him?"

"Yep, and as I was telling him he pulled me close and kissed me. It was the most incredible kiss . . . my whole body vibrated. He is so hot, Nettle, and I know he is the one for me."

* * * * *

Alarms started going off at 3 a.m. They had been instructed not to bring anything with them this time. Joan had gotten up to make coffee.

Nettle made sure she and Chrissy had their radios. Pulling into the bus station parking lot, Nettle heard the radio go off.

"Welcome, gang," a familiar voice said.

"Ollie, is that you?" Nettle inquired. "Where are you?"

"We are all waiting on you. As soon as the others arrive, have everyone get in the black limousine. The keys are under the mat. Drive downtown to the Bank of America Plaza building's parking lot, get on the elevator, and go to level five. Someone will be there to meet you."

"OK, will you be there too?"

"You will see me in a little while; just follow the instructions to a T."

"Yes, sir," Nettle said.

Just five minutes later, Sam and Carver pulled up in the parking space next to them. Immediately following were Tenya, Tay, and Cory. Everyone got into the limo as instructed. When they arrived at the bank plaza, a gate blocking their access immediately started to rise. Two men in dark blue suits were there to greet them. Even Sam remained quiet. Everyone was on edge—wondering where they were going and who these men were. They went up to the fifth floor and were immediately met as promised. They were then taken down a long hall to another elevator. One of the men punched the sixteenth floor, the top floor. When the elevator opened and they saw the huge, elaborate room, everyone gasped. The view of the other buildings was beautiful because it was still dark outside and the city was lit up. There were computers everywhere, a huge projector screen in the middle of the room, and numerous control stations. It almost looked like the inside of a space ship. Over to the side sat the most elaborate couches and chairs they had ever seen. There was a huge conference table with more than twenty chairs on the right.

"Come in," they heard a female voice say, but they did not see anyone. They entered, and as the door behind them closed, they could hear it lock.

CHAPTER 19

Undercover Hierarchy

The Bank of America Plaza building was familiar to Carver because he had worked there as a teller during the summer. He was telling them about the building, when suddenly, out of nowhere, a very refined woman walked over and introduced herself as Debra, their personal assistant for the day.

"If anyone needs anything, please let me know," she said. "I also want to make sure I know who everyone is. So let me see if I get this correct." She pointed to each one of them separately, calling out their names.

Cory winked at her and gave her one of his flirtatious grins.

"Well, I have seen each of your pictures and read each of your bios. I know that you, Tenya, don't like asparagus and that your father moved to the United States from Cameroon, Africa, and raised you and your sister in Texas. I know that you, Tay, want to be with your girlfriend, Jackie, every waking minute and that your parents adopted your nephew, Jay, and they are raising him now. I know Chrissy is majoring in broadcast journalism, was voted senior beauty in high school, and grew up in Colorado. She is a runner and a cheerleader and has a dog named Freckles. I know that Josh and Tommy have been friends since grade school and would take a bullet for each other. Josh loves peppermint pie, basketball, and video games, and he is majoring in political science and government. Tommy loves fried chicken, mashed potatoes, and green beans, and has a heart for volunteering. I know Sam is a jokester and an excellent marksman, but can have a really serious side when needed. I know Carver has a really high IQ and helps tutor underprivileged kids on the weekend. I know that Cory has two younger brothers and has had dreams of playing football since he was five years old. He is also the tallest man in his entire family. And most importantly, I know that Nettle has powers she is not even aware of, and that they are going to blow her mind when she taps into them. I know that you all have been chosen to go on the greatest mission this world has ever seen and will each play an integral part in that mission."

"Wow, now that was pretty incredible!" Sam declared. Debra smiled.

"General Kerwin will be out in a minute to speak with each of you," Debra said, in a quite serious tone, as she walked away.

You could hear a pin drop as they sat waiting on the general to arrive. The air was thick with anticipation, and everyone knew that this was probably the most top-secret information in the world right now. A few minutes later, the general arrived. Nettle and Chrissy stood to greet him, and everyone else followed suit. He made his way around, introducing himself to everyone and shaking hands.

"Did Debra get you everything you need?"

"Yes, sir," Sam piped up. "She knew when I was born and how much I weighed." Everyone chuckled at Sam's humor; he had a way of making everyone feel a little more at ease.

"Well, great. We always do our homework, especially on a mission as serious as this one. Why don't we move over to the conference room table; I have a few others who will be joining us in a few minutes.

"Before we get started, I want you all to know that you can completely trust everyone involved in our mission. If anyone other than the people you meet here today asks you anything about the mission, you are to say you know nothing. If you should happen to get kidnapped or caught, immediately take this little blue pill. It will keep any type of truth serum from working." As the general was speaking, Debra handed them each a packaged blue pill.

"OK, this is really serious," Tay said under his breath.

"Does anyone need to exit now?" the general asked. No one dared move.

"OK then, let's get started." General Kerwin lifted up his watch to his mouth and spoke directly into it. Without delay, two other men entered the room, along with Officers Cothern and Holmes. Each marched over, saluted the General, and sat down. Lastly, Ollie came out from a corner office.

"Now that everyone is here, please watch the screen," General Kerwin said. Instantly, dark shades started covering the windows all around the building. A giant screen slowly came down in the center and lit up. Even the people on the computers turned to watch. A gentleman with what sounded like an English accent appeared on the screen.

"Hello, everyone, my name is Joseph Petrus. General Kerwin reports directly to me. He will keep me updated on the progress of the mission. Nettle, you will have access to my direct number; the only other person who has this access is General Kerwin. It is very important that no one knows of my existence. Do you all understand?" They all shook their heads yes. Nettle could feel her stomach tightening a little. *Who is this guy? No one has ever seen or heard of him before.* But he sure spoke with authority.

"Our world is under transition. As your new commander and chief, I am determined that we meet the challenges of this mission responsibly and directly. In contrast to the murderous vision of these violent extremists, we are partnering together to forge an alliance that can't be broken. You are about to encounter top military protocol. No civilians have ever before been allowed to perform a mission such as this. You are also about to witness a mystery from the unseen realm—which few, while here on this earth, will ever encounter. We will confront and defeat any aggression that gets in our way."

Joseph seemed stern, yet confident, in this mission. He assured his listeners of their assignments and thanked them for their obedience. He told them they would be rewarded for their participation. Then he exited the screen.

Tommy touched Nettle's leg under the table and squeezed a little.

Josh grabbed Chrissy's hand and held it tight, letting her know he was there with her, and that everything was going to be OK.

"This is Special Forces Officer Jason Prosper. And this is Special Forces Officer Stefan Stone," General Kerwin announced to the room. "Jason and Stefan are highly trained and skilled in hostile-takeover combat. They will be with you on every mission. You are to take orders directly from them." Nettle was relieved to know there would be someone from the military with them.

"May I ask a few questions?" Chrissy asked.

"Sure," the general said.

"Are you going to explain to all of us in more detail what this is really all about? Are our lives going to be in danger?"

"Yes and yes," General Kerwin answered. "Anytime you walk out your front door in life, you are not guaranteed another day. This mission, which will be called Operation Seeker, will have its risks, but one thing I promise you: we will protect you as much as possible. But there might be times where it will be up to your own intellect and supernatural powers."

"But what if we never discover our supernatural powers?" Chrissy asked. "I mean, Nettle doesn't even know what hers are yet, and she is the one with the most knowledge."

"Don't worry about that, Chrissy. When the time is right, they will be imparted to you."

"Are you going to train us for this mission?" Carver asked.

"These extremists have the ability to pose catastrophic threats that could directly threaten our security. I don't know if I could ever train you enough for that. But I do know that if you rely on your gut instincts and listen to what we do tell you, your chances of survival are much greater. Our goal is to destabilize their threats and find out where they are hiding their ballistic missiles and/or weapons of mass destruction. We want to deny the aggressor the ability to achieve his objectives and facilitate a transition to stable governance. We will guide you as much as we can, and the rest will be up to you," General Kerwin said.

"Yeah, a bunch of football players, a cheerleader, and a chick with special powers. Who would've ever thought it?" Sam said. Even the general laughed at that.

"Who is their leader?" Tommy asked.

"As of now, Mohammed Darius, the supreme leader of Iran, along with our president and the prime minister of England. The ambassadors are simply there in case Darius needs to be overruled on certain issues."

"Well, I have a question," Tenya said. "Why in the world would the United States, knowing that most of the Arab world hates America because they have been taught that we are infidels from childhood, allow this to happen and partner with them? That's really stupid on our part."

"Well, Tenya, unfortunately, most of the world does not realize, believe, or even understand that this is a spirit war! There is no point in trying to convince them because the eyes of their understanding have been blinded. So in saying that, Ollie, why don't you tell them what you know and believe is going on out there."

Ollie stepped forward. "Yes, sir. Twenty years ago, a very powerful gentleman by the name of Caiphus Creed called a meeting together with many global politicians and leaders from around the world. They were some very rich and powerful men. I was in my early thirties then, and my best friend was a man named Bobby Fanelli. He, at the time, was head of the mob and a very powerful man. Bobby had many governmental connections. He was invited to the meeting, and, for some reason, allowed me to attend with him. I was never in the mob, and looking back on it, the only thing I can figure out was that I guess he just trusted me. We had been friends since we were children. The first meeting I attended, they talked about the world becoming one big, global society. They made it very clear at the time that the goal was universal civilization. All of them felt that the world should be one big country.

"They wanted all of humanity to be one big family. I thought to myself at the time, 'How would countries like Vietnam, Cuba, Russia, China, North Korea, and Iran ever agree to that?' Their thinking was to convince the people that they needed a renewed commitment to family life and moral values in order to bring peace globally. Then, they would establish a call for social and economic justice. Thirdly, oil . . . we all need oil. Everyone there seemed to know it would work. They called it a New Global Neighborhood. Then they went on to say they would propose peace to Israel at first. And then . . . annihilate them. They really don't consider Israel a threat; they consider it more the equivalent of a rodent.

"The group had assembled several physicians, chemists, nuclear physicists and biologists who were put in charge of creating an odorless gas that, when released, would spread very quickly and kill people very easily. They were also told to start developing a virus that could spread fast enough to destroy an entire neighborhood within minutes. Part of me was blown away, but another part of me was very intrigued. Little did I know that I would end up running the whole outfit years later! But you must believe me when I say that it doesn't matter if our nation is being run by Republicans or Democrats; there is another faction that is controlling it all. Our people are just ignorant pawns."

"What happened to Bobby?" Nettle asked.

"I stopped hearing from him. He is either living undercover somewhere deep in the jungles of South America, or else they killed him. I really don't know. I tried to find out when I was at the cave, but no one would talk."

"Well, I thought the mob had kind of vanished by now," Chrissy said.

"Oh, they are still around, but they lay very low. The guy who is running it now, Randy Dorn, has a very different approach."

"What does the mob get out of it?" Tenya asked.

"It is all about the Benjamin's for everyone involved," Ollie said.

"So, who is this Creed dude?" Sam asked. "It sounds like he is the instigator in all this."

"He is a billionaire who controls most of the banking world, the pharmaceutical world, and the petroleum world. He is from Egypt and lives a very low-profile life. He makes Bill Gates look poor. We have kept our eye on him for a long time now. It is men like him who helped put men like Mohammed Darius in power," General Kerwin explained.

Nettle's mind started wandering and she found herself thinking about Jackson and how scared he must be when, suddenly, the big screen dropped down again. General Kerwin began showing everyone a picture of the desert location. He showed them the farmhouse and the cave and the large bronze statue they all seemed to be bowing to.

No one spoke because this was the moment that made it all seem surreal. There was no turning back. There was no going home now.

CHAPTER 20

Unlocking the Power

As the sun began to rise, Jackson lay in bed, thinking that something must have happened to Nettle and Tommy since they did not come back to the desert. He wondered if they would ever come back. It felt like it had been months since he had been locked up in the cave. Just as he was mulling these thoughts over, he heard someone opening the door.

"Arlice, get up and come with me!" Ransom demanded.

"What's the matter?" Arlice asked.

"Your other boy is sick, and if you don't come and cure him, he's going to die."

"What?" Arlice said, frenzied.

Arlice and Jackson followed Ransom to the hospital. They were amazed at all the sick people in hospital beds. *Who were these people and what was wrong with them?* Arlice hastily scouted the place to see if he recognized anyone. Ransom opened the door to a small private room, and there lay Stephen, almost lifeless on the bed.

"Stephen . . . Son, are you OK?" Arlice asked as he tried to hold him in his arms. Stephen barely could turn his head to look at his dad.

"He needs more insulin, and we have decided not to give him any,"

Ransom said coldly.

"Are you crazy? He will die if you don't give him his insulin."

"We want you to use your powers and cure him," Ransom said.

"They are not my powers," Arlice responded abruptly.

"Well, whosever they are, if you want to see your boy live, you had better conjure them up."

"It doesn't work like that. And besides, I need to be alone with him."

"Fine, but you do understand that, before long, you will be doing this for us whenever we want you to? If you just go along with it all now, I will see to it that your boys live; otherwise, I'm not sure what will happen to either of them." Jackson looked at his dad with concern. Ransom walked out and closed the door.

Before Arlice had a chance to do anything, a nurse peeked in.

"Hello, my name is Wendy. If you need anything, please let me know," she whispered, a pressing tone to her voice.

"Thank you," Arlice replied, wondering why she was whispering.

"Jackson, I would like to introduce you to your brother, Stephen."

"Hi, Stephen, don't you worry about a thing. Dad will make you better, and then we can get out of this place." He was so excited to know he had a little brother. His eyes filled with tears as he tried to encourage him. Stephen tried to smile but could hardly move.

Arlice turned and looked at Jackson. "Son, can you believe with me?"

"Yes, sir, I can."

"Supernatural powers are ours to have in the kingdom. Our kingdom is not of this world, and our abilities are not either. We are like aliens here, Son, and if we obey the voice of Parakletos, we have all the power we need. Arlice began speaking over Stephen. Immediately, Stephen sat up in bed. He smiled really big and then gave his dad a really big hug. Arlice wasn't sure how well Stephen would remember him, but Stephen acted as though he knew exactly who he was. Arlice decided to play Ransom to get what he needed.

"I knew you could do it," Ransom sneered gleefully as he stepped back into the room.

"Yes, and I will be willing to do more of it if you allow the three of us to live at the farmhouse together."

"The farmhouse?" Ransom questioned. "That is where all the world leaders stay when they are here."

"Yes, but if anyone is sick I can heal them."

Ransom knew this might actually be a good idea, and once they had Nettle, she could see how well they were all being treated.

"OK, fine," Ransom said. "You will stay in the cave until Saturday. Then I will move you. But Stephen stays here until then. I want to make sure what you did lasts."

"Very well, but I am holding you to your word," Arlice insisted.

Jackson began barraging Ransom with questions as he escorted them back to their room.

"What's down all the other halls?"

"Well, the blue hall is where we keep all the seekers. The red hall is where we keep all our weapons. The green hall is where the hospital is, and houses our rooms filled with pleasures. The yellow hall? Well, that hall is top secret." Ransom rattled it off like it was no big deal. As soon as Ransom locked them back in their room, Arlice began writing down what he had just told them.

"I guess he thinks that we will never leave this place and that eventually we will all be on his side. But he also might be lying. You never know about him," Arlice said.

* * *

General Kerwin had finished explaining everything and had just asked Nettle to come with him and sit tight; he would be right back. Nettle sat down in a huge, soft black chair that was so big her feet barely touched the ground. No sooner had she closed her eyes when the door opened and in walked Joseph Petrus, the man in the video.

Nettle stood up to shake his hand.

"I was not going to introduce myself to you yet, Nettle, but I felt this prompting to go ahead and impart some things to you personally."

Impart? . . . "Like, what?" she asked.

"Positional information." Nettle wasn't sure what Joseph meant, exactly, but she was ready to listen. She believed this was going to be another part of the answer to her seeking and she was anticipating the arrival of new information with, now, even greater expectancy.

"What I am about to tell you, many mortals of today only vague-ly understand," Petrus began. "There is a twisting of truth going on in the atmosphere of life. Deception fills the earth, and its participants are many. You see, the unseen realm has a hierarchy just like on earth. This positional information is crucial to your undertaking. Elyon is the king. He is the highest-ranking official in the kingdom. The Prince of Life, his son, is leader and commander of the earth's chosen kingdom citizens. He has ultimate delegated authority and power, which he holds only for those who accept him and his position. Parakletos is the one who transmits information to the citizens. He fills in all the blanks, supplies all the answers, and renders each one their powers. He is the most con-troversial of this trio among mortals who believe in and accept them. Only a few understand his power. You must show them Nettle . . . you have been chosen to lead them with genuineness. I have given you the keys. Now go unlock the doors."

And with that, he departed.

As he spoke, Nettle knew everything he was saying was true. But she was also thinking, *Who is this guy? Is he a spirit-being himself? Why me?* Nettle knew this was a moment in the history of her life that would never be forgotten. She could hardly stay standing.

General Kerwin came back in and escorted Nettle back to the others. Tommy and everyone else immediately noticed a massive change in her countenance.

"You may leave now," the general said. "Be aware of your surround-ings at all times. We will be in touch, so keep your radios close by. Jason and Stefan will escort you all back to your vehicles."

"That was it?" Chrissy said. "I was expecting more information than that."

"That was just a confirmation meeting. There will be more—lots more," Nettle said with utmost confidence. "There is no need to worry. Just be at peace with it all for now."

* * * * *

After dinner, a special news report was announced. Beth La'mon, the SBC news anchor, came on saying there was a very serious nuclear threat from Russia against Israel. They watched as President Clemmons tried to calm the situation by informing the nation that he was talking with Russia's prime minister, Igor Mutko, and everything was stable. He felt certain that by tomorrow, the issue would be resolved.

"Oh boy," Josh said. "Here we go again. It's probably all a facade."

"Well, whether it is or not, we need to be on high alert," Nettle said. "They might be calling us sooner than later."

"So why aren't we seeing Benjamin Meir, Israel's prime minister, speak out?" Josh asked. "The media never even mentioned his name. I wonder what he's planning on doing about this."

"Our world is changing very quickly," Richard said. "It's taken years to get to this point, but now I have a feeling that all hell is about to break loose, and I mean literally. Evil spirits are everywhere. Their mission is to murder, embezzle, and destroy."

"What are you talking about, Dad?"

"I am talking about the outer realm's hordes. I have been studying this for the past few months. Man's struggle is not against man, Tommy. I know it may appear that way, but the fight is against rulers and cosmic powers in the outer darkness. There are spiritual forces of evil surveying the atmosphere. They have a chief prince who deals in wiles and strategems. They watch for certain moods or emotions to launch their attack. They commence their master marketing plan with a deceptive essence that entices people through their feelings. It looks, sounds, and feels good . . . at least in the beginning."

"Whoa . . . that's awful," Chrissy said.

Tommy was thinking his dad was now sounding like Nettle.

"Yeah, I just read that when you operate out of any extreme emotion to an excessive measure, then you become a target for this evil power," Nettle said.

"Can you give us an example?" Chrissy asked.

"Like extreme anger, intentional self-pity, or harboring unforgiveness. Even the constant mulling over of depressing thoughts or out-of-control worry will open doors for his attack. We have to be cognizant of his schemes, because he deals through our emotions," Richard said.

"He's right. There is a battle raging, and the chief enemy is looking for team members. His diabolical ploys can be defeated only when we put on our panoply," Nettle said.

"OK Nettle, I need that repeated in simple terms, please," Chrissy requested. "What do you mean when you say, *panoply?*"

"I just mean his schemes can be defeated when we understand our power. We have literal armor or panoply; we can put on to fight in this other kingdom. Most people are aware of the dark evil spirit but only from the standpoint of television or movies. However, the dark spirit has consequences that are dangerous. Many times they hide themselves in instruments of pleasure. For instance, they camouflage themselves in certain video games, fiction novels, paranormal-activity entities, movies, music, certain board games, and many humanistic spiritual religions. They lure you in and then attack you later. They always mix a little truth with the lie . . . and a lot of pain after the pleasure," Nettle said. "But, our kingdom is so far superior to what this sinister spirit has to offer that it isn't even comparable. The problem is that this evil force has blinded the hearts and minds so well that humans only know how to live by what they feel or think. They cannot separate truth from their mortal souls. No one is teaching people about the kingdom and its authority. It is pitiful."

"I understand your aggravation, Nettle," Josh said. "But you have to realize the problem is that most don't understand how to obtain the kingdom. They have never tapped into the supernatural side of the kingdom. We are just now learning about it ourselves."

"Yeah, all they recognize is defeat," Tommy interjected.

"But it is still up to the individual. Parakletos will never force himself on anyone," Nettle said. "Deception is just that—deception. You aren't aware of it." Suddenly, she heard her radio go off. She excused herself and went back to her bedroom.

"Nettle, are you there?"

"Yes, Ollie. I am here."

"Get everyone ready. You must go tonight. Be at the bus station in two hours. Have Tommy and Josh tell the others in person. Do not, and

I repeat, do *not* call them. Take only two vehicles. When you arrive at the station, Jason and Stefan will be there to meet you to execute the plan." Nettle could feel her heart start to race. *Now?* She was not expecting to have to go right now.

"Be careful, Nettle."

"Yes, sir," she responded. Nettle sat there a bit stunned. *Am I ready to live up to everything I have just been telling everyone?* She got up and marched back into the den with a look of trepidation on her face.

"I have something very serious to tell you all."

That got everyone's immediate attention.

"I just received a radio call from Ollie, and we have to be at the bus station at midnight tonight. He wants us to tell the others, but only in person."

It was almost as if they were all moving in slow motion. It took them a minute to comprehend Nettle's words and move into gear. They grabbed a few things, hugged Pastor and Mrs. Jones, and headed out the door to go tell the others. Their adrenaline began to kick in.

CHAPTER 21

I Can Fly

Arlice woke up from an interesting dream and saw it was around 1 a.m. Perplexed and preoccupied with it, he couldn't go back to sleep. He glanced over at Jackson; he was now glad to know both his sons were OK. He wanted desperately to escape and start a new life together. Those thoughts quickly disappeared as his dream pressed heavy on his mind. *I need to go outside for a breath of fresh air.* He sprang up from his bed and rang the buzzer for the guard to come. Convincingly, he persuaded the guard to let him go outside.

By now Nettle and the group had made it to the desert. Stationed at their posts, Stefan was about to give the order to move in closer when suddenly he whispered for everyone to stand back.

"Over there, look, it's Arlice," he whispered. As Arlice moved closer in their direction, Stefan pointed a laser directly on Arlice's chest. Immediately realizing someone was out there, Arlice froze. Nothing happened, so he took it as a sign to move forward. Arlice carefully gave a thumbs-up signal so that whoever it was could see him. He walked back over to the guard and asked to go back inside to the restroom in order to write a note for whoever it was outside.

"What did that mean?" Tay asked.

"I don't know, but let's wait a few minutes before we proceed," Stefan ordered. He quietly radioed Jason and his team to let them know they had spotted Arlice over at the cave.

As the guard escorted him in, Arlice took a quick peek in at Jackson, quickly grabbed a pen, then proceeded on to the restroom. Once inside, he took a paper towel and began writing instructions for whoever was out there. He shakily wrote down the location of his room, explained that Stephen was in the hospital, and provided its location. He also noted that they were being moved to the farmhouse this Saturday. Then he flushed the toilet and went back out to the guard.

Once outside again, he headed as far out as he could and sat down under a huge tree to look up at the stars for a minute. He hoped to see his family again. The moon was bright, and there was a gentle breeze; the stars lit up the desert sky. Arlice began to dig with his hands to bury the note. Stefan, through his night vision goggles, could see that Arlice was trying to dig a hole.

Over at the farmhouse, the others had split up to surround it. Sitting in the dark, reflecting on her dream, Nettle began remembering how she could fly. She kept in mind how she soared above the desert, overlooking everything. Something clicked. *That's it. One of my special powers is that I can fly!* It was a profound moment of revelation—one that she found herself truly believing.

She quietly stood, lifted her arms up into the air, and said, "I don't just know I can fly, I *believe* I can fly." There was something deep inside of her that had never believed anything so strongly in her life. This was the moment, the pivotal millisecond, to test her faith in the supernatural kingdom. She had no doubts or misgivings about it. This was a huge piece of the puzzle in her search for answers, and she was about to blow man's theology away. As she stretched her arms above her head, she could feel her body leaving the ground. Her thoughts catapulted to the time one mortal man walked on water and another was transported between cities. If that was obtainable by defying gravity, then flying was no hard task for King Elyon to make happen. As she soared above the earth, she felt exhilarated. She knew that somehow she had just entered into a realm where most mortals never go. She was so caught up in the fact that she was flying that she almost forgot she was on a mission. She began searching everywhere for guards, but she couldn't find them anywhere. She left the farmhouse area and headed off to look over by the cave. She landed in the top of a tree. Looking down, she could see a man sitting on the ground, digging a hole. She immediately recognized Arlice. Quietly, she whispered his name. Arlice immediately stopped digging. He cautiously looked up and saw her at the top of the tree. He stopped everything he was doing and just stared, completely amazed.

"What's he looking at?" Sam asked Stefan.

"I think he sees something," Stefan said.

Arlice turned to see what the guards were doing. Still talking and laughing, they were paying no attention to Arlice. Arlice showed Nettle the paper towel in his hand.

"Just leave it on the ground," Nettle said. "I will get it. Don't bury it, just set it in the hole you have already dug, and go back and distract the guards so I can pick it up." Arlice nodded his head and stood up. He pushed the note down as far as he could to get it out of sight.

"What's he doing now?" Tenya whispered.

"I don't know," Stefan responded. "Just stay put. No one move."

"Whatever he saw up in that tree made him head back toward the cave," Tenya said. As Arlice approached the guards, he slipped and fell. The guards instantly rushed over to him, giving Nettle enough time to fly down, get the paper towel, and fly back to the top of the tree.

"Whoa, did you guys see that?" Tay whispered rather loudly.

"Yes, we saw Arlice fall down. Now be quiet, Tay," Tenya said.

"No, not Arlice, bozo—Nettle. I saw Nettle fly down out of that tree, pick up Arlice's note, and then fly back up into that tree!" Tay said.

"What?" Tenya whispered loudly. "Jackie must have slipped something in your food, dude. That's absurd."

"No, I'm serious. I saw Nettle fly down out of that tree and get that paper!"

"Good grief, it is her," Stefan responded. "Nettle is up in that tree; I can see her."

"I told you, and she can fly. I saw it with my own two eyes," Tay said, a bit more boldly, now almost bragging.

The guards helped Arlice up. After brushing himself off, he hobbled back to his room.

Jason began gathering his group to meet Stefan's group by the cave, but he could not find Nettle. Just as he was about to radio her, she landed beside him.

Jason stood speechless.

"I found Arlice, and he gave me this note. I thought you might want to read it."

"Where did you see Arlice?" Jason asked, a perplexed look on his face. By this time the others had arrived at their positions.

"He is over at the cave, and I flew over there," Nettle said.

"What did you say?" Tommy asked.

"I flew," Nettle said, yet she was quite humble about it.

"That is awesome," Chrissy said.

"Are you serious?" Tommy asked, hugging Nettle as if to say: *Let's do this!*

"Let's move," Jason ordered. They made their way to the other group. Jason asked Nettle to tell the others what happened.

"Well, Arlice was outside the cave sitting under a tree trying to bury a note. I flew up in the tree and whispered for him to leave me the note. He went back, acted like he tripped and fell, the guards ran over to him, and I flew down and picked up the note."

"I told y'all she could fly. I saw you fly down out of that tree and fly back up," Tay said.

"Did you really do that, Nettle?" Tenya asked.

"Yes, Tenya, I can fly. But the most important thing is that Arlice told us where he is located."

"We need to inform General Kerwin of this information," Jason said. "We can head back now. It doesn't look as if anything else is going on here now, and once we extract Arlice, he can tell us more."

"Wait a minute," Cory whispered, looking around as if he heard something. "Look, over at the farmhouse: someone's coming out the front door." They quickly ducked and watched as Ransom escorted three men from the farmhouse to a car parked in the driveway.

"Oh, great, he's with President Clemmons, Prime Minister Dunn, and that dude from China," Sam said.

"What are they doing out this late?" Chrissy asked.

"I don't know," Jason said. "Be very still. Nettle, do you think you can follow them and meet us back at the bus stop later?"

"Sure, I can try," Nettle said. "I'm not sure what all I can do yet except fly, but if I run into a problem, I will radio you."

"She's only flown once," Tommy said. "Do you really think that's a smart idea, since it is dark and she hasn't done it much?"

"I can do it, Tommy. I promise to be very careful. Maybe where they are going will give us a clue to what is going on here."

"Great. The rest of you come with me, and let's get out of here," Jason instructed.

Ransom drove the three gentlemen down the farmhouse driveway. He headed back down the mountain road, taking off at a high speed. Nettle began to realize how incredible flying was. It was almost inconceivable, she thought. *Never in a million years would anyone believe this unless they saw it,* Nettle said to herself. She realized for the first time that this kingdom offered its seekers the ability to do almost anything as long as they truly believed.

The desert could be very dark at night. Nettle stayed up high and far to the rear as she followed the vehicle's taillights. In a flash, she realized she was following three of the most powerful men in the world. *What are they about to do, who is about to be affected, and what is going to be my role in all of this?*

Coming out of her thoughts, Nettle stayed behind the vehicle. As the vehicle made it to the edge of town, Ransom pulled over and settled the vehicle in a small area known as Tremer Park. Nettle only wished she could be invisible so she could hear what they were saying.

CHAPTER 22

Thy Kingdom Come

Nettle landed in a tree just above their car and waited to see what would happen next. Immediately, another vehicle pulled up. It looked identical to the car that kidnapped Jackson. Nettle soon realized it was Hawk driving this second car. He opened the door for the same local police officers Nettle had dealt with earlier. Officer Whitmore, Detective Gibbs, Detective Moll, and one other gentleman she did not recognize stepped out of the car.

Ransom, President Clemmons, Prime Minister Dunn, and President Mai Fan Zhoo of China exited Ransom's car and sat at a large picnic table on the other side of the tree Nettle was nestled in. She was thrilled she would be able to hear what they had to say. Ransom and Hawk continued pacing the place, making sure no one else was around.

They give me the creeps, Nettle thought. She began listening carefully to hear the conversation below. Detective Moll started by saying the leaders could count on his police station for complete cooperation to help execute the plan. He mentioned that they had two men in their station who might cause some problems. He shared their names—Officer Cothern and Officer Holmes. But, he said, he felt certain they would eventually come on board.

Nettle noticed another vehicle pulling up to park. This one was a limousine. She found it a little hard to believe they chose to sit out in the open, even though it was only 4:30 a.m. and still dark. Surely they weren't going to be here long, she thought.

Nettle's heart immediately started beating faster when she realized the last group of men walking up from the limo was the four kings. The leaders of the entire regime were right below her. There stood Mohammed Darius, Faisai Salam, Charles Otto, and Constantine Alexander. *This can't be good.* President Clemmons introduced them to the officers.

"We have now confirmed that 90 percent of all transformed seekers are on board with 'Operation Dying Breed,'" King Darius began. "Our plan worked, and we have convinced them to completely believe in our glorious transformation of nations. We now know our technique will work on all seekers. The devastations will leave the people hopeless and we will become their hope. The only thing you must prepare yourself for are the uninvited constituents around the world."

"What do you mean by that?" Officer Whitmore asked. "I'm not quite sure I understand."

"Then let me explain," Darius said, quite calmly. "You see, many people will not understand at first what is happening. Some will be scared and some will be skeptical. We must give them total security again and obtain a peaceful environment across the globe. Then, once we gain their loyalty, we have no choice other than to see to it that they understand the importance of belonging. In order for us to merge our societies and cultures together, we must have a common bond or common thread. Then we introduce our spiritual system. People are not afraid of faith like they are of politics, so we must make sure that we present everything with compassion coupled with supernatural events. Then they will feel safe."

"How will we make that happen?" Whitmore asked.

"It is fairly easy," Darius said, smiling. "We have invented a numerical system that will keep track of our followers. Everyone who wants to join our new global community and spiritual system will be able to identify each other through our new system. This will unite us and make us one big, happy family. They must understand that this is all for one and one for all. All outsiders will have a difficult time surviving."

"I think we will find that most all will comply," President Clemmons said reassuringly. "This is for everyone's good. All of us here love the people of the world. We want to end hunger, poverty, and lack. This new global neighborhood will give them that. Most religions will support us. God is the God of all of us anyway . . . right? Most all will happily come on board. We all know there is only one way anyway . . . right?"

What in the world is that supposed to mean? Nettle thought, still listening from her perch.

"He's right," Darius said. "There will be a small few who are willing to die for their dogmas. I admire the poor fools. At least they are willing to stand up for what they believe in, unlike most. Those unfortunate fools will lose their heads." Nettle noticed he was having a euphoric moment. "Anyway, enough of all that talk for now. We want peace and I will personally see that peace will be our main objective for the whole world."

"However, in order to obtain our New World, we will have to get rid of some of the population in order to make this work," President Clemmons added. "Remember, 60 percent of the world's population lives in Asia, which is why Mai Fan Zhoo and Tatsu Kan are important to us. They will help us win their people over." Nettle suddenly realized that the other man who got out of the car was Japan's president, Tatsu Kan.

"But what about North Korea?" Whitmore asked.

"They are one of our closest allies now. You have nothing to worry about there," King Salam answered.

"The world has yearned for this transition to take place since the beginning of time," Clemmons continued. "All along, man has been preparing for this merger." He looked intently at Officer Whitmore and in Detectives Moll's and Gibbs' eyes. "The reason the three of you are here today is because one of our new global headquarters will be here in the Arizona desert. The main headquarters will be overseas, but we will also have many hidden branches across the globe.

"We are promoting the three of you to top-ranking police officials for the new global governance in this part of the neighborhood. Your titles will be changing when the transition takes place. You will be employed by the World Government Council. Your salaries will be one million dollars a year and you will report directly to King Constantine of Greece, who will oversee all military police officials. All police will now be part of the Global Military Militia."

The two detectives looked at each other and grinned. Whitmore, though, could not get a very uneasy feeling out of his gut. He knew his wife was not going to like this one-global-belief thing, but he just smiled, letting them all believe he was in on the deal. The money and the position sounded good, but something inside of him felt that all of this would not turn out well.

"Two months from tonight, the world news will be announcing disasters all over the globe," Darius announced. "We will stage these disasters by country. Then, within seventy-two hours, we will announce the new plan to merge our world. People will be preoccupied and devastated with all that took place; they should go along rather peacefully with our proposal."

"How are you going to stage fake disasters all over the world?" Moll asked.

"We are not going to stage them. They will be real," Darius said. "Tiny pockets all over the world will feel the devastation, and this will make the people need a strong leader to save them. That is where we come in."

"Where will the devastations be?" Whitmore asked.

"Do not worry about that. The people will never know what hit them. We will immediately set up police stations all over the world to bring the people in to receive their new personal ID numbers as well as their new financial packages. Everyone who understands the advantages of this new global community will prosper, and those who don't, won't."

"You mean they will be jailed?" Whitmore asked.

"The executions will be the responsibility of the police stations," Darius answered.

Whitmore tried to smile and act as though he thought this was a great plan. Both Moll and Gibbs commended King Darius on his excellent strategy.

Nettle was about to throw up on all of them as she listened to every word. She wished they had named the places they were going to devastate, but it looked as though Darius wasn't going to be giving that information out tonight. *These men are pure evil.* Nettle had a hard time believing her very own president was buying into all this. This was a guy the nation loved, she told herself again and again. She even voted for him.

"Next Saturday, all kings, generals, and colonels will be convening at the farmhouse," President Clemmons said. "Ransom will pick the three of you up to attend as well. It will be our last assembly before we meet here again in two months for the completion of our project. Tell no one of the things you have heard here today. You are dismissed."

The men all shook hands and got back in their vehicles to leave.

Nettle sat in the tree, stunned at what she had just witnessed. Her emotions were rattled because she was quite tired, but knew she had to get this information to General Kerwin quickly.

When she finally arrived, Jason was waiting outside for her. He motioned for her to get inside the Hummer, as everyone was waiting anxiously to hear the news. By now it was 6:30 a.m., and they were all tired and hungry. Nettle hugged Tommy.

CHAPTER 23

Waiting

"Welcome," General Kerwin said as he greeted them at the entrance to the headquarters. "Let's go to the conference room; we have food waiting for you there." It was all sinking in to everyone just how serious this was and that the whole mission was dependent upon common, everyday, young adults—college students. As General Kerwin opened the door to the conference room, there sat the most incredible display of food any of them had ever seen.

As they were filling their plates, they noticed officers Cothern and Holmes, Ollie, Dr. Wallace, and two other gentlemen sitting down, already at the table.

"I am glad everyone could make it this morning, and we are all anxious to hear what you found out, Nettle," General Kerwin began. "Jason told me that your trial run to scout out the place went well and that you were able to retrieve a note from Arlice."

"Yes, sir, we did, and it was good to find out that they are all OK. The note informed us Arlice would be moving into the farmhouse this weekend," Nettle said.

"Great. That will make it a lot easier to rescue them. What else took place?" General Kerwin asked.

"They plan on killing a lot of people in two months in order to bring their New Global Neighborhood to pass. They want to rule the world, from what I understand, both politically and spiritually."

"Yes, she's right," Kerwin said. "Their goal is to bring together emerging economies to stabilize the global financial market, or at least that is what they will tell us. Then, they will reform our monetary system by forming a one-world currency. They believe that today's key economic challenges require a collective and ambitious action, which the New World Government Council is able to bring about. Once they have this 'under control,' they will have built up their military and the local police will be involved and working directly for them."

"Yes," Nettle said. "I heard them say that they were going to pay one million dollars a year to Officer Whitmore and detectives Moll and Gibbs, and that they would be at the helm of all police. Darius told them they will report directly to the king of Greece."

"Correct," Kerwin said.

"I don't quite even comprehend why they would want to kill their own people in order to make all this happen," Tommy said.

"To create mass confusion in order to weaken people's defenses, so they can usher in their agenda," Ollie said.

Everyone sat in silence for what seemed like close to a minute.

"But we are going to stop them, right?" Nettle asked.

"Yes, you are," spoke the gentleman at the end of the table.

Nettle had been eyeing the tall, dark, mysterious-looking man dressed in a military uniform and sitting at the end of the table. The general had not introduced him to anybody. He stood up, and everyone's mouths dropped, as he was more than ten feet tall and had the most incredible wings attached to his back. He was a sight to behold and had the most majestic presence they had ever witnessed. Everyone instantly knew he had great authority and abilities that were not from this world. No one could take their eyes off of him once he stood up.

"I have been sent to patrol the earth—to protect the great name. I reveal myself to you today for one purpose: a prophetic warning. The kingdoms of this world will be shaken. Let yourselves be built into a spiritual house. Do not be surprised at the fiery ordeal that is taking place among you to test you, as though something strange is happening to you. For the time has come for judgment to begin. You have all been chosen for this assignment since the foundation of the world. Spiritual militias fighting the earthly stratagems—but your special powers will be much more effective than any earthly tactic or ploy."

"What special powers?" Sam asked. "Only Nettle has those."

"I'm afraid you're wrong, Sam."

This creature even knows my dad-gum name, Sam found himself thinking.

"Every kingdom citizen has the ability to have them, but only if they choose to believe. When the time comes and you do that, you will automatically know what to do with them."

"Excuse me, sir. May I ask who you are?" Nettle said. She couldn't take her eyes off of this magnificent being. She had never seen anything like him, and he was definitely not human.

"My name is Michael, and I am the archangel of war. I have come to bring a sword against anyone who threatens the chosen ones."

"So, you are not human?" Carver asked.

"I am the commanding officer in the army of the highest king, Elyon: the top-ranking official assigned to watch and protect the kingdom. Your eyes have been opened for a season to observe the war. Two kingdoms are about to collide on schedule, and you are being granted permission to see into our world."

"Awesome!" Sam replied.

"I am here today for one purpose, and that is to prove to you there is another kingdom, as you have thought. You have chosen, by conviction, to believe, and because of that, you will do great exploits. But remember, *your belief* will be the only thing that keeps you moving forward."

And with that, Michael disappeared into thin air.

"Are you beginning to understand?" General Kerwin asked. "We are in a different kind of war and have been since the Ancient of Days destroyed the earth-curse. Go home now and get some rest. Prepare yourself for war. I will be in touch."

"But what about this Saturday when they all meet again?" Nettle asked. "Aren't we going to do something then?"

"I don't know right now," General Kerwin said. "My orders have not been given yet. I do not move until instructed, and you should not either.

"As soon as I know more, I will let you all know. You are dismissed."

But he turned to Nettle to give a special word to her.

"Nettle, do not move ahead of your gift; it won't work. Wait on the timing. It is the most important thing," the general said.

"Yes, sir," Nettle said.

Waiting . . . Something I'm not great at.

Everyone loaded back up in the Hummer, and Jason drove them back to their cars.

For the moment, sleep was mostly what was on everyone's minds.

CHAPTER 24

China

The next morning, Arlice was anticipating the move from the cave to the farmhouse. Jackson rolled over and popped his eyes open to see his dad staring at him.

"Dad, where did you go last night?" he asked. "I woke up and you were gone. I thought they had taken you."

"No, Son, I woke up after a dream I had and called the guards to go outside for a breath of fresh air. I just felt an urge to go outside. When I got out there the strangest thing happened. I looked up and spotted Nettle up in a tree."

"I knew it," Jackson said. "I knew she and Tommy would come find us."

"Not only did they find us, Jackson . . . Nettle can fly."

"Fly? Now that is *tight*. I want that to be my gift."

"It will only be a matter of time now before we are rescued," Arlice said. "I left Nettle a note, and I'm confident she will deliver it to someone she can trust to help us."

"I know she will rescue us. I had a dream that she would save everyone out here."

* * *

"You know, Chrissy, I am totally convinced now that our purpose is intricately designed by our creator. All a person has to do is stop, ask, look, and listen for it. I believe the greatest tragedy in life is not death; it is a life without knowing your ultimate, higher purpose. I want to discover the original intent of my existence," Nettle said.

"I guess a life without a clear purpose is just an experimented life," Chrissy said, deeply in thought. "What I mean by that is, without purpose, activity has no meaning, and time and energy are misused. Purpose determines what is right and protects us from doing something wrong at the expense of what was designed for us. I guess finding and fulfilling your assigned purpose really is a critical step in life. It should be our top priority to find our purpose."

"Yes!" Nettle declared. "I am so glad you are starting to see it."

* * *

Nettle quickly got dressed and frantically drove back to Corridor Mountain. The puzzle was halfway complete. Nettle now knew what she had seen and experienced was no match for any scholar, philosopher, genius, atheist, unbelieving evangelical, or any form of religious dogma. She now knew that there are not multiple gods, there is only one, and he is a King. She realized this was never about a religion, as the world had been taught, but about a kingdom and any person's place in it. *No wonder our generation doesn't feel like man's traditions or institutions offer them the real deal . . . most don't. Man has been searching for eons trying to prove or disprove all the messages when all they had to do the whole time is ask. Parakletos would always answer.*

* * *

General Kerwin's phone rang, and it was President Clemmons calling.

"Hey, Todd, how are you today?"

"I'm great, Paul, and how are you?" the general replied.

"Tired, but I had a great meeting this morning I need to tell you about. The police station in Arizona is on board, and it looks as though our meeting at the farmhouse is on for this Saturday. I am about to board Air Force One to head back now, so let's have dinner tonight in the Oval Office. I have a lot to tell you."

"Sounds great. See you around seven?"

"Seven it is," President Clemmons said.

As a young boy growing up in Michigan, Todd Kerwin had a very abusive father. There were many nights he was locked in a closet after being severely beaten. His mother was so fearful her husband might kill them both that she chose to remain silent and not confront the monster she was married to. Despite the abuse, Todd knew that his dad was mentally ill. One day his neighbor invited him to a youth gathering. The man speaking was from the Bahamas, and he spoke about a supernatural kingdom. Todd was convinced, and from that moment on believed he, too, could live in this kingdom. So the nights young Todd spent in the closet, from then on, became intense conversations with this king. It was there he was introduced to Parakletos. Todd figured out at a very young age that humans were not created to live for themselves but to live for a kingdom purpose. As he grew older, he realized that all the talk on leadership means nothing if one is led in the wrong direction. He realized he had to lay down his own will and allow Parakletos to be his guide. Parakletos would show him a world where nothing would be impossible: a world where almost everything is supernatural.

One night, at age twelve, Todd prayed hard to be taken somewhere else besides the tiny 3x6 closet he was trapped in. It was then that Parakletos answered his prayer. Todd was immediately transported to a stunning, bright room filled with music and fresh-smelling flowers. It was daylight, and he could see a beautiful ocean outside. He knew he was somewhere else besides Michigan. It was from that point on that Todd's life dramatically changed. His gift, like Nettle's, was way out of the ordinary, so being in Arizona one moment and in Washington, DC, for dinner the next moment was no problem for him.

He didn't need Air Force One.

* * *

Back at the cave, Ransom and Hawk were preparing for the upcoming meeting. They made sure the bronze altar was polished and that the farmhouse was cleaned up. Ransom informed Hawk that Arlice and his children would be moving into the farmhouse that weekend.

"Hawk, I want to hold a gathering this afternoon with everyone. Go and announce that we will meet at 4 p.m. Hey, and before you go, I will let you in on a little secret. I am going to have Arlice heal Denise Clemmons this weekend. That will catapult you and me to a whole new level in the eyes of the president," Ransom said gleefully.

"Awesome," Hawk remarked before he headed out the door. He immediately went to the PA system inside the cave and made the announcement about the afternoon meeting.

Denise Clemmons, the first lady, had a rare form of cancer and had only been given a year to live. Ransom knew that if Arlice could heal her, it would elevate him in the eyes of the president to one of great trust. He yearned for the approval of Clemmons.

Ransom went and got Stephen out of the hospital and led him to Arlice's room. "He can stay here in the cave with you for now. Your room will be ready to move into this weekend." Ransom shut the door and left. Arlice grabbed Stephen and held him tight.

"Daddy, can we go home and see mommy now?"

"We will soon, Son. We will all go home soon." A tear welled in Arlice's eye as he looked at both his sons together.

* * *

Nettle sat down on the corridor bench and began asking questions. This time . . . silence. Nothing at all. Just as she was about to leave, she heard the word . . . *China*.

"China?" she said out loud. "What do you mean? Are you telling me to go to China?" Nettle waited again, but no response. She drove back to Tommy's house, wondering what had been meant.

Obviously, this was another key in the journey.

CHAPTER 25

Mystery Man

Back at Operation Desert Seeker headquarters, Ollie was excited about meeting with General Kerwin. He knew a secret that just might be to their advantage.

"Todd, I think I know someone that would be a vital asset to us if we could find him. He helped build the underground cave and all the tunnels. He designed the whole thing. I cannot remember his last name, but his first name is Sky and I believe he lives in Missouri somewhere. I know he was an engineer and an artist, so maybe we can find him and talk to him."

"Absolutely," Kerwin said. "I will get Debra on it right away."

"I'm not sure he will help, but we can at least feel him out," Ollie said.

It wasn't long until Debra found Sky, or at least a gentleman who fit his description. She informed General Kerwin and Ollie that when they ran a background check, they found out he was a Muay Thai expert, a highly trained sharpshooter, and that he spoke five languages: English, Spanish, Chinese, German, and Farsi.

"Wow, that's impressive," the general said as he was looking over Sky's credentials. "What is he doing for a living now, and is he still in Missouri?"

"His name is Sky Mullins, and he is thirty-two years old. He lives in Missoula, Montana. He owns a gun shop there and teaches German and Chinese at the University of Montana part time. He loves to hunt, fish, and snowboard and lives alone up in the Blue Mountains. He has no criminal record, but he does have an engineering degree from the University of Central Missouri. His IQ is like 150, so no wonder he speaks five languages and designed an underground city for the military," Debra said.

"Do you think he knew what was going on out there?" General Kerwin asked.

"I don't know," Ollie said. "But he had to design a lot of weird and interesting things not to question that something was up."

"Well, we're going to find out," Kerwin said. "I want you and Stefan to take a trip to Montana tomorrow to see him. We will brief you on what to say tonight and the signs to look for."

"Sounds great," Ollie said.

Debra scheduled a plane for early the next morning. Ollie felt certain that Sky could help in a very significant way—if they could talk him into it. They knew positioning everything effectively was crucial.

* * *

Back at the cave, Ransom was getting ready for his meeting. Arlice glanced at the clock, realizing it was almost 4 p.m.

"This meeting today will give me a chance to see just how many people have been brainwashed," Arlice told Jackson.

"Do you know any of them personally?" Jackson asked.

"I know a few of them well enough to know if they've changed. There was a gentleman named Dan who had an amputated leg that grew back out. He should definitely recognize me.

"I want you boys to stay very close to me. Do you understand?"

"Yes, sir," Jackson said.

"OK, Daddy," Stephen said. The intercom went off announcing the time, and one of the guards unlocked their door and escorted them down to Clement Hall for the meeting.

Arlice found a back row seat and sat Jackson and Stephen on each side of him. He noticed several of the people who had been at the healing service, but they didn't seem to recognize him. Arlice spotted Dan, the amputee, sitting a couple of rows in front of him.

Ransom began his speech, and one would have thought he had won the lottery. He was almost giddy as he began to talk.

"Welcome to the most important meeting of your lives. As you are all aware . . . shortly you will become part of a New Global Community of Peace, where your lives will be transformed forever. Your loyalty is now to the kings until the Great One appears."

A loud noise startled everyone; Arlice noticed a large bronze statue being rolled into the room. Instantaneously, everyone started to get down on their knees and bow. Arlice and his two sons were the only ones still sitting. Ransom glanced back at Arlice, giving him a sort of grimaced look. Arlice became conscious of how desperate he was to get his children out of that place. The room roared as the people shouted.

"This Saturday you will move into your new jobs," Ransom announced. As soon as the people heard this, they shouted again and clapped profusely. It was almost as if they acted robotic. Arlice could not believe the fervor of the participation. Finally, Ransom ended his speech and everyone was dismissed to go. Arlice took Jackson and Stephen's hands and quickly led them over to Dan, the amputee gentleman.

"Hey, Dan . . . it's Arlice. Do you remember me? I was the one who prayed for your leg to grow out." Dan looked at Arlice as if he had no clue who Arlice was. He made no facial expression at all.

Turning away, he quietly mumbled, "Yes, I remember you, but they must never know that." As he walked away, Arlice saw Ransom staring at him, so he quickly acted as if he was just trying to get the kids to follow him back to their room. Once they got inside, they settled down to talk.

"Dad, didn't he say yes, he remembers you?"

"Yes, Jackson, but we can never let anyone know that. Ever!"

"Yes, sir."

"But it does let me know that there might be a few others who still haven't been completely brainwashed; they are just pretending. That tells me they have been scared bad enough to betray their convictions. We have got to find them and help them escape too."

"Why would the government do this to people?" Jackson asked.

"Because, Son, it is about men wanting power and control. They are greedy human beings. They are full of themselves and don't care about anyone else. Some people are so corrupt they will do anything to get what they want—even murder."

This was enormously unsettling to Jackson. He knew he had to find his powers so he could help everyone escape.

* * *

Ollie and Stefan landed in Montana; they had been trying to find Sky Mullins all day. They had gone by the university as well as his home, but he wasn't at either place. They decided to grab a late lunch and park close to his cabin and wait for him to arrive. A few hours later, just before dusk, he drove up. They approached his door.

"Can I help you?" Sky said, barely cracking his door.

"Hello, Sky. I am Oliver Cook and this is Stefan Casey. If you don't mind, we would like to talk to you about possibly helping us with a situation we have encountered in Arizona."

"What about it?" Sky asked.

"Well, we seem to have a problem that cannot be resolved without your help. We have found out that several people have been kidnapped and are being held hostage in the cave you designed."

"What cave?" he said—almost convincingly.

"The one in Arizona: the government cave you designed and built while I was there," Ollie said.

At that point, Stefan pulled out his government ID, and Sky looked down to check it out.

"Why don't you come inside?"

"Thank you," Ollie said. Ollie and Stefan quickly stepped inside.

"So, what's this about?" Sky asked.

"It seems as though we have some rogue politicians," Ollie said.

Sky grinned pretty hard; he was thinking about the ones he had encountered out there.

"You're telling me?"

Immediately, Ollie became very serious. "They have kidnapped a hundred people or more out there. We know they have plans to destroy part of the human race in order to convince people to join arms and embrace the New Global Neighborhood. Their plans are very extreme and include the annihilation of over one billion people worldwide." As Ollie was talking, Stefan was watching Sky's body language. He could tell he was a bit uneasy, but not opposed to having this conversation.

"Well, what do you think I have to do with that?"

"We know that you designed and helped build the cave."

"Now, how do you know that?" Sky asked.

"Because I was there when you did it," Ollie answered.

Sky looked a little bewildered, but still did not display much facial expression.

"I used to be in charge at the farmhouse but got fired several years ago because I was a drunk," Ollie continued.

"What makes you think I want to get involved and help you?" Sky said.

"Because one would think that you value the ability to live freely up here in these mountains without being told what to do. Am I correct?"

"You are," Sky said.

"If you want to keep those freedoms, along with your guns, your hunting and fishing abilities, and even your job for that matter, I suggest you at least hear us out," Stefan said.

"OK. Go."

"We need the floor plans and for you to explain how the cave and the farmhouse connect to the underground city. We need to know the details about all the secret passageways that you designed."

"How do I know you are not being followed or that you are the good guys in all of this?"

"That's a good question," Ollie said. "The government doesn't know that we know about any of this."

"I thought you *were* the government," Sky said.

"Look, if we were bad, we would just coerce you to go with us," Stefan said.

"They sure would not have sent me," Ollie said.

That got a little of a chuckle from Sky.

"The scary part is that our own president is involved in this takeover plan," Stefan said.

"So, whom are you both working directly for?"

"Someone who is very high up—someone who is going to stop this horrendous plot. He needs you to come back with us and help us form a team to rescue the kidnapped people and stop the hostile takeover."

"Look," Sky said. "I am an engineer and that's all. I don't mind giving you the plans, but I really have no desire to get any more involved than that. I smelled a rat the moment after I won the bid to build the thing. They knew I was a loner type of guy who lays low and really doesn't want much attention. That's why they chose me. Plus, I was right out of college, so they knew the money would lure me in."

"Yes, but you're also very smart, and we know you are a skilled sharp-shooter, proficient at Muay Thai, and don't mind fighting if you have to. Your parents are both deceased, you don't have a girlfriend, and the only thing you really have affection for is your dog Maui."

"Wow, you have done your homework." Sky paused, but only for a moment. "OK. So when do we leave?"

Sky thought about what they said and knew that if he didn't go along now, somewhere down the line he would probably be forced to.

"Tomorrow morning at seven o'clock," Stefan said.

"I will have to let the university know so they can get a substitute for me."

"No problem," Ollie said. "Just tell them it is a family emergency and that you will be gone for two to three weeks."

"We will meet you at the airport in the morning . . . Don't be late," Stefan said.

* * *

"Well, that was easier than expected," Ollie said as they left.

"I think he is smart enough to know that if he doesn't come along now, there will probably be a later experience that won't be fun."

"Yeah," Ollie said. "You are probably right on that one. Let's go get something to eat and get back to the hotel and get some rest. Our plane leaves very early tomorrow."

CHAPTER 26

The White House

General Kerwin knew his meeting with President Clemmons was vital to finding out certain key things he needed to know in order to move forward. As he arrived back in Washington, DC, for dinner, he was deliberating on what to say to get the president to tell him the key initiatives. Sounding convinced about his belief in the president's plan was his number one concern. While putting on his dinner attire, the general began mulling over his speech in his head.

President Clemmons had ordered General Kerwin's favorite meal and had Chef Diane prepare chocolate molten cake for dessert. When he arrived, the president hugged the general's neck.

"Good to see you, sir. Is everything still on schedule as planned?" Todd asked.

"I have a lot to tell you this evening," President Clemmons said as he poured himself a beer. "We have decided to meet again this weekend. Full on with everyone there. Every king, ambassador, general, and colonel will be there, along with the three other key players we have put in charge of security. We will announce the new agenda and new line of attack."

"The other three?" General Kerwin questioned.

"Yes ... Officer Whitmore, Detective Gibbs, and Detective Moll."

"Oh, I see."

"We have made it very clear to Gibbs, Moll, and Whitmore that if they leak any of this, they are dead men."

General Kerwin grinned and tried to look enthusiastic. *So we are threatening our own people now.* Fortunately for Todd, they were interrupted by their food being served. Chef Diane personally brought it down herself. General Kerwin noticed that Paul winked at her. *What was that?*

"This looks delicious," the general said, trying to act as though he was clueless. "Thanks for the invite."

Diane asked if they needed anything else. General Kerwin quickly spoke up and told her they did not, then thanked her. Staring directly at the president, she flung her hair around and proceeded to leave the room. Paul stared at her the whole way out.

"You know, Todd, I have thought a lot about what we are doing. I wanted to meet you here tonight to get your opinion on it all. What you think means a lot to me." Todd wasn't sure whether this comment was planned or sincere. His curiosity was piqued, however.

"This is something you have dreamed of and have worked for all your life," Todd said. "You are on the cusp of having all your dreams come true. Just think, Paul Clemmons, supreme ambassador of the New World Order. It doesn't get any better than that."

"You are right, Todd, and just think, you will be right there with me. Todd Kerwin, general of the Transnational Global Alliance," he said as he lifted his glass to toast. "We aim to deliver social justice around the world, resolve global problems, and regulate the economic power of international capital for the good of all." Todd smiled as they toasted while the president gave the most chilling laugh he had ever heard.

"You know the sad part, Todd?"

"What's that, sir?"

"The sad part is that Denise might not be there with me. She has been feeling really bad lately. The cancer is spreading quicker than they thought."

"I'm so sorry, Paul. I don't know what to say."

"Don't say anything. I brought you here to tell you good things, not sad things. Anyway, I wanted to talk to you about Israel. I know King Darius secretly wants them destroyed, but I have been trying, covertly, to talk to them. At first, I could not get Benjamin to cooperate at all. But now, I might be the very one who helps assist King Darius and Benjamin Meir in signing a peace treaty between Israel and the Arab nations."

"Really? That would be interesting."

"I know Darius and General Mutko are in a pact together, and I know that one day Russia and many other Arab nations will probably invade them like a beast of power. But for now, I am doing everything I can to spare them. Benjamin should be grateful."

General Kerwin decided to test Paul and ask a few daring questions.

"Mr. President, do you ever think about the end of the age as we know it?"

"You mean the end of the world? Not really," the president said. "I think that is a bunch of farce talk. I think that's something those ol' Christians and fearmongers publicize so they can propagate their material. That is their line of greed. There is no way anything could ever destroy the whole world. That would take an act of God, and I don't think God would do such a thing. Do you?"

Trying not to raise any red flags, Kerwin responded, "I suppose not."

"Good. Now let's talk about your role in this. That is the whole reason I invited you here tonight in the first place."

"OK."

"I have been thinking. I want you to play a larger role in this whole ordeal."

"Like what, sir?"

"Like you being the front man for the new International Interfaith Organization."

"In what way?" Todd asked.

"You would be the global religious voice uniting the myriad of religions with peace and safety centers. You would start with the youth and unite them according to their traditional values as you submerge their cultures together under a common goal. I would like it if you would put together a team to travel to the top major churches in America and other religious institutions around the world, informing them that their roles will be changing."

"Roles . . . changing? I'm not sure I understand."

"Yes. Once the devastations take place, we would like for you to inform the churches that the government is now going to embrace the church, or mosque, or just whatever they all call their own assemblies. We are going to allow the youth to lead. They will have to choose from their congregation one whom they want to follow. He must be between the age of twenty-one and thirty. If they can't make that decision, then we will pick the person for them. The religious organization of tomorrow will be led by those more inclined to follow our lead—the youth!"

"In what way? May I ask?"

"We are now going to give them more privileges. What I mean by that is they will now be an active part in communicating to the people what the government wants to implement around the world. No more separation of church and state; that's what they have all been screaming for, right?"

"I am not sure I am following you, Paul. What do you mean? I thought that was unconstitutional!"

"It won't be unconstitutional under the New Global Community. In fact, this is an opportunity of a lifetime for all religious groups. They will now be at the forefront of spreading the news to everyone about the new One World religion through their church, mosque, temple, or whatever you want to call it. We have already convinced the Vatican to help. We expect every religious organization to support our endeavors."

"How do we know they will *all* agree?"

"You will tell them they will no longer be supported by the people financially. They will now receive money from our new government. More money than they have ever imagined. No more 501c3's; no more nonprofits. They will now be able to reach millions of people globally and bring them into the fold. And they will be completely supported by the United Nations zone."

"But don't you think they are going to balk when the existing leaders have to step down after they have built the church?"

"That's what I know you will figure out, Todd. Just show them their alternative."

"Why do you think this is a good idea?"

"It's all the same God, just different paths to get to him. This will be the start of a loving, peaceful world, with everyone on the same page."

"OK, if you think so, sir," Todd said. "'Operation Religious Recruit' it is."

"Great. Then you'll do it?"

"Sure, I'll do it."

The door opened and in walked Chef Diane with their chocolate molten cakes. Paul took a bite and told Diane it was the best she had ever made before. A seductive smile, another wink, and it looked as though Paul was smitten by the chef. *Denise would not like this at all.*

"I am so fortunate to have a friend and advisor I am able to trust. You are the one person that I know I can tell everything to," Paul said.

"Mr. President, you know I will support you in all that you do. I have always done so in the past and will not stop now."

"Then can I share one secret thing with you before you leave?"

"Sure, Mr. President, what is it?"

"I just want you to know that I recently converted to Islam." Todd instantly made sure his facial expressions did not show any concern.

"Well, congratulations, sir. That is great."

"I thought you would be happy. I know this will only help in my relations with King Darius and King Salam. You should think about converting too."

"But I thought that we will all soon be one."

"Well, we will, and let's just say this is a good choice."

"Have you told Denise or anyone else?" Todd asked.

"No. The time has not been right yet, but I will tell Denise and the girls soon. When the mood is right, I will let the kings know as well."

The two men shook hands.

"Remember, I trust you with my life . . . don't let me down."

"No, sir. I won't," the general said.

General Kerwin left, very discouraged. He radioed Nettle, requesting the group meet at noon tomorrow. The usual pickup would occur.

CHAPTER 27

Hands-On Basic Training

"I have called you all here today to tell you something very important," General Kerwin began. "For those of you who don't know, sitting next to me is my wife, Mabry, and my son, Lee. Sitting to my right is Amanda Patterson, the mother of Stephen Beasley and previous girlfriend of Arlice, Jackson's dad. Next to her are Angela and Judy, Dr. Wallace's nurses. His other nurse, Wendy, is at the compound, working in the hospital there undercover. And last, but certainly not least, is Sky Mullins. Sky is the one who designed and engineered everything out in the desert. We briefed Sky this morning and he has agreed to help us. He will share with us all the details and intricacies of the compound. I have also invited a few other people that some of you might know."

Debra calmly opened the door and escorted in Jackie, Jamie, Brooke, Sarah, and Nancy. All the guys' mouths dropped open because they could not believe their girlfriends were there. Following them in were Richard and Joan Jones. No one said a word. Had a pin been dropped, the noise would have echoed around the room.

As they were being seated, Debra proceeded back to the door and let in a gentleman who looked very familiar. Dressed in full uniform, everyone saw he was a five-star general, but who was he? He was followed in by those who were obviously his assistants. General Kerwin stood at attention, saluted him, and everyone else followed suit.

"This is Lieutenant General Dale Howard, the national security advisor to the president of the United States and his assistants, Malone and Grace." Instantly the meeting intensified.

"First, I want to thank everyone for getting here on such short notice. I have asked you all to come because of a meeting I had last night with President Clemmons. I am more concerned now than ever. The reason your friends and family are here is to let them know the seriousness and danger of this mission. They will be required to stay here at the headquarters this Saturday as you go on your discovery mission, as well as on the day of the actual takeover. We felt this would be the best place for their safety. Once the mission is accomplished, then you all will come back here and stay for a few days until things clear. Is that understood?" General Kerwin asked.

"Yes, sir," they all replied in unison.

"Last night, the president informed me of a new role I will be playing. Once the devastations take place, he has asked me to meet with many of the top spiritual leaders and ask them all to step down. They will then promote someone between the ages of twenty-one and thirty to run their new spiritual institutions. He wants me to assure them they will have great influence in the International Interfaith Organization, since it will be mandatory that everyone join. The church will soon become the mouthpiece to the people for the government. If the religious leaders don't go along with the new strategy, then I am afraid they will no longer be in business. The way they will keep up with this is by assigning everyone a personal pin number they will use to transact business with."

"But that's not right," Sam said.

"Yeah, I thought we would always have freedom of religion, no matter what God you worship," Cory said.

"Not in the new government. If we don't stop this endeavor, life will never be the same again. There will be no place in the world you can move to improve your circumstances. I invited General Howard here today to let you know there are others at the helm of our government who are on our side. General Howard has assembled a small group of Special Forces that will be protecting you when we decide to move in. I wanted you to meet him and his team today because he will be an integral part of leading your mission. So, may I introduce to you all, Lieutenant General Dale Howard." Everyone stood again, this time clapping.

"This is a bunch of right-wing Christian conspiracy crap," Jackie whispered to Nancy, who seated to her right. "My Aunt Lisa was right about not believing any of their rhetoric. I can't wait to hear this guy's next theory."

"Hello, and thank you all for your complete support," General Howard said. "It is critical that you prepare exactly as you are told. This will be an extremely dangerous mission. That is why we have called your loved ones here. We need to make sure you all understand the seriousness of this operation. It is literally up to the few of you to stop this global takeover. Never in the history of our nation have we ever relied on civilians to complete a government operation. However, this is really kingdom work, and we need kingdom citizens to join the ranks, seize the opportunity, and destroy our enemies," Howard went on.

"They must be talking about the devil's work," Jackie said again to Nancy, mocking his theory and smiling quite superficially. Nancy just gave her a 'please-be-quiet' look.

"The second reason we called you here today is because there is a very important meeting scheduled for this upcoming Saturday at the farmhouse. General Kerwin found out that President Clemmons will be taking his wife, Denise, who is ill, to the meeting. We find this a bit unusual. This means something is changing. You can bet there is an ulterior motive behind the change. We just need you to find out what is taking place. On a different note, the president informed General Kerwin last night, confidentially, that he recently converted to Islam."

"What?" Nettle exclaimed. "You have got to be kidding me . . . surely not."

"I am afraid so. But this must not, and I mean *not*, leave this room. The president feels this will help him in his relationship with King Darius and King Salam."

"What does that mean?" Chrissy said.

"Oh, I don't think you have anything to worry about, Chrissy. He has never practiced religion of any sort his whole life. This is strictly a political move on his part. The only person who will be upset about his decision is his wife, Denise," General Kerwin said.

"Does she know yet?" Chrissy asked.

"No, not yet, but I have a feeling he is going to tell her this weekend."

"We plan on sending you back out there this Saturday," General Howard said. "General Kerwin will be there and can look for Arlice and his boys in the farmhouse. We are counting on Arlice to know where the rest of the seekers are."

"What if Arlice doesn't know where everyone else is?" Josh asked.

"We are determined to find them, but if we don't, then we have no choice but to go ahead as planned."

"As planned?" Tommy questioned.

"We will destroy the entire compound." As soon as the words came out of General Howard's mouth, you could have heard a pin drop. Silence filled the room; their minds were racing with thoughts of destroying people's lives. This was not what they were expecting to hear.

"Why do we want to do that?" Chrissy asked, hoping for a solid, truthful answer.

"If our mission fails to accomplish what we plan, we have no other choice. Remember, Chrissy, these people plan on taking over the world and killing millions of innocent people through nuclear and viral devastations. Eventually, all seekers' lives will be in danger of death, too, if they don't conform to the New World structure. This will be the one time that we have all of them in one place," General Howard said.

"Yeah, right," Jackie whispered to Nancy. "These guys are nothing but extreme fundamentalists with authoritarian ambitions, lying in wait to posture their moralistic extremes to the rest of the world. I've got to get out of here and let someone know."

"Why don't you just let the general know right now?" Nancy said, this time aloud. "Excuse me, sir? My friend Jackie has something to say to you," she said, turning her head toward Jackie.

"Well, I personally think that you guys are the evil dignitaries. Our world has been corrupted far more by religious literalists than any other group. You elegantly and persuasively work each day to obliterate the separation between church and state and to supplant science with your irrational, dogmatic, ancient philosophies that aren't even relevant in today's society. Maybe you should take a look at what they are trying to accomplish. It might be better than anything you guys have ever come up with—or done—before."

Immediately, Jackie's tongue began to cleave to the top of her mouth. She could no longer speak. Her frantic eyes gave way to the panic of the realization of her newfound mouth structure. She fell on the floor, gripped with fear. Dr. Wallace came in and removed her from the room with the help of Angela and Judy. Tay didn't move. He was scared for Jackie.

Nettle quickly caught a glance of a supernatural being in the room. She was the only one who saw him. Suddenly, he disappeared. Nettle knew then there was no match in power for the kingdom force.

"Finding everyone will be up to you guys. If we can save them, we will," General Kerwin said, trying to comfort them a little after what had just happened to Jackie.

"You will be protected by a team of Special Forces, along with Jason and Stefan. You will be dressed in the same brown camouflage uniforms to allow you to recognize your team easily. Here is a picture of the Special Forces group. Memorize their faces and names; you will be tested on this." Malone, General Howard's assistant, handed out pictures of the team.

"From left to right are Zac, Cade, Bailey, Harrison, Tanner, Cameron, Tyler, Chris, Julio, Miguel, Will, Connor, Hunter, Adam, Chase, Miles, Drew, Taylor, Trip, and the other Tanner. They have been briefed on everything about you guys and will recognize you easily. Our Special Forces team is tasked with six primary objectives: unconventional warfare, foreign internal defense, special reconnaissance, direct action, hostage rescue, and counter-terrorism," Howard specified.

"And don't forget you have me," Sam said, chuckling.

"Oh, that's a big relief. I forgot about you, Sam," Chrissy said sarcastically.

"Now I would like for Sky to show you all the layout of the place,"

General Kerwin said. As a screen came down, Sky got up to show them the blueprints of the whole compound.

"As you can see, the farmhouse is actually three stories high. I am guessing they are putting Arlice and his kids in the Kennedy Room on the third floor because we designed it for a hostage situation. If not there, then next door is the Korinne Room, but it doesn't have a kitchen, so I really think he is in the Kennedy Room. The downstairs conference room is where they will convene. Ransom's bedroom is down there and so is President Clemmons'. There is nothing about the farmhouse that makes it look suspicious if anyone should discover it. However, it has a transparent film cover around it, so that when the switch is turned on, it becomes invisible. This is just in case someone gets suspicious about anything; then they can just make it disappear. Or, at least, appear that way."

Josh and Tommy glanced at each other.

"In the dining room there is a secret door that leads down to the underground cave. From the cave there are many channels to the underground city, and that is where they will probably all go when the devastations take place. It is protected from any kind of radioactivity, nuclear bombs, or anything that we could be attacked by. It is truly a small underground city and can hold up to one thousand people and their vehicles if it had to. There is enough food to feed a thousand people for five years. Another secret door exists in the president's bedroom on the first floor. That door goes straight into the underground city. Only the President and General Kerwin know about it—and me, of course. King Darius does not even know it exists. It is in his closet, but you can't see it with the naked eye. The president has a pair of glasses that allow him to see it, and he is supposed to keep them on himself at all times while he is there. He is the only one who has the glasses.

"I designed the cave to house military equipment, a hospital, and a bunch of extra bedrooms. In two of the rooms in the cave, they had me design large cages. They wanted locks on them. I thought that was kind of strange, but I didn't ask any questions at that point," Sky said.

"I have a question," Tenya said. "Who hired you to build and design all this? I know it was the government, but whom specifically?"

"That is a good question," Sky said. "It was the Chickasaw Indians . . . " Everyone had a puzzled look on their face. "No, that was just a joke, man. Seriously, it was a man by the name of Gavin Samuelson. I figured this must be a very important job and was honored to get it. It wasn't until all the weird requests came that I became suspicious. Gavin was kind of a jokester guy and was really fun to hang out with. However, I really watched what I said around him. He liked the booze and the women a lot. He was always joking about taking them to his private cave. He always made me feel a little uneasy when I was around him. When it came time to pay me, I grew even more suspicious. A gentleman by the name of Randy Dorn ended up paying me. I didn't know who he was, and I didn't ask any questions. I was just glad to be through and be going home a rich man. I later found out Dorn was a mob guy. General Kerwin informed me this morning he is the head of the mob. But no one knows who Gavin was. Not even the two generals here. We think he used a fictitious name and is somehow connected to King Darius, but we're not sure. He did not look American, even though his name was. And he was definitely not the Ransom in the picture that you all know.

"Anyway, the cave has four halls, and each one is color-coded. The blue hall is the one with all the bedrooms, and the general thinks that is where all the seekers are. I know it is where all the guards and employees stay. The red hall is where they are keeping all their weapons. The green hall is where the hospital is, and that is the hall I designed all those cages in as well. It also has bedrooms down it. The yellow hall is full of offices and where I think their above-ground headquarters are. The control room and situation room are in the underground city. It was only to be used in case of a disaster. As far as I know, no one lives or stays there, but that could have changed.

"There is access to the underground city from each of the halls in the cave. In the green hall, the secret door is in the hospital, in the nurses' station storage room. Down the red hall, the secret door is in the only closet down that hall, third door on the right. Down the yellow hall, it is in the first office on your left; the sign above the door says International Alliance and inside that office is a closet and the door is inside it. That door is always unlocked. Down the blue hall, it is in the hall bathroom behind a built-in shelf holding the paper towels—just push the metal back and the whole wall will open up." Sky easily rattled all of this information off.

"I sure hope I can remember all that," Tay said.

"Don't worry, you will have all this information to take home and study," General Kerwin said. "In fact, Debra, would you please pass out the information now?"

"Yes, sir," she said, passing out the Operation Seeker blueprint to everyone.

"One thing that you should all know, something no one else knows but me, is once you are in the underground city, if you should ever get kidnapped and placed inside the city, I designed two ways out that no one knows about but me. I only did it in case I was ever sequestered and needed to escape. They will never find them. I am only telling you this in case Operation Seeker goes bad."

"OK, here is the plan," General Kerwin said. "All the kings, generals, and colonels will be arriving this Friday. They will all land in their private planes and be picked up from Davis-Monthan military airport. The meeting will begin Saturday morning at 8 a.m. sharp. You guys will arrive shortly before that."

General Howard took over: "The additional envelope Debra is passing out now has your final instructions on Operation Desert Seeker. Take it home and memorize it tonight. Everything you need to know is in there. Do not utter a word about any of this. Lives are in danger here, and your silence is vital. We are finished here today with everyone except the mission group, so the rest of you can go home now. We will see you all tomorrow evening."

Once the others left, Joseph Petrus entered the room. Nettle was anxious to hear what he had to say.

"I came today to tell you something very important," Petrus began. "But before I do that, I want you to know that Jackie is OK. She is still unable to speak, but we will take good care of her as she remains here with us. Now, I want to warn you that you will experience things out there that will test your beliefs. Evil will be lurking everywhere, and there are men there who will be able to perform signs and wonders empowered by the dark angel. If you see great marvels, do not get distracted from your mission. As you study the plans and learn the strategy, remember, all people at one time or the other will encounter opposition and come face to face with their fears. Out of this, however, if allowed, they always discover their purpose and make a huge difference in the world we live in, both for themselves and others. May you all go forth equipped with your panoply and with Parakletos' guiding," Joseph said. There was an air of finality in the way he spoke.

This dude is different, Tommy thought. His thoughts were interrupted when Joseph looked intently into Nettle's eyes and began to speak.

"Do not be afraid. You have been gifted because of your certainty." With that, Joseph turned and left the room.

"What is our panoply again?" Chrissy asked.

"Your armor," General Kerwin answered.

"Are there any more questions?" he asked the group.

General Kerwin and General Howard said their good-byes, and Jason and Stefan gathered everyone up and drove them back to their cars.

CHAPTER 28

Kingdom Dogma

That next Friday was spent in deep contemplation, in study. Each person reflected on their lives and what was at stake going forward. Each one determined to discover their power. This group of college students, who used to think that football, cheerleading, and partying was exciting, suddenly had their eyes opened to the real truth. A whole new paradigm, a whole new world. Never before had they been faced with such grave circumstances. But the time was ripe, and as each one *asked*, each one *received*. Their powers were revealed and this was far more exhilarating than anything previous in their lives. What was next?

Upon arriving at the headquarters that evening, General Howard greeted them at the door and told them that General Kerwin had already left for the farmhouse.

"Have you all studied your instructions?" General Howard asked.

"Yes, we have, and we are ready for the operation," Tommy said.

"Debra will help you all to your rooms and I will see you at dinner."

Everyone settled in and then proceeded to the dining room. The food was delicious as everyone ate with great anticipation of this night's meeting. General Howard stood up and tapped his glass with his spoon. The room got quiet, and everyone turned their focus to him.

"Now that everyone has finished eating, would everyone please follow me?" He led them all to a huge meeting room that was set up classroom-style.

"I am about to introduce you to two people who you will recognize, but you must not tell anyone—and I mean *anyone*—that they are here and involved with us." Debra opened the door and escorted in Arizona Governor Jeff Morrey and Senator Rostene Waller, also from Arizona. As they sat down in the front row, the lights immediately went off, and down came the big screen. Instantly, the viewers could see the cave and its entrance. There were two guards out front and a woman dressed in African clothing talking to them.

"That woman is Lulu Zuma from South Africa. She is one of the colonels," General Howard said. The camera panned over to the farmhouse, where a car was pulling up. They watched as all the dignitaries arrived. Governor Morrey and Senator Waller walked over to the podium to address the room.

"These are the few gentlemen and the lady that plan on taking over our world," Senator Waller began. "They are highly skilled communicators and build their governance on influence and persuasion. They will convince the populace that they are purely concerned with their well-being and that everything being done is for the good of the citizens. They understand that most people read at a sixth-grade level, so understanding politics for most is difficult. Most people are just plain uneducated in governmental affairs. These politicians have the uncanny ability to make wrong seem right and right seem wrong."

"Yes, and the deceived will be your everyday commoners, such as your educators, your economists, your philosophers, your bankers, your religious leaders, your business leaders, your next-door neighbors," Governor Morrey added. "Do not be fooled! Hitler once said, 'If you tell a big enough lie and tell it frequently enough, it will be believed.' He also said, 'And the victor will not be asked if he told the truth or not.' But his most famous quote was: 'What luck for the rulers that men do not think.' Senator Waller and I just wanted you all to know that we are in the kingdom with you and if you ever need us, we are here for you."

"OK, troops, your time has arrived," General Howard told the group. "The Special Forces team will do its best to protect you. We will be watching you from the control room and giving Jason and Stefan their orders from here. Remember, General Kerwin is there in the farmhouse. If anything gets too bad for him, he can just leave and teleport himself to another location, so don't be worried about him. Your goal is to locate Arlice, his children, and the seekers and possibly find the underground city. Once we know where everything is located, the Special Forces team will perform the extractions at a later time. If you happen to get caught, take your blue pill immediately! Do you all understand?"

"Yes, sir," they all replied.

"You are all dismissed. I will see you in the morning at 5 a.m. Good night."

Trying to sleep was near impossible. Nettle tossed and turned all night, realizing that she had involved all of her dearest friends on this mission. Tommy felt responsible for including his football buddies and was now having second thoughts. Chrissy was praying that she would not have to shoot anyone, and Josh was hoping that he could protect Chrissy and get her out safely. No one slept very well as they all lay in bed thinking about their mission. Finally, alarms started going off at 4 a.m., and everyone was rather quiet. Dressed in camouflage, the team loaded up their artillery and equipment and headed to the desert location. As they neared the premises, Jason motioned for all the Hummers to pull off into the wooded area. Emotions were high and everyone was ready to roll.

* * *

Ransom was up early, preparing for the day. He headed over to the cave to get Arlice, Jackson, and Stephen and bring them back to their new room in the farmhouse before anyone else was up.

"Thank you very much," Arlice said.

"You are welcome, but don't get too comfortable yet. I need you to cure someone this morning."

"Who?" Arlice asked.

"Don't worry about that. Just do your job and you will get to stay here a while," he said before exiting.

"Wow, this is nice!" Jackson said upon arriving at the farmhouse. "I like it so much better here. It even has a kitchen."

"Me, too," Stephen said. Arlice surmised that Ransom must have had a plan to begin with to allow them to move to the farmhouse. He had a notion something important was taking place today because of all the extra security and vehicles. He could only imagine what and whom it was.

Eight o'clock in the morning arrived and all the dignitaries convened in the conference room. Anticipation was high as they approached the advancement of their coming kingdom.

"I hope that everyone had a good night's rest," President Clemmons said. "It is great to see everyone and I am looking forward to our meeting. Today we have many beneficial items to discuss. Very soon our lives will be changed forever. The planet as we know it will be dramatically different, and our road to new leadership will emerge quickly. We are about to revolutionize our world and make history. Just think, our people will finally be united and world peace will be on its way. No more war and no more famine. No more poverty. We will finally have an earth filled with equal opportunity and fairness." Everyone clapped and cheered loudly at the president's speech.

* * *

"Dad, can you hear that clapping?" Jackson asked.

"Yes, I can. It sounds almost like people are having a party this early in the morning. I wonder who is here. We will ask Ransom when he comes back." As soon as Arlice spoke those words, the door opened and in walked Ransom with a woman who looked very familiar. Arlice could tell she was very ill since she had lost most of her hair.

"This is the man I was telling you about," Ransom said to her. "He has the power to cure you. All he has to do is conjure up the formula and speak something over you, and bam . . . you will be cured." Jackson looked up at his dad to see his response.

"So, Arlice, do your thing and cure this woman!"

"Hello there, ma'am. My name is Arlice," he said sticking out his hand to shake hers.

"I am Denise. Nice to meet you."

"You don't need to know her name. Just cure her!" Ransom seemed to be losing what little patience he had.

"It's OK. He can know my name."

"Are you Denise Clemmons?" Arlice asked.

"Yes, I am," she said.

"OK, that's enough. I didn't bring her here to chitchat. Now, just cure her, I said."

"Look, Ransom, you can't just conjure it up. I have to pray for her, and I need to be alone with her."

"Well, that's impossible. I am not leaving the president's wife alone with you."

"Ransom," Denise said. "It's OK. What is he going to do? This place is packed with military personnel, and he doesn't seem like the kind of guy to take me hostage."

Arlice spoke up. "Look, Ransom, you take both my boys and give me fifteen minutes alone with her, and I will cure her." Ransom thought for a couple of seconds and decided to oblige him for the sake of his expected outcome.

"Fine, but you get fifteen minutes, and that's it."

He grabbed both boys' hands rather abruptly and took them out of the room.

CHAPTER 29

Underground

The clock was ticking as Arlice hoped to get answers from the First Lady. Denise looked around the room and surmised that Arlice and his boys were being held there against their will.

"Who are you, Arlice?" Denise asked.

"Just a guy who likes to set people free and they have me and my children hostage out here."

"Are you spiritual?"

"Yes, if that is what you like to call it."

"I am a seeker too. Well, at least I used to be. But to tell you the truth, I find it kind of irrelevant for today. I know there is talk of miracles, but I have never seen one."

"Well, ma'am, it is not about seeing miracles. It's about participating in a true, spiritual kingdom and knowing your rights as its citizen. Elyon never meant for us to have a religion . . . he has a kingdom and he is the ultimate king and he wants us to rule in his kingdom as ambassadors. It's not religion that brings you closer to the relationship with King Elyon; it is accepting his son, the Prince of Truth, and communicating with Parakletos, who relays his messages. He is the one who bridges the gap."

Denise was listening. She had never heard it explained that way before. She wanted to know more but knew this wasn't the time.

"Well, what did you do for them to take you hostage?" she asked.

"Cure people," he said.

"What?" she responded.

"Look, Denise, I don't have much time, and the story is rather long and complicated. I can tell you this: I am a good person and I love my boys very much, but whatever is going on here your husband is involved in, and it is not good. Has the president shared anything with you?" He knew he was probing; he knew he had to take this risk.

"No, but he has been focused on something else a lot lately. It's as though he doesn't want me to know yet, and he usually tells me everything. I think it is because I am sick, and he doesn't want to burden me with it."

"Well, you must get it out of him. You might be the only person that can save our nation."

"Save our nation? I don't even feel like getting out of bed most days."

"Well, that is going to change," he said. "Let's get you well, and then I need your help."

"OK, you will make a strong advocate out of me if I am cured."

Arlice commanded the sickness to leave her body . . . and immediately, Denise was cured.

"Oh . . . my. Oh my!" she exclaimed. "Oh my gosh, oh my gosh, I can feel the difference. Oh my goodness . . . What did you just do? What did you just do to me?"

"He made you well, Denise. Rejoice!" Arlice said. "We don't have much time. I think Ransom plans on keeping us here forever, hoping that I will go along with them. If I don't, then I think he might get rid of me and my children. Please, Denise. I need your help."

"Well, I am sure that after Paul sees that you cured me, he will make them let you go."

"No!" Arlice said. "Their goal is to kill people like me, especially ones who have special powers. They also want to kidnap a girl by the name of Nettle. She has special powers too. I promise you their intentions are not good. I know he is your husband, but we are in a time and place where those that don't believe . . . well, their minds are blinded to truth. You won't be able to trust them, even if they are nice people. Please listen to me, Denise. I need your help and the United States of America and our world do too," he begged.

Denise could see that he was desperate. She knew he wasn't a crazy man, since he had just cured her cancer. She still wanted to see proof, but she knew something was different in her body. Suddenly she could feel the hair on her head start to grow. She touched her head.

"OK, here is my personal cell phone. Keep it on vibrate and do not answer unless it is me, and don't call anyone. I will call you when I have a plan."

Ransom swung the door open, and Denise stood up and shouted: "I am cured!"

"Nice. . . . Here are your boys. You can stay here a while longer now that you have obeyed."

"Come on, Mrs. Clemmons. I will escort you back to your room." Denise smiled at Arlice and his boys as she left the room.

"Mrs. Clemmons, did Arlice ask you anything about why you were here?" Ransom asked her as they headed down the hall.

"No, he just focused on making me well. Why?"

"I just don't want him to nose into our governmental affairs; it is none of his business."

Denise sensed right then that something wasn't right, and that Arlice was telling the truth. She quickly changed the subject; she did not want Ransom to think she was suspicious of anything. She needed to find out from Paul what was going on. She entered her bedroom and used their private phone to text him. She requested his presence at their next break.

* * *

Ransom headed back to the meeting to see if anyone needed anything. He arrived just in time to hear the president making an important announcement.

"I have a very special announcement to make this morning." You could see on the president's face he was excited to share the latest news. "Our plans have changed. We have decided to move forward with the devastations this weekend. King Darius, King Salam, King Alexander, King Otto, Ambassador Dunn, and I have decided to move the disasters up ahead of schedule." The whole room started to mumble—those in attendance were clearly agitated because they had not been consulted.

"Why in the world would we do that, and why weren't the rest of us included on that decision?" raved Lulu Zuma of Africa.

"Yes, this is not what we agreed to at all," said Dan O'Donnell, England's chief of staff.

"We are asking because we all thought that major decisions would be voted on by the entire assembly," said Hamid Patel of India.

Tatsu Kan of Japan and Mai Fan Zhoo of China shook their heads in agreement.

"If I could, I would like to answer that question, please," King Darius said as he stood to his feet.

"Sure, go right ahead," President Clemmons said.

"My fellow constituents, may I first say that it is my honorable pleasure working with all of you. I know that we all have the same goals, desires, and ambitions for our world; otherwise we would not all be sitting here today. The reason we chose to move the disasters ahead of schedule was because we felt the timing was better now. The element of surprise is always best, even among us. We think there might be an inside informant, so we wanted to remove all chances of leakage on the timing of the devastations. We thought it best to tell you after you arrived here."

General Kerwin's heart started to beat a little faster. *An inside informant. Did they know? There's no way.* He sat up straighter in his chair, keeping a closer eye on everyone.

"As you have all agreed, we have a ranking order in the new system. I felt as your leader that this decision was in the best interest of our world. It was too difficult to get us all together to discuss this urgent matter before now, so we made the decision without all of you being there. I trust you all understand this decision is in your best interest. Whenever I make a decision, it will always be with your best interest in mind."

"We understand, sir. We just thought we agreed that any major decisions were to be made by all of us, and this is a pretty big decision. I am not saying that we, or I, are opposed to the decision you made, just a little concerned that we were not all involved, that's all," Lulu Zuma said.

"In the New World, there will be times when decisions must be made quickly, and the only ones who can oppose those decisions would be ambassadors Clemmons and Dunn," said King Darius rather piercingly. "We are all in agreement that this is the best policy and structure for our New Global Neighborhood as it stands right now. So, moving forward, is everyone now clear on the decision-making process?" The air was thick, even intense, but Lulu and everyone else shook their heads in agreement. They could all sense that this was how it was going to be, and there was no point in arguing with King Mohammed Darius. Lulu felt a little uneasy about this new decree.

We need to get our new laws in writing and have a vote before all this goes down, she thought.

Her intuition was stirred . . . and all of a sudden something inside did not feel right to her.

"OK, now that we have cleared that up, let's talk about the devastations," Darius continued. "Remember, the missiles can never be traced to the starting location. No one will ever know they came from Arizona or the United States. We will move to the underground city tomorrow and do all our press releases from there. It will take the world by surprise, and no one will question us once we announce our global plan. President Clemmons has secured a local woman—Erica Webb, from WBN-TV—to cover the story. She thinks she is coming here to cover a new tropical plant that might contain a chemical we can use in the future to make fuel with. She doesn't know it yet, but instead, she will become part of our entourage. She will provide the first coverage of our New Global Neighborhood."

"What about our families?" General Mai Fan Zhoo asked. "I thought last weekend we agreed to have them here with us." General Zhoo's concern was obvious; he had a daughter secretly attending a university in the United States under a fictitious name, and he wanted to make sure he got her to the compound before the terrible devastations began.

"Yes, you are correct, but that has all changed now. Our new target date is tomorrow, Sunday. You must call your families today and tell them not to leave their homes at all."

"I am not sure I like this," Tatsu Kan of Japan said. "Family is very important to me, and I prefer to be with my family when this goes down."

"And if you can't?" Darius questioned. His eyes had a piercing look to them as he asked this question.

Colonel Kan could tell this was not going well and that King Darius was adamant about moving forward. He also harbored acute fear in his heart about going against Darius's wishes, so he backed off.

The air remained thick with tension. General Kerwin hoped that these men and the woman, Zuma, realized the danger of giving Darius control. He looked at his watch and knew that his team should be arriving any minute. He must relay this new information to them and General Howard as soon as possible. General Kerwin was concerned about the leak Darius had mentioned. Was he bluffing, or was there really a leak? He was confident it was not from his team.

"Why don't we take a thirty-minute break, so you can all take care of whatever business you need concerning your families. We will convene back here at 9:30 a.m.," Darius instructed.

CHAPTER 30

A Miracle

General Zhoo headed straight to call his daughter, Noel (her American name), to get her on the next flight to Arizona. She had twenty-four-hour security, but he instructed her to come alone. She must sneak out without them knowing. This was his only daughter, and she was very close to her father. He coached her on how to get to Tremer Park, and he would have someone there to pick her up.

General Kerwin had stepped out to call General Howard and inform him about the change of plans.

President Clemmons headed straight for his bedroom to see what Denise wanted. He opened the door—and found her on her knees.

"What's wrong?" he asked.

"Paul, I need to talk to you."

"OK, what is it?"

"I know that you are here for a specific purpose and that you have been working on something very diligently and secretly in the last year. I know there are many things that you cannot tell me, but you and I both know that my illness is an aggressive one. There is one thing that I want to make sure of, and that is where you stand. Do you believe in an afterlife, Paul?"

Clemmons could tell that this was heavy on her heart and that maybe this was the time to tell her that he had converted.

"I do believe, Denise. I believe that there are many kingdoms and many paths to God. In fact, I have just made a new commitment to my faith."

"You have?" she asked.

"Yes, I have recently converted to Islam and feel very good about it."

"But they don't believe in multiple paths to God. They only have one God."

"Well, I don't know what all they believe. This is really more of a political move as it is spiritual."

"Then you have not renewed your faith." Denise knew that the feeling of horror she felt . . . she could not allow it to be expressed on her face.

"Yes, I have made a new commitment to follow Islam."

"You mean Allah."

"I guess."

"What caused you to do that?" she probed.

"Look, Denise, something is about to take place that you and I have been waiting for our whole lives. I can't tell you now; I don't have time, but I can tell you that I am about to be put in a position to help rule the whole world."

"What do you mean?" she asked.

"I mean just that. I am meeting with several top leaders from around the world here this weekend, and we have devised a plan to help our world become a better place. We are going to strengthen the world economy by creating a one-world monetary system. We're going to eliminate the global healthcare crisis, help create more jobs, and most of all give people a one-world religion so that they can bond together instead of fight about their religious differences."

Denise felt her stomach cringe as he was talking. She could tell by his enthusiasm and excitement that he believed this with his whole heart.

"And what is this one-world religion going to be?" she asked.

"It will be one of great peace, great harmony, and the gathering of all mankind."

"Will it be Islam?" she inquired.

"Not exactly," he said.

"Then what will it be?" she prodded.

"It will be a religion for all people. It will be a safe place that will have distinct rules and regulations for all to abide by. Its roots may be Islam and some of the doctrine from that, but as a whole, it will be the religion of and for the people. In fact, King Darius is going to appoint someone who will form a peace treaty with Israel for seven years while we work all this out. So in essence, Denise, all humans on earth will be at peace. No one knows that yet, so you cannot tell anyone that." Paul knew she would be excited to hear about peace for Israel.

Denise knew immediately that Paul was changing. Power and greed for distinction and making a difference in the world had taken over his logical thinking and blotted out his upbringing and values. However, it was good to hear about Israel. No one knew that Denise's roots were Jewish. Her mother's parents had fled to the United States under an assumed name. Her mother's parents' name was really Levi. But they had gone by Dubose until her mother married an American man whose last name was Hartsell. She was Denise Hartsell until she married Paul Clemmons.

"Paul, what if you're wrong about this New Global Neighborhood and religion? What would it take for you to believe that? Would a miracle change your mind?"

"Like what?" he asked.

"Like me being cured?"

"Well, I would have to say if that happened I might have to figure out why it happened."

"What if you saw blind eyes able to see, or if a man rose from the dead, or an amputated leg grew back? Would that change your mind?"

"Why are you asking me all this, Denise? I don't know the answers to your questions. I have never seen those things happen and probably never will, so it really is a moot point."

"But what if . . . what if your new direction is wrong?" she said. "If you did find out it was wrong, would you try and stop it?"

"Denise, that is absurd thinking. First, I don't have time to change it."

"What do you mean?"

"Look, things are about to change really quickly. I brought you here this weekend because of that change. The world is about to become one over the next few days, and your husband is going to be at the helm of the New Global Neighborhood. It's here, Denise. It's what I have been schooled for my whole life. We have finally done it, and we have just got to get you well so you can share in it with me and our girls."

Denise knew that even if she told him right then that she was cured, he would dismiss it. He was too caught up in the lure of power, prestige, and prominence. He craved success. He had bought the lie hook, line, and sinker. What was she going to do now? She knew that Ransom would ask if she had told him she was cured, so she realized she had to say something.

"Well, today I had something happen to me that was miraculous."

"And what was that?"

"There is a man here who prayed for me, and I think his prayers healed me."

"Oh honey, that is awesome. How do you know?"

"I know because I feel it, Paul. I can tell in my body. And my hair started to grow. I could feel my scalp tingle."

Paul hesitated for a minute, thinking about what she had just said.

"What if your new way is wrong, honey?" Denise asked. "What if all religions are wrong? What if this kingdom rule is correct? What if he does have kingdom citizens here on earth able to perform miracles?"

"Well, then he better step up quickly, because as far as I can see, there are sixteen people who are about to start ruling this so-called 'kingdom' called earth, and I am one of them. It will no longer be 'We the people of the United States,' but 'We the people of the world.' This is my mark, sweetheart."

"I understand your excitement, honey, but I just want to make sure this is the right thing for us."

"I'll tell you what, Denise. You go down to the cave and have Dr. Shinall check you out, and bring me back the report. Then you and I can talk about this later. I need to get back to the meeting."

"OK, sweetheart, but one last thing I want to ask you. Do you know the gentleman named Arlice they are holding prisoner here?"

"No, I don't know him personally, but Ransom and King Darius seem to think that he and some others of his kind will get in the way of the new system. Darius feels we need to help refocus them to the wonderful benefits we are about to encounter."

"You mean kidnap them and brainwash them?"

"No, Denise. That's not what it is."

"Well, I know that you have this man and his two children upstairs being held hostage against his will, and Paul . . . he is the one who cured me."

"OK, I hear you. Just go get checked out, and we will talk tonight."

* * *

The meeting reconvened, and Paul could not help but think about what Denise had just said. Surely she was wrong. He did want her well, but it was too late to stop the agenda, especially now that they planned on starting the devastations tomorrow. He had to focus on the meeting until he knew for sure about Denise.

He had to remember this was going to be his time, his chance, to own it all. He was going to have to see some pretty miraculous things for that to change his mind.

CHAPTER 31

Satellite View

The teams had parked their Hummers and were already in place. Stefan and his team—Tay, Tenya, Carver, and Cory—were stationed close to the cave and were instructed to try and find the kidnapped seekers. They were to gather as much information about the cave as possible. Jason's team—Nettle, Tommy, Chrissy, Josh, and Sam—were surrounding the farmhouse trying to find out where Arlice was stationed. If possible, they were to extract him and his children, unless it jeopardized the mission. No one knew yet of the change of plans for the devastations.

General Kerwin had informed General Howard about the change. He only hoped this young group of college kids could stop this evil empire. When the president walked back in, General Kerwin could tell that something new was on his mind. He had known him too long not to recognize it.

* * *

Jason and Stefan received the new orders but were instructed not to say anything yet, only to start their mission. Nettle flew up into the tree closest to the back of the farmhouse to peek in the window. She immediately saw the First Lady knocking on one of the doors, so she waited a few minutes to see what she was doing. It looked as if she was talking to someone. *I wonder who is in that room,* she thought. *What is she doing? Why isn't she going into the room instead of talking through the door?*

Nettle watched as Denise headed back down the stairs, exited out the back door, and began walking toward the cave. Chrissy and Josh both spotted her, so Josh decided to follow her. He hid behind some trees and watched as the guards left their post to escort her into the cave. *Now's my chance,* Josh thought. *I wonder where Stefan and the guys are.* He knew they were supposed to be guarding the cave, but this was a chance to go inside, and he had to take it. He remembered Tommy talking about trip wires, so he was very careful upon entering.

"What's he doing?" Sky inquired back at the headquarters; all were watching via satellite.

"I don't know, but he had better be very careful," General Howard said as he tried to radio Jason. Josh remembered the secret door to the underground city was in the closet on the right down the red hall. Just as he approached the silo room, he heard people coming. Immediately, he stepped inside a nearby bathroom, went into the last stall, locked the door, and stood on top of the toilet. Two men entered as Josh watched through the crack in the stall door. He didn't recognize the men at first, but then he suddenly realized one of them was King Darius, the king of Iran. *Why is he over here?* He knew if they saw him, he would be kidnapped or killed. He quickly got out his blue pill. *Why aren't these men at the farmhouse in the meeting with everyone else?*

"You know, Ransom," King Darius began.

Ransom? That's not Ransom. This guy looked very different from all the pictures Josh had seen of Ransom. This guy had white, blondish hair and was clean cut. *Maybe there are two Ransoms,* he thought.

"When we attack the world, everyone will know what I stand for. There will be times that the others don't see things my way, but I know I can trust you. I have told the others about the change of plans to attack tomorrow, but I could tell that a few are not happy about it. I want to make sure that things go as planned and that nothing stops our mission.

Anyone who tries to stop our plan will ruin your place on the throne with me," King Darius said. "So they must be annihilated."

"Yes, sir. I will never allow that to take place. Nothing will happen to you or our weapons, sir, I promise."

"After I leave I want you to take the red dragon down to guard the arsenal. Make sure no one—and I mean no one—enters that room. You are my loyal assistant."

"Yes, sir. And I will never let you down."

"Good. Let's take a look at the missiles, and then you can go get the beast." As King Darius washed his hands, Ransom turned to use the bathroom. Josh stood as still as a statue, holding his breath, waiting for him to leave. Sweat began to roll down his forehead. Quietly he peeked out as they finally left the bathroom area and walked toward the missile room.

There is no way that is Ransom, at least not the Ransom we know. Josh began to ask and believe for his special powers right then and there. Instantly, he received them.

"Whoa . . . " As he looked around, he could now see through walls. He watched as they walked over to the weaponry room.

"Dear God," he said under his breath as he saw the massive arsenal. "That is enough missiles to destroy half the world." He studied everything a few more minutes then took off to inform Jason about what he saw.

* * *

Denise had finished with all of her medical tests and started back to her room to wait on the results. She knew she was cured, but would this be enough for Paul to stop this whole ordeal? For the first time, the First Lady was scared for her life, her family, and her country.

* * *

Lunchtime arrived and General Kerwin went outside to stretch and take a walk. He immediately called General Howard. "I really think this might be a bluff, sir. I think he just wants to see who's loyal to him and who's not. I will get back to you later when I have a better feel for everything and know for sure the plans will be executed tomorrow."

"I sure hope you are right; we are not prepared to fight this soon. Jason just radioed me that Josh snuck into the cave a few minutes ago and overheard Ransom and King Darius talking. Josh said that Ransom had changed his entire look. He said that if King Darius had not called him by name, he would not have recognized him at all. He had blond hair and was very clean cut."

"That's odd," Kerwin said. "Is he sure it was Ransom? Because Ransom has been in the meeting with us, and he still looks the same."

"Not a hundred percent," General Howard admitted. "But Darius called him Ransom."

"Well, again, Ransom has been in the meeting with me almost the entire morning."

"Then I am not sure," General Howard said. "I am just letting you know what Josh saw. We may smell a rat here."

"OK," Kerwin said. "I am aware and will call you back when I find out more."

* * *

Stefan unexpectedly spotted Dr. Shinall walking out of the cave in his white coat. He handed the guards what looked like a note. It appeared as though he was instructing them on something. Surprisingly, they both left their posts and began walking toward the farmhouse.

"Let's move," Stefan said urgently. "Follow the plans," he said as they all approached the entrance of the cave. Carver and Stefan took the blue hall; Tay took the green hall; Tenya, the yellow hall; and Cory, the red hall. Their goal was to find the seekers and the secret passageways to the underground city. As Carver and Stefan rounded the corner to the blue hall, Stefan shot the guard with a sleeping agent, so it looked like he had just fallen asleep. There were no other guards in sight. It was lunchtime, and Stefan could hear them in what was probably the break room, laughing.

"Well, this isn't just a coincidence," Carver muttered.

Stefan and Carver scurried down the blue hall and started knocking on a few doors, pretending to be guards looking for someone.

"Who is it?" a female voice asked.

Stefan looked at Carver as the voice responded again.

"Who is it?"

As they both stood motionless waiting for the door to open, their hearts were beating fast. Stefan motioned to Carver that he was going to stay back out of sight. All of a sudden the door opened and there stood an older woman.

"Can I help you?" she asked.

Realizing Carver was in a camouflage uniform, she immediately thought he was one of the guards.

"I was just guarding the place, and I thought I heard a strange noise from your room. I wanted to make sure everything was all right."

"Yes, sir, everything is all right," the woman said. "I was just working on the plans."

"Oh, I see, you mean the plans for the new agenda change?" Carver asked bravely.

"Why, yes," she said. "How did you know which plans I meant?"

"Well, the president told me," Carver said. "May I come in?" Stefan could only hope that Carver was executing a decent plan.

"Do you work for the president?" the woman asked as she stepped aside and swung the door open for Carver to enter.

"As a matter of fact, I do."

"Well, I didn't know the president knew about the plans," the lady said. "I thought this was only for Redimir and King Darius at this time."

Carver had to think quickly. "Yes, ma'am, it was only between them at first; then they decided to let the president in on it. What is your name?" Carver asked.

"My name is Ruth. I have been very good, so Redimir chose me to help with the plans. I have never seen you out here before," she said.

"Well, I usually guard the farmhouse," Carver said, still thinking quite quickly on his feet.

"Oh, I have never been to the farmhouse, but I hear that King Darius is here today, so I hope I get to meet him."

"Well, you just might," Carver said. "Are you a seeker?" Carver knew he might be risking everything asking that question. But he felt as though she was willing to give him the answer.

"Well, we don't use that term anymore," she said. "I am a citizen of the New Global Neighborhood, the NGN. I was chosen to help because of my good behavior and administrative skills. I am an architect, and I know how to draw."

"Oh, that's great. I'm sure you have done a great job, then."

What is your name, sir?"

"My name is Kaylon." Carver thought quickly enough to use his middle name.

"Well, nice to meet you, Kaylon."

"It is nice to meet you too, Ruth. Are you drawing the escape plans?" Carver continued.

"No . . ." she said, hesitating. "I am not sure I can tell you what I am drawing."

"You know, you remind me so much of my grandmother, and her name is Cula. She lives in Texas. She is a wonderful woman, and I miss her so much." Carver thought if he could get Ruth to trust him, then he might get some important information from her that would help them. Ruth smiled as Carver described his grandmother; she felt quite comfortable around him.

"Well, I guess I can let you see my drawings, but you can't tell anyone."

"Yes, ma'am. I promise not to say a word."

She walked Carver over to the table and opened the plans. Carver couldn't believe his eyes. It was a map of the world, and she had different cities marked for something significant.

"What are those markings?" Carver inquired.

"Well, when King Darius gets rid of all these people, he plans on setting up new political offices in these areas. I am just mapping out those offices and then designing the buildings for them. He wants every building to look exactly alike."

"Oh, that is awesome!" Carver said, feigning enthusiasm. "You did a fantastic job. Are there others here like you that are helping with the plans for the NGN?"

"Yes, Kaylon, there are a lot of people that are now citizens, but I don't think that many of them get to do as much as I do. They just stay in their rooms until we go out to worship or grow the gardens. We are all very happy now under the new system."

"You mean the rooms down this hall?" Carver asked.

"Yes, Kaylon, the rooms you are guarding. You should know that."

"Well, this is my first time to guard the cave; I am usually at the farm-house. I wasn't aware of where their rooms were."

Ruth had now begun to look a little skeptical.

"They are all down this blue hall," she said.

"Well, I'm not sure what the big secret is. I think everyone pretty much knows about the new offices."

She looked at him intently. "I don't think so . . . I was told the president didn't even know."

"Well, President Clemmons knows," Carver said.

"Well, Redimir and King Darius must have changed their minds, because they were planning on killing Ambassador Clemmons and Ambassador Dunn. The ambassadors are the only ones who have power to override Redimir and King Darius, and King Darius doesn't like that. At least that's what Redimir told me. He also told me that if I was good, I could help him and work for him."

Carver wasn't sure who Redimir was, but didn't want to act like he didn't know. "Well, that is great. I'm sure you will do a fine job."

"Well, that's good to know they aren't going to kill Ambassador Clemmons. I always liked him," she said.

Carver now knew he had to get out of there quickly. Just as he was about to think up a plan, there was a knock at the door. Carver's heart dropped. As Ruth got up to answer it, Carver held his breath. She opened the door, and there stood Stefan.

"Oh, sergeant," Carver said. "I am sorry I have taken so long. I was just talking to Ruth here about my grandmother in Texas and forgot about the time. Ruth, I want to thank you for inviting me in, and good luck with your plans. I will see you later."

"OK," Ruth said. "It was my pleasure."

Carver practically pushed Stefan out of the way to get out of there. He didn't want him to call him by name since he had given his middle name.

"We have got to get out of here quick. They plan on killing the president," Carver muttered to Stefan, under his breath, as they quickly began walking.

"What?" Stefan said. "When?"

"I don't know, but I think soon." As the two ran back down the hall to meet up with the others, they could see the guards heading back. They barely had time to get out. Stefan could only hope the others had made it out already. They met back at their strike point; everyone was there waiting.

"We were starting to get worried about you guys," Cory said. "Thank God you made it out. Look, the guards are back now. Tay was the only one who made it down a hall besides you guys. The rest of us could not get past the guards.

"Did you see anything important down the green hall?" Stefan asked Tay.

"Yes, I found the hospital and the rooms where some of the seekers are. There are about twenty rooms that I think they are in."

"How do you know?" Stefan inquired.

"Each room had the words 'New World Citizens' written across the doors, and I assumed that was them."

"It is them," Carver said. "That is what they have all been brainwashed into thinking they are." Carver then went on to tell them about Ruth and the information she disclosed. Stefan radioed General Howard to let him know what Carver had found out.

* * *

The guards had delivered the envelope to Denise Clemmons, and she decided to wait until Paul came back and let him open it. She knew that the results were going to be negative. She knew she was cured and wanted him to see that no one had tampered with the envelope. The

President had just finished eating lunch and went to check on Denise again. He walked in to see her smiling.

"I have the results."

"Well, what do they say?" he asked.

"I don't know; I left them sealed for you to open." She handed the envelope to him and held her breath as he opened the letter. He began reading and saw that everything was negative. The report went on to say that there was no cancer in her body anywhere; in fact, everything, including her blood work, was perfect.

"See, Paul. I told you he cured me."

The president sat there a little speechless. "I have always thought belief was really only in the mind of the individual. That's why it was so easy for me to convert. I never in my wildest dreams thought it was for real. If this had not been you getting cured, I still wouldn't believe it, and even still I am a little hesitant."

"Paul, it is real, and I am cured. We have got to tell others about this so they can experience the kingdom."

"No Denise. Please, be quiet. You don't understand. I am involved in something that is way beyond this. I can't just go out there and say, 'Gentlemen, my wife just got healed and this kingdom thing is real, so you all need to convert.'"

"I am not asking you to do that, but you have to tell me what is going on here, Paul. Are our lives in danger?"

"Well, they weren't before now."

"What do you mean?" she asked.

"Well, all the seekers' lives will probably be in danger because they will never conform to the New Global Neighborhood, much less the New World religion. Especially if any of them have experienced anything like you just did."

"What do you mean?"

"People that are like Arlice, that believe in this kingdom thing."

"Well, how will the government know who is and isn't like Arlice."

"Just don't tell anyone, Denise. Do you hear me?" he said, avoiding her question. "You have to give me time to work this out. Did you only see Dr. Shinall?"

"Yes, I only saw Doctor Shinall and his nurse, Wendy."

"You have got to go back and tell him the president of the United States commands that he and his nurse keep silent about this. Go, now, before he has the chance to tell anyone. We will talk more tonight when I am finished. Go on. Get over to the cave now!"

Clemmons left to return to the meeting, and Denise quickly headed back to the cave.

* * *

Stefan had already radioed Jason, requesting him over at the cave. As they gathered around, Stefan apprised them of everything that went on inside. Just as Carver was about to tell them about Ruth, Tay whispered rather loudly.

"Look, the First Lady is going in the cave again."

"What's with that?" Cory asked.

"We are not sure," Stefan said. "But something unusual has to be going on."

"Have you guys found Arlice yet?" Tay asked.

"Maybe," Jason said. "Nettle flew up in a tree and saw the First Lady talking to someone through a closed door. We think maybe he is in there."

"Why would she be talking to Arlice?" Cory asked.

"We don't know. It may not be him at all."

"I thought she was really sick," Tenya said.

"It doesn't look like she is very sick to me," Chrissy said. "Maybe Arlice healed her."

They watched as Denise walked up to the guards again, and they let her past and into the cave.

"I wonder if she is going to the hospital?" Nettle asked.

"Who knows, but we need to find out if she will talk to us," Stefan said. "So once she is in, I will take the guard on the left, and Jason, you take the one on the right. Carver, you go back in and see Ruth and see if you can get the information we need about the president. Josh, you and Tommy head for the missile room and see if you can get in and see what types of missiles they have. Chrissy, you go down the green hall and check out what the First Lady is doing. See if she is at the hospital. Cory, Tay, Tenya, and Stefan, you stay here and guard the place. Nettle, you and Sam come with me back to the farmhouse, and let's find Arlice. Remember, the guards will only be down for thirty minutes, so hurry and watch your time."

"I will count to three, and on three, shoot," Jason said to Stefan. "OK . . . one, two, three." Jason and Stefan successfully shot the guards with quiescent tranquilizer bullets; they only needed one shot each.

"Remember, when they wake up, they won't remember a thing," Jason said. "Now let's move."

CHAPTER 32

New World

Tommy, Josh, Carver, and Chrissy headed inside the cave. Once they were inside, Jason, Nettle, and Sam darted back to the farmhouse. Everyone else stood watch. Approaching the rear of the farmhouse, they heard the back door start to open. Immediately, they took cover. Out walked President Clemmons with Arlice. Jason motioned for Nettle to fly up into the tree above them to hear their conversation.

"Arlice, I will make this quick. I know you cured my wife's cancer this morning because the hospital verified it. How did you do that?"

"Well, sir, power belongs to those in the kingdom," Arlice answered.

"Look, I don't have time for fluff. How did you do it?" Clemmons asked again.

"I told you, sir . . . It is given to all kingdom citizens who believe in it."

"Well, Denise is upset because they have you and your kids locked up in that room. I owe you for saving my wife's life, so I'm going to help you get out of here."

"Oh, that would be great, sir! I would appreciate that very much," Arlice said.

"Who put you there? Was it Ransom?"

"Yes, sir, it was. He doesn't seem like a very good person, if I might say so," Arlice said.

"Well, he just does what he's told," Clemmons said. "I don't know how I am going to do this without anyone finding out, but I will discuss it tonight with my wife and get back to you tomorrow. I promise to get you and your kids out of here as a favor for curing my wife, but you can't tell anyone about it. Do you understand this?"

"I understand, sir, and I won't."

"Do we have any more like you locked up out here?" the president asked.

"I know there are many locked up out here, sir, but most all of them have been brainwashed. I haven't a clue as to whether they have extraordinary powers or not."

"Well, I don't think we would brainwash anyone, Arlice. We just want them to understand we have their best interests in mind. We would never intentionally hurt anyone."

"Well, that is not what has happened here, sir. I can assure you of that," Arlice said.

"Let's get back inside before anyone sees us," Clemmons said.

"OK, sir. Thank you again."

"Just keep your mouth shut, OK?"

"I will, sir," Arlice said.

They walked back inside, and Nettle flew to the door to catch it before it shut completely. There was a bathroom right off the entrance, so she went in and stayed inside the stall for a few minutes to make sure no one saw her. Jason radioed Stefan and texted General Kerwin to let them both know that Nettle was inside the farmhouse.

Nettle quietly went up the stairs to the third floor and immediately heard Jackson's voice inside the room. She knocked quietly on the door.

"Who is it?" Arlice asked.

"It's Nettle. Can you hear me?"

"Yes," Arlice said. "We can hear you."

"Nettle, it's you! This is Jackson. I knew you would come back for us."

"Yes, Jackson. We did. Arlice, I overheard what the president said to you outside. I was up in the tree listening."

"You like those trees, don't you, Nettle?" Arlice said, grinning.

"We were going to try and get you out of here today, but since the president is going to do it, it will be much safer for you guys that way."

"OK," Arlice said, the conversation continuing through the closed door. "But if things go wrong, please don't forget us."

"We won't," Nettle said. "At least I know where you are now. I will talk to you later," she said. "Bye, you guys," Nettle said. As Nettle was saying this, she heard the door right next to Arlice's room start to open, so immediately she flew up to the corner of the ceiling and froze in place. The man coming out of the room had two short—yet-monstrous—creatures on a leash. One had two heads that rolled back and forth as it growled. The other had all kinds of horns sticking out of its head. Its eyes were red like fire, and it had a long tongue that kept rolling in and out of its mouth. He placed them both in front of Arlice and Jackson's room and locked them down. Nettle could see that their teeth looked like a great white shark's teeth; they were terrifying to behold. The man left, and Nettle flew away and back into the restroom.

Great! Now how is the president going to get Arlice out of there? Just as Nettle was about to open the bathroom door, she heard two men coming around the corner, talking. She quickly shut the door. Both men stopped at the back door, and Nettle recognized their voices. They were Ransom and Hawk.

"I want you to make sure no one gets near Arlice's door tonight. He has healed the president's wife, and I don't want anyone to get any strange ideas," Ransom said. "I had Scientist Frank put the creatures outside the door just in case. I have to get back to the meeting now. You just make sure that room stays guarded."

"Will do, boss," Hawk answered.

* * *

At the cave, Carver knocked on Ruth's door, and she welcomed him back in.

"Hey, Ruth, may I ask you a question? I was thinking earlier about what you said about killing the president."

"Yes."

"Do you know why they originally planned on doing that? Did anyone tell you?"

"I think we have been warned not to get too attached to anyone, remember?"

"Yes, and I am not attached to any of the men in charge. I just think Paul Clemmons will be of great value to us later. What were they planning on doing to him, anyway?"

"I am not sure I can tell you that. I just know they were planning on getting rid of him and his wife, along with Prime Minister Dunn, this Sunday when they set off the disasters."

Disasters on Sunday . . . I got the answer to that question, Carver thought to himself.

"But how . . . ? Everyone will be here and will know if something happens to all of them."

Ruth looked around as if to make sure no one else was listening, and then whispered softly.

"You know . . . the deadly virus. They were going to serve it to them at breakfast in the underground city on Sunday morning, then just bury them in the underground cemetery."

"Have you seen the underground city?" Carver asked.

"No, but the professor says I will one day soon." Ruth was starting to have her suspicions arise with all of these questions from this guard she knew as Kaylon. She had been taught to be very aware of everyone. *Maybe Kaylon is on the opposing side,* she began to think.

"Have you seen the statue yet?" Carver plunged ahead, though he was nervous about how far he was pushing things with Ruth.

"Yes, we worship at the altar. You should know that."

"I do. I just wanted to make sure that you did."

"I know everything, including that you are not a real guard."

Carver's face suddenly turned ashen.

"What do you mean?" he asked.

"I went looking for you earlier, and you were nowhere to be found. I asked the other guards about you, and they said there is no guard named Kaylon here or at the farmhouse. But don't worry, I did not tell anyone about you," she said.

Carver had to think quickly since he did not know whether she was going to turn him in or help him.

"So, who are you really?" she asked.

In a split-second, Carver knew he had a choice to make. He opted for gut-level honesty. "My first name is Carver, my middle name is Kaylon, and I am a seeker. I am trying to find Arlice and the other seekers so they don't get killed. I want to help you and the others seekers escape."

"Why would we want to do that? We all like it here."

"Because they are brainwashing you all into believing a lie," he said.

"What lie?"

Carver looked at his watch and realized he only had ten minutes before the guards would be waking up.

"Ruth, I really like you a lot, and I need your help. I need to know how to get to the underground city and if there is another way out of here besides through the cave opening."

"There is another way, but first you must tell me the lie."

"Well, I don't know the whole story, but I do know that seekers can have special powers—and I mean out-of-the-ordinary powers. King Darius and the president and about sixteen others know this, so they want to exterminate seekers for good. As a result, they kidnapped a bunch of you and brainwashed you into believing what they are doing is good. But it is not good, Ruth. They want to rule the world and take all the power away from the people. They are making it sound good now by making a lot of promises to you, but they are lying."

"Just like you did to me earlier," she said, her eyes narrowing.

"Yes, and I'm sorry. I just felt I had no choice in order to help save you and all the other seekers. I wasn't sure who you were at that point."

Carver wasn't sure how Ruth was taking all this information. He decided to probe further to see what she remembered.

"Can you remember life before you were kidnapped? Can you remember being a seeker? Do you remember Arlice healing those people before everyone was shot at?"

"Stop!" she said adamantly. "I don't want to remember those things. I am a citizen of the New Global Neighborhood, and you must go now before I have to report you. I like you, Kaylon . . . Carver, but you are wrong. They love us here and only want to help us. The professor believes in me, and I am here to help him make his dreams come true. King Darius rules and his dominion will be forever and ever. Hail to the graven image and the beast."

It was as though she sounded robotic. Carver felt a chill.

"Look, Ruth, I am here to help you and your family . . . " As soon as the words tumbled out, Ruth turned on him.

"Guards, guards!" Carver immediately sprang up and started running to get out of the place. She followed him, screaming at the top of her lungs.

"Guards, guards!" she screamed, not too far behind him. Carver barely made it out and back to Stefan's team.

Not seeing guards anywhere as she rounded the corner, Ruth turned and went back to her room.

CHAPTER 33

The Green Hall

Chrissy had hidden in the bathroom down the green hall, across from the hospital. She was waiting for Denise to come out of the hospital when she realized she only had a couple of minutes to get back before the guards woke up. As she opened the bathroom door, there stood the blond-haired Ransom whom Josh had spoken about. He stopped dead in his tracks, seeing her in a camouflage uniform.

"Who are you?" he demanded.

Chrissy boldly shot a question back at him. "Who are you?"

Captivated by her beauty, he quickly responded, "Ransom."

Chrissy immediately knew this was not the Ransom who had tried to kidnap Nettle. He had blond hair, an accent, and was extremely good-looking.

"How did you get past the guards?"

"I am a guard," she replied. Immediately, Ransom grabbed Chrissy by her arm and started pulling her toward the cave entrance to see if the guards were there.

"Look, I am here to escort the First Lady back to her room. Stop pulling me, please. I think I twisted my ankle."

"She is here for me." The female voice responded from behind them.

Ransom turned to see the First Lady of the United States.

"I have been very ill," she said as she walked toward Ransom and Chrissy. "I wanted to get some pain medicine," she said, glaring into Ransom's eyes. "And this must be the beautiful young lady my husband sent over to assist me back."

"Yes, ma'am, my name is Chrissy, and I am the one who was ordered by the president to follow you to make sure you are OK because of your illness."

"Well, that would be nice, since I have not been feeling too well." Chrissy could tell Ransom was not happy with this idea, but he did not want to get Denise suspicious about anything, so he allowed her to go. He wanted to know more about Chrissy since he had never seen her in this place before. Enthralled by her beauty, he determined he would discover more about her later.

"Very well!" Ransom said as he pushed Chrissy, faintly, toward Denise. The two women immediately headed off to the farmhouse. They walked past the guards, who were now awake, as if everything was fine. Ransom followed them to the entrance of the cave.

"That is the Ransom I saw this morning," whispered Josh to Stefan and the others.

"Well, that's not the Ransom who kidnapped Nettle," Tommy said.

Denise Clemmons and Chrissy entered through the back door of the farmhouse. Nettle, still in the bathroom, heard the door open and heard Chrissy's voice.

"Thank you so much for rescuing me from that man," Chrissy said to Denise.

"You are welcome, but don't say anything else until we get into my room."

"What in the world are you really doing here?" Denise asked once she closed the door to her bedroom.

"Before I tell you, can I please ask you a couple of questions?"

Hesitantly, Denise agreed.

"Do you know there is a plan for a hostile world takeover?"

"I know there is a plan for a global community. I am not sure it is hostile."

"Are you a seeker?"

"That is kind of a personal question, don't you think?" Denise answered, an eyebrow raised.

"Well, I need you to answer it, because it has a lot to do with my answer to you as to why I am here." Denise could tell that Chrissy had some information that she was dying to tell her if she knew she could trust her. But could she trust Chrissy? That was the biggest question going through Denise's mind. She decided she would.

"Yes, I am a seeker. Why?"

"I am a kingdom citizen, destined to provide you a way out of the misfortune that you are about to encounter. I have authority from another world that supersedes the earthly kingdom. You must trust me; I will not lead you astray."

"Well . . . what do you mean, *misfortune*?" Denise asked.

"There is a plan to annihilate all kingdom citizens as well as all of Israel. The goal is to establish a one-world administration and creed. Soon all governments will be united through devastations across the globe. The plan will appear peaceful at first. Then the mission will change. It will turn evil. The two kingdoms will collide. "

"So you are asking me to go against my husband?"

"I am asking you to stand up for what's right—no matter whom you have to go against." Denise actually liked her boldness.

"These people have kidnapped a little boy named Jackson. He is my friend and I am here to help rescue him," Chrissy continued.

"All by yourself?" the First Lady asked.

"Possibly," Chrissy answered.

"Well, that is very brave. Are you looking for his dad, Arlice, too?" Chrissy's eyes got really big. "Yes, I am. Jackson is Arlice's son."

"Yes, I know," Denise said. "Why don't we give him a call, and you can speak to him." Denise picked up her phone, dialed Arlice, and handed the phone to Chrissy.

"Hello?"

"Arlice, is that you?" Chrissy asked.

"Yes. Who is this?"

"My name is Chrissy, and I am a friend of Jackson's. Can you put him on the phone, please?" Arlice handed the phone to Jackson.

"Hello?"

"Jackson, this is Chrissy, and I am here to help you, buddy."

"Yes, I know, Chrissy. I just spoke to Nettle. She is here too."

"You did? Where is she?"

"She was outside our door here in the farmhouse a few minutes ago."

"Hold on just a minute." Chrissy turned to Denise: "Do you know where they are keeping Arlice and Jackson, and can we go there right now?"

"Yes, I know the room, but it is locked."

"That's OK. We must go there right now." Chrissy turned back to the phone. "Jackson, tell your dad I will be up there in a minute . . . bye," she said, quickly ending the call.

As soon as Denise and Chrissy made it to the third floor, they spotted the creatures.

"Oh, my heavens!" Denise exclaimed. "What in the world are those?"

"Chrissy," Nettle whispered.

"Nettle . . . Jackson said you were here."

"Who is this?" Denise Clemmons asked.

"She is my best friend, and she can fly. Arlice heals, and Nettle flies."

"And what do you do?"

"I control nature."

Nettle looked at Chrissy as if to say, *You go, girl.*

"Well, I think I would have to see that to believe it."

"Not a problem," Nettle said. Without hesitation, she flew up to the ceiling and back.

"Dear God!" Denise said in awe. "I am beginning to think I am not on planet earth."

"Well, that might be partially true," Nettle said, smiling really big.

"Did you know your husband is going to help Arlice, Jackson, and Stephen escape?" Nettle inquired. "I overheard him tell Arlice this afternoon, out back under that big, old tree."

"What made him want to help Arlice?" Chrissy asked.

"Arlice cured me of cancer this morning, and I went over to the hospital and had the doctors check me out. The report came back negative.

All the cancer is gone, and I showed Paul the report. Then I asked him to help Arlice, and he said we would discuss it tonight. I guess he decided to go ahead and tell Arlice. But how in the world, now that those creatures are there, is he going to get them out?"

"We will figure it out," Nettle said.

"Well, Ransom has definitely seen me," Chrissy informed Nettle.

"How?" Nettle asked.

"When I went in the cave to follow Denise, I ran into him. But Nettle, Josh was right; it is not the same Ransom. This one is very good-looking ... but, I believe, way more evil. I think this guy has special powers from the underworld."

"Really?" Nettle said.

"Yes, and my instincts tell me he controls more than we know."

"Whoa . . . what do you mean?"

"I just mean this is a different guy altogether, and he seems very influential."

"Do you know this Ransom, Mrs. Clemmons?" Nettle asked.

"I don't know much of anyone here; this is my first visit to the farmhouse. I did meet the other Ransom, the dark-headed one, this morning when he introduced me to Arlice. He truly gave me the creeps. I just met the blond Ransom when Chrissy did. He also gave me a bad feel; I am not sure what he does here, but I will find out.

"You girls have to get out of here now!" Denise said, as though the seriousness of the entire situation had just dawned on her. "This is way over any of your heads, and if you get caught. . . . " She shook her head.

"That's fine, Mrs. Clemmons, but before we go, you need to know something. The world leaders meeting with your husband right now are planning on setting off disasters all over the world tomorrow. They plan on killing millions in order to persuade the world to buy into their new agenda. But you cannot let your husband know I told you that. You must get him to tell you."

"What!?" exclaimed Denise.

"That is why he brought you here, so you won't get hurt."

"But I have daughters out there!"

"You have to convince the president to stop this plan," Nettle said.

"Let him know there are others who will help him if he decides to do the right thing. Here is my phone number. Call me if you convince him."

Denise was left with so many emotions inside. She was ecstatic about being cured but was deeply troubled for her husband and country. She could not believe all that she had just seen and heard, and now she had to figure out what to believe and how to get the information she needed from Paul.

As Denise stood looking out the back door, she felt someone walk up beside her. She turned around, and there stood the dark-haired Ransom.

"Hello, Ms. Clemmons. I see you are still feeling well. Have you told the president about your situation yet?"

"Yes, and he was very grateful to you for introducing me to Arlice."

"Did I hear you talking to someone before I walked up?"

"Uh . . . no. I was just looking outside at how beautiful it is and mumbling to myself. I haven't been out much lately, and I was enjoying the view."

Suddenly, a thought popped into her mind that she felt she should act on.

"Ransom, is there another gentleman working here named Ransom?"

"No, I am the only one here by that name. Why do you ask that?"

"When I went to the hospital to get checked out, I thought I heard one of the guards call another man Ransom. Maybe I was wrong. No big deal," she said.

"Well, I will walk you back to your room," Ransom said. "I am just glad that I could be of service to you today and hope that the president is happy as well. He has not said anything to me as of yet, so I wasn't sure you had told him."

"Well, I am sure he is just waiting for the right time. I know he is very grateful. Thank you again, and I will see you later," Denise said as she turned to go into her room.

Denise had not been in her room very long when there was a knock on the door. It was Caleb, one of the guards, coming to see if she was OK, and to see if Chrissy was still there, following his orders.

"Yes, I am just fine. Chrissy is off duty now and has gone home, but thank you for checking on me. Can I ask you a question before you leave? Do you know both Ransoms who work here? One has dark hair, and the other has blond hair."

"No ma'am. There is only one Ransom who works here, and he has dark hair."

"Then who is the gentleman that sent you over here, the extremely blond gentleman?"

"That is Professor Redimir Bean."

"Oh, I see. So, he is not in charge?"

"In charge of what?" he questioned, looking as though he had no idea what she was talking about.

"Of the cave," she quickly said.

"No ma'am."

"Well, thanks for clearing that up."

"You are welcome."

I know he told Chrissy his name was Ransom. This is getting stranger by the minute. Denise couldn't wait for Paul to get back to the room to ask him questions. Caleb walked back to the cave and went straight to Professor Bean's office and knocked on the door.

"I am sorry, sir, but the girl who escorted the First Lady back to the farmhouse is no longer there."

"Where is she?" Redimir asked.

"The First Lady said she is off duty now and has gone home. Sir, may I ask you something?"

"What is it?" he said.

"Well, the First Lady thought your name was Ransom, so I corrected her and told her it was Professor Redimir Bean."

"Good," Redimir said. "You did well." And with that, he quickly shut his door.

CHAPTER 34

Coup De Main

"Mayday! Mayday!" General Howard shouted. "Get out now. Mission compromised!"

Jason, Nettle, Chrissy, and Sam had just made it over to the rendezvous point by the cave. As they heard the general's warning, they spotted armed men coming out of the woods from seemingly every direction.

"Down!" Jason shouted. He looked over at the girls.

"Quick, Nettle, get behind that huge tree, put Chrissy on your back, and get out of here . . . go! Sam, you follow me." Chrissy hopped on Nettle's back, and they flew back behind the farmhouse and up into a tree to hide.

Jason radioed Stefan. "Mayday, mayday—you are about to be ambushed. Split up and crawl out fast. They have weapons!" Jason then tried to reach Zac and Cade from their Special Forces team to come help. Stefan immediately told his team to do the best they could and get back to the Hummers.

"Be sure and swallow the blue pill if you get caught," he reminded them all.

Tommy's heart was racing as he was trying to get away. Tenya, Tay, Carver, and Cory had split up, crawling on their bellies to try and find a way out. Cory suddenly stood straight up, knowing an abrupt distraction would allow his friends to escape.

"*Wicked!*" Cory stood up and shouted as he heard every gun in the place lock, cock, and aim on him.

"Whoa, Whoa . . . " Cory said as he held his hands up. "No need to kill a man just for looking around and trying to find his possessions. Come on guys, give me a break here."

Agitated and frustrated, Jason had tried several times to reach Zac and Cade to inform them they were being ambushed, but there was no answer. Crawling side by side, Jason and Sam discovered a gigantic hole underneath a large bush. Diving in it, they covered themselves up with leaves and debris. Before they were completely dug in, Josh crawled by, and Jason grabbed him and pulled him in. They all lay motionless and silent.

The men made their way to Cory, guns aimed and ready to fire.

"Who are you and what are you doing out here?" Max asked, the leader of the Special Forces team.

Pretending to be stoned, Cory responded . . . very s-l-o-w-l-y. "Dudes . . . it's cool, man . . . it's cool. I was just looking for my stash and a good place to grow some weed."

"What is your name?" they demanded.

"My name is Cory, Cory ten Boom. You guys look awesome. Can I do whatever it is that you do?" They seemed to miss the ten Boom comment.

All the others could hear Cory since he was deliberately talking loud. They realized he was distracting the men so they could all escape.

"How did you get out here?" Max, the captain, requested.

Cory made up the first story he could think of.

"My buddy, Sean Michael Da'Laru, dropped me off earlier. He's coming back later this afternoon to pick me up." Cory was counting on Zac and Cade and their Special Forces team to come out at any minute.

"So he just left you out here?"

"Yeah, man, isn't this a cool place? I mean there is water to drink and woods galore to plant in. It is like a desert oasis, dude. You know what I mean?" Cory laughed, hoping they were buying it.

"Well, this is government property, and you are not allowed to be here."

"Oops," Cory said, putting his hand over his mouth. "I didn't know that, man. I will leave. Sorry about that."

"Well, it's not that easy," Max said. By this time Tay, Tenya, Carver, and Tommy had made it far enough away to be able to get up and run. As they were all gathered around the Hummer, Tommy noticed Stefan, Jason, Josh, Sam, and the girls were missing.

"Hey, where are all the others?"

"I don't know. I thought they were crawling out too," Tay said. "Well, we can't go anywhere without Stefan. He has the keys."

"What happened to all our Special Forces guys . . . Zac and Cade and the rest of the team? I thought they were supposed to be there to help us," Tenya said.

Nettle and Chrissy watched as they handcuffed Cory and led him over toward the farmhouse.

"Look man, I am sorry. I promise not to grow any weed out here. Can't you just let me go home?"

"I'm sorry, but I have to take you to our superior and see what he wants us to do."

Max called President Clemmons to come outside, telling him it was urgent. Clemmons, however, in turn asked Ransom to take care of it as he did not want to leave the meeting yet. Ransom quickly got up to go check things out.

"Who in the world is he?" Ransom demanded.

"I'm Cory, and man do you have a cool place here, dude." Cory swirled his head around and smiled really big.

"He is just a stoned kid we found out here looking for a place to plant some weed. His buddy dropped him off and is supposed to come back here and pick him up later."

"Was anyone else with him?" Ransom asked.

"No, sir," Max said.

"Did anyone else see you capture this guy?"

"No, sir," Max said.

"Who ordered you guys out here?"

"We are the Special Forces team the president called in earlier today to guard the compound. We had just arrived and were trying to get familiar with the place when we heard what sounded like several voices, but this guy is all we found. I think maybe he was just talking to himself."

"I didn't know the president called in any Special Forces teams."

"Yes, sir, he did. And I am Captain Max, sir." Ransom held out his hand to shake Max's hand and introduced himself.

"Yes, Ransom, the president spoke of you, and he told me to get a hold of you if I needed anything, sir." This made Ransom stand up very tall, since what he really wanted was the approval of the president, and he wanted it desperately.

"I will take Cory from this point and question him myself. Thank you very much for all your help," Ransom said. "What is your assignment from this point on?" Ransom was suspicious of the president possibly calling them there to rescue Arlice.

"Just to guard the cave, sir," Max responded.

"OK, great. How many of you are there?"

"There are six of us, sir."

"OK, you can get back to that assignment now. I will take care of this kid."

"Yes, sir," Max said. Ransom took Cory by the arm and proceeded to walk him back over to the farmhouse area.

"Don't play me for a fool, you ignorant boy," Ransom spit out as soon as they were alone. "I know there are more of you out here. And I will get it out of you one way or another."

"Dude, there is no one out here but me. But I can get some more people out here if that's what you want." Cory was laughing, doing his best to act completely stoned.

* * *

Nettle told Chrissy to remain in the tree, and that she would be back to get her. When she flew over the farmhouse, she could see Ransom taking Cory around the back. She flew down feet first and hit Ransom

231

so hard in the head that he fell to the ground, knocked out.

"Run, Cory; get out of here," she said. Cory took off and rounded the other side of the farmhouse and headed back down the main road. Nettle knew the new Special Forces team was still lurking around the cave, and she was worried about the others. She flew quite high over the entire place but couldn't see a thing. As she searched hard for her own Special Forces team, she didn't see them anywhere. She tried radioing both Zac and Cade, and still, no answer. *Something doesn't feel quite right.* She flew back up to get Chrissy and radioed General Howard.

"Good job, Nettle. Cory is getting away. Ransom is still down, but when he gets up, he is going to be extremely angry and wonder what in the world happened to him. You must get out of there now."

"Sir, I hate to interrupt, but where is our Special Forces team? We have tried to radio them and they don't answer."

"Yes, I told them to leave earlier when I found out that the president had called in his own Special Forces team. I knew they would get caught, and that would jeopardize the whole mission. So right now you guys are on your own. You need to get everyone out of there and get back here ASAP."

"Yes, sir," Nettle said.

Nettle and Chrissy flew back over the cave one more time, but all they could see were the two guards, Caleb and Kenneth.

"They have all moved inside now. I wonder what they are up to in there. Let's go see if we can find the others now," Nettle said to Chrissy as they flew over to the rendezvous site. Nettle and Chrissy quietly landed.

"Psst . . . Nettle, over here." Nettle turned and saw Stefan squatted down.

"Get down, both of you. You must get out of here now. Our Special Forces team is gone, so we are out here alone. Here are the keys to the Hummer. Now you guys get back as quick as you can and get everyone out of here. Stefan assured her he would make it out OK.

Cory arrived at the Hummers and couldn't stop talking about how Nettle had knocked the holy mess out of Ransom's head, helping him get away. Nettle and Chrissy landed at the Hummers and instructed them on their new orders from Stefan.

"We can't leave now," Tommy said. "Jason, Josh, and Sam are still out there too."

"What if they all get caught? They will need us," Tay said.

"Yeah, and I can't leave without Josh," Chrissy said.

* * *

Ransom started waking up and could feel a huge knot on the back of his head. He was still dizzy-headed as he began looking for Cory. He could not figure out what had just happened. *That kid must have had some help*, he thought. He ran inside and into the meeting, frantically yelling.

"Something's going on here. I was just attacked outside and knocked out by something. It came from the sky and literally knocked me out. The young man I was bringing back inside escaped. He is probably part of the attack. I think we have terrorists outside. They must have gotten insider information that we are all meeting here today."

General Kerwin looked over at President Clemmons to get his reaction, then over at Mohammad Darius to see his. He was wondering if something had gone wrong with the mission, and wanted to dismiss himself to go check it out, but knew that wasn't possible.

"The guy said he had a buddy coming back here to pick him up. I don't know what hit me, but I think we need to take cover soon, just in case."

"There is nothing to worry about," Clemmons told the group. I called in additional Special Forces today to guard the place. If anyone is out there, they will find them."

"Why don't we take a thirty-minute break?" King Darius suggested. "General Kerwin, please come with me."

CHAPTER 35

The Transition

General Kerwin could not imagine what in the world King Darius wanted with him as they walked outside toward the cave. He knew he had to play the game strategically and not let his opponent outwit him.

"I wanted to bring you with me so you could talk to the Special Forces team the president ordered here today. I also want to show you something very special."

"OK," General Kerwin said. "And what do you want me to advise the Special Forces team to do?"

"Ask them if they have seen anything or anyone who looks suspicious. Tell them to radio you if they do, not Ransom or the president. Also tell them to surround the farmhouse and guard it immediately." Todd radioed the Special Forces team leader, Max, and gave him the instructions. Immediately, they left the cave and moved back to the farmhouse.

* * *

President Clemmons went quickly to check on Denise. He had not been able to get their conversation out of his mind.

"Paul, we need to talk now."

"OK, what is it, honey?"

"I need you to tell me what is going on here."

"Well, first I want you to know that I have spoken to Arlice and called in a Special Forces team to take him out of here this evening after everyone is asleep."

"Well, there might be a small problem with that."

"What are you talking about?"

"There are huge science-fiction-like creatures outside his door, guarding his room. Paul, this is serious and unbelievable at the same time. This is the twenty-first century; what are those creatures doing living in it? I saw them, Paul, with my own eyes."

"Yes, I know about the creatures. They were designed by our scientists."

"Then they are robots?" Denise asked.

"Well, not exactly," the president said.

"What do you mean by that, Paul?"

"They were bred by two different animals and then injected with a special formula that turned them into these creatures."

"Dear God," Denise said. "Well, can you get past them and help Arlice and his kids?"

"I will figure it out, Denise. I promise."

"Second, I don't trust that Ransom man. He is not a good person, Paul, and I know he is the one who put those creatures outside their door. Do not, and I mean do *not*, let him know your plans for Arlice. Promise me?"

"I promise," Paul said.

"Now, please, tell me what is going on here with all these foreign presidents."

Paul looked at his wife with a heavy heart . . . despite his intentions in these evil plans, she remained very precious to him. He decided it was time to tell her the whole truth.

"We are about to bring the whole world together through unusual devastations across the globe. This will unite the people and prepare them for the New Global Community." Denise remained calm so she could get the rest out of him.

"How are you planning on accomplishing that?"

"Well, that is the secret part. I cannot tell you that yet," Paul said.

"Sweetheart, I have loved you since high school, and we have always shared everything together. I know you are deep in this process. I understand you think this is what we need and what you have always wanted . . . but Paul, not at the expense of people's lives."

"Who said anything about people's lives, Denise?"

"You did, by telling me it is a secret."

All of a sudden, Paul's voice and demeanor changed dramatically.

"Look, I am getting the guy and his kids out of here for you, Denise. That is enough for now. Please, be content with that, and know I would never do anything that would jeopardize our relationship or the lives of those we love."

"But what about my healing, Paul—it is real!"

"What about it?" he asked.

"You know it's real; you know there is more to this than meets the eye. We were warned of this . . . "

"Warned of what?"

"Warned of becoming one. Can't you see it?" she asked.

"That's nonsense, Denise. That is not what this is. King Darius would never mean harm to anyone."

"Come on, Paul, you know he is anti-Semitic. For God's sake, Paul: I am Jewish!"

"I don't have a problem with the Jews, Denise!"

"Then promise me this: find out more about this peace treaty and when he plans on offering it. I assure you I will be satisfied with the answer if you feel it is sincere. OK?" she asked.

"OK, but that's it . . . no more questions."

"Well, I have one last one."

"What is it now, Denise? I need to get back to the meeting."

"That girl Arlice talked about—Nettle. Why do you guys want her?"

"I am not sure that we do . . . " The president seemed to be hesitating.

"Arlice told me that she had tremendous powers like him and that they were looking for her."

"Well, I am sure it is for a good reason, sweetie. She can probably help us."

"Help you *what*, Paul?"

"Look, Denise, I don't know every little thing."

"Well, maybe you should, Paul. You are the president of the United States of America, and you have a duty to protect our country and the people in it." As she said that, she turned and walked away from him, and he quickly turned and left to go back to the meeting.

General Kerwin had followed Darius into the cave. He was a little uneasy, but knew he had to act as though committed to the plan. Where was this guy taking him? He did not trust Darius at all. He could sense that something was up his sleeve.

"General Kerwin, can I trust your president?" Darius asked, finally turning to face him.

"Why would you ask me that, sir?"

"I just would like an answer, please."

"Yes, you can trust President Clemmons. He is a man of his word and believes wholeheartedly in the New Global Neighborhood."

"Do you?"

"Of course I do. Otherwise, I would not be here."

"Come, let me show you something." General Kerwin was starting to get a little upset, since he could not figure out why Darius would be asking him these questions or where he was taking him. He followed him down the green hall and into the room that Tommy had discovered earlier.

"See those two dragons?"

"Yes," General Kerwin said.

"They are like me—part mortal and part science. They have the power to destroy anyone or anything that gets in their way. They are mystical, magical, and will kill on demand."

Kerwin was wondering where this was going. All of this was making him a little uncomfortable.

"This room is filled with many treasures, and there are many people who would become very rich if they had just a tenth of this wealth. But I have total power over this wealth and over who gets it. You see, General Kerwin, I want you to be able to share it with me." Darius began walking over to a secret door beside the dragons. "I have a few gentlemen I want you to meet." Darius reached for the door, and in walked detectives Moll and Gibbs and Officer Whitmore.

"What is this all about?" Kerwin asked.

"You see, Todd, there will always be those you can trust and those you can't," he said as he walked over toward the dragons. "Humanity doesn't understand the importance of universal law and the New World arrangement yet, nor do they understand the power of the unknown kingdom. But you do, General Kerwin. You understand it very well.

"Come here." King Darius motioned for Officer Whitmore. The officer rushed over to Darius with a huge grin on his face, hoping the king would reward or honor him in some way. Immediately, Darius grabbed him and put a dagger to his throat.

"In my kingdom, I can either saw his head off or I can feed him to the dragons, because I am king. My friend, today is your lucky day, because the general gets to choose your death."

"Hey, wait a minute. I am on your side. I don't want to die. I want to live in the New Global Community," Officer Whitmore said, clearly in full panic. Detectives Moll and Gibbs were standing there like dead men, too scared to make a move.

"Don't let him do this to me. You guys are my friends," Whitmore pleaded.

"Oh, Officer Whitmore," King Darius said. "Don't you know that friends are only friends when you can provide them something? You are not their friend now. I am."

General Kerwin immediately decided to call his bluff.

"Why don't you feed him to the dragons, sir? I'd like to see that."

Darius smiled and said, "Very well, then." He opened the cage and swirled Officer Whitmore around, still with the dagger on his neck, as if he were going to follow through with the choice.

"You are fortunate today, my comrade. Your life has been saved by the general. If he had chosen the knife, I would have killed you." He pushed Officer Whitmore away; Whitmore fell to the ground. "Americans, you are a funny breed. You hate pain or to see anyone hurt. You always try to rescue people! Well, it is not that way in my kingdom. My kingdom thrives on pain. We love to see the deserving suffer and die. That is the way it should be."

It was at that moment that General Kerwin saw the evil in Darius's eyes. Detectives Gibbs and Moll helped Officer Whitmore up; he was still in shock at what had just happened. King Darius dismissed the officers. They returned back to the room to wait for "Operation Takeover."

"You are right, King Darius. Life as we know it is like a matrix, and only a few get to peek in. The good and evil of it is that the players are real, and the game is on, and may the best man win." General Kerwin laughed hard to let Darius think that he was not afraid of him and to appear as if he was on his side.

"Good, my friend. You understand both worlds."

"Intimately."

"Well then, let's get down to business and show them who's boss," Darius said.

"Let's do it," Kerwin said.

* *.*

As they walked back to the meeting, General Kerwin was trying to figure out that whole ordeal. *Was he just trying to see if he could trust me? Or was he trying to build fear in me to make sure that the president and I stay on track?* Whatever it was, Kerwin knew for sure that Darius's world was not one he wanted anything to do with. As they walked back into the meeting, everyone was waiting anxiously to hear the remainder of the plans.

CHAPTER 36

In The Hole

Jason slowly peeked out to see if it was safe to move, while Josh and Sam remained hidden. It was now dusk, so Jason walked around carefully to confirm things were clear. He glanced over at the farmhouse and saw Hawk escorting a beautiful Chinese girl who looked to be around twenty years old toward the cave. *It doesn't look as if she is being forced against her will. I wonder who she is.*

"It's safe," Jason whispered to Josh and Sam. "You can inch out now." But just as they started crawling out, they spotted the kings, generals, and colonels walking in the direction of the cave.

"Be very still. Don't move until everyone is over at the cave," Jason instructed.

Tommy and the rest of the team decided to make their way back toward the cave. Totally disobeying their orders, they were determined to go back and help. Nettle flew ahead and landed behind a gigantic boulder close to the cave's entrance. She could see all the politicians, including Denise, walking toward the cave's entrance. Nettle settled behind the boulder to see if she could hear what they were saying. *I wonder why they are all going into the cave now?* Nettle saw the First Lady going in with them. Suddenly, she heard her name being whispered. She looked around, but couldn't see anyone.

"Nettle: right here," the voice said.

"Tommy?"

Instantly, she felt something touch her arm. "Tommy, is that you?"

"Right here," he whispered.

"Oh my gosh, Tommy. You are invisible!"

"Yep, this is really going to help us. I received my powers from Parakletos earlier today. I am very excited about using them."

"Oh, wow. That is awesome. Has anyone else received their powers yet?"

"Yes, I think so."

"Have you told them about yours?"

"Yes."

"Now you can find out what is going on without anyone seeing you."

"Wait. Who is that girl with Hawk?" Tommy asked.

"I don't know; maybe she belongs to one of the politicians. You have got to follow them into the cave and find out what they are all doing. Just stay close to General Kerwin and out of everyone's way. You have to make sure the First Lady is safe as well . . . if you can."

"Can you feel me?" he asked.

"I can feel you. I just cannot see you."

Tommy walked right up to the president and the other world leaders; no one flinched. It was the coolest feeling in the world to be invisible. He stayed close to General Kerwin, who was next to President Clemmons and Denise. He continued to follow everyone inside.

Nettle decided to walk back to the rendezvous point and stay with the team. She figured walking in the outer woods would be safe since Tommy had come that way. Suddenly, she felt as though someone was behind her. She turned, but didn't see anyone.

"Tommy Jones, is that you?" She continued to walk toward the rendezvous point when, suddenly, someone grabbed her violently from behind. She thrashed about trying to see who it was. He held her tight when, abruptly and without warning, he plunged a needle into her neck. Immediately, Nettle passed out.

Ransom picked her up and threw her over his shoulders. "I knew there were others out here," he muttered out loud. "I just never dreamed it was my little Nettle. The president and King Darius will not believe this, and I will surely get a raise now," he said to himself. He had a sense of satisfied self-importance as he began carrying Nettle toward the cave.

* * *

Jason, Josh, Stefan, and Sam had rendezvoused with the rest of the team and were hoping that Tommy could gather valuable information now that he was invisible.

"OK, once Nettle gets back, we will devise another plan," Jason said. "I saw her start walking back through the woods a few minutes ago."

"Oh, no, this doesn't look good," Cory said. Everyone turned and saw Ransom carrying Nettle over his shoulder.

"He has drugged her," Jason said. Everyone watched as Ransom took Nettle inside the cave.

"The first thing he will do is search her," Jason said. "He will find her radio and, probably, her blue pill. He will then know the government is in on it." Jason quickly radioed General Howard.

"Mayday, mayday . . . they have Nettle."

"Yes, we see that."

"We also know that Tommy is invisible and apparently is inside the cave now. We can wait and see what he does, or we can go in, sir," Jason said.

"It is getting dark, and I am afraid we won't be able to see you all very clearly much longer," General Howard said. "We can't let them have Nettle, so you guys must find a way to get her out. When they find out the government is in on it and using her, they will either kill her or torture her. Does Tommy have a radio?"

Just as General Howard was asking that question, Chrissy spotted the blond Ransom coming out of the entrance of the cave. She knew that the only way to save Nettle was to get more people inside the cave. Chrissy sensed that he was attracted to her, so she made a daring—but rash—decision. She sprang up and started running toward the cave.

"Chrissy!" Josh whispered loudly. It was too late to stop her. They all watched in shock.

"What on earth is she doing?" Jason said in utter disbelief.

"Trying to save her best friend," Josh answered.

No one dared move. Jason and Stefan sat with guns aimed and ready to fire in case something went wrong. As she approached the cave, the guards turned and looked at the professor as if to say, *What do you want us to do?*

"It's OK," he told them. Chrissy walked straight up to him—and grabbed him and kissed him passionately.

"I have been waiting for that since I met you," she said, looking him straight in the eyes. This took him so much by surprise that he was speechless. After coming to his senses, he finally spoke.

"I thought you had gone home," he said.

"Getting you out of my mind has been impossible. I came back hoping you would appear again, and here you are," Chrissy said, convincingly. Dumbfounded, but led completely by his feelings for her, Ransom grabbed Chrissy's hand and walked her inside the cave.

"Whoa, Josh. What was that?" Sam asked. "I didn't know Chrissy was like that."

"Like what?" Josh said in a rather defensive tone. "She is just trying to rescue her best friend. So don't go there, Sam."

"Dude, what? I wasn't going anywhere."

"Yes, you were," Tay said. "Not the time for it now, man," he continued.

"OK, I was just a little surprised by the move, that's all," Sam said. "I guess we all have different weapons. Who is that guy anyway?"

"That is the Ransom guy I saw in the bathroom with King Darius," Josh said.

"Oh, OK, man," Sam said. "I sure hope Chrissy knows what she's doing."

"Yeah, me too," Josh said.

* * *

Tommy had followed the group down the green hall. King Darius opened the door to a conference room and led everyone inside. As they were seated, Darius approached the podium but was interrupted by Ransom bursting through the door.

"Look! I've got her . . . I just knew something was going on outside, and I was right."

"Who is that?" Darius asked.

"It is Nettle, the one we have been looking for, sir."

King Darius smiled.

"Is she dead?" President Clemmons asked.

"No sir. I just injected her with a sleeping agent so I could bring her here. That way everyone can see we have terrorists outside."

"I hardly think that she is a terrorist, Ransom," President Clemmons said. He was thinking about Denise and what she had said to him about Nettle and Arlice.

"Why don't you take her to the hospital, put her in a room, and keep an eye on her there until we get through with our business here? We can question her when she wakes up," President Clemmons said. General Kerwin was delighted to hear President Clemmons suggest this. Ransom looked a little dejected, but agreed. He wanted them to be more thrilled that he had captured Nettle. King Darius gave Ransom the nod to proceed, realizing this was a confirmation to push forward as planned. He did not want to let on about his enthusiasm as a result of her capture.

Tommy, watching from the back of the room, was taken back. He immediately followed Ransom down the hall to try and rescue Nettle. Out of the blue, he decided to trip him. As Ransom started to fall, Tommy caught Nettle, laying her down so she wouldn't get hurt. Lifting up his fist, he pelted Ransom in the face, knocking him flat. As Ransom started to get up a second time, Tommy drilled him again. This time, he nearly knocked Ransom out.

Tommy threw Nettle over his shoulder and started running the other direction. All Ransom could see was Nettle's body, up in the air, moving away from him. Lightheaded and still dazed, Ransom started yelling loudly.

"Help! Terrorists! Help, they are attacking me. Help!" He pulled himself up and started to chase Nettle's floating body. Tommy knew they had to hide fast, so he took Nettle down the red hall and entered a door that ended up being a large closet. He quickly locked the door and pushed a shelf over it to secure it. He was furiously searching for Nettle's radio.

* * *

In the meantime, the blond Ransom walked Chrissy to his office, and she noticed that the sign on the door said "Professor Bean."

"I didn't know you were a professor," Chrissy said.

"Yes, my real name is Redimir Bean. Some Americans call me Ransom instead. I prefer Redimir." That explains it, Chrissy thought.

"Where are you from?" she asked, trying to discern his accent.

"Originally from Russia, but I have lived in both Egypt and Syria and different parts of Europe until moving to the compound. I have lived here for several months now. I sometimes present at the university here."

"So, you work here too?"

"Do you know what 'here' is?" he asked.

"I think it is a military cantonment . . . of sorts?"

"This is about to be global government property, and I work for the world government."

"Wow, that's awesome. I love a man who understands world politics," she said, moving closer to him and touching his arm. Redimir was totally enamored by Chrissy's beauty, but also instinctively cautious.

"I had a great conversation with the First Lady. After my shift was over, I remained here to see if I could find you." She was trying to get a feel to see if he believed her. Chrissy was good at acting.

"So, you guard the place?" he asked.

"Yes, I guard the farmhouse. But today they have special dignitaries here, the First Lady being one of them, and I was assigned to her."

"Why didn't you tell me that to begin with?"

"I don't know. I think I tried, but you were a little rough with me."

"What else did the First Lady tell you?" he inquired.

"Not much . . . just that the president was working on something very global that the whole world will benefit from."

"Yes, that is correct. And I work directly for that New Global Community."

"Oh, so you don't work for the president of the United States?"

"No," he declared quite harshly. "I work for King Darius." Sensing her concern, he immediately tried to lighten things up by smiling and gently grabbing her hand.

"Well, I have never met anyone from Russia before, but I am so glad I have met you," she said, a rather seductive look on her face.

All of a sudden, without warning, alarms started sounding down every hall, and Chrissy knew something must have gone extremely wrong.

"What is that?" she questioned.

"You must come with me now!" Redimir quickly grabbed Chrissy's hand and led her over to one of the secret passageways to the underground city.

"Where are we going? What's wrong? What are the alarms for?" she asked frantically as they were running down a long hall.

"Do not worry; you are safe with me," he assured her. At the end of the tunnel, Redimir opened a door, and when Chrissy saw what was inside, she could not believe her eyes. The place was enormous, exquisite. It looked like the Emerald City out of *The Wizard of Oz*. The sight of it was astounding. Redimir grabbed her face and told her to look directly into his eyes. She could see he was very serious, and she knew her safety was dependent on listening to him right now.

"The world is about to change drastically. You must decide if you want to live or not. I will allow you to live here only if you become my wife. Otherwise, I must discard you."

"Discard me? What have I done?"

He grabbed Chrissy again—violently—and shook her sternly to make her understand.

"I know you are a spy, but I will give you a second chance right now only if you become my wife. You must then follow me and all my rules."

"You are wrong. I am not a spy."

Redimir slapped Chrissy hard across the face.

"Woman, do not beguile me. Give me your answer now!" Chrissy knew at that moment that she had made a very huge mistake. She had moved out on her own emotions to help save Nettle without the instructions of her superiors or Parakletos. She knew that she must either answer yes at this point or try to call his bluff. That is, if it was a bluff.

"Yes, I want to be with you, but I don't want you to slap me anymore, and I'm not a spy!" He quickly pulled her over to what looked like an apartment, opened the door, and made his way over to a closet.

"You must change clothes quickly, and stay put," he warned her. "If you try to escape, I will have you executed."

Redimir turned and walked out of the room and locked the door. Chrissy began to cry. Upon peering into the closet, she realized he wanted her to change into a burqa, a Muslim woman's garment.

After putting it on, she felt extremely scared. She lay down on the bed and began to pray for her safety.

CHAPTER 37

Mayday, Mayday

"Mayday, mayday! Jason, can you hear me?" Tommy had found Nettle's radio and was desperately trying to get a hold of Jason.

"Yes, Tommy, I hear you. Where are you?"

"We are in big trouble. I have Nettle, and we are hiding in a closet down the red hall. We need help. Sirens are going off everywhere. All the kings and other dignitaries are down the green hall."

"Did you see Chrissy?" Jason asked.

"What?"

"Chrissy!"

"No!" Tommy answered. "What is she doing in here?"

"She went in trying to help Nettle."

"Great. Now I have to rescue her, too?"

"You just worry about Nettle right now; we will get Chrissy. You must get out of the cave . . . now! You need to radio Sky on channel twenty-three and find the secret passageway in that closet down to the underground city and escape from there. It is too dangerous to go out into the cave now."

"Yes, sir, will do."

Tommy radioed Sky for help.

"Take the escape hatch under the rug," Sky radioed. "When you get into the underground city, go toward the sign that says, 'Gateway to Paradise.' It will be to your left. Head down that hall, and when you arrive there, radio me and I will lead you guys out." Tommy moved the shelving and lifted the rug. Nettle began waking up and was somewhat disoriented. She began to try and get up.

"Hey, sweetie, you were drugged and are still groggy. We are inside the cave and have to get out quick. You just hold my hand and follow me." Tommy grabbed Nettle's hand, and without saying a word, she followed him down a flight of stairs into the underground city. Her legs were still wobbly, but she was able to run. As they entered, their mouths hung open, and they could not believe their eyes. It looked like paradise.

"Shhh . . . " Nettle said. "Do you hear that? I hear someone yelling. Listen . . . it sounds like Chrissy. Come on. We have got to find her." They ran toward the screams. When they got very near—the screams were on the other side of a door—they raised their voices, just a bit, to try and communicate with her.

"Chrissy, it's Nettle. Where are you?"

"I'm in the apartment-looking room beside the huge tree." Tommy tried to open the door, but it was locked. He looked around and could not find anything to open the door with. He tried using his weight to break the door down, but it wasn't working.

"Tommy, we have the power to open this door." Tommy had never seen Nettle come across so intense and serious. She had definitely recovered from her sleep-induced state. She looked sternly at the lock with an authority he had never seen before and began to speak . . .

"Behold, I have been given dominion and power, over the fish of the sea, over the birds of the air, over the cattle and everything that creeps on the ground, so that means I have authority over the lock on this door. So in the name of the Commander of all hosts, the Giver of truth, my King, I command you, lock, to open." Nettle reached and turned the doorknob—and it opened. Chrissy was standing there in her burqa and grabbed Nettle, holding tight.

"What in the world do you have on?" Nettle asked.

"It doesn't matter. We can discuss that later," Tommy said. "Come on, we have got to get out of here now." As they ran toward the exit, they could hear voices approaching.

"We need to find a sign that says, 'Gateway to Paradise' in order to get out of here," Tommy said.

But it was too late; the voices were too close. They had to turn and start running back toward the city.

"Wait, stop. What are we doing?" Nettle said firmly. "Tommy, they can't see you, and I can put Chrissy on my back and fly to the very top of the rafters. You can just walk right by them, and we can leave once they are gone. Come on, let's go." Chrissy hopped on Nettle's back, and they flew up into the rafters. Tommy, invisible, turned around and ran back to see who was coming.

* * *

President Clemmons decided to step aside and order the rescue of Arlice and his boys now, since everyone was in the cave. He secretly radioed Max with the instructions to execute that plan.

Obeying the president's command, Max had his covert team storm the inside of the farmhouse. He and his first lieutenant, Brock, stayed outside in case of any other threats. Reaching the top of the stairs, the team spotted the creatures guarding the door. While radioing Max for new orders, Scientist Frank overheard them. Peering out his peephole, he released the creatures.

The unit opened fire, but the bullets were useless, seemingly repelling off the creatures. It was as if they were made of steel. With the push of a button, Scientist Frank released two more creatures that came from behind the men. They began pouncing all over the team, ripping and peeling skin off the men and eating them alive. It seemed as though the creatures were everywhere. Hearing the dreadful sounds, Max opened the back door and followed Brock in, dashing up the stairs. Horrified, he watched as a creature grabbed Brock and bit off his head. Max barely escaped. He made it into the woods. Confused about his orders, he decided not to radio the president. He was mortified at what he had just witnessed and wasn't sure, now, what the assignment had even been about. *What is this place?* He was aghast.

Arlice had covered his sons' ears; they could hear the ghastly sounds of the men being killed. Once all the men were dead, Scientist Frank directed the creatures back into the room so he and Hawk could head on down to the underground city. Immediately, Hawk walked out of Scientist Frank's room and opened Arlice's door in order to escort him and his children down to the underground city with them.

"I am truly sorry your kids had to hear that. Radicals came to rescue you, but to no avail," he said, a disturbing tone in his voice. All of a sudden, Jackson jumped up and flew toward Hawk, hitting him in the head with his feet so hard that it knocked him out completely. Scientist Frank took off running down the back steps and out the door.

Arlice was stunned. "Son, you can fly!" He grabbed Stephen, and they quickly started running in an attempt to escape.

"Once we are outside I want you to take Stephen and fly back to Tucson to safety. You hear me?"

"Yes, sir." They made it down to the bottom floor and out the back door.

"Dad, if Tommy and Nettle parked in the same place that we did last time we were here, then I know where they will be parked if they are still here. We are not too far from them. Let's try to get there first," Jackson shouted.

Arlice followed his son through the woods, praying for their safety the entire time.

* * *

King Darius had ordered a lockdown of the city. President Clemmons kept trying to reach his Special Forces group, but there was no answer. General Kerwin approached him to ask what he was doing.

"I can't get the Special Forces team I ordered here to answer." General Kerwin merely shrugged, as if to say he didn't know what was going on.

"Did you get Arlice and his children to safety yet?" Denise whispered in Paul's ear.

"I don't know. I sent the Special Forces team over to rescue them, but

I am not getting a response back at all. Even if they didn't get them out, I am sure they will be OK. They have food and water, and the guards will help them if they need anything." Denise frowned since she could not help but worry about the man who cured her. Her emotions finally got the best of her.

"What is going on here, Paul?" she yelled, hoping to get a straight answer this time. "What *is* this place?" General Kerwin stood there, waiting to see if he was finally going to tell her.

"Look, Denise, we think there are terrorists that might be trying to sabotage our mission."

"Your mission to take over the world?" she said so loudly that every-one could hear. King Darius walked over, and feigning politeness, told "Ambassador" Clemmons that he needed to take control of his wife.

"Excuse me?" Denise said, this time even louder. "No one controls anyone in America, not even my husband," she said, as she stared him down. Denise could see that all the others were now listening, and no one seemed to be standing up to this man, not even her husband. Dari-us rolled his eyes and slowly turned to walk inside the large conference room. Everyone followed.

"Look, Denise, everything is going to be OK. I promise," Paul Clem-mons said. "Come on, let's go sit down." She glanced over at General Kerwin with a conspiratorial look in her eyes. He knew he could not say a word or they might suspect him of something. As soon as they were seated, the door then opened and in walked Ransom. He gave a momentary look at the president and then walked up and whispered something to Darius. They both nonchalantly glanced over at President Clemmons; General Kerwin knew it was not a look of endearment.

Todd realized the mission was starting to unravel, and it had barely just begun. Somehow, he thought, he must dismiss himself and get a hold of General Howard. But first, he wanted to hear Darius's plans be-fore he made a move. King Darius motioned for everyone to be seated as Ransom approached the podium.

"We are under attack," Ransom said. "I have been knocked out twice, and both times I never saw the person. I had captured our enemy, Net-tle, and was about to take her in for questioning when I was hit again.

As I tried to get up, I saw her being carried away over an invisible person's shoulder. It was as if she was traveling in thin air." General Kerwin knew then that Nettle was, at least, out of their hands.

"Hawk has just informed me that our own Special Forces team attempted to rescue Arlice and his kids, whom we held hostage here at the farmhouse." Denise carefully turned her eyes over to Paul, who didn't flinch. She realized this action had now made Paul a huge target.

"Hawk reported to me that he was knocked out and that Arlice got away," Ransom continued. "I figure they are on the property somewhere. I am going to have Scientist Frank send the creatures out to kill them. I move that we should proceed with our plans immediately!"

"Wait a minute," Lulu Zuma said. "We must not rush into this if we don't know for sure we are under attack. From whom would this attack be coming?"

"She's correct," General O'Donnell of England said. "Do we know for sure we are being attacked? I haven't seen or heard anything except the alarms going off."

"If it is a bunch of young people like you think, Ransom, how in the world can they hurt us?" Colonel Zuma asked. "It's not like they have nuclear warheads or machine guns or anything of that sort. How would they even know about our mission anyway?"

It was then that Darius walked up to the podium next to Ransom.

"I have been informed by another that a group of radical students are on our property, and they are trying to gather information," Darius said. "It is my understanding they might be working for the United States government." At that point, everyone's focus was on the president and his chief of staff.

"This could possibly jeopardize our plans, so we have no choice but to move forward sooner than we originally scheduled," Darius went on.

"Do you really think these students are that dangerous?" Ambassador Dunn asked.

"All of this kind are dangerous," Darius quickly answered.

"That's right," King Salam of Iraq said as he stood to walk to the podium. King Alexander and King Otto also stood up and walked toward the podium to support Darius.

"Our fellow constituents, you must remember: they will never agree to our New Community. Since we all are here, we must take a vote now to move forward with our plans even sooner," King Otto said.

President Clemmons knew he had to speak up now and save himself.

"Look, I can personally assure you that these students, if they are seekers, are not part of the United States government at all. And Ransom, if you are talking about Arlice and his children, I ordered the Special Forces team to retrieve them because I was going to ask Arlice how he cured my wife, then thank him for doing so. As I recall, you are the one who took my wife to Arlice and allowed him to heal her in the first place."

"Is this true, Ransom?" Darius questioned.

"Yes, sir, it is. I knew he could do it, and I thought the president would be glad to have his wife well. I didn't think there would be any harm in doing so, sir."

"Oh Ransom, you poor, foolish American," Darius said as he carefully and skillfully pulled out a large knife. Without any hesitation, he grabbed Ransom and slit his throat. Denise screamed as she grabbed Paul's arm. The other kings moved back out of the way.

Officer Whitmore moved to the back of the room, now fully aware of just how dangerous this man was. Ransom fell to the ground, grabbing his throat, with a look of disbelief and utter horror on his face as he lay there bleeding to death, gurgling in his own blood.

*　*　*

"That can't be good," Nettle said upon hearing the scream. "I wonder if Tommy is OK in there." Nettle radioed General Howard and told him about the blood-curdling scream she had just heard. She informed him that she and Chrissy were together and that Tommy was in the room, invisible, listening to whatever was going on.

"We have researched Redimir, and we cannot find anything other than he is the son of a high-ranking military official in Russia," said General Howard. He graduated with top honors from his university. He has traveled to Syria and Iran quite frequently. But there are no ties to radical Islam that we can see."

"Well, he told Chrissy that she had to marry him, and then he made her dress in one of those Middle Eastern woman's outfits. It's pretty creepy."

"You must be very careful, Nettle," Howard said. "If things don't go as planned, tell Chrissy to go back and convince Redimir she was forced to go with you guys. Have her pretend she really desires to be with him. That way, maybe she can still help us . . . and live."

"OK, I will tell her."

"Oh, great. The last thing in the world I want to do is be slapped around by some psycho who plans on destroying the world," Chrissy said, tears springing in her eyes.

"Don't worry, Chrissy, we are not going to get caught." Nettle sought to reassure her best friend.

* * *

"Someone clean this mess up."

Detective Moll stepped forward to pull Ransom to the other side of the room while Gibbs went to get something to clean up the blood. By this time, Ransom was dead.

"I told you guys that he is crazy," Officer Whitmore said to his two partners in law enforcement and in this scheme. "We are in way over our heads and need to rethink this."

"Why would you think that?" Gibbs asked. "This is what we have all been waiting for, you idiot, and you better not mess it up for any of us, or it will be you whose throat gets slit." It was then that Officer Whitmore knew the power of Darius. He had convinced good people to follow him completely. He was beginning to realize that what his wife, Robin, told him was coming true. Was this the beginning of the end? *Dear God*, he thought, *please help me if it is.*

It was the first time Officer Whitmore had hoped there was a God.

CHAPTER 38

The Curse Unveiled

Officer Whitmore was beginning to rethink his decision of becoming involved with this New World regime. After cleaning up the mess, he walked over and sat down on the other side of Denise Clemmons; she and Paul were sitting by themselves toward the back of the room. Denise was still clutching Paul's arm and was very scared of what was about to go down. *How could Paul have been so deceived? Where had it all gone wrong? Was he that mesmerized by this corrupt establishment?* As she thought about this, she could not get her four daughters—Elizabeth, Alice, Lyla, and Trish—off of her mind. She knew she had to stand up for what was right, even if it cost her life. She could not deny the fact that she had just experienced a miracle. Was this the way her life was to end? Was this part of her ultimate plan?

She was Denise Clemmons, the wife of the president of the United States—a woman of great influence, with several degrees, and who had hobnobbed with the world's elite. But that was all so trivial now. How had she been so misled on how to spend life on earth? She was having a tremendous epiphany as her life flashed before her. She remembered the quote, "All the world's a stage." Well, the curtain was pulled back, and it was show time, and she was a very inexperienced actress now in what truly mattered. *How many people really know the truth? How many people even care to discover the real truth? Nettle and Chrissy are so young, yet they have journeyed to find it. If only I had paid attention to the signs I was given throughout my life.*

She had been more concerned about her own dreams and goals being fulfilled than with figuring out what she had been put on earth for. She never had a clue that she was supposed to ask what her assignment on this earth should be. She had always been taught that self matters first and to do whatever you have to in order to get what you want and to get ahead in life. *After all, the person that has the most toys wins . . . right?* But this is where it all had landed her: alone, scared, against all odds, and about to face the possibility of death in an entirely different way from what she had ever thought. What mattered most now wasn't what she owned.

Denise thought about her Jewish roots and the Catholic Church. What truths had she learned? She had never really read the ancient writings, so how could she possibly know the whole story? *This is not about a religion, for God's sake, it is about a relationship and a kingdom that has no end! If only people knew that Elyon has a specific purpose and job for each one of us . . . That he cares about each person individually. He has a specific assignment designed with supernatural gifts for every person on earth who walks in faith. He actually places part of himself within each of his followers when they choose to accept his kingdom. And while he rebukes those who act religious, he is all about love and relationship . . . not condemnation and judgment.*

Something inside Denise rose up like never before as she realized this unbelievable truth. Parakletos was imparting revelation directly into her. This was her assignment; this was her destiny! She began to get excited; she felt a rush of assurance in her heart. It is never too late to discover it, and it doesn't matter how bad someone has been in the past, or the things they have done wrong before. *I am going to make a difference, no matter what the cost.* Silently, she asked for more wisdom.

Glowing, she sat straight up. Paul looked over at her and saw this incredible radiance on her face.

"Are you OK?" he said.

"Yes, I am fine, and I hope you will be too, Paul." He wasn't sure what she meant by that, but Denise had realized that his liberation was up to him, and there was nothing she could do to change that—and for the first time in her life, she was fine with it.

Quietly, Officer Whitmore leaned over and whispered to Denise.

"If you want to get out of here, I will go with you."

What did that mean? Was this a ploy?

"These people are evil and we must get out of here before it's too late!"

Denise immediately got up and headed to the restroom. Tommy got up and followed her.

"Mrs. Clemmons?"

"Yes, sir?"

"Oh, I am not a sir. My name is Tommy Jones." Suddenly Tommy appeared to her.

"How did you do that?" she asked.

"It's a long story, but more importantly, we have to get you out of here now. Nettle and Chrissy are waiting on me to help you. I don't think this King Darius likes you very much, and I'm worried you might get killed. I know the way, so if you will, follow me, please."

"Wait . . . what about my husband? I think he might want to come too."

"I don't think we can risk it. Paul has made his decision, just like you."

"Well then, we have to get Officer Whitmore. He just told me he wants to come."

"OK, then, go back in and tell him, then you guys meet me at the sign that says 'Gateway to Paradise,' over to the left side of the main room, after General Salam's speech is over. That is the hall to the exit of the underground city. Oh, and by the way . . . General Kerwin is on our side. If the president really wants out, he will help him."

"We will be there. Or, at least, I will."

Denise went back and sat down to wait and hear what Salam was saying before she invited Officer Whitmore to go with her. Tommy, once again invisible, had followed her back in.

* * *

Redimir had gone to get Ruth and escorted her to the control room. He knew she was totally converted and was proof that his plan would work on these people.

"These plans look very good," he told her. "You have done well, and we appreciate all your hard work. I have made sure your position with me in the NGN will be one of great prominence."

"Thank you," Ruth said. "May I ask you a question?"

"Yes."

"Are you aware that there are people lurking around this place acting like they are guards, but are not?"

"What do you mean?" Redimir asked.

"Well, I had one of them come to my room earlier today to try to get information from me. I yelled, but no one seemed to hear me. I did not want to get too far from my room, so I went back."

"Was it a beautiful, blonde-haired girl?" he asked.

"No, it was a young man named Carver."

"Did you say Carver?"

"Yes, and he was dressed in army fatigues. He told me he was a seeker."

Redimir thought about Chrissy's attire. "They are a bunch of young idiots trying to find out what we are doing here. I plan on destroying them, so you don't have to worry about a thing."

"Oh, I see. Is everything still going to go as originally planned?" she inquired.

"You mean with President Clemmons?"

"Yes," she nodded.

"Of course," Redimir said, smiling cunningly. "Only it won't be tomorrow morning. It will be another time. Why do you ask?"

"Because Carver said you had changed your plans."

"I see," Redimir responded. "Well, you don't worry about Carver or the president; I will take care of that situation myself."

"I just hope you catch and destroy them all."

"We will, dear Ruth. We will."

* * *

King Salam from Iraq was encouraging the leaders on how they were eventually going to divide the nations up into ten kingdoms. Everyone was listening intently. It seemed that every time a new king spoke, the plans would change. King Salam informed them there would be a governor over each kingdom, but that King Darius would be the sovereign king over all ten kingdoms. This was very different from what they had been told before, but no one dared say a word against it. It was as if fear had struck all hearts.

Motionless, they were letting these kings usher in a totally different kingdom rule than originally planned.

Still invisible, Tommy walked right up to Darius and debated knocking the holy crud out of him right there, on the spot, but knew he couldn't. He watched as Darius began whispering into his radio. A few minutes later, in walked a debonair, blond-headed guy whom Tommy had never seen before. Maybe this was the Ransom that Josh was talking about. He walked up to where Darius was sitting and sat down next to him. King Salam continued his speech about the new "epicenter for social justice" and the infrastructure that would be needed and formed to create this massive transformation.

"We are at the beginning of a global shift," King Salam continued. "The world will never be the same again once we implement our plans. We must allow the devastations to take place first, and then the people will be more likely to follow our lead. This is a momentous moment in time, and you all should be proud of your involvement. This is an electrifying age for us, a world history-making event. But for those who are anti-government, it will be a chilling, galvanizing, and horrific time down the road. Those simple-minded, ignorant puppets . . . how misguided their spirits, and how poor their lives will become. But we will not let them know that at first. Our goal will only be peace. One can only hope they see the light at that point. But for you, and all the incumbents involved in the shift . . . it will be a transnational world, a world without borders or limitations. It will be a true global community." The group cheered and clapped as Salam roared forth his speech.

"Next, King Darius has a little surprise for you," he gleefully proclaimed.

King Darius turned and nodded at General Sahaad of Saudi Arabia. Immediately General Sahaad got up and walked out the door. Tommy was right behind him. He noticed General Sahaad was walking back to where the girls were hiding, so he followed him. Just as he got to where he knew Nettle and Chrissy were, Tommy quickly appeared—and then disappeared—so they could see that he was there.

"Did you see that? Tommy is behind that man," Chrissy whispered.

"Yes, I saw him," Nettle said. I wonder where he is going."

"Who knows?" Chrissy said. "But I bet it is not good."

Tommy followed Sahaad into a room filled with creatures. The general waltzed over and unlocked one of the creatures to take back with him. This was by far the ugliest and scariest-looking creature of them all. Tommy followed Sahaad as the general led the creature out into the main area. He decided to stay a good distance behind the general just in case the creature could smell his scent. He opened the conference room door, and Tommy followed him in again. As they entered the room, the creature let out a terrible roar, and everyone turned and gasped.

It was then that Darius motioned for Professor Redimir Bean to come up to the podium alongside him. Tommy watched as this handsome, stately, and sophisticated-looking man approached the podium.

CHAPTER 39

Global Community Arises

"Good evening to all of King Darius's constituents. My name is Redimir Bean. Some know me as Ransom." Everyone looked a little confused since they had never seen or met Redimir before. However, his good looks and presence were almost intimidating. He spoke with a slight accent; it was not easy to tell where he was really from.

"I am King Darius's assistant, and I want you all to know that today will mark the beginning of many miracles. They will be hidden until the proper time to reveal them. But today you will witness one. I will show you what I am talking about in a moment. But first, let me start by telling you that the people who seek to destroy us are not the true seekers of the world. The true seekers are each of you and the ones who support the global change and dogma—*which are one and the same*. The phonies are the deceived ones. Though they may have special powers, the real power of the 'True One' is much greater. Let me show you."

Redimir confidently walked over to Ransom's lifeless body on the floor. Then he effortlessly picked Ransom's corpse up in his arms. You could have heard a pin drop in the room as he stood there holding Ransom.

"What you are about to witness is only the beginning of things to come," he remarked proudly, effortlessly. He spoke as if it took no effort to hold up the body. Immediately, the side door opened, and there was Hawk, rolling in a bronze statue. For the first time, Tommy could see that it was a statue of Darius. They rolled it to the center of the room as General Sahaad walked the beastly creature alongside him.

"Hail to the anointed one," Redimir began to chant. While the others joined in, Denise observed that her husband of thirty-one years was chanting along with them.

The chant grew louder and louder; the room's atmosphere was filled with a wicked presence. Then Redimir slowly began raising Ransom's body over his head with a strength that was superhuman. It was as if Ransom weighed only ten pounds. The tension in the air was immense. Suddenly, what sounded like bongo drums began to play, but there was no one visibly playing them. Redimir began to chant.

"Oh, great and mighty one, allow his spirit to come back." Then Redimir slowly lowered Ransom down, and before their eyes, Ransom's spirit emanated back to life. The whole room was motionless. It had been at least a couple of hours since Ransom's death. Denise sat there, dumbfounded, and thought, *Wow, this is how they will be deceived. How do you compete with that?*

Chills ran down Tommy's spine as he watched in utter horror. All he could think was: *If this is a foreshadowing of what is to come, then there just might be a universal war.*

Redimir set Ransom down, and Ransom immediately fell on his face to worship him. Every single person in the room except Denise and Officer Whitmore bowed down to Redimir, King Darius, the statue, and the beast, worshiping them.

"Get up, Ransom, go and transgress no more," Redimir spoke, in an almost haunting tone.

"Thank you, oh thank you, my anointed one," spouted Ransom in nearly childlike tones. He went and sat down by Hawk and looked almost like a zombie—more zombie than human. The beast roared, and the room was filled with praises to the beginning stages of a new kingdom.

Denise knew this was the moment to get out of there.

"Do you want to come with me?" she hurriedly whispered to Officer Whitmore.

"Yes," he said.

"Then let's go," she said. Tommy quickly followed them out the door.

"Run this way," Tommy said, appearing right before their eyes.

It startled Whitmore.

"Just run," Denise said. "We will explain everything later."

As they entered the main area, Chrissy hopped on Nettle's back and they flew down, joining them. They feverishly ran to the area Sky had instructed them and spotted the sign that read: "Gateway to Paradise."

Jason, Stefan, and the others anxiously awaited the rescue.

"Whoa . . ." Josh said. "They are in trouble. There are four huge creatures lying down guarding the door, and Nettle and Chrissy are running right toward them. They have to turn back now!" he yelled at Jason. "They won't see them until they are right up on them. Stop them, Jason: tell them to stop!" Josh yelled. He was almost hysterical.

"Mayday, Nettle, mayday," Jason said, calling Nettle on the radio.

"Stop!" Nettle yelled loudly. Everyone stopped as she answered the radio.

* * *

Paul was looking for Denise but didn't see her anywhere; nor did he see Officer Whitmore. He knew in his heart she was trying to escape at that very moment. He hoped Darius wouldn't notice she was gone. He motioned for General Kerwin to come sit by him.

"Where is Denise?" the general whispered.

"I don't know," Paul answered. Just as Kerwin was about to ask another question, they were interrupted by Darius.

"I have been informed by security that somehow people have infiltrated our city, but do not worry, we will seize them. But because of this, I have given the orders for Redimir to proceed with the devastations within the next hour. We must move ahead in case any were able to escape and attempt to reveal our plans." Everyone looked a little confused, and General Kerwin looked around for Redimir but did not see him anywhere. He figured he was on his way to begin the process.

"Oh, great King Darius, I plead with you to hold off until we can reach our families again and update them," Tatsu Kan begged. "They think it is tomorrow."

"It is too late, Colonel Kan. The orders have already been given."

"But if there is no immediate threat, why can't we wait until tomorrow as planned?" Kan asked. General Kerwin knew he had to do something, so he quickly got up and left.

Once outside the room, he immediately transported himself to the nuclear arms room in the cave. But it appeared they had moved all the warheads and everything else out of the room. Kerwin knew King Darius was serious. He walked over to the room next door, only to find a beautiful young lady sitting at a desk.

"Excuse me, who are you?" he asked.

"I am Noel," she responded.

"What are you doing?" he asked, not at all sure who she was.

"I am waiting on my father to arrive," she answered.

General Kerwin knew he did not have much time, so he had to let this situation go.

"Well, stay put until he gets here, OK?"

"Yes, sir," she answered.

"Think," he said out loud to himself. *Where would they be?* He transported himself back to the city, right outside the Control Room. He slowly cracked open the door and could see Redimir and all the others looking at the devastation sites on a huge screen. He radioed Nettle.

"Hello," Nettle answered.

"Have you guys left the building yet?"

"No, sir, we can't. There are huge creatures blocking our way out. We are trying to figure out where to go."

"I need you guys to head to the apartment where they were keeping Chrissy earlier, and I will meet you there."

"What about Denise and Officer Whitmore? They are with us."

"Tell them to go back to the auditorium and wait it out; otherwise, they might be killed." Denise overheard and did not want to make that move, but the general insisted, so they agreed.

Denise and Whitmore were about to re-enter the conference room when Whitmore took off running. Denise yelled for him to come back, but he was adamant that he could not and continued to run.

King Darius noticed Denise entering the room but paid no attention to her. The president was relieved to see her but said nothing as she sat down on the other side of him. Denise remained silent, wondering what General Kerwin was planning to do.

Everyone made it to the room where Redimir had been holding Chrissy earlier.

"I only have a few minutes, but here is the plan," General Kerwin said. As soon as he began speaking, it felt as if the floor was starting to vibrate. The carpet shimmied like it was moving, so Tommy pulled out his gun and aimed it at where he thought the floor was about to explode. Then all of a sudden, from underneath, from a secret passageway in the floor, out popped Sky, along with Josh, Sam, Carver, Tay, Tenya, Cory, Jason, and Stefan. Stunned to see them, Tommy quickly helped them inside.

"What are you doing here, Sky?" General Kerwin asked, a bit surprised.

"General Howard's team transported me out by helicopter to help you guys escape. I know some other exits besides the ones I told you about, like this one. I created a couple of more just in case I ever was taken captive and needed to get out myself. I never told anyone about them, not even you guys. Come on, let's get you guys out of here," Sky said.

"We can't leave just yet," Kerwin told the group. "They just announced they are about to attack the whole world tonight, and we have to stop them."

"There is a guy here named Redimir with special powers too," Tommy said. "He literally raised Ransom from the dead after several hours of the guy being dead. I watched it with my own eyes. No telling what else he is capable of. He is as powerful as this King Darius, or maybe even more so."

"So, what's the plan?" Sky asked.

"I need Chrissy to find Redimir," General Kerwin said, looking at her as if she was their only hope at this moment. "You must tell him Nettle forced you to go with her but that you really want to be with him. I need you to convince him of your desire for him and spy out his plans. Make up some fake tactics of ours and reveal them to him to convince him you are truly on his side. You know where this escape tunnel is now, and no one knows of it except us, so use it if it gets too dangerous. I'm sure he will bring you back here later."

"Yes, sir," she said hesitantly. Nettle was worried about this plan. Chrissy was not as daring as she, and she didn't want her friend in this much danger. She would rather it be her.

"Put this in your ear," he said as he handed her a tiny earpiece, "and we can communicate together. Keep your burqa on and wrap your headpiece tightly so no one can see your earpiece."

"Yes, sir," she said.

"Redimir is in the control room getting ready to launch the missiles. Tommy, you follow her into the control room and get as much information as possible. Your job is also to protect her."

"Here are several mini radios I brought for you guys to use," Sky said.

"Fantastic," the general said as he took one from Sky and handed it to Tommy. "Be careful no one hears you talk on it."

"Yes, sir," he said.

"Nettle, I need for you to remain in the rafters and be there to help Chrissy and Denise in case they need you."

"Have you all discovered your special powers?" Kerwin asked.

"Yes, we have all received them," Josh informed him.

"I can walk through walls," Sam said.

"I can see through walls," Josh said.

"I have superhuman strength," Cory said.

"I have X-ray vision," Tenya said.

"I have supersonic hearing," Tay said.

"As you know, I can turn invisible," Tommy said.

"I can walk across water, through fire, or on thin ice," Carver said.

"I can control the weather," Chrissy said.

"Well, good, because I think Redimir is full of power," Kerwin said.

"OK, Josh, I need you and Sam to go and look through the walls of each room and find the missiles or nuclear warheads or anything else important. Sam can enter in and check them out and see if they are turned on to launch."

"General?" Sky interrupted. "I built two other secret exits as well. One is in the control room, and I put it there in case the president ever needed help getting out. It is behind the huge map of the world. You must speak a special code word for it to open, and it will lead you out, all the way underground, to the pond. The code word to open it is *cucumber*."

"Oh, nice one," Sam said.

"To close the door, you simply say, *close*. Both exits are sound-activated, so I had to select a password that no one would be using. The other exit is in a room they wanted me to build that has a jail cell. It is a secret room on the top floor. I built a passageway out, inside the wall. I placed jutted-out pieces of rock there so you could scale down inside the wall, and it takes you underground and out to the pond as well. I placed it inside the jail cell on the backside wall. I painted a mural of the sky with a rainbow, and at the bottom is a pot of gold. You knock on the pot of gold three times and it will open. There will be steps leading you down and out; you must be careful or else you could fall off the steps and get killed in that exit. To close it, you just say *close*."

"Great job," General Kerwin said. "Everyone clear on the exits now?"

"Yes, sir," they said, nodding.

"OK, now I want Stefan, Cory, Tay, and Tenya to go over to the farmhouse and see if Arlice, Jackson, and Stephen were extracted. If you find them, bring them back to this exit outside, and wait until you get further instructions. You must not get caught. Remember, there are still Special Forces guarding the farmhouse, I think. I want Jason, Sky, and Carver to go back outside and guard this secret entrance to this place and wait for further instructions. Jason, keep in touch with Stefan. If they have a problem at the farmhouse, go and help them. I will inform you of the disasters when I know more. Until then, be safe! Oh, and watch out for the creatures outside."

* * *

General Kerwin transported himself back to the hallway just outside the meeting room and then walked into the meeting again.

* * *

"OK, Chrissy, let's go," Tommy said.

"You guys please be careful," Nettle said.

Everyone left for their positions. Suddenly Nettle spotted Officer Whitmore being escorted by the two guards, Caleb and Kenneth. She watched as they led him up the stairs. *I bet they are taking him to the jail cell that Sky was talking about.* She watched until she could not see them anymore. A few minutes later, they came down without him.

Tommy followed Chrissy to the control room. Still dressed in the burqa, she knocked on the door. A woman dressed in a similar burqa opened the door.

"May I help you?" she asked.

"Is Professor Bean here?" Chrissy asked, taken back by her attire. The woman looked at Chrissy—intently into her eyes—as if to say, *Run. Get out of here.* She seemed full of fear, but Chrissy persisted. The woman shook her head and then allowed Chrissy to enter the control room. Tommy was invisible, right behind her. Chrissy instinctively looked for the world map, just in case she needed to escape. She was grateful that the two places she would probably end up in had escape passageways.

The other woman stayed far behind, curiously watching to see who Chrissy was.

CHAPTER 40

Deception

Redimir was working feverishly, almost in a trance-like state, to get everything ready for the attack. The room was buzzing around him as everyone prepared for an earth-shattering, catastrophic event. Chrissy slowly approached Redimir and gently touched his arm; he turned abruptly and slapped her across the face, nearly knocking her earpiece loose.

"What was that for?" she screamed. The whole room turned and looked. Tommy just about lost it but remained composed. Everyone in the place became extremely quiet.

"For trying to escape," he said.

"I am here, now, aren't I?" Chrissy said. "I didn't voluntarily leave. I was forced by the others. But I want to be with you; that is why I escaped them and came here." Chrissy was very convincing. Choosing to believe her, Redimir's whole countenance changed; the other woman just bowed her head in anguish at Chrissy's seemingly poor choice.

"You must sit down and be very quiet," he said to Chrissy. Tommy gently touched her arm.

Whew, she thought to herself. *Thank God he is here with me.*

"I know their plans," Chrissy said. That got Redimir's full attention.

"Proceed," he said.

"Their plan is to rescue the kidnapped students. That's all. But not today . . . later, so you have nothing to worry about right now," she said trying to find out if the students were there too.

"You mean the four high school girls?"

Chrissy immediately knew they had kidnapped them as well. "Yes. They don't care about the rest of everything going on here, whatever that is; they just want to rescue the students. I originally came to help. Then I met you, and for some reason that I am not even sure of, that all changed. The minute I looked into your . . . "

"Enough!" Redimir said. Chrissy stopped speaking, realizing he did not want what she was about to say said out loud.

"Well, they cannot have the seekers, can they, Ruth?" Redimir looked over toward his most transformed seeker.

"No, Professor, they cannot."

"Go make sure that Kaylee, Emery, Jean, and Allie are in their proper places. Now!" Redimir ordered. Ruth jumped up and went to check on the high school students.

"May I speak with you in private for a moment?" Chrissy asked. "Please?"

He looked around, and everyone was busy with their plans. *What are you doing, Chrissy?* Tommy thought. Redimir grabbed her hand and mostly dragged her to a small storage room. Tommy could not get in before they shut the door.

"Redimir," she said, as she took off her headscarf, totally forgetting about her earpiece, "I am crazy about you." As she was speaking, he grabbed her and kissed her so long and passionately that Chrissy was taken for a brief moment.

"Please believe me. I want to be with you and help you. I am not sure what you are doing, but I want to be by your side," she said. "Do you believe in love at first sight?"

As he looked at this beautiful, blonde American girl, the type that he had been taught all his life to detest, he could not help but long for her. He had never seen or been with a woman as alluring and beautiful as Chrissy. Her soft, tan skin, her deep blue eyes, and the way she expressed her desire for him made him want her even more.

"We will be married tomorrow, and then I will have my way with you," he said, nearly emotionless.

"'Way with me.' What does that mean?" Chrissy asked.

"We become one," he said.

"Who will marry us?"

"King Darius will. Now come, and I will show you what we are about to do."

"Wait!" she said, grabbing his arm. "Do you have other wives?" He hesitated for a moment, knowing it was not custom for that to happen in America.

"Yes, but none as beautiful as you, for you will bear my children and be the first in line to receive my riches and have my passions. I will tell you all my secrets tomorrow as you lie down with me."

"Is that one of them, the woman who let me in the door?" Chrissy asked.

Redimir was not used to a woman being as assertive as Chrissy. "Yes, that is Omar; she is the only wife here with me." *Oh Lord, what have I gotten myself into?* Chrissy thought. *I have to get out of here; this was not a good idea. I can't marry this evil man, and I sure can't sleep with him. Josh would never forgive me, and I would never forgive myself.*

"How many more wives do you have?" she questioned.

"I have two more—a total of three wives."

"Three!" Chrissy exclaimed.

Then Redimir pulled Chrissy close, put his mouth on her ear, and breathing very heavily, said, "I will fill your basket with grapes, and your cup with wine, and your mouth with pleasantries, and then you will be consumed with my love for you, and you will know that my heart burns with passion for you and you alone."

Chrissy had to focus her mind on the mission as his words dripped like honey into her ears, and her body *felt* his words. He was very convincing.

"Chrissy!" whispered General Howard rather loudly in her other ear. "I heard that. Is your headpiece still on?" Suddenly, Chrissy panicked. She quickly pulled away, making sure her long hair was over her ear and covering her earpiece. Redimir would kill her immediately if he knew she was working for the United States government. She had been caught up by his presence, his good looks, and his aggressiveness. *He is going to deceive the world,* she thought. *He is so evil, yet so debonair, smooth talking, and attractive; he almost had me spellbound.*

"Now put your headscarf back on and come with me," Redimir demanded. She obeyed rather quickly and sighed deeply as she followed him back into the control room.

Whew . . . that was close. She had forgotten about her earpiece. Tommy was glad to see she was OK. She sat down and listened to Redimir as he told everyone that they would launch the first three missiles at 2 a.m.

That is only a few hours away. Chrissy was furiously trying to figure out what she could do to stop him.

"We will fire three missiles every fifteen minutes from that point on," Redimir said coldly. "Our first three targets are China, India, and Russia. The next three are Iran, Pakistan, and Brazil. The next three are the Ethiopia, Japan, and England. Then we will hit Indonesia, Bangladesh, and Nigeria. The next targets are Greece, Germany, and France. Next will be Mexico, Egypt, and Turkey. The next will be Syria, the United States, and the Philippines. Then, our final target of the morning: *Israel.*" With that last one, there was more a ray of hope in his eyes than anything else. "Eventually, I will sit and rule my kingdom from there. In a matter of two hours' time, our world will no longer be separated."

Tommy touched Chrissy's arm as she held her breath, knowing that if she didn't escape, tomorrow she could be Mrs. Redimir Bean—or dead. Her stomach turned.

* * *

Stefan led Cory, Tay, and Tenya as they made it over to the farmhouse.

"Hey, where is the Special Forces team?" Tenya asked.

"Yeah," Tay said. "I don't see one of them."

Stefan ordered Cory to go over and kick in the back door. They went inside and up the stairs only to find no one there. Once Scientist Frank made it to the underground city, he was ordered by Redimir to go back and release the creatures outside of the compound. Captain Max was the only one who had escaped. He had run deep into woods, mystified by what was happening and hoping there were no creatures outside. Stefan, Cory, Tay, and Tenya searched the entire farmhouse—only to find no one there.

"Something's not right," Stefan said. "I just feel that things are not what they appear."

CHAPTER 41

The Situation Room

Darius announced that it was time for everyone to proceed to the Situation Room. The atmosphere was beyond tense, and no one dared say a word. These, the world's elite politicians, were about to emerge as transnational leaders. They had built a bridge to the future, and now they just had to make sure their execution was flawless. Stomachs were churning and nerves were on edge as they took their assigned seats in the Situation Room in the midst of the magnificent underground city.

Nettle quickly radioed General Howard, Stefan, and Jason to inform them of the transfer into the Situation Room. General Howard told her that Officers Holmes and Cothern had just arrived in the desert to help the team and had spotted Arlice, Jackson, and Stephen next to the Hummers.

"They are all heading your way and will meet you at the secret passageway to Redimir's apartment. Stephen is being brought back here. You need to know that Jackson can fly, just like you, so we allowed him to stay in order to help out with the mission. Can you make it over to Redimir's room to let them in?"

"Yes," she answered.

"We have equipped them with laser guns to kill any creatures that you might encounter. The lasers will kill them immediately."

* * *

After about an hour of searching the grounds, Josh and Sam finally found the missile room within the city. Josh peered in and could see the missiles, but not much else.

"I'm going in," Sam said. He walked right through the wall; out of nowhere, a giant flying dragon soared down from the ceiling and landed right in front of him.

"And just where did you come from?" Sam said out loud.

"Sam, get out of there now!" Josh yelled.

"I think I can take this thing."

"No, get out of there now, Sam!" The dragon opened its mouth and fire came out, nearly burning Sam before he skidded down onto the floor to avoid the flames.

"Whoa, dude," Sam said, as he decided, and rather quickly, that Josh was right. However, he wanted to try at least once to hurt the dragon. He pulled out his knife and threw it at the dragon's eye, piercing it perfectly. The dragon roared loudly, spinning around hysterically. Fire was going everywhere. It was out of control. Sam frantically went back through the wall.

"Dude, you're crazy!" Josh yelled as they started running back.

"Gotta' love it," Sam yelled back, his heart about pounding out of his chest.

"You are out of your mind, Sam," Josh declared. "Being a linebacker has messed with your brain!"

"It's what I live for, man. Love that adrenaline!"

Nettle had met the others, let them in Redimir's apartment, and told them to stay there while she went to find Josh and Sam. As she rounded the corner, she saw them running as fast as they could.

"What's wrong?" she asked. I was beginning to get worried about you guys."

"Sam tried to fight a fire-breathing dragon. He threw a knife and jabbed him in the eyeball, and the dragon started roaring and spinning around like a mad man. It was wild, and Sam's crazy!"

"Yeah, well, that will teach that dragon to mess with me again," he said proudly.

They headed back to Redimir's apartment to see if the others had made it there yet. They sat down to wait.

* * *

King Darius led all the world leaders into the Situation Room via the control room; all had been set up theater-style. Tommy followed close behind to determine the next move. Darius strode to the podium.

"I want to make it very clear that all of your families will be safe. As we proceed with the disasters tonight, you must be strong and concentrate on your future. This is what we have all been waiting for, my friends. You are about to enter into a world of tranquility, synchronization, and liberation." As he was speaking, his eyes seemed to turn an almost red-like color. It was the most peculiar thing Tommy had ever seen. He could sense this man's evilness as he stood there listening to him speak. There was a chill in the air, and Tommy felt as though his hairs were standing on end. The more Darius spoke, the more threatening he appeared. Tommy was desperately trying to devise a plan to stop this mad man and the catastrophic devastations from taking place. *Was this the beginning of the end?*

"You must understand that we have to proceed tonight with our agenda. From this point on, Redimir, my loyal assistant, will be my mouthpiece to the people. You can trust him completely, for he is a man of great prestige. You witnessed one miracle today, but you will see many more in the years to come. He is the great Imam Redimir, and he will show the world many signs and wonders to prove his holiness. Once the devastations are over, then Redimir and I will televise our New Global Community plans. Ambassador Clemmons and Ambassador Dunn will be alongside to assist us. I have chosen General Kerwin and Pope Constantine to assist the ayatollah and King Alexander in establishing the new ruling religious parliament, so once we have everything under control, these gentlemen will move forward in announcing to the world our new 'calculus of culture' in the sacred sector. We have it planned to implement in just three-and-a-half years."

Denise, a Roman Catholic by faith, cringed as she heard this news. *The Pope? How can this be? Have they deceived him, too? I must warn him.*

"In forty-eight hours, each of you will broadcast your extreme concern for our world. You will begin to set the stage for congruency. You will be televised from the room next door. Here are your speeches. Please use your great influence to reassure the people that everything will be all right and that all world leaders are connecting now better than ever." Darius began to pass out the speeches.

"How will we get the information to the news media if everything is going to be down, now that we have moved things up?" Lulu Zuma of Africa asked.

"Don't worry about that, my dear lady. We have already worked all that out."

Denise couldn't stand it any longer.

"Your plan will never work," she stood up and shouted. "The people will see right through it and know this is a political scheme."

"Denise, what are you doing?" her husband asked.

"I can't sit by and allow you all to do this. I don't concur, and I can't believe you all are allowing this power-hungry, ego-driven Hitler to sway you. Your eyes are blinded to the truth, and may God have mercy on your sightless souls."

Darius nodded at the two guards, Caleb and Kenneth, in the back of the room.

"My dear Denise, I am so sorry you feel this way, as we have no malevolent plans for our beautiful world. We only have plans that are true, plans that are noble and just, plans that are lovely and of good report. And if there is any virtue and if there is anything praiseworthy, it is our plans. Meditate on these things I am saying, and you will be spared."

"Spared!" she screamed. "And you think sparing me is noble, you insidious devil?"

"Denise!" Paul yelled. "For God sakes, stop!"

The guards grabbed Denise by the arm and pulled her away. Darius, waiting to see Paul's reaction, which would let him know of his loyalty, was glad to see that he did not make a move to help his wife.

Tommy was sweating by this point, trying to figure out whether he should follow Denise or not, hoping that Nettle would spot her from the rafters as she was escorted out. As he struggled to figure out what to do, the door opened and in walked Redimir, with Chrissy and his other wife right behind him.

Caleb and Kenneth escorted Denise into the main lobby and began moving toward the jail. As Nettle, Josh, and Sam were waiting on the others to arrive, Nettle peeked out the door and, luckily, spotted Denise. She quickly shut the door.

"Whew . . . that was close," she said, her heart skipping a beat. "They have Denise. Sam, will you follow them and find out where they are taking her?"

"No problem," he said.

"Please be careful, and don't get caught." Sam snuck out the door and quietly followed the guards with his gun in hand. He watched as they opened the door to the jail and took Denise inside. Sam waited for the guards to leave, then entered the room. Immediately, he spotted the mural escape hatch Sky had told them about. There sat Denise and Officer Whitmore inside the cell.

"Who are you?" Whitmore asked. "And how did you do that?"

"My name is Sam, sir."

"Let me guess. You are a seeker and that is one of your powers," Denise offered.

"Good guess, my lady," Sam said. "I am here to save you."

"Do you have a key to the cell?" Whitmore asked.

"No, sir, I don't have a key. I have better than that. There is an escape hatch right there beside you. It is very dangerous, so you must be careful." Sam explained how to proceed down the escape route and told Denise and Whitmore the location of the Hummers so they could wait there for help.

"Here is one of my guns in case you need it, and remember there are creatures around here that can kill you, so be very quiet and very careful when you get outside. Stay close to the road." Sam gave them very clear instructions as to where the Hummers were parked.

"We will, and don't worry. The First Lady is in good hands," Whitmore said.

"She better be, or later I will hunt you down and kill you," Sam, ever the wild man, said. Whitmore, looking a little perplexed at this, knocked on the pot of gold three times, and the door opened. He and Denise quickly crawled through to escape.

"Good-bye," Denise said to Sam. "Thanks so much, and we will see you soon." They closed the secret passageway door and Sam headed back to Redimir's room.

* * *

The others arrived, and Nettle quickly helped them up the hatch. She hugged Jackson tightly. She was glad there were more people to help.

"Nettle, did they tell you I can fly like you?"

"Yes, and that's awesome, Jackson, but you must be very careful. This place is very dangerous. We have to wait for our orders before we do anything."

"OK," Jackson said. "No problem." Nettle informed them that everyone had been escorted to the control room and that Tommy and Chrissy were both inside that room now.

"Chrissy has on a long, black burqa, so make sure you remember that," Nettle said.

"Do you think they know how many of us are here?" Tenya asked. "Surely they can see us on their monitors."

"General Kerwin told me this is the only room not seen on the monitors," Nettle said. "It is Redimir's private apartment. That is why we meet here. He also radioed me on our way over here and told me a kidnapped man named Dan found a way through their radio system to get a hold of him. They are in contact now. Dan told him there are eight more seekers assigned with him in the monitor room who are not brainwashed. Their names are George, Karen, Don, Brianna, Bethe, Donna, Kris, and Lexi. We must try and save them, too. They are taking shifts, and Dan is not reporting that you guys are here except for me, Chrissy, and Carver, whom they already know about."

"Great, we can now move around freely," Tenya said.

Suddenly, Sam appeared as he walked through the wall. "Hey guys, Whitmore and Denise are headed toward the Hummers to wait on help. They are safe, so you need to call someone to pick them up."

Jason immediately radioed General Howard to let him know so he could get someone out to retrieve them. He informed Howard that he believed they should make their move now.

He told him all the government officials were in one room and that they needed to strike right away.

CHAPTER 42

The Exit

Denise and Officer Whitmore made it safely down to the pond without sounding off any alarms. They scanned the place, and it looked clear, so they took off running toward the Hummers through the edge of the woods. Just as they were nearing their destination, a giant, four-headed creature jumped in front of them. Denise screamed hysterically. Its heads were bobbling profusely. Whitmore began shooting at each one.

"Run, Denise," he yelled, hoping she could escape. She didn't want to leave Whitmore, but knew if she stayed, they might both be killed. He fired several shots at the creature, which only seemed to irritate it. Suddenly, another creature appeared out of nowhere, and this one had huge, fang-like teeth. Whitmore realized that he was in great danger, so he began to pray out loud for help. He prayed for strength, knowing he was about to die, since he only had a few more bullets. Suddenly, out of nowhere, a strange high-pitched sound began to resonate. Both creatures acted as though the deafening sound had taken control of them. They began to swing their heads around and around, giving Whitmore time to run away. As soon as he was out of sight, he began calling for Denise.

"Over here," he heard a voice yell. Max jumped down out of a tree just as Denise appeared from behind it. "Come on," Max said, and they all ran toward the Hummers.

"Oh my gosh. You had a miracle," Denise said to Whitmore.

"Who are you?" Max asked.

"I am Officer Whitmore, the deputy chief of police for Tucson."

"I am Special Forces Captain Max Brown. The president called me in for help. My whole team was killed by those awful creatures. What is happening here?"

Before Whitmore could answer, a helicopter arrived and was so loud he couldn't talk. They all hopped in and were swept away by a very different-looking gentleman.

"What's going on here?" Max asked again.

"You will soon see," said the strange-looking man.

"Who are you, sir?" Max asked.

"I am the chief of mission, and you have now entered a war zone in which Operation Seeker is in place. You must tell no one of anything you saw here today, is that understood?"

"Yes, sir," Max said, feeling compelled to salute.

* * *

Arriving back at headquarters, everyone applauded as the First Lady entered the room. General Howard escorted her, Whitmore, and Max into the conference room for questioning. Officer Whitmore went first and shared all he could about the hideous plans. He informed them of the devastations that would be taking place in a very short time. He was extremely remorseful for what he had done and wanted to help as much as he could. He asked if he could speak to his wife, Robin. He just wanted to hear her voice.

Denise relayed all that she had witnessed. She kept her composure as she spoke of her husband's loyalty to Darius. She had no choice. She had a duty to protect her country. She confirmed everything that Whitmore had conveyed. General Howard was most impressed at the First Lady's character and fortitude. She deserved a medal of honor in his book.

Next, they brought in Max, who had not been warned about the creatures. He told them all he saw and what orders had been given.

* * *

Back in the Situation Room, Redimir was now seated in the front row, waiting to speak as King Darius was still addressing the group. It was 1:45 a.m.—only fifteen minutes until the first missile launch. Tommy, noticing the time, knew he only had a few moments to strike. He had heard that the devastations would start at 2 a.m. and that the United States would be hit shortly after. He walked up to Chrissy and whispered for her to go to the restroom so he could follow her and get out of the Situation Room and into the Control Room. She agreed.

King Darius motioned for Redimir to come forward and update the group. As he was walking to the podium, Chrissy headed for the door.

"My darling, where do you think you are going?" Redimir quickly asked. But Chrissy kept walking. She reached to open the door, and then turned to face him.

"I am going to the bathroom, my dear sir."

"You must wait for a few minutes; I have something very special to show you right now."

Tommy slipped through the door as Chrissy stopped and turned around. She stood against the wall by the door as Redimir glared a hole right through her. Getting back on track, Redimir directed them all to the screen.

"As you can see on the screen, we have China, India, and Russia lit up. In exactly twelve minutes we will launch our first missiles. On the screen to your right, you will be able to see the local television stations broadcasting the catastrophes live." Chrissy could not believe her eyes. As chilling as it was, there was something inside her that left her with a strong will to fight this man. She was hoping that Tommy had a plan. She was ready to help in any way she could.

Nettle and the entire group had made it to the Control Room. Josh peered inside and reported that nearly everyone was sitting at their posts with their backs to them.

"It looks extremely quiet in there," Josh said. "No one is moving around, and I am afraid that is a bad sign. Sam, I think you can walk through the wall right now and open the door for us, because no one is looking in this direction. I don't see Redimir, Chrissy, or any of the kings. Something just doesn't look right. I see what looks like several pictures of three countries on the big screen. It looks like Russia, China, and India are lit up on the map."

"I bet those are the first few countries they are going to hit," Nettle said. "We have got to stop them."

"OK, I'm going through," Sam said. He walked through and no one noticed him except Tommy.

"Great, no one saw him," Josh informed the others.

"Sam, it's me, Tommy. You duck down and I will open the door. We have exactly six minutes until they launch the first missiles." Tommy quietly opened the door for the group to enter.

The instructions were to take over.

Quietly, they all snuck in. Tommy watched as each person walked silently to his or her position. Jason, Stefan, Sky, officers Holmes and Cothern, Carver, and Sam bravely positioned themselves around each side of the room. The others—Arlice, Jackson, Nettle, Josh, Tenya, Tay, and Cory—remained on the floor in the back.

They were prepared for the showdown.

"Everyone please put your hands up now!" Jason shouted. As heads turned around to see what was happening, Tommy was scurrying around, trying to find which person was controlling the nukes. Suddenly, bullets started flying.

"I'm crawling over to that door to see what's behind it," Josh said to Arlice. As he opened the door, Chrissy was standing right there.

"Josh?" she said.

He looked up at her frantically. "Come with me now!" he whispered rather loudly, trying to grab her hand. Chrissy immediately looked over at Redimir. Everyone could hear the noise coming from the other room.

"I can't," she said, closing the door in his face.

Redimir watched her slam the door shut.

"In exactly two minutes, our world will change forever," Redimir announced. He was practically glowing.

From the sounds of gunfire on the other side of the wall, General Kerwin realized the group was inside and engaged.

"Was that gunfire?" Ambassador Dunn asked. The room they were in was soundproof, and you could not hear anything except what was heard when Josh opened the door.

King Darius jumped up to speak.

"My fellow constituents, do not worry. Everything is under control." He ordered Redimir to go next door and check it out. The gunfire had stopped as Josh crawled back over to the others. Redimir opened the door and could see a few of his men down and others with their hands up in the surrender position. Instantly, Redimir pushed the release button to the hidden cages inside the control room and released three huge creatures. As the cage doors opened and the creatures came into the room, Jason yelled out new orders.

"Kill the suckers!"

As gunfire was blazing, Redimir made his way over to the main control panel and launched the first three missiles. Tommy saw him and tried to get to him, but it was too late. The place was in turmoil; the creatures were extremely difficult to kill, even with laser guns. One creature grabbed Carver and threw him across the room, breaking a few of his ribs. Jason summoned the rest of the team to fight. Josh made his way over to Nettle, Arlice, and Jackson.

"You three get out of here, now!"

"No," Nettle said. "Come on, Jackson: we can fly over these creatures' heads and distract them while the others shoot them."

She and Jackson took off and started soaring around the creatures' heads and pounding them in the eyes. Stefan was able to take the first one down. Tay made it over to Carver to see if he was all right, then helped him up. Tommy grabbed Redimir and threw him to the floor, all the while anxiously trying to figure out how to stop the missiles. Redimir rose and set off the alarm, summoning more people to come and assist. Tommy, still invisible, hit Redimir again as Josh and Sky showed up to help.

"Let me have him!" Sky yelled. As Redimir stood up and turned around to face Sky, his appearance changed so freakishly, so drastically, that even Sky backed off. He suddenly knew that everything the general and Ollie had talked to him about was true. There was another world.

Josh stood there frozen as Redimir approached him, thinking about the danger Chrissy was in by being associated with this evil character.

"Get out of here, man," Sky shouted to Josh. Tommy yelled at him too. Josh had heard of some strange, spiritual things before, but never anything this wicked. All of a sudden, the room began to fill with the most ghastly yellow smoke and the most repulsive smell one could imagine. Tommy pulled Josh's arm, urging him to run so they could get out.

"Abort Operation Seeker, abort now!" Jason screamed.

The Control Room crew put on their gas masks for protection while all the others were gasping for air as they tried to get out. Immediately, the doors were locked from the inside, and only a few of them made it out.

Those who remained began to pass out from the gas.

CHAPTER 43

Missiles Launched

The first low-yield missiles had been launched. Each soared over the earth and spiraled toward its target, prepared by their makers to cause havoc in India, Russia, and China. The low-kiloton usage would do the damage needed without annihilating the whole population. It would cause severe climatic changes, but the evil men concluded that it was the price to be paid for ultimate control. All the kings, generals, and colonels watched as China, India, and Russia were hit. The large mushroom cloud emitted devastating radiation. Smoke, debris, and fire were everywhere.

Oh dear Lord, General Kerwin thought. *I have got to stop this before the next few countries are hit.* He transported himself into the control room and suddenly realized he couldn't see anything because of the yellow smoke.

Immediately, he transported himself again, this time to Redimir's room, hoping someone was there to give him some answers. No one was there. *Where are they?* Kerwin went back to the Control Room, holding his breath, and saw several people lying on the floor. He spotted two creatures lying dead and one being put back inside a chamber. Redimir was typing feverishly on a control panel. He launched the next three missiles to Indonesia, Brazil, and Pakistan. General Kerwin transported himself to the Weapons Room, pulled out several gas masks, took one for himself, and dropped the others off in Redimir's apartment for the others. He immediately transported himself back to the Control Room, walking directly over to Redimir.

"Can I help you?" he asked.

As Redimir slowly turned, his eyes were a bright, glowing red, and his face looked like bronze. His eyebrows were tilted upward, and his tongue slithered in and out of his mouth like a snake. His ears became almost pointed, and his forehead protruded. General Kerwin could see the demons in him, but he was not at all afraid.

"What are you doing out here?" Redimir asked.

"I just came to see what all the commotion was, and to ask if I could help."

"Where is everyone else?" Redimir asked.

"Still in the Situation Room," Kerwin answered.

"I am about to launch all the missiles at once," Redimir said. "I need you to leave. Go back with the others and tell them my plan."

"I can't do that," Kerwin quickly answered.

Redimir turned to strike Kerwin. Just as he lifted his arm to strike, the general disappeared. Redimir turned back around and hit the launch button to release the next six missiles. He launched the strikes on Iran, Pakistan, Brazil, Ethiopia, Japan, and England. He subsequently began to queue the next three to launch on Indonesia, Bangladesh, and Nigeria.

All those in the Situation Room, including Chrissy, knew something had gone wrong, since they saw six missiles being launched, instead of three, in less than the fifteen minutes as planned. No one dared to move, not even Darius. The president noticed that General Kerwin was gone again and now suspected that Todd was not on his side. His best friend, closest confidant, and most loyal advisor had betrayed him, just as his wife had. This infuriated the president, so he stood up.

"Long live King Darius and his notorious brotherhood," Paul Clemmons chanted. It was apparent at that moment that demons were entering his soul.

* * *

The news media from Russia were the first to report the attack. The kings, generals, and colonels watched as the horrified media tried to figure out what was happening. It was 9/11 all over the world, now. The chaos was rampant as the reporters went on to announce that many small cities were utterly destroyed. They were burning with fire, and hardly anything was left of them. The Situation Room was silent as they watched the bombs explode in parts of Iran, Pakistan, and Brazil . . . then Ethiopia, Japan, and England. No one dared move or speak; they just watched in silence and utter shock while pockets of their countries and people were being destroyed. Next hit were Indonesia, Bangladesh, and Nigeria. Hysteria could not even begin to describe the world picture at this point.

Nettle, Tommy, Josh, Jackson, Arlice, Carver, Sam, and Sky made it safely back to Redimir's apartment. Carver was in excruciating pain from his broken ribs, but luckily, he was the only one hurt. General Kerwin had transported himself back to Redimir's apartment to find them all gathered inside.

"Where are the others?" he asked.

"They didn't make it out," Sam reported. "They locked the doors right after these guys got out, and I was able to go through the wall."

"So, who got left behind?" Kerwin asked.

"Jason, Stefan, Tenya, Cory, Tay, officers Holmes and Cothern. The gas got them and they passed out," Sam said, stunned.

"And Chrissy is also still in there," Josh said. "I tried to get her to come, but she just shut the door in my face."

"She must know something," Kerwin said. "We have to act fast since we don't have much time. The gas won't kill you; it will just make you pass out, and then sick to your stomach when you wake up. I was able to get four gas masks, so I want Sam, Tommy, and Josh to put them on and come with me. The rest of you get out of here now—and that's an order. Nettle, you radio General Howard and tell him what is happening, and then take the Hummer and get out of here. Here are the keys. Have the general send two more vehicles and park them so that we will all have a way out later. Now, go!"

Nettle, Jackson, Arlice, Carver, and Sky headed out the escape hatch.

"This is not good," Nettle said. "This was not supposed to happen."

"Well, there is a reason. We just have to trust," Arlice said. "We just need to focus on getting back to get help. They began running down the main road to avoid any creatures in the woods.

* * *

General Kerwin, Tommy, Josh, and Sam headed back to the Control Room to rescue the others.

"When we get back up to the Control Room, Josh, you look in and tell us what you see going on. Sam you go in first and open the door for us."

"Yes, sir," Sam said.

"Tommy, since you are invisible, I need you to come with me over to Redimir and take him out. Can you do that, son?"

"Yes, sir, not a problem," Tommy said, his heart pounding.

"Sam, you and Josh head straight for the Situation Room and grab Chrissy. If you have to shoot someone in self-defense, then do it. Just get her out! Got that?"

"Yes, sir!"

"If the doors are still on lockdown, they won't open. If that's the case, then Sam, it will be just you and me. I will transport in right after you. I will go after Redimir, and you go after Chrissy."

"Yes, sir," Sam said.

"Our main objective is to stop Redimir from launching any more missiles."

Carefully approaching the Control Room, they saw that it was clear to proceed. Josh peered inside and reported that everything looked normal again. No one was lying on the floor, and the smoke was gone.

"I don't see our guys at all, or any creatures for that matter," Josh reported.

"Well, keep your gas masks on anyway, just in case," General Kerwin said.

"Oh, I see Redimir now. He is looking up at the giant screen," Josh said. "Everyone else's back is to us, so I think if Sam goes in now, it will be OK."

Sam walked through the wall. General Kerwin quickly transported himself inside. As Josh watched, he told Tommy, "So far, so good." Sam tried to open the door, but it was locked. He shook his head no, so Josh and Tommy knew they were not getting in. Josh watched and relayed everything to Tommy. He kept an eye on Sam as he approached the Situation Room. General Kerwin advanced toward Redimir.

Once Sam entered the situation room, Josh couldn't see him anymore. For some reason, he could not see inside the Situation Room at all. *They must have some special coating on the walls or something,* he thought. The instant Sam walked in, several guns were cocked and pointed in his direction. He knew that if he turned around to flee he wouldn't have time to get through the wall before being shot. Slowly and carefully, he held up his hands in the surrender position.

Kerwin quietly made his way over to Redimir. Steady and cautiously, he reached for his gun, when . . . a huge **crack**! Someone had shot Kerwin from behind.

"Oh my God," Josh said, panicking. "General Kerwin just got shot. The guy sitting down at the desk right behind Redimir pulled out a gun and shot him in the back."

"Is he OK? Who was the guy?" Tommy asked, aghast.

"I don't know. He hasn't turned around." All of a sudden Josh's face displayed the most repugnant look.

"Oh my God, it was President Clemmons. He shot the general. We have got to get Sam and Chrissy and get out of here now!"

Josh looked scared, as everything was starting to unravel.

* * *

"Welcome, big boy, why don't you come over here with all of your friends?" Ransom said to Sam. At the click of a button, the wall in the back of the Situation Room became invisible. Sam saw the other half of his team in a small jail-like room with bars. A few of them were still passed out on the floor. He waved at them, but they just sat there, mouths open, in dismay and disbelief.

"Why don't you have a seat right here by me," Ransom said as he patted the seat. "You and I can watch our world become one." Sam cautiously sat down, and for the first time in his life, was speechless. With a gun pointed directly at his head, Sam hoped that General Kerwin would be bolting through the door soon. If not, then what would their fate be? Sam knew he had to think of something even if it cost him his life. His gun was strapped to his ankle, but he had to choose the right time to use it. He was ready to massacre them all.

"Maybe we can use you as an example to the world of what not to do," Ransom said, as he motioned for Colonel Chatel of France to come forward.

"What's that supposed to mean?" Sam asked.

"That means you made a huge mistake, boy, coming in here like this."

"My name is Sam, and you don't know who you're messing with."

"Yes, yes, I am so afraid. I can't stand it right now," Ransom uttered pompously.

Sam looked around the room into each of their eyes. Glancing around at each of them, he caught Lulu Zuma secretly winking at him. *What was that?* Sam thought. *Was that a signal that she might help me? He wasn't sure, but maybe, just maybe, she was on his side.* As he turned to look behind him, he noticed the two women standing in the back of the room. One of them must be Chrissy. *OK, I have to think. How do we get out of this?*

Suddenly, right before his eyes, he watched the screen; it was showing six more missiles heading for their targets. The countries lit up . . . Greece, Germany, France, Mexico, Egypt, and Turkey.

You could cut the tension in the room with a knife. The devastation of this evil agenda was so evident to anyone who was decent, even cocky Sam.

"Keep your eyes on the screen," Ransom demanded. Sam watched as the final missiles were launched at Syria, the Philippines, and the United States of America. The people clapped and cheered. Everyone watched as Darius strutted to the front of the room.

"Perfect . . . things are perfect," he bellowed with glee. "Redimir, along with Ambassador Clemmons, has done an excellent job at keeping the enemy at bay. General Todd Kerwin will no longer be working with us!" Darius exclaimed. No one dared ask what happened, but all assumed General Kerwin was now dead. Sam concluded that with General Kerwin out of the picture, their lives were in grave danger. He watched the world burning and began to feel sick to his stomach. Until now, Sam had more or less looked at this as an amusing game. Now, everything had changed. He realized for the first time that he would be the one they would use to torture as an example to everyone else.

At Ransom's prompting, Peter Chatel hit Sam violently on the head with the butt of his handgun.

Sam tried hard not to flinch, but it almost knocked him out. He remained calm.

"If you try and do anything, there will be more where that came from, big man. You understand?"

Sam just nodded.

* * *

"I don't see Sam coming back out, and we can't get in. What should we do now?" Josh asked Tommy.

"I think we should leave and go get more help. General Kerwin is probably dead, and we need to touch base with General Howard," Tommy answered with obvious reservation.

"But what about Sam and Chrissy and all the others?" Josh asked.

"I don't know, man, they could be dead too, and I'm afraid if you and I stay around any longer, we might be next. We can't get in anyway. I think we need to go get help," Tommy insisted.

"OK, let's go," Josh said.

"Wait, I have another idea. Why don't we do this?" Tommy said. "You go get help, and I will stay, remaining invisible, to see what else I can find out. They will never know I am here, and maybe I can help out in some way until you get back with assistance. Go back to Redimir's room and get out of here."

CHAPTER 44

The Power of One

Josh headed back toward Redimir's room, removed his gas mask, and carefully opened the door to make sure no one was inside. The place looked clear. Approaching the escape hatch, he bent down to remove the rug. Suddenly, someone grabbed him from behind, placing a chemical-filled rag over his nose and mouth, causing him to pass out.

Meanwhile, Ransom had grabbed Sam's arm, pulling him over to the jail. Opening the door, he pushed him inside. Chrissy stood watching. *Oh God,* she thought. *They have caught nearly everyone. What in the world am I going to do?*

"Are you OK, man?" Jason asked Sam as he was dumped inside.

"Yes, I'm OK, but they shot General Kerwin," he whispered.

"Where are the others?" Jason whispered back.

"Tommy and Josh are still outside the Control Room waiting to get in." Instantly, a loud, unexpected noise caused them all to look. Hans, a government aide, threw Josh inside the jail cell on the floor. Chrissy nearly screamed, but contained herself as she saw Josh fall to the ground. He was out cold. Jason and Sam rushed over to make sure he was still alive.

"He's OK," Jason whispered. "He is still breathing."

Sam held his thumb up for Chrissy to see, so she would understand that he was still alive.

Sam whispered, "I know that Nettle, Arlice, Sky, Carver, and Jackson got out. Tommy is probably our only hope right now because he is invisible." As they were talking, they noticed another huge screen being lowered. Everyone became quiet as all attention was focused on the new screen. It was showing . . . the United States of America.

"I'm outta here while they're not looking," Sam said. "I'm going through this back wall to get help."

"Be careful. These guys are everywhere," Jason said.

"I'll be back with ammunition," Sam said as he easily slipped through the wall, heading for Redimir's room.

* * *

Tommy was waiting for something to happen when a beautiful Chinese girl walked up to the Control Room door, punched in a code, and opened it. Tommy slipped right in behind her. He watched as she proceeded to go inside the Situation Room. *Who was that?* A huge picture of Israel was now up on the main screen. The United States was on the other big screen. He knew his country was about to be hit. Searching for General Kerwin, he spotted him lying on the floor. Tommy began to take his pulse. He was still alive. Tommy wasn't sure how much longer he would survive since he was losing a great deal of blood. He whispered in the general's ear. General Kerwin barely opened his eyes; he was going in and out of consciousness.

"General, it's Tommy. Can you transport yourself to Redimir's room? I can meet you there and get you out of here." General Kerwin barely shook his head yes, and instantly, he was gone. Tommy jumped up and headed for the exit door when he saw Redimir walk out. *Oh crap*, he thought. *I hope he is not going to his apartment.*

Tommy walked out behind him and followed him. Sure enough, he was headed in that direction. Tommy knew he had to do something fast. In his quick attempt to shoot Redimir, Tommy tripped and stumbled, shooting him in the leg, instead of his back. Redimir went down;

Tommy ran up to him to finish him off when Redimir's blood emitted a fume so putrid, Tommy had to move away. He could barely breathe. He took off for the apartment and locked the door. He turned around, and there was Sam, picking up General Kerwin to get him out of there. Tommy appeared to them both.

"He can't transport anymore; he is too weak," Sam said. "Come on man, we have got to get out of here."

"Where is Josh?" Tommy asked.

"They got him," Sam said.

"What!?" he cried out. "Then you go, Sam, and take General Kerwin and get him to safety. Here are the keys. Since I am invisible, I'm going to stay here and see if I can find the others and help them escape. If you see they sent other vehicles for our rescue, then leave my keys under the driver's seat floor mat."

"OK, dude, they are all inside the Situation Room in a small jail."

"OK. Thanks, man." Sam picked up General Kerwin and carried him out through the tunnel. When Sam got outside, he radioed General Howard on General Kerwin's radio.

"Mayday, mayday, this is Sam. I have General Kerwin, and he has been shot."

"Get him to the Hummer. There is help waiting." Sam knew it would be a long haul but remained hopeful as he carried General Kerwin across his shoulders.

Redimir dragged himself to his apartment and called for help. Tommy sat invisible, watching to see what he was going to do. The stench had gone. Immediately, Dr. Shinall came in to work on his leg.

"I called you here for a reason," Redimir told the doctor. "Stand back," he said as he got an amazingly wild look in his eyes. Placing his hand into his own leg, he pulled out the bullet. Then he touched the wound again and healed it instantly. Dr. Shinall was dumbfounded, and at once, bowed his knee to Redimir. Tommy could not believe his eyes. *Who is this guy that he can heal himself?* And then Redimir became extremely angered.

Staring at Dr. Shinall, he shouted, "From this point on, the seekers are as much a target as the Jews in Israel. I will call this 'Operation

Annihilation,'" he said quite sadistically. Dr. Shinall dismissed himself, speechless at what he had just witnessed. He headed back to the hospital to inform Wendy, his head nurse, about this unbelievable incident.

Redimir, without delay, got up and walked back to the Control Room and pushed the door to the Situation Room wide open. Tommy followed close behind. Everyone stood and cheered. Redimir paid no attention to their applause. He walked straight to the jail, unlocked the door, and stood with his face as cold as stone.

"Who wants to die first?" he demanded.

Lulu Zuma quickly petitioned King Darius. "Sir, most of them are just young people. Let's just keep them locked up," she pleaded.

Chrissy panicked. Walking directly over to Redimir, she whispered in his ear.

"No!" he yelled. "One must die, and now you will do it," he said as he grabbed her, forcing her inside the jail.

"I will not allow a bunch of stupid youth to interrupt King Darius's plans without payback." Seeing this, Tommy, still invisible, rushed over to Redimir and struck a blow to his face. Redimir let go of Chrissy and fell back, grabbing Tenya as he fell. Gaining his balance, he swiftly pulled Tenya closer. Taking out his knife, he held it to Tenya's throat.

"I don't know what that was, but I can assure you I will find out!" he yelled. Everyone watched in stunned terror.

"Wait!" Chrissy screamed, overwhelmed at all that was unfolding.

"I will tell you all their plans if you will just let them all live," she declared. "I love you and want to be with you, but they are my friends. They don't even know what all is going on here." Everyone's eyes were now on Chrissy. King Darius was waiting to see if Redimir would listen to the woman.

"Oh, you foolish woman; you just killed your friend, and maybe yourself," Redimir said. With that, he pushed Tenya back and pulled out his gun to shoot him.

"Wait!" a voice screamed. "Please allow me to shoot this man."

Redimir turned to see a striking young Chinese woman plead to assist him.

"General Zhoo, is this the daughter you were telling me about?" King

Darius asked.

"Yes, my king."

Noel slowly walked over to Redimir with an enticing, sexy look on her face. Her tight black leather pants gave off an even more villainous air. Seductively, she took the gun from his hand and pointed directly at Tenya and fired. But Jason had calculated the move and leaped in front of Tenya to take the bullet. He fell to the floor, face down. The whole room exploded.

Redimir was enthralled by Noel's courage and immediately wanted to know her better. In the minds of all these world leaders, Noel would now be heralded as a hero since she had killed one of the so-called "terrorists." Only Colonel Zuma and Ambassador Dunn remained silent.

"That was your fault," Redimir said, glaring at Chrissy. She began to cry as she ran to the back of the room. Redimir's wife tried to console her. Jason was down. Josh, upon rising, tried to get Chrissy's attention, but she was too upset to even notice him. Then, instantaneously, the jail became invisible again by the wall.

Focusing everyone's attention back on the huge screen, Darius stood to speak. "Soon the whole world will be in the palm of our hands."

"Hail, King Dairus; Hail, Redimir," the others started chanting.

"Go now, and get some rest," Darius instructed the others. "Tomorrow we will announce the new cataclysmic evolution . . . our transition to a better world, our New Global Neighborhood."

Everyone left the Situation Room except Darius, Redimir, Omar, General Zhoo, Noel, and Chrissy.

As Redimir approached Chrissy, her heart was beating furiously. Trembling with fear, she decided to question his authority again.

"Why did you let her do that? You killed an innocent man."

Paying no attention to her question or her emotional state, he grabbed her arm, pulling her alongside him.

"I have a new plan. King Darius is going to marry us—right now."

"But I want to wait until tomorrow. I am too mad over what just took place."

"No, we must do it right now."

Chrissy felt she had no choice in the matter. She walked over with

Redimir, looked Darius straight in the eyes, and told him to proceed.

King Darius pronounced them husband and wife.

"Now, go back to the room and wait for me. I will be there shortly."

Tommy followed Chrissy as she walked back to Redimir's apartment, whispering to her to keep walking and act as though he was not there.

"You must go out the escape hatch immediately and get away before he gets back to the room. I will radio General Howard to send someone to get you. If you don't, you are going to have to sleep with him tonight."

"Well, I'm his wife," she said, and it sounded quite sarcastic. "And if I leave, then he will kill them all. I am sure of it, and I can't let Josh die."

"I will figure out what to do. You just get out of here," Tommy demanded. As Chrissy and Tommy moved the rug to open the escape hatch door, they suddenly heard a noise from below. Carefully pulling on the hatch to open it, to their surprise . . . Nettle appeared.

"Nettle, what are you doing back here?" Tommy nearly shouted.

"I'm going to rescue all of you. That was the dream, and that's what is going to happen."

She turned to her best friend. "Chrissy, I need you to swap clothes with me. I'm going to pretend I'm you."

"No, Nettle, this guy is supernatural," Tommy said. "I shot him and he healed himself. You are no match for him."

"But Elyon is, Tommy . . . I am not afraid of him."

"Things have changed, Nettle," Chrissy said. "King Darius just married us, and he is planning on being with me here in a few minutes. I don't think this is a good idea. We both need to get out of here, and fast. He will be here any minute, I am sure."

"You both have to trust me on this," Nettle said. "Chrissy, please give me your burqa and then get out of here. Tommy, if you want to stay here invisible, that's OK. But you have to follow my lead on this."

* * *

Back in the Situation Room, Redimir was discussing the plans for tomorrow with King Darius, General Zhoo, and his daughter. King Darius was quite enamored with Noel and admired her ability to be able to kill so easily. He believed she would be a valuable asset to their team. He could see it in her eyes—the involvement in the communist youth programs in China had served her well. She was a pleasant surprise.

They all parted, excited over the prospect of announcing their New Transformational Global Agenda to the entire world in just a short amount of time. This was a day they had been anticipating for a very long time.

* * *

"You can get up now, Jason," Stefan said, inside the rear jail cell. Everyone watched Jason as he sat up. He had been shot at very close range but had his bulletproof vest on. The shot knocked him out of breath, but it had not killed him, as all had thought.

"It's time to swallow the blue pill," Stefan announced. "We cannot afford for anyone to be taken in the middle of the night and questioned, so I believe we must swallow the pill now."

"Wait," Josh said. "If it works immediately, then let's wait and see what they are up to. We can always swallow it as soon as they come to get us, if need be. Who knows, Tommy might have a plan to get us out of here shortly."

"I think he's right," Officer Holmes said.

"I agree," Jason added.

"OK, but have it ready just in case something should go down quickly," Stefan said. Everyone agreed, and they all lay down on the floor to get some rest.

* * *

Just as Chrissy was about to exchange her clothes with Nettle, the front door swung open, and in stepped Colonel Lulu Zuma.

"You didn't lock the door?" screamed Nettle.

"Quick, come with me right now," Colonel Zuma said. "I want to help you."

"It's OK. We can trust her," Chrissy said. "She can help us get the others out."

"Hurry, you have to get out of here before he gets back," Colonel Zuma commanded. Tommy told the girls to leave with Zuma and that he would take care of Redimir when he returned. Nettle informed Tommy that General Howard wanted Redimir alive, if possible, so he could question him. She and Chrissy quickly followed Lulu Zuma up to her quarters.

Tommy began to rummage through Redimir's apartment, gathering a few things to help protect himself since Redimir was capable of withstanding a bullet. He found a baseball bat, some rope, and duct tape.

Just minutes after Nettle and Chrissy left, Redimir opened the door to his apartment and shouted for Chrissy. He immediately started walking through the apartment, looking for her and calling her name. Just as he rounded the corner to his bedroom, Tommy swung the bat, hitting him in the head from behind. Redimir fell. Tommy picked him up and laid him across the bed, checking his pulse to see if he was still alive. Upon detecting a pulse, Tommy rolled him across the bed and started tying him up. After he finished, he sat down and began thinking up scenarios in case Redimir woke up. First, he wanted him to answer some questions. Then he would give this evil man a fatal blow and kill him. He felt it best to override the orders. He sat nervously anticipating what would come next. He had certainly never killed anyone before. But he sat there with full confidence that he was about to do the right thing.

* * *

Sam made it back to the Hummers with General Kerwin. Help was waiting; Dr. Wallace and his nurses, Angela and Judy, scrambled to provide expert medical care. Kerwin was barely hanging on, and Sam was worried that he might die before they got back to headquarters.

CHAPTER 45

New Life Begins

Colonel Zuma rushed the girls inside her place.

"How did you know we were here?" Nettle asked. Just as she was about to explain, there was a knock on the Colonel's door. Nettle and Chrissy looked at her with great concern.

"Don't worry, this is someone else who is going to help us get out of here," Zuma said. In walked Ambassador Dunn of England.

"What is going on here? I thought you both supported this 'new global initiative' thing."

"We did, originally," Colonel Zuma said. "We thought we were doing the right thing for all our countries—until this weekend."

"Colonel Zuma and I do not agree with King Darius's world take-over. We can see that this is heading toward a horrible dictatorship, not a world of peace. We want to help you and your friends in the jail to escape with us. Is there anyone else here with you besides them?"

"No," Nettle quickly spoke up. She needed to make sure this wasn't a setup before she told them anything important.

"Well, we have to act quickly if you want to see them alive again," Colonel Zuma instructed.

"It might be too late," Chrissy said with a saddened face. "When Redimir shows back up in his apartment and I am not there, he will probably put this place on complete lockdown and head straight to that jail room."

"That's why you have to go back," Ambassador Dunn said.

"No! She can't go back," Nettle cried. "He is crazy, and he might kill her. She is his wife now, and he will want to sleep with her."

"Look, I overheard Redimir talking about Chrissy to King Darius, and he sounded almost giddy, if evil can be capricious in that way," Dunn said. "We have to distract him so I can get the rest of your friends out of that jail. I need Chrissy to go back to Redimir and convince him that she was very nervous about tonight, so she took a walk." Speaking directly to Chrissy, he detailed the rest of the plan. "When he finally falls asleep, you get out of there and meet us at the exit that goes back into the cave."

"But what if he tries to sleep with her?" Nettle asked.

"Then you must say that it is against your religion until a priest marries you both. Be adamant about it," Dunn said. "He is a religious man, and I really believe he will listen to you. He has no idea what your religion's rules are. Just be adamant. But remember, no matter what happens, you are saving the world."

"And Chrissy, if he tries anyway, then dismiss yourself to the bathroom, get to the escape hatch, and get out of there," Nettle said. "If he does listen to you, then wait one hour, and after he is asleep, go out the hatch and I will be waiting to fly you back to the Hummers. Got it?"

"Got it," Chrissy said. "I think I can do this."

"Nettle, you come with us to the jail," Dunn said.

"Did you say *fly*?" Colonel Zuma asked.

"I will tell you guys about that later," Nettle said. "Just don't worry about us. We will get out of here and back to Tucson by ourselves. When you get the others out, you all just leave."

"OK," Zuma said. "I hope you are right, but I think you should stay with us."

"OK, let's move," Ambassador Dunn said. "Colonel Zuma, if we get separated, we will all meet at the cave exit. I have already removed the creatures."

"Chrissy, please be very careful with that man. He is *evil*," Nettle pleaded one final time.

Chrissy walked slowly back to the apartment and opened the door. She didn't see Redimir in the front, so she walked back to the bedroom. As she opened the door, there he lay, tied up on the bed.

"Chrissy," Tommy whispered loudly.

"Tommy, is that you?" she said. Tommy appeared—sitting on the bed right next to Redimir.

"I hit him in the head. I didn't know where you guys went, so I decided to stay here and wait."

"Is he dead?"

"No, but I hit him pretty hard. If he wakes up, I am going to ask him one question then kill him."

"Well, Ambassador Dunn of England and Colonel Zuma of South Africa have switched sides. They are helping the others escape. They are all on their way to the jail cell to let them out now. Nettle told me to appease Redimir, and then, after he went to sleep, to escape through the exit in the front room."

"OK, then maybe I should just go ahead and kill him now while he is still out cold. I can just crush his skull," Tommy said.

"Well, not while I am standing here," Chrissy exclaimed.

"OK, I can wait. I am going to find Nettle and make sure they all make it out. You stay here, and I will be back to kill him when he wakes up," Tommy instructed. "Don't worry; he can't escape. I tied him up really well."

"All right, but don't be gone too long. I don't want him to wake up without you here."

"I'll be quick," Tommy said, heading out the door.

Chrissy moved over to the chair and kept an eye on Redimir. She started praying that the others would make it out safely. She started dozing off, when all of a sudden, she heard Redimir moving.

"Chrissy, is that you?" he said. Chrissy's heart felt like it was going to explode.

"Yes, it is me."

"What is this? I am all tied up."

"I just walked in and found you like this. I don't know what happened. I was just sitting here waiting on you to wake up."

"Someone hit me from behind and then must have tied me up."

"Are you OK?" Chrissy asked, extremely nervous and not knowing what else to say.

"I am fine." No sooner than he said that, and Redimir suddenly appeared standing in the corner of the room.

"How did you do that?" Chrissy asked. She realized then she should have let Tommy kill him. He approached her and she froze, wondering what he was about to do to her. He grabbed her by her headpiece and pulled her close to him, her face almost touching his.

"I have been waiting all day and night for my time to be with you alone," he said, slowly removing her headpiece. Chrissy's long blonde hair fell down around her face. She stood as still as a statue as he moved his mouth to her neckline and kissed her up and down her neck. As Redimir was making his move, Chrissy spoke up.

"I really want to talk with you right now about a lot of things. I am so tired and a little shaken by all that has gone on, and I just want to get to know you better before we consummate our marriage . . . please? In my religion, we need to be married by a pastor for it to be legal."

"OK, then we will play a little game while you get to know me better," he said.

"What kind of game?" she asked.

"Come over here, my love," he said, grabbing her hand and pulling her to the bed. Next, he slowly unzipped her burqa, and it dropped to the ground. Chrissy now stood there in her T-shirt and boots.

"You are truly beautiful," he said. Chrissy knew this was not going as planned and prayed that Tommy would be back soon. Redimir carefully picked her up and placed her on the bed. He took the rope and began to tie her up so she could not move.

"What are you doing?" she questioned.

"I am playing a nice little game with you since you like to disappear so much," he said, finishing tying her up from head to toe.

"Now you can get some rest, since you are so tired."

"I don't like this," she said. "I feel trapped, and I don't like not being able to use my hands."

"Do not worry, my princess. I am not going to hurt you. I am just protecting my property to make sure no one else tries to steal it." As he sat down on the bed staring at her beautiful face, she began to think of questions to ask him about his past, pretending to care about him and acting as if she truly wanted to know more. But what Chrissy could not get off her mind was . . . *how did he get out of that rope and appear on the other side of the room?*

She told herself she must find out the answer to that question.

* * *

Tommy had caught up with Nettle, Colonel Zuma, and Ambassador Dunn and secretly followed them to the covert entrance to the Situation Room. Once inside, they closed the door and walked into the jail cell. Everyone was asleep, so Nettle went over to Josh and woke him up.

"Whoa," he said, pulling himself to consciousness. "What are you doing here, and who is he?"

"This is Ambassador Dunn, and he is going to help get us all out of here. Quick, help me wake everyone up." Josh and Nettle proceeded to get everyone up, and quietly, they all followed Ambassador Dunn through the back exit door. Colonel Zuma was standing guard at the entrance.

"Where is Chrissy?" Josh asked eager to know.

"She is with Tommy in Redimir's apartment," Nettle answered, not knowing Tommy was overseeing their escape. "I am about to go get her and fly her back to Tucson as soon as you guys are safe."

"Well, I am coming with you too," he said. "I am not leaving Chrissy, you, or Tommy here alone."

"OK, just make Jason and Stefan aware of your plans."

"Will do," Josh said.

* * *

As they approached Redimir's apartment, Josh and Nettle said their good-byes to the group. After everyone else headed off, Tommy appeared to them both.

"I had a sneaky feeling you were here, too," Nettle said. "So where is Chrissy?"

Tommy told them about knocking Redimir out and that Chrissy was watching over him in the bedroom. As they quietly opened the door and proceeded down the hall, they could hear people talking.

"He's awake," Tommy whispered. "Let me go check it out first. You guys hide in the first closet down the hall, and I will be back in a minute." As Tommy carefully peeked into the bedroom, he could not believe his eyes. *What in the world? How did this happen?* He could see Chrissy's burqa lying on the floor and Chrissy lying on the bed, tied up. He stood there listening to them talk for a moment, trying to think of what to do. He knew he could not let Josh see this, or Josh might jeopardize the whole thing by trying to rescue her. Chrissy was asking Redimir about his life, and he was answering her questions politely.

Suddenly, Tommy noticed the baseball bat in the corner of the room where he had left it. He decided to go for it—to club Redimir once again—this time with the intent to kill. He tiptoed over to the bat and quietly began to raise it up to strike him. It startled Chrissy when she saw only a bat in the air, and Redimir turned just in time to catch the bat in mid-swing. Chrissy screamed.

"That was Chrissy screaming," Josh said to Nettle. "I'm going in."

"No, wait," Nettle pleaded—but it was too late. Josh opened the closet door and ran to the bedroom. Redimir's strength was superhuman, and once he grabbed the bat, he broke it in half. Tommy fell back and hit the table.

"If you don't show yourself, I will kill her."

About that time, Josh rounded the corner and Redimir looked over at him. Tommy immediately jumped up and grabbed Redimir around the neck, trying to choke him. Nettle entered the room and frantically began trying to untie Chrissy to get her loose. Redimir broke Tommy's grip and turned toward Josh. Instantly, Josh forged his two fingers right into Redimir's eyes, trying to poke them out. Redimir made the eeriest scream they had ever heard, and smoke started coming from his nostrils. As Nettle got Chrissy loose, Tommy and Josh were wrestling Redimir to the ground.

"You two get out of here, now!" Josh yelled.

Nettle and Chrissy ran to the escape hatch.

"Go!" Nettle told Chrissy. "I have to go help them since I can fly, but you had better go this time, or he will kill you." Chrissy climbed down the exit as fast as she could and headed toward the Hummers. Nettle re-entered the room, only to find Josh and Tommy knocked out completely, lying on the floor.

"Well, well, if it isn't my dear little Nettle . . . it's you I have been waiting for this whole time. Finally, you have arrived for me. You only thought I wanted your best friend," he said as he jeered eerily. "I don't care a thing about her, but I knew I could get you if I used her. And look . . . here you are!"

"You let them go free, and you can have me," Nettle said sternly.

"Oh, but I already have you," he said. "I know you will not leave Tommy."

"Try me!"

"You see, Nettle, we are alike, you and me. We both have supernatural powers, and we are both very passionate in what we believe."

"I am nothing like you," she said. "Now let them go or . . . "

"Or what?" he said, a horrible grin on his face.

"Or else I will leave," she said. Tommy began waking up but felt very dizzy, and his vision was blurry.

"What did you do to us?" he asked.

"Nothing that won't wear off in time," Redimir said.

"Tommy, you listen to me," Nettle said. "You pick up Josh and you guys get out of here, now. I have this handled."

Tommy leaned over and tried to wake up Josh but he wasn't moving.

"You better not have hurt him, or I will jack your plans up so bad," Nettle said, and this time she had a huge grin on her face. Tommy stood up but felt extremely dizzy. He tried picking up Josh but fell over again.

"When will this wear off?" Nettle asked.

No response.

"I'm outta here," Nettle said. As she turned to walk out, Redimir assumed she was serious.

"Wait," Redimir pleaded. "I will sit calmly right here on the bed until they are back to normal and can leave. I will let them go if you stay." Gradually, Tommy started getting his balance back, and Josh eventually woke up.

"What's going on?" Josh asked. "Where's Chrissy?"

"Chrissy is safe, and you and Tommy are about to leave."

"You know we can't do that," Tommy said, clearing his head.

"Well, if you want our relationship to continue, then you best scramble now. I mean it, Tommy Jones; I am not kidding you." Tommy could see the seriousness in her eyes. This was one time he was going to have to fully trust Nettle—fully trust Parakletos.

"Come on, man," Josh said. "She knows what she is doing. Remember the dreams?"

"OK, Nettle. I sure hope you know what you are doing."

"I do. Now, good-bye," she said rather sternly, keeping her eyes on Redimir the entire time.

Tommy and Josh went through the escape hatch quickly, trying to think about what to do next.

"So, what is it that you want with me?" Nettle asked.

"I want your powers, of course."

"And you think you know what they are?" she snapped.

"All of them," he said. "You have all of them." Nettle instinctively knew she could do more than just fly—but she wasn't sure yet about all of her other powers.

"Why don't you come with me, and I will show you the kingdoms of this present world—the one we are about to encounter. When you see what I have to offer you, I think you will be pleased to work with me. And . . . don't knock it until you understand it, my dear."

"I will never work with you, Redimir. Anyone who plots to kill people so they can take over the rest of the world and rule it is not someone that I would ever work with."

He laughed as he slowly got up and stood before her.

"Today will mark the beginning of a new humanity, and the people will eventually listen to me and King Darius. Your own president is a joke now, and we have no use for him, either. He thinks we are on his side, but he is completely deceived. He only thinks he is a brother . . . " Redimir laughed, quite loudly.

"So what are you saying?" Nettle asked.

"I am saying that it's my world now, and those who don't go along will eventually be executed. That includes all your friends we have locked up in the jail." Nettle knew that Ambassador Dunn and all the others should have escaped by now. She just hoped Tommy and Josh had really left.

"So what's your plan now?" she asked, trying to get as much information as possible.

"The plan is to announce world peace, and then, just when everyone thinks things are OK . . . **bam!**" he said rather loudly, making Nettle flinch. "We will wipe the Israelis off the face of the earth . . . along with anyone else who stands in our way." Nettle had never seen such intensity in someone's face and gestures before. She knew that he meant business and was serious about Israel.

"Just when everyone thinks 'peace, peace,'" he said in an almost dreamlike state. "Then those dreadful rodents will be wiped off the face of the earth." He laughed hideously.

"Excuse me?" Nettle said. This angered Nettle more than anything. This wasn't about a political regime. This was a spiritual prophecy being revealed right before her eyes. As he spoke, he started moving toward Nettle. She stood firm and unflinching as he made his way past her.

"Come with me, and I will show you the map." Nettle decided that she would follow him to the Control Room; perhaps she could get critical information from him. As they were walking, she suddenly had this uncanny feeling they were not alone. *Is Tommy following? Surely this is just my imagination.* As they entered the Control Room, Caleb and Kenneth grabbed Nettle by her arms, holding her tightly so she could not fly. She fought, desperately trying to break away from them.

"Nettle . . . my darling Nettle. It is of no use for you to try to get away. I have now placed everything on lockdown and am about to blow up the whole outside compound. I'm afraid that Josh and Tommy might not make it home . . . or anyone else, like Chrissy, for that matter.

"Oooohhh," he said, his eyes becoming red again. "The bomb will reach all the way into Tucson, and we will lose some of our own."

Now Nettle was *praying* that it was Tommy she had sensed. She knew that not enough time had passed for everyone to get back to headquarters so that they wouldn't be killed. She had to stall for time . . . she had to think of something.

* * *

Ambassador Dunn, Colonel Zuma, and the others had made it to the vehicles. The first group—Stefan, officers Cothern and Holmes, Cory, Tay, Tenya, and Colonel Zuma—had already taken off; they were heading back to headquarters. Only Ambassador Dunn and Jason were waiting on Chrissy, Nettle, Tommy, and Josh.

Chrissy finally arrived and began telling them what had happened.

Suddenly, there was a knock on the Hummer door. It was Josh. He got in and held Chrissy tight.

"Redimir has Nettle, and Tommy would not leave her. I think if we wait a little longer they will be here."

"We can't wait any longer," Jason said. "I just received orders to come back immediately."

"But what about Tommy and Nettle? You can't leave without them," Josh demanded. "I would not have gotten in this Hummer if I had known that. Let me out; I am going to wait for them."

"Look, Josh, if they escape, Nettle can fly Tommy back. They both have a radio to apprise us of their whereabouts, and we can always come back if necessary," Jason said. He began to start the engine. "Nettle is smart—they will figure out how to get out of there."

After traveling for about fifteen minutes, Jason's radio went off.

"Mayday, mayday." It was Tommy calling from a closet inside the city. Jason answered the call. Tommy was whispering.

"You have got to take cover now. I just heard Redimir tell Nettle they are about to bomb the whole outside compound as well as part of Tucson." Just as Tommy got the words out of his mouth, everyone heard a loud explosion.

"I think it's too late, man; it's too late!" Jason cried.

Static instantly filled Tommy's radio. He stood there, stunned, a single tear running down his check. His best friends were in those Hummers, and he had no way of knowing if they were dead or alive.

Dear God, these people are truly evil. They are of the devil himself. Tommy's stomach churned in anguish.

What would he tell Nettle now?

The second book of the Seekers trilogy, Sealed, will release in 2015. Make plans to get your copy and find out what happens with Nettle, Chrissy, Tommy, Josh, and the rest—and whether Darius and Redimir and their evil intentions can be stopped.

To find out what your own 'super powerful gifts' are, please visit our website at www.readseekers.com and take our motivational gift assessment for free.

For more information about the Seekers trilogy, and to learn more about Liz Morris, go to our website at www.readseekers.com. You can also share your thoughts on the upcoming series and enter a chance to win up to $10,000.